About the Author

Rachel Armstrong has always loved making up stories and has never wanted to be anything but an author. She writes contemporary romantic fiction ranging from rural to suspense. Rachel enjoys creating epic feel-good stories and has a weakness for an adventurous holiday escape. Helping her characters find their happily-ever-after is her life's joy.

Rachel lives in Townsville, Queensland, with her border collie, Jacob, where she helps people live their best lives as an exercise physiologist. In her spare time, she is either reading on her treadmill or plotting out her next novel while grooving at Zumba. Rachel's a keen traveller and has enjoyed many holidays exploring historic London, flying through the Grand Canyon, and hiking volcanos in Bali.

Rachel enjoys connecting with readers on social media and through her website.

www.rachelarmstrongauthor.com.au

RACHEL ARMSTRONG

The Man From
Shadow Creek

**Pink Paws
Publishing**

First published 2023
ISBN 978-0-6453555-2-9

Published by
Pink Paws Publishing
Rachel Armstrong
Townsville QLD 4810
Australia

A catalogue record for this book is available from the National Library of Australia
www.librariesaustralia.nla.gov.au

For Jill Staunton

Dear Reader,

Welcome back to Elizadale! Three months have passed since Ana found her home with Liam and now, her sister has arrived in town to help plan the wedding. Natalia is a young GP keen to establish herself in a rural practice and she hopes Elizadale will provide her with a fresh start like it did her sister. But she didn't count on having her own romance with Liam's cousin, Adam.

Adam and Natalia's story has troubled me for some time. Originally, it was told in a different light, but new ideas develop, the world changes, and even though it was a tough journey, I'm glad that I discovered what the core of their story was and am proud to be able to tell it.

Adam and Natalia have both experienced sexual harassment. Their situations are different and they've each responded in keeping with their character. However, while Adam and Natalia may both be suffering, their shared experiences help them conquer their pain in a way I hope is respectable and reflective of society. Please note, this book contains no graphic detail of abuse, rather it focuses on the emotional response to inner turmoil, which is the heart of romantic fiction.

Yet a Shadow Creek book isn't complete without a furry friend, so I'm excited to introduce you to Rusty. Adam's dog is a Jack Russell, but he shares similar characteristics to my fox terrier, Timmy. Timmy may have been my mum's baby, but he protected us against snakes and was a skilled rat catcher. These are traits I have brought out in Rusty, although the little farm dog doesn't particularly like cuddles. Maybe he's in need of a mummy?

I hope you enjoy Adam and Natalia's emotional journey to their happy ending as they open their hearts to achieve dreams that they never thought possible.

Happy reading,

Rachel
xoxo

Prologue

Adam Maguire never needed to justify a night out with his mates, but at least his birthday provided a legitimate excuse. The shots may have been too much though, which was probably why Cade had bailed on him. Typical. The man ordered the sambuca, then he piked out.

But the night was still young, in the literal sense of the wee hours, when he and his new friends left the Royal Hotel.

'To the park!' the foreign guy called. Adam couldn't remember his name. He'd just met the bloke and there were many overseas workers who passed through Elizadale. 'Nothing better than partying in nature!'

Adam swigged from the rum bottle as they walked, the warm liquid filling his belly to battle the cold evening. Or morning. Whatever. Adam didn't particularly care as he stumbled into Elizadale Memorial Park.

The pretty girl beneath his arm pressed her hand to his chest. 'Steady there. If you fall over, there'll be no picking you up.'

'I'm good.' He pulled her to his side and pressed his mouth to her temple, inhaling her sweet scent of shampoo and roses. 'You sure you don't want rum?'

She shook her head, her dark hair swishing. 'You know I don't like rum.'

'Dunno why.' He took another swig. 'Rum's gooood.'

Laughing, she squeezed him around the waist. Adam hadn't planned on hooking up tonight, and if he hadn't already started on the shots when he'd met her at the pub, he may have taken the woman home. But it was too late for that and he wanted to dance.

'Anyone got music?' the foreigner asked. 'Should get some Trollfest playing around here. They're good for drinkin'.'

'Nah, mate, this is 'straya.' The other man laid his hand on the foreigner's shoulder. 'We sing Slim.'

'Yes!' Adam cheered and thrust the rum into the other bloke's hand. 'Drink up, bud. We'll teach this Euro bloke about good music.'

His mate lifted the rum, but the other woman in their group quickly snatched it away.

'What do you think you're doing? Don't share your rum. It's your special birthday present.'

'Aww, come on,' Adam said, grasping the bottle as she thrust it back at his chest. 'I'm just being friendly.'

She smiled widely and shimmied closer. 'If you want to be friendly, we can ditch this lot and go back to my place.'

She pressed her mouth to his and forced his lips apart as her arms snaked up around his neck. Adam blinked, his hands tightening around the bottle between them. He drew away and stumbled backwards. 'No. I told you, I want to party.' He took another gulp of rum. 'And we're not … I don't want …'

'Leave him alone.' The warm, kind woman wrapped her arm back around his waist. 'We're having fun here and Adam's not going anywhere with you.'

'Stay out of this. What's between Adam and I—'

'There's nothing between you and Adam. And he's not leaving.'

Adam shook his head. 'No. I'm not.'

'We wanna dance!' The foreigner spun around on the grass holding his vodka bottle in the air. 'Come on!'

A familiar guitar riff sounded from the other bloke's phone and Adam grinned. 'Hell yeah! Line 'em up!'

'Fine.' The woman threw her hands in the air. 'Be like that.'

Adam wrapped his arm around the guy's shoulders, forgetting about the woman as he sang Aussie classics at the top of his lungs and shared his bottle of rum. The music didn't stop. Nor did the drinks. There was laughter. More kissing.

Next thing Adam knew, light speared into his consciousness. He squinted, his throat dry and head pounding as the grass itched at his back. Groaning, he rolled over and glanced around.

The park? What was he doing in the park?

Adam winced. Fuck, he felt like shit. His head, his guts. Had he drunk the *whole* bottle of rum?

He shivered, his bare skin cold against the grass. Where was his shirt? He curled his toes. No shoes. Pants? Yes, he was wearing pants. Thank fuck.

Gritting his teeth, Adam forced himself to sit, blinking until the dizziness eased. There was no sign of his shirt. Nobody else around. He'd slept there. Alone?

Bile rose in his throat, and he dropped his head into his hands. What the fuck had happened last night?

Reaching into his pocket, he pulled out his phone. It was mid-morning and he had missed calls from his brother. Groaning, Adam called him back.

'Hey,' Jack said, sounding rightfully pissed. 'Where are you?'

'The park.'

'Why?'

'Dunno. Can you come get me?'

Jack made a sound Adam had heard many times before, a mix of a grunt and a sigh, likely accompanied by an eye roll. 'You had a big night, then?'

'Must have.' Exhaling, Adam ran his hand down his face. 'Can't remember, though. Where were you?'

'I left after dinner when you and Cade went to Smithy's.'

Adam scratched his head. That made sense. He'd had dinner with Jack and their friends at the Royal Hotel, then he and Cade had moved on to the other pub, Smithy's. But after that ... he couldn't recall a single thing.

'You 'right, mate?' Jack asked.

'Dunno. Feel like shit.' Adam's gut tightened and he forced out a breath. 'You coming?'

'I'm on my way.'

They hung up. Adam pushed to his feet and his vision blurred. Rubbing his eyes, he scrolled through his phone and called Cade. His mate answered after a few rings, yawning. 'How'd you pull up?'

'Where are you?'

'Home. Why?'

'Did you come to the park?'

'Why would I go to the park?'

Adam frowned. 'Well, I did. You weren't here?'

'No, I left you at Smithy's with a bunch of farmers. You were talking about going back to the Royal. Don't you remember?'

'No. I don't even know how I got here. Head's all fuzzy and—'

'Shit, mate.' Alarm filled Cade's voice. 'What the fuck did you drink?'

Chapter One

Natalia Hamilton strolled off the plane and into Cairns Airport, ignoring the flutters in her belly. She'd already overthought this move and enough was enough. She'd arrived in North Queensland and would soon be in her new home of Elizadale.

A small town.

A small *rural* town.

A small *rural farming* town.

Where she'd be stuck for two years.

Natalia sighed. Yes, she'd never imagined she'd leave the raging metropolis of Sydney, but Elizadale had its advantages—fewer people, a sense of community, and tight-knit friendships. If she couldn't find value in her work and respect as a doctor in a small town, where would she?

Emerging from the airbridge, she heard her name called. 'Nat!'

'Ana!'

Natalia grinned as her sister ran towards her. Embracing, they swayed from side to side, holding other tight. It had been far too long since Natalia had seen Ana. She'd moved to

Elizadale in January and a lot had happened in the seven months since. Not for Natalia, but Ana had settled in as a schoolteacher, had met a bunch of lovely people, and was now engaged to Liam Maguire, the tourism director of his family's banana farm, Shadow Creek. There had also been the incident when Ana's ex-fiancé had sought revenge upon her after they had released him from prison, but Natalia didn't want to think about that. Rick was serving out his longer sentence, and Ana was happy.

Natalia drew away. 'I've missed you!'

'Me too! It's been ages. You look great!'

'I went to the salon before I left.'

'Good, because our hairdresser is closed for almost *ten weeks*! Can you believe it? Claire's gone away to do a beauty course.'

'Ooh, sounds promising. Maybe we'll be able to get our eyebrows done.' She looked Ana up and down. 'You look great too. I guess the engagement adds this extra glow? Now let me see the ring!'

Ana's grin turned cheeky as she bounced on her toes and extended her left hand. 'Don't you just love it?'

Natalia's breath caught as she grasped her sister's fingers. She'd seen a picture, of course, but it was nothing like the real thing. The three-quarter carat princess cut diamond sparkled beneath the airport lights.

'It's stunning. I'm so happy for you!' Ana deserved nothing less than the wonderful man and home she'd found in Elizadale. Natalia only hoped that one day she might find the same things.

She swallowed a laugh. If only. It'd take a special man for her to make such a commitment. A man who didn't bother with pretence and who saw past her 'pretty face'. A man who was strong, kind, had a sense of humour and was downright sexy—at least in his own way.

But since such a man didn't exist, Natalia had decided it was easier to swear off them entirely. Men weren't worth the effort.

'Thanks.' Ana looped her arm through Natalia's, grabbed her suitcase, and led her away from the gate. 'I'm excited. And I'm so glad you're here! Just wait until you see Elizadale. This town, these people … But seriously, Nat—' Ana's face sobered '—you in a small town?'

Natalia's chest tightened. Ana's concerns weren't unfounded since Natalia thrived on the class and buzz of city life, but she'd needed a fresh start and a new town provided that.

They stepped onto the escalator. 'Yeah, but it's only for two years. You inspired me, Ana, and a fellowship in rural medicine can take me far. Besides, I want to work in a place where I feel valued, not where I'm just another disposable doctor.'

'I know. You want to feel needed.'

The tension inside Natalia loosened. 'Exactly. And you made Elizadale sound like the place to do that.'

Besides, Doctor Joanne Brennan had hired her on merit, which was more than Natalia could say for her previous job. Her boss, Doctor Mason Canning, had destroyed her rosy picture of life as a doctor.

* * *

After leaving the airport, Natalia admired the rainforest as Ana navigated her hatchback up the Kuranda Range. Everything she'd heard about North Queensland's beauty appeared to be true as trees she couldn't name speared into the bright blue sky. Natalia wouldn't call herself a nature enthusiast, but she liked the outdoors and would enjoy exploring the walking trails during her time off. Give her a scenic track through a national park and she could walk all day.

'I haven't visited many of the towns around here,' Ana said. 'I planned to during the Easter holidays, but Liam had just opened The Bent Banana.'

'How's that going?' Natalia asked, keen to visit the new café.

'Fantastic. Business is good and we've had great comments about the dog-friendly section and our diverse menu. Our gluten-free apple crumble muffins are our bestsellers.'

'Anything vegan?'

'I told Liam that if he asks nicely … you might give us your pineapple cake recipe.'

Natalia laughed. 'You think I'll give that away? It took me ages to nail that one!'

'Oh, come on! Wouldn't you like to visit The Bent Banana and eat something other than the fruit salad?'

'No, I love fruit salad.' Not that she had a problem sharing her recipe, Natalia just loved to tease. Of course she would help Liam if he wanted her to because finding vegan-friendly cafés was challenging enough.

Soon, the rainforest disappeared and they entered barren, dry country.

'We've definitely left civilisation,' Natalia muttered, questioning her sanity as she glanced around at the savannah north of Mareeba.

'Well, this *is* cattle country, but there's a lot of diversity. Mangos, avocados, and bananas are the biggest crops around here. And people in Elizadale are lovely. Tomorrow, you can come to the pub for Friday Frenzy and meet Meg, Isabella Brennan, and the Maguires. Meg's thrilled that you're here.'

Natalia didn't doubt that Ana's friends would be as welcoming towards her as they'd been her sister. It was one part of the move she'd been looking forward to as working long hours hadn't left her much time for socialising.

Almost two hours after leaving the airport, they arrived in Elizadale. The lush parkland to Natalia's left curved around footpaths and play equipment while large trees lined the highway. They passed the golf course on their right, one pub, and then the infamous Royal Hotel.

'There's The Bent Banana,' Ana said, pointing out Natalia's window towards a brick building with a massive concrete banana out the front. 'And this is the main street, Riley Road.' They turned at a cluster of shops and drove by sporting fields. 'Elizadale Medical is down that way. There's the school and community centre. You'll *have* to come to yoga.'

'Try to stop me. But you're right, Ana. Elizadale is beautiful.'

It may not be what she was used to, but she could make this work. It was only for two years and Cairns wasn't far away if she desperately needed entertainment. Besides, she had Ana, and that's all that mattered.

Ana pulled into the driveway of Jackson Villas—a group of five double-storey townhouses built of sand-yellow brick. She parked outside the one at the far right, the unit angling in towards the rest.

'Here we are! No one's lived here since I moved out.'

Natalia stepped out of the car. 'They look nice. Elizadale Medical seems to be behind them, is that right?'

'Pretty much.'

'I know I should get myself a car, but I'll be happy walking for a while.'

Ana rolled her eyes, and Natalia smiled. She'd relied on public transport in Sydney and didn't mind walking, so she'd never bought a car. Considering the size of Elizadale, she probably didn't need one here either.

'A car will be helpful,' Ana said as they grabbed the suitcases. 'But yes, this place is lovely. The only problem is the stairs. They're hard and slippery and I strongly recommend that you don't have sex on them.'

Natalia followed Ana to the door. 'Thanks for that. Great advice too considering I have no one to have sex with.'

'You never know. Elizadale's full of single men and we both know you like to date.'

Natalia winced. Once, maybe. But now … 'I told you, I've sworn off men.'

Ana dismissed that with a wave of her hand. 'You say that now.'

Letting that comment go, Natalia followed Ana inside. With space to move about, neat furniture, and a roomy kitchen, it was homier than the tiny units she'd squeezed into in Sydney.

Natalia sank against the breakfast bar. 'Yeah, this place will work for me.'

'I enjoyed living here, but I love Liam's more.'

'So, when do I get to give Liam the older sister scrutiny and decide if you can marry him or not?'

Ana laughed. 'I'm sure you'll approve, but I'll pick you up at seven for dinner. His parents and sister are coming too.'

'Sounds nice.' Natalia crossed the room to hug her sister. 'I'm not crazy in coming here, am I?'

Ana squeezed her. 'You're not crazy.'

Natalia inhaled, then released her breath slowly. She knew that what had happened to her in Sydney could happen anywhere, but Elizadale had given Ana a fresh start and newfound joy in life. Besides, Natalia could practise medicine, read books, and exercise anywhere. Small-town life wouldn't be forever.

She would be fine.

Chapter Two

Adam Maguire lacquered his brush with oil, set the lathe to spin, and added the final touch to the red cedar trinket dish. The wood turned from dull red to glistening mahogany in an instant, and his chest expanded. It never failed to impress him how he could transform a hunk of useless wood into something useful. Piece it together right and he could create furniture for people to dine at. With the correct chisels, he could shape decorative items to be gifted to loved ones. Over the years, he'd learned various techniques and experimented with new ideas, enjoying the challenge he imposed upon himself.

Not that he knew why. He'd never set out to work with wood. He'd needed to fill in a subject at school and woodwork had been more appealing than IT. But the satisfaction of completing a project well done was addictive, and Adam had needed that over the past few weeks.

He stopped the lathe and admired his work. The bowl made the perfect piece to take to Elizadale Homewares this afternoon where he would pitch his business plan. He should have done it years ago like everyone had told him to. The two ladies who owned Elizadale Homewares had asked—almost begged—him to on many occasions. But had he listened?

Ha! Adam didn't listen to anyone. He ran off his own steam, did what he wanted, and didn't care what anyone thought. He had a reputation for a poor attitude and getting into trouble. Adam had been the 'bad boy' of Elizadale for most of his life and had worn the title with pride.

But trouble wasn't always good, which he'd learned the morning after his twenty-eighth birthday. Six weeks had passed since he'd woken hungover in Elizadale Memorial Park and his questions still raged.

How had he ended up there? Who had he been with? What had he done?

He hadn't a clue. But he knew he didn't want to repeat the experience, so he was turning a new leaf and going into business.

Placing the bowl on his workbench, Adam sawed off the base that had attached the bowl to the lathe and sanded it smooth. When he was satisfied, he completed the oiling and laid it beside the other items he'd created these past few weeks—bowls, vases, and candlesticks. He'd start small because he was confident that he could deliver a supply of basic homewares, which would be necessary if he was going to make a success out of this. And he had to. For too long he'd been woodturning for no reason other than to please himself and his family. He'd crafted the massive tables at his mother's tourist retreat and his cousin Liam's café. People had always admired his work, but he'd shrugged off the compliments. Working with wood was simply a way to pass the time when the farm was quiet and his mates were busy.

But if a man wanted to make something of himself, then he had to play to his strengths.

Grabbing a rag off the bench, Adam wiped his hands and left the shed, grinning as he crossed the front yard towards his house by Shadow Creek. His family had farmed this land for generations and this spot had always been Adam's favourite, so there'd been no question about the location when he'd built. Like wood, he had a love for water and had always found the creek comforting. During the wet season, the water would rise and rush past his house, creating a spectacular sight from his elevated position that protected him from flooding. He'd fenced off a large yard, the surrounding scrub provided privacy, and the gap in the tree-lined creek offered a spectacular view of the banana farm.

The house was a simple four bedroom because, like any sane man, he'd built for the future. And yes, his brothers and sister had laughed at him for it. But just because a man didn't seek commitment in his twenties, that didn't mean he never would.

Tossing the rag onto the verandah, he pulled his dusty shirt over his head. He'd go to town, ask Sue and Heather if they'd sell his woodwork, and get his life sorted.

Adam yanked open the door and frowned when his Jack Russell, Rusty, wasn't there to greet him. But Adam quickly saw the reason for his dog's absence when his gaze landed on Jordan Kelly stretched out along his lounge.

Naked.

Adam drew to a halt, the screen door crashing closed behind him. His shoulders stiffened and hands tightened around his shirt. Fuck, he wished he was still wearing it as Jordan's eyes zeroed in on his bare chest. Her lips parted in a toothy grin.

'That's a sight I like to see, a man eager to join me.'

Exhaling, Adam dropped his shirt and shoved his hand

through his hair, trying to look anywhere but towards Jordan. This situation wasn't unusual. Whenever she was lonely or in the mood, Jordan would invite him around or turn up unexpectedly. In the past, he'd usually gone with the flow, most of the time without complaint. But lately, he'd felt nothing and had been turning down her booty calls since April.

Why she kept showing up, he had no idea.

'What are you doing here, Jordan?'

'Aww, are you still playing hard to get?'

'I'm not playing anything. I told you on the weekend I'm not interested anymore.' And the weekend before that, and that …

'Oh, stud …' She stood. Adam's gaze darted to hers as she moved towards him. It wasn't an effort to stop his eyes from straying down her body. 'I'm sure I can change your mind.'

Never. Not again. He didn't want to be a regular hook-up. An easy lay. They were over. Sure, sometimes it'd been convenient to have an arrangement with her, but she'd had the same arrangement with many other men. He'd never judged her for it because he'd known what he was getting himself into. She'd lured him back in after Ana had come to town, which had resulted in another fist fight with her brother Paul Kelly. When she'd taken up with some other bloke a week later, Adam had barely batted an eye.

Then he'd watched Liam fall in love with a smart, beautiful woman, and Adam had considered there might be more to life. When Jordan had come to him one rainy night in March, she'd left him feeling empty and he'd seen the light. Meaningless hook-ups were no longer fun, and it had delighted him more than he could say to realise that. So, the next time she'd called, he'd told her no. He wasn't interested.

Since his birthday, he'd been more determined than ever to avoid her.

Jordan reached for him, and he stepped back. 'I don't have time for this. I'm busy.'

She sniggered. 'Doing what?'

'I have places to be. Wood to work.'

Her fingers brushed the waistband of his jeans. 'I'll play with your wood.'

Adam clenched his teeth, his skin prickling. 'Not that kind of wood.' He stepped out of her reach.

'Oh, come on,' she whined as he moved around the lounge. 'You know I'm much more fun than that junk you keep in the shed.'

'It's not junk,' he muttered, spying her clothes on the lounge. Adam gathered them up and thrust them at her. 'Now, please leave.'

She huffed out a breath and took her clothes. 'Are you serious?'

'Yes.'

Her eyes steeled. 'Fine. Be like that. Just know that next time you're horny, I might be busy with wood too.'

Then, clutching her clothes to her breasts, she turned and strode out of his door. Naked.

Adam flipped the lock behind her and let out a deep breath. Bloody hell. Rubbing his hands down his face, he strode through the house to the back door where Rusty was scratching at his locked dog flap demanding to be let back in.

'Sorry, mate.' Rusty darted inside. 'She's gone now.'

Rusty ran to the front door to double check though. Adam left him to his guard-dogging, shoving the incident from his mind as he showered and left for his meeting at Elizadale Homewares.

He didn't know why he was nervous as he walked in and greeted the owners, Sue Riley and Heather Knowles—sisters, avid craftswomen, and two prominent figures of the community.

'Ooh, you have more things for us?' Heather asked, a twinkle in her eye.

Adam swallowed as he set the box down. 'Yep. Although I was hoping I could do it more regularly. I want to make something of my woodturning and was wondering if we could strike up a deal?'

'Oh, that's wonderful!' Sue clapped her hands together and beamed at her sister. 'Isn't it, Heather?'

'Yes! I've been saying this for years, Adam.'

He nodded slowly. 'I know. But I'm serious now. I still have work to do on the farm, but I enjoy making things and after whipping up some bowls the other day, it clicked. I could make a business out of this.'

'You can, Adam. You're incredibly talented.' Sue picked up the mango bowl he'd brought and examined the various shades in the grain.

Heather nodded. 'The items you've made us before have always sold quickly.'

'People love handmade homewares. And with your cousin's new café taking off, we're seeing more visitors pass through Elizadale. Knickknacks sell well.'

'And furniture.' Heather shot him a pointed look. 'You could make a killing with tables.'

The tension in Adam's shoulders loosened. 'I have slabs of rose gum that would make nice coffee tables, so I could do that.'

'And we'll gladly sell them,' Sue said.

Adam managed a smile. 'All right, then. So—'

'You have yourself a deal.' Heather extended her hand. 'If you deliver it, we'll sell it. As long as you do so regularly.'

Adam swallowed. 'I will. I'm also happy to take suggestions. Or commissions. I'll give you a steady supply of bowls and vases, but I've considered ordering in parts to make clocks too.'

Sue beamed. 'Clocks would be fantastic!'

'Absolutely.' Heather placed her hand on Adam's arm. 'You've made an excellent decision, my boy. I'm proud of you.'

Stupidly, Adam's chest expanded. He'd known Heather and Sue all his life. They were his mother's age and Sue's daughter Meg was one of his best friends. 'Thank you.'

'What did your mum say?' Sue asked.

'She's pleased and wants me to make more things for the retreat.'

'I'm sure she does. Will you sell through Liam's tourist centre too?'

'Not the stuff I'm selling you, but I've carved some banana souvenirs for him. I figured The Bent Banana needed some.'

'I'll need to get one of those,' Sue said.

'Of course you will. Now—' Heather cleared her throat '—let's talk business.'

Nodding, Adam followed the ladies out of the store and into their office. Already, he felt changed. And scared as all shit. He'd always had dreams, but since when had he ever achieved anything of substance?

Chapter Three

Natalia and Ana didn't stop talking as they unpacked. She hadn't brought much with her, just clothes and a few treasured possessions. Smiling softly, Natalia placed Surge Duck in the shower. She'd been six when her father had given her the yellow duck with a stethoscope around his neck, and in that moment, she'd decided to become a doctor just like her daddy.

A week later, her daddy had died.

'Just another house, Surge.' God knows they'd both seen many. 'But hopefully, we can make a difference while we're here.'

She'd harboured her medical dreams during childhood, but her motives had changed by the time she'd started university. She'd studied medicine because she wanted to help people, something she'd forgotten while working for that awful Mason Canning.

Shuddering, Natalia left the bathroom. Never mind that now. She was in Elizadale where she looked forward to working with long-time town physician Joanne Brennan. Natalia would learn the ropes and build a good rapport with the community. In a small town, a solid reputation was vital.

After unpacking, Ana drove Natalia to the supermarket to buy some much-needed essentials.

'You'll need to visit a few stores to get everything. Vicki Hall is the baker and she's keen to know everybody. She's Meg's aunt and the sister of our town's representative with the Mareeba Council, Ron Riley.'

Natalia nodded. She'd heard of the Rileys and their leading influence in Elizadale.

'Then there's the fresh produce store, the hardware store, and Claire Taylor's hair salon.' Ana parked the car and they climbed out.

'And tomorrow I get to meet your friends?'

'Yep. Although …' Ana stopped walking, her gaze lingering over Natalia's shoulder. 'Looks like you might meet one now.'

Natalia turned at the rumble of a motorcycle and watched as the man parked, kicked down the stand, and switched off the bike. His blue jeans stretched over strong thighs and broad shoulders filled his leather jacket. Then he lifted his helmet and ran his hand through his dark hair. Natalia's breath caught.

Hello!

Swinging off the bike, he grinned and lifted his hand in a wave. Ana waved back. Natalia didn't move.

'Hey, cuz.' He strolled over and enveloped Ana in a hug. 'Good to see you. Who's your friend?'

Natalia's cheeks heated. Wide smile, dark eyes. *Oh yes …*

Ana glanced at Natalia. 'This is my sister. Nat, meet Adam Maguire. Liam's cousin.'

Adam Maguire. Yes, she'd heard about him. Elizadale's notorious bad boy who got into fistfights with the Kelly brothers and kicked out of the Royal Hotel. The man who'd helped rescue Ana when she'd been abducted and beaten by Rick Newman.

The man Ana had failed to mention had shoulders like Adonis and should be in a toothpaste ad as he flashed her a smile and offered his hand. Natalia took it, her fingers tingling and toes curling inside her sandals.

'You couldn't be Ana's *older* sister.'

Her blush deepened as he released her hand. 'Ahh … yeah, I am.'

'I told you Nat was coming,' Ana said, glancing at Adam with a frown.

'You tell us lots of stuff I half listen to.'

He actually drawled, and Natalia stifled a laugh. Ana rolled her eyes.

Adam turned his gaze back to Natalia. 'So, what brought you up here?'

Ignoring her developing arrythmia, Natalia recovered her voice. 'Apparently, Elizadale's a great place for fresh starts.'

'Your sister would agree with you there.'

'Yeah …' Ana cleared her throat. 'We have some groceries to buy, so we should go.'

'I'll see you around, then. Tomorrow, right?' Adam's gaze shot to Ana. 'You *are* bringing Natalia to Friday Frenzy.' It was not a question.

'Of course.' Ana's tone was light, but her eyes flashed.

'Good. I'll see you ladies then. It was nice meeting you, Natalia.'

She shivered as the syllables of her name rolled off his tongue and he turned and swaggered away. Her breath escaped in a whoosh and her gaze fell to his backside. Damn, he looked good in those jeans. Sexy as sin with his lazy gait and fine glutes.

Natalia turned to Ana, who was still frowning. 'What?'

'Don't even think about it.' Ana turned on her heel and strode into the supermarket.

Natalia followed. 'Think about what?'

'I saw it.' Ana snatched up a basket. 'Don't go there, Nat. I know he's bloody gorgeous and incredibly charming, but you don't want to get mixed up with Adam Maguire.'

'What? Like every other girl in town?'

Ana spun to face her. 'I thought you'd sworn off men!'

'Well, yeah, but ...' Natalia blew out her breath. 'Okay, I know what you've said about him. Bad boy and all that. But God, Ana! Have you seen his smile? His eyes?' Not to mention the rest of him, but Natalia wouldn't say that out loud.

'Yeah, I know. He's gorgeous. Tall, dark, and incredibly sexy. But forget Adam, Nat. He's not for you.'

Ana marched down the aisle. She'd mentioned Adam many times on the phone and, yes, he always seemed to get into trouble. He was popular with the ladies and apparently, he'd partied far too hard on his birthday and had woken in the park with no recollection of how he'd got there.

But while Natalia didn't approve, she'd be the last person to judge someone for their past. Thousands of other men did the same things—or worse. And while Adam might be hot and she could notice, he was *not* her type. She'd always been attracted to the more academic types. Men with smooth good looks and a serious personality.

'Ana, surely he can't be too bad.'

'Nat, only an hour ago you were telling me you weren't interested in dating. Men use you. They're only interested in your looks.'

Natalia's heart plummeted. She'd said all of that and more because it seemed like that's all the men she'd dated were interested in. A good time. Sex. Scoring with a woman who looked like her. Natalia wasn't vain, but her beauty was obvious every time she looked in the mirror. She'd inherited her Russian grandmother's looks with her golden blonde hair, bright blue eyes, and clear complexion. The many hours a week she dedicated to various forms of exercise kept her body slim, limber, and strong. Once, she'd even enjoyed doing her hair, makeup, and wearing nice clothes. Taking pride in her appearance was something she'd valued. Until Mason Canning had whispered that he longed to unpick her braided hair while his eyes had absorbed every plane and groove of her body in her favourite plum work pants. After that, Natalia had lost herself. And her confidence? That had vanished too.

'I know. And I meant every word. But it's not like I *want* to swear off men.'

Ana smiled softly. 'I know.'

'I just don't think that I can—'

'Trust anyone to like you for you?'

'Yeah.' Her trust in men was hanging by a thread and until she worked that out, she couldn't risk even a fling.

Not that she did flings. She might be female enough to admit that her hormones had gone haywire over Adam, but attraction had no right to rule her head and now that her body had stopped tingling from his sexy smile, her rational mind had returned.

She was the new doctor and she needed to build a respectable, approachable image. It was the one thing she sought above all else. 'I need to focus on work and settle into town.'

'Yes, that's a good idea. Now, let's finish this shopping so we can get you home.'

'Okay. Then I'll have time to go for a run before dinner.'

Laughing, Ana wrapped her arm around Natalia's shoulders. 'Glad you're thinking straight again.'

* * *

Natalia couldn't be happier for her sister when she arrived at Ana and Liam's house. This was everything Ana had ever wanted with lush tropical gardens dotting the expanse of green lawn and shaded by towering gum trees. Natalia stepped out of the car to the sound of a kookaburra calling as she admired the modern-style Queenslander.

'Wow, Ana. It's beautiful.'

'I know, right? Our dogs love it, and I enjoy working in the gardens. I'm even learning the names of trees.'

'That's more than I ever plan to do.' Natalia followed her up the cute T-shaped steps. 'Although I've always wanted to grow my own herbs.'

'Why not try it?'

Natalia considered that as Ana dropped her keys onto the hall table. Perhaps she could?

She followed Ana down the hallway and into the open-plan kitchen and living area. Natalia smiled at the border collies, Steph and Louis, who sat watching them through the screen door. She'd missed Louis and longed for a cuddle, but first, she turned her attention to the man who greeted them in the kitchen. His face lit up with a fantastic smile as he returned Ana's embrace.

'Liam, this is my sister.'

'Hello, Natalia.' Liam took Natalia's hand in a friendly shake. 'Great to meet you in person.'

'You too.'

Liam opened the fridge. 'Would you like a drink? I have

water or I can make you a cup of tea? There's some flowery thing Ana bought for you.'

'Hibiscus tea,' Ana said.

'Yeah.' Liam grinned. 'It's pink. Looks weird but tastes good.'

'It certainly does,' Natalia agreed. 'But I'll be okay for now, thanks. Ana, is there anything I can do to help with dinner?'

'No, it's fine. Unless Liam screwed it up while I was gone.' Ana peeked into the oven.

'I wouldn't burn your delicious food. I don't like going hungry.'

The front door opened and there were greetings all around as Liam introduced Natalia to his family. Cliff was her definition of an Australian farmer with hard tanned skin and he greeted Natalia with a smile that mimicked his son's. Deborah was pretty, blonde, and delightful as she declared she'd love anyone that her precious daughter-in-law did. Liam's sister Lucy—tan, lean, and beautiful—greeted Natalia like an old friend.

'I'm so glad you're here! Now, Ana might get a move on with wedding plans.' Lucy clapped her hands together. 'I'm so excited.'

Natalia smiled. 'I'm sure it's going to be wonderful.'

'It'll be a lovely day,' Deborah agreed.

Liam offered his dad a beer and the men moved onto the deck as wedding talk filled the kitchen. With the date for September and it already being July, the big day would arrive in a flash.

'Liam and I finished the guest list last night.'

'Are you inviting anyone from back home?' Natalia asked.

'Just Mama.'

Lucy took a swig of her beer. 'Liam's asked Adam to be his best man.'

Natalia's eyebrows shot up. This wedding just got better.

'I didn't doubt that,' Ana said. 'He loves all his cousins, but he and Adam are the closest, being the same age and all.'

'That means Adam will be your partner, Nat.' Lucy flashed her a smile and heat unwillingly rose in Natalia's cheeks.

'Yes, Nat met Adam at the shops earlier,' Ana said, disapproval lacing her tone.

Natalia shrugged. 'He seemed nice. Very charming.'

'Adam's a good boy,' Deborah said fondly.

'And I think that morning in the park was a wake-up call,' Ana said as she turned towards the oven. 'Now, let's serve up dinner.'

Chapter Four

A bitter wind blew across the verandah as Adam sat with his elder brother, Jack, to plan their trip to Innisfail for the Banana Growers Council workshop next weekend. They agreed to drive down late Friday afternoon, then sat in silence, enjoying their beers while insects buzzed in the bushland. Light from inside Jack's house formed patches of gold on the concrete but otherwise left both men shrouded in darkness.

'I got Sue and Heather onboard. They'll take my stuff.'

'Doubt it'd have taken much to convince them.'

'Yeah, yeah. I know.' Yet his meeting with Sue and Heather seemed like a lifetime ago after running back into town and—

'So, I met Ana's sister.'

Adam kept his tone casual, even though he felt anything but. Since the big black unknown that was his birthday, he'd avoided women outside everyday interactions, but Adam hadn't been able to shake the stunning image of Natalia Hamilton from his head all afternoon.

Hell, she was something else. He'd never seen a woman with a more delicate face, all soft cream with pink cheeks, sparkling blue eyes, and clear of makeup. Natalia was taller than Ana and carried herself with grace and elegance, which he found attractive. He also hadn't failed to notice her strong, well-sculpted body. She must work out because she was without a doubt the sexiest …

Grimacing, Adam drank his beer. What was he thinking? He was attracted to Ana's sister? The beautiful, smart doctor from Sydney? That would never work. Natalia Hamilton would have more class and self-respect than to give a bad boy like him a second look.

Bugger.

'Yeah?' Jack asked mildly. 'What's she like?'

Adam lifted his shoulder and stared out into the darkness. 'We didn't say much, but she seems nice. Looks like Ana. Except a lot more … I dunno. Prettier, I suppose.'

'Well, Ana did say she was prettier.'

'Yeah, but I thought she was pulling my leg!' Adam clearly remembered Ana's teasing remark about her sister being 'prettier' than she was. 'Natalia … she's bloody stunning, mate.'

Lines formed between Jack's eyebrows. 'You better not be thinking of doing anything with Natalia. Ana would kill you.'

Adam scoffed. 'She wouldn't kill me. She loves me too much.'

'I haven't met her, mate, but I don't think Natalia's a woman you can fool around with. She's Ana's sister. Don't do anything to piss either of them off.'

'Who said I want to fool around with her?'

'Your reputation, mate. You may want to turn a new leaf, but change doesn't happen overnight.'

Adam's jaw clenched. He hated that bloody reputation. Once upon a time, it'd been cool to be the kid who would wag school and could score alcohol underage. He'd done as he'd liked, broken rules, and he hadn't given a shit what anyone else thought. As a teenager, he'd been a hero.

But now, he was frustrated. There were rules he had to live by and a job he had to do. Drinking was getting old and women … yeah, he'd been with a few, but some had been more serious than others. Especially Grace White, his one steady girlfriend three years ago. But he hadn't realised how good she'd been for him and had let her slip away. Now, she was happily dating local publican Luke Smithfield.

So yeah, he'd spent many years being young and stupid, but he regretted little.

Then there was the birthday incident.

Adam downed his beer, though it did little to settle the unease prickling between his shoulders. It might irritate him, but he'd been grateful for the wake-up call. He wanted to pour his focus into his new business and make something of himself. He needed to stop messing around in life and *never* get so blind drunk again.

Because blind he had been. He'd put himself in a vulnerable position and that's what worried him. He might have been a little easy and loose in his behaviour, but he'd never blacked out before, which made him wonder if it could have been drugs somehow. He'd never touched those, so he wouldn't know. And if someone *had* slipped him something, then he considered himself lucky he'd woken alone without any obvious harm done.

He wouldn't risk that again. Now, he was starting afresh. So, Jack saying that Adam would want to fall around with Natalia only pissed him off.

'Beer?' Jack handed him another one and Adam sighed gratefully.

'Thanks.' He twisted off the cap and took a swig. 'And I'm not saying that having some fun with Natalia wouldn't be enjoyable, but I don't want to be that bloke anymore. Not that I want to try for anything deeper. With Natalia or anyone. I'd fuck it up for sure.'

'Probably. Doesn't mean you can't give *dating* a shot if you want to squash your reputation. You know what dating is, right?'

'Do you?' Adam snapped before he could stop himself. Not that he cared. If Jack wanted to be a bastard about it, Adam would be one right back. He didn't know what the hell his brother was thinking when it came to Meg Riley. He was sure Jack loved the woman and Meg clearly adored him. But anytime Adam mentioned it, Jack shut down, so Adam had long given up on getting any answers out of him. And now, Jack and Meg hadn't said a single word to each other in fourteen days. It was driving Adam nuts and if it went on any longer, he'd lock them in a room together until they sorted their crap out. Everything was wrong with the two of them not speaking, but since neither of them wanted to admit they'd been wrong—Jack had been—the silent treatment was irritating their friends more than it was the two of them.

But Jack didn't bite.

'Doubt Natalia would go out with me anyway,' Adam said, 'as I'm sure Ana's told her stories. And if she hadn't, she would have by now.' Adam grinned as he recalled the way Natalia had checked him out. 'She'd be asking about me for sure.'

'That confident, hey?'

'I had her blood humming. I know when a woman's attracted, mate. It's one of my many gifts.'

'Sure it is.'

Adam laughed. 'Yeah. Nat's a woman with "serious" written all over her, but there's no harm in being friendly. As Meg says, my charm wins over the ladies.'

'Yes, you think you're so charming.'

'Meg finds me charming.' Adam let that statement hang too, but again, Jack ignored him. His brother took another swig of his beer and stared out into the darkness. 'Jack … you could apologise.'

'I have nothing to apologise for.'

Adam rolled his eyes. 'I don't care either way, but I think that's what Meg wants. The sooner you apologise, the sooner you'll be in a better mood and stop pissing me off.'

'Then don't give a shit about me.'

'You're my brother! I do give a shit about you. Just say you're sorry, then everything will go back to normal and there won't be a deep freeze when we go to the pub. Seriously, mate. It's not cool.'

'There wouldn't be a deep freeze if she hadn't got all cranky.'

'You could've kept your mouth shut.'

'But I was right!'

Adam sighed. This was where things got difficult. 'Yes, what you said was right, Meg going out with Scott was a bad idea. But telling her that was wrong.'

'She's my friend! I was looking out for her. You'd have done the same if someone you cared about was getting too close to that wanker.'

Bitterness laced Jack's tone, and Adam bit back a grin. He'd love to tell his brother he wouldn't need to be jealous if he just asked the woman out, but Adam wouldn't waste his breath.

'Yeah, I care about Meg,' Adam said. 'But I didn't go all macho on her when she went to dinner with another man. You did.'

Jack exhaled between his teeth. 'Just … shut up.' He stood and tossed back the last of his beer.

'You know I'm right. I'm not the only one with girl problems, mate. Just say you're sorry.'

'I'm not sorry.' Jack tossed his empty bottle into the old oil drum and stalked inside, slamming the door behind him.

That had gone well.

Placing his hands on his knees, Adam pushed himself to his feet. Jack's stubbornness didn't surprise him. His brother knew nothing about women.

He tossed his bottle away and turned to the door. 'I'm off then! Enjoy your sulking.'

There was no reply, but Adam hadn't expected one. Slipping behind the wheel of his Toyota Hilux, he started the engine and turned onto the main road of Shadow Creek—the once cattle station now banana farm his family had operated for generations. Natalia slipped back into his mind and Adam's body heated—both a welcome and worrying sensation. He wasn't a stranger to desire and usually, he embraced it. Except …

His hand tightened around the wheel. He couldn't go back to the way he'd been, acting on impulse without a care in the world. It was terrifying enough to have one gap in his memory. He couldn't risk that again. He needed to get his life on track. The farm would always be there, but he wanted more. Something that was only his. Liam had his booming café and Lucy ran popular horse-riding tours at their tourist retreat, High Ridge. His younger brother Michael was a successful builder and his little sister Lily was eighteen months away from her dream of becoming a vet. Surely, he could create a career from his passions too.

But trying to do that and date at the same time? No. Multitasking had never been his strong suit. He'd commit to his business first. At least if he fucked it up, the only person he'd hurt would be himself.

So, he'd get busy and make more bowls. And vases. He'd put flowers in a vase. Give it to Natalia.

Shit.

* * *

Jordan Kelly sank against the kitchen counter and cracked open a cold can of Coke. Damn, she wished it was beer, but the Coke still had the satisfying fizz and caffeine hit to soothe her frustrations.

What the fuck was going on with Adam Maguire? Why didn't he want to hook up? For years, she'd been able to rely on him for a good time. But these past few months, he always seemed to be 'too busy'. With what, she didn't know, as making that wooden junk couldn't be too time consuming. And Adam thrived on partying, fun, and sex. He couldn't turn her down forever. She had her ways and would convince him. And once she dangled the bait …

Jordan slammed the can on the counter. Fuck, her plan better work. Otherwise, she was screwed.

Jaw clenching, she reached into the cupboard above the stove and popped open a blister packet. Grabbing the Coke, she tossed back two tablets. She may have been told years ago that she no longer needed the anti-anxiety medication, but right now, Jordan didn't give a damn. She couldn't let Adam toss her away like this. Despite his devil-may-care attitude, there was one thing Adam had that she needed. Honour. No matter what wrong he did, he always owned his actions. If she made him believe her problem was *his* problem, then he'd take responsibility for it. Sure, she may have fucked up and she wasn't happy about it, but there was too much at stake for her to fail. And it would be all right once she had Adam on board. She couldn't have the bloke she wanted, so Adam would do. If she needed to trick him to protect her secret, then so be it. It wouldn't be a burden to be tied to him for the rest of her life. This turning a new leaf thing was utter nonsense. Men never changed. Adam Maguire was a bad boy, always would be a bad boy, and dammit, she needed to keep him that way. Otherwise, she would lose everything she held dear, and no fucking way would Jordan let that happen.

She'd get Adam back. Tempt him. She might not have much going for her in smarts or career, but she had skills and men never said no.

Not until Adam had, anyway.

Chapter Five

Natalia enjoyed her first night in Elizadale, the evening peaceful with the windows open to the cool breeze. At the sound of her alarm, she sprang out of bed, changed into her tights and hoodie, then headed out into the darkness for a run. No matter what, there was nothing, *nothing*, that prevented her from running every morning. Except maybe a six am flight like yesterday, but those didn't come around often.

Ana had shown Natalia the pathway that circled Elizadale, so she began her jog in the driveway and headed up Stuart Road to the parkland on the east side of town. Dawn peeked over the hill on the other side of Shadow Creek as pop music pumped through her earphones. Jogging towards the golf course, Natalia's gaze strayed over the land beside her. Shadow Creek didn't look like a banana farm when all she could see was bush, but she didn't stop to wonder where the beautiful rows of fruit plants were. She rarely thought when running as it was her 'me time'. Time to let go, destress, and protect her heart. Men and romance weren't the only threat to it. Everything she did was about protecting her heart, hence the exercise and vegan lifestyle. But neither was a burden as she enjoyed moving and loved food.

Forty minutes later, Natalia skipped inside her new home and sat down to her favourite breakfast of soaked strawberry and cinnamon oats with a side of chia pudding and apple slices. She had plenty of time until she was due at Elizadale Medical, so she lay on the floor to stretch, then showered and considered what to wear for her informal meeting. Eyeing the black corporate dress with medium-length sleeves and pencil skirt, part of her wanted to be a little daring. Why not start her new job on a good note? The dress still had the tags on it, after all.

Her fingers brushed the soft material and Natalia's belly clenched. Maybe not today. Instead, she grabbed her favourite charcoal pants, white embroidered blouse, and slipped them on over her delicate bra and knickers set. Natalia might have lost her glamour on the surface, but she'd never sacrificed her love of lingerie. It had remained her guilty pleasure, a comfort whenever she'd been feeling low, and all at a discounted rate considering her mother managed a Bras 'n' Things store.

Natalia sighed as she stepped outside and locked the screen door behind her. She missed her mum, who was now alone in Sydney. But Nadia had only encouraged Natalia's move, for which she was grateful as she arrived at Elizadale Medical early and stepped into the empty waiting room. Two doors stood closed to her right and the white walls contained posters featuring familiar health information. She approached reception and introduced herself to the young woman.

'Lovely to meet you. I'm Grace White, the nurse.' Grace stood and rounded the desk. She looked about Natalia's age, wore her brown hair in a ponytail, and was slender and fit. Not surprising since Natalia knew her to be the local yoga teacher.

'Nice to meet you too.'

'You're Ana's sister, hey? I like her. We used to be neighbours, but I recently moved in with my boyfriend. Anyway, we're excited to have you here. We haven't had a second doctor in years.'

The door behind them opened and two women emerged. Natalia recognised Joanne Brennan from their Skype calls as she farewelled her patient. Grace returned to the other side of the desk as Joanne beamed and extended her hand. 'Hello! So glad you're here.'

Following Joanne into the consultation room, Natalia couldn't stop smiling as they exchanged pleasantries. But as she sank into a chair and glanced around, Natalia's doubt rose again. What had she been thinking, applying for rural medicine? Sure, she wasn't afraid of more training, but now that she'd arrived, the challenges were quite clear with a lack of specialist and allied health support.

'So, how do you like Elizadale, Natalia?'

Shaking away her thoughts, Natalia tore her gaze from assessing the consult room to meet Joanne's. 'I've only been to the grocery store and Ana's place, but I've liked what I've seen. Ana's taking me to the pub tonight to meet her friends.'

'Ana's lovely and so are the Maguires. You'll probably meet my daughter, Isabella, there too.'

'Yes, Isabella and Ana are good friends.'

'They are. So—' Joanne leaned forward and gestured vaguely around the room '—I'll show you around, and like we've discussed before, you'll need to think of this place as more than just a general practice. We're almost a mini hospital as we deal with minor emergencies and serious issues after hours. For anything major, we'll assist while waiting for the ambulance, which is about forty minutes away in Mareeba.

Mainly, we work as GPs and gain extra skills where we can. Grace has her certificate in radiography and she's taught Emma how to use the x-ray machine, so she'll teach you too.'

Natalia nodded. She'd never taken x-rays, but she would learn.

'Monday is our pathology day,' Joanne continued, 'so Grace does phlebotomy in the morning and that's when we schedule minor procedures.'

'That's one thing I'd love to work on, my excision technique. We rarely did them at my previous workplace.'

'I'll keep that in mind. If we need an urgent sample during the week, though, we can still get it to Mareeba. They're our closest referral hospital for basic surgery and maternity. Most specialists are in Cairns. Townsville is our closest major hospital for anything serious. Brisbane is for burns, transplants, and anything Townsville can't take.'

The map formed in Natalia's head, the distance stretching further and further. Brisbane was fifteen hundred kilometres away. Townsville was six hours by road. It certainly put things in perspective when last fortnight she'd been working ten minutes away from the Royal Prince Alfred. She'd done her internship at St Vincent's and had started her GP fellowship at a prestigious city surgery.

But prestige wasn't everything. Prestige could make people arrogant or feel entitled. Natalia didn't need that. Here, she could know her patients. She would see them at the supermarket and know them by sight. Sure, small towns generated conflict-of-interest problems, but it couldn't be worse than what she'd already experienced.

'We do all the routine things here,' Joanne continued. 'Grace and Emma are wonderful nurses. Emma's also a midwife and runs our baby health clinic. We like women to go to Mareeba to give birth, but sometimes things don't go to plan. James Nelson operates the pharmacy and our receptionist, Nikki, is off today, but she's a godsend.' Joanne stood. 'Let me show you around.'

Natalia followed Joanne through the two consultation rooms and the procedure room. The ward was small but well-equipped with everything they needed. The pharmacy shop supplied locals with all the regular paraphernalia, and James kept a supply of prescription medications.

When she and Joanne returned to the waiting room, hope had replaced Natalia's earlier apprehension. There was so much she could do here. So much she could learn. She'd become valuable to this town and could make a world of difference.

Shaking Joanne's hand, she couldn't stop smiling. 'Thank you again for this wonderful opportunity.'

'I'm looking forward to having you here. I'll see you Monday.'

Grace glanced up from the desk. 'Actually, Emma and I were wondering if you'd like to go for a welcome drink at the Royal later? You can bring Ana and Liam if you like.'

Natalia already planned to go tonight, so why not arrive earlier to spend time with her colleagues? 'Thank you, that sounds lovely.'

'Excellent! We'll see you at five.'

Natalia almost skipped home. Everything was coming together. She would achieve her Fellowship in Advanced Rural Practice at this small-town surgery, which must be a nice place to work since Joanne had been there for thirty-odd years. Ana said she'd been the doctor who'd told Deborah she was pregnant with Liam! Natalia would never get that in the city. She might love the hustle and bustle, the shops, the culture, and the opportunities, but deep down, she longed for intimacy. She wanted to invest herself in the community's health and know her patients as individuals instead of just a name on a chart.

She'd find that here, she thought as she strode down Riley Road and glanced around Elizadale. Sure, there might be little entertainment and shopping, but that didn't matter. She could adapt. And for the first time in forever, she might even be happy.

* * *

Natalia squeezed inside the corner entrance of the jam-packed Royal Hotel. The colonial-style pub had high ornate ceilings and a wraparound verandah, but renovations boasted a modern wooden bar, glass-fronted fridges, and booths along the side wall. The double doors lining Abbott Street opened to the cool breeze—a testament to the time before air conditioning—while the neighbouring room contained the bistro, a jukebox, pool table, and dance floor. It was there where she found Joanne and Grace, who introduced her to the rest of the group. Natalia had heard a lot about Joanne's husband David, as he was a teacher who worked with Ana. Their daughter, Isabella, worked part-time at The Bent Banana, had recently celebrated her twenty-first birthday, and was as pretty as a pixie with her platinum blonde hair.

'I'm so pleased you're here!' Isabella said. 'Ana's spoken about nothing else.'

'Me too. I hear we're neighbours.'

'Yep. If you're ever looking for something to read, feel free to stop by. I have plenty of books and love to share.'

'I may take you up on that. I love reading too.'

Natalia met Emma Knight, the nurse/midwife, and when Ana and Liam arrived, Grace began the celebrations.

'I'd just like to say that we're so pleased to welcome Natalia to our team. We hope you thrive here and love Elizadale as much as we do.'

'Thank you, Grace. I'm sure I'll enjoy working with all of you.'

'It's helpful that you have family here too,' Emma said, glancing at Ana and Liam.

'You didn't have anyone to bring with you, Nat?' Grace asked, raising her eyebrows.

Shaking her head, Natalia sipped her sparkling water. 'No, I haven't been so lucky with men. Too many bad experiences, I'm afraid.'

'Yeah, that was the same for me,' Grace said. 'Then I found Luke. You just need to wait until the right one comes along, I suppose.'

'That's what they keep telling me,' Isabella muttered. 'But you never know, you might end up like your sister and meet the love of your life.'

Ana beamed while Natalia fiddled with a coaster. She didn't know about that. Love was a onetime thing, and she wasn't planning to settle down in Elizadale.

Grace grinned and crossed her arms over the table. 'Yeah, I'm sure that once the blokes see you around, you'll be beating them off with a bat. You're very pretty.'

Natalia's stomach knotted, but she forced herself to smile. It wasn't anything she hadn't heard before and Grace didn't mean any offence, but she hated the unease that swarmed in her belly by the comment. Once, she'd been used to compliments, but now … 'I dunno—'

'Natalia doesn't like to admit she's absolutely stunning,'

Ana said gently. 'She's very modest and doesn't enjoy comments about her looks.'

Natalia's shoulders relaxed. It wasn't exactly the truth, but Ana's defence was better than sharing the unpleasant details of her past.

Grace's eyes widened. 'Oh, I'm sorry. I didn't mean—'

Natalia held up her hand. 'It's okay, honestly. Besides, the fact I'm new here would undoubtedly generate interest.'

'You'll be the talk of the town,' Emma agreed. 'But if you *are* interested in dating, my brother Cade's sort of single.'

Natalia smiled. Sort of single? What did that mean? Not that she was interested.

Then a deep voice reverberated down her spine. 'Hey there.'

Adam Maguire pulled up a chair at the end of the table. His white T-shirt stretched across his broad shoulders, clinging to every groove and plane of his chest with sleeves short enough to display his strong, tanned biceps. Natalia shivered. Damn, he was hotter than she remembered.

'What you doing here, mate?' Adam slapped his hand on Liam's back. 'You're out with a bunch of pretty ladies and didn't invite me?'

'We're celebrating Natalia joining the medical team.'

'Sounds good.' Adam's dark gaze strayed around the table. 'So, what are we talking about?'

'How Natalia will be the talk of the town when word gets out that the new doctor's pretty and single.'

Natalia froze as the words tumbled casually from Grace's mouth. Heat rushed into her cheeks. *Oh God. Kill me now.*

She almost didn't dare look as a slow grin stretched across Adam's devilishly handsome face. 'I'll say. She sure is.'

Natalia's skin itched, yet strangely enough, her pulse

steadied because the way he looked at her … it wasn't in a *bad* way. The rock music, clatter of balls on the pool table, and chatter in the bar faded until there was nothing but the simmering interest in Adam's dark eyes.

Because of your looks.

Blinking, she shoved that thought away. *That's the fear talking. It isn't true.* Because alongside his interest, there was cheek, wickedness, and temptation lingering, all of which were welcome.

'I think we've actually come to the end of that discussion.' Ana's stern voice drew Natalia out of her daze and she exhaled, grateful for her sister's level head. 'Is the rest of the group here, Adam?'

'Think so.'

Joanne pushed back her chair. 'Then it's time David and I head home and let you kids have fun.'

Everyone made a move. Natalia thanked and farewelled the nurses, then followed Ana, Liam, and Adam into the main bar. Her embarrassment and panic had faded, but she loathed her reaction to a little male interest.

Could Mason Canning have screwed her up that badly? God, she hoped not.

'Jack's still in a grumpy mood,' Adam warned them.

'I'm not surprised. Everyone.' Ana took Natalia's arm as they arrived at the booth. 'This is Natalia. Nat, this is Meg, Jack, and Michael.'

Everyone stood to greet her. Adam's brothers, Jack and Michael, shook her hand and Ana's friend Meg Riley pulled her into a tight hug.

'I'm so happy you're here! Ana's talked so much about you.'

Meg was exactly as Ana had described, outgoing and pretty

with wavy blonde hair and a passionate soul. She was also a teacher and charitable with her time since she was on every committee in town.

'She's talked about you too.'

'So, come! Sit!' Meg slid into the booth and pulled Natalia down beside her. 'We need to learn all about you.'

* * *

Adam sat in the corner and drank his beer while Meg claimed Natalia as her new best friend. Every nerve in his body fired until he felt like he was being tortured. Not by the twenty million bloody questions, because he rather enjoyed learning about Natalia, but by the woman herself. She spoke in a soft manner and moved in a smooth way that captivated him. He couldn't take his eyes off her as she relaxed, smiled, and twirled the straw in her glass.

And she wasn't even dressed up! Not like Meg and Ana. Natalia's blue top was loose, plain, and sadly covered everything. Her golden hair was pulled back in a ponytail and she wasn't wearing any makeup.

Adam smiled into his beer. He liked that and admired her simplicity, although whether or not a woman enhanced her appearance didn't faze him. Sometimes those touches made them look nice, but hell, Natalia didn't need any of that. She was stunning all on her own. Flawless. Far too beautiful to ignore. Or to be put in the 'friends' zone.

Hell. What was it about Natalia that pulled at him so quickly? *Never* had he wanted to know someone more.

He liked what he learned, though, as the women chatted. Natalia loved dogs but didn't own one, enjoyed reading, and was keen to explore the surrounding national parks. Reading wasn't his thing, but he could take her to the parks and share his dog.

Then she spoke of her time at university, her experiences in the emergency room, and her passion for musical theatre and Adam crashed back to reality.

They were unsuited. Opposites. She city, he country. She intelligent, he … not so much. She good and he bad. He didn't deserve her and needed to put a lid on his raging desire.

Then again, why should he back out of a challenge? He never had before. And was he mistaken, or did interest flicker in her crystal blue eyes every time their gazes crossed? Could he possibly stand a chance?

'You'll come to yoga then?' Meg asked.

Natalia nodded. 'Definitely. I love yoga.'

'And even though you don't have a dog, you should come to agility training on Sunday.'

Adam suppressed a groan. Great. Now he'd need to bathe Rusty before agility. Rusty wouldn't like it, but he'd need to take one for the team. The last thing he wanted was his dog smelling like rats around the woman he wanted to impress.

Within the hour, Natalia was one of them and although Adam longed to get in on the conversation, for once, he had nothing to say. But he didn't mind not being the centre of attention. Natalia was far more interesting as she talked, laughed, and delicately closed her lips around her straw. Her company brought a warmth to him that he liked. Perhaps a little too much.

Yeah, he was totally screwed.

Chapter Six

The next morning, Natalia buttoned her black trench coat and left for Ana's house on foot. Honestly, why would she need a car? It took ten minutes to walk to Ana's, work was around the corner, and if she picked up a few grocery items at a time, her feet would serve her well. Come summer she might feel different, but she'd worry about that then.

Strolling along Station Drive, she gazed out over the scrub that was Shadow Creek and lifted her hat from her face. How did people on such vast farms live? It seemed like a whole other world being so far out of town. What about utilities? Did they use rainwater? A bore? She understood the whole septic tank system, but were they on the power grid or did they rely on solar?

Natalia shook her head. Nope, she was far happier living in town. For as far as she could see, Shadow Creek was a cluster of overgrown scrub with a few trees. Ana had said it'd once been a cattle station but that they'd switched to bananas a few decades ago. Natalia smiled, liking that. And since she liked to consider where her food came from, she'd be interested in learning about how they grew bananas. Were all the people who worked the farm tough and rugged like Adam?

She dropped her gaze and kept walking. What was wrong with her? Yeah, he was gorgeous, but what was it about his rebel edge that enticed her so much? Adam Maguire was *not* like the men she'd known. Or dated. He *wasn't* everything she was sick of—clean cut, businesslike, and boring. He was different. A farmer. Bloody sexy. And from what she knew about the day they had rescued Ana from Rick, Adam was also warm, considerate, and, in Ana's words, a 'true gentleman'.

But she couldn't afford to let her guard down and become another mark on his bedpost.

Although …

Her subconscious quickly whacked her upside the head. She didn't do flings, but she'd never had a long-term relationship either. And if he asked her out, she couldn't promise she'd say no.

Catching sight of the golf club, Natalia drew to a halt. Dammit, she'd walked right past Ana's house. Shaking her head, she turned back, strolled up to the door, and rang the bell. Dogs shuffled and nails scraped against the wooden floor, then the handle turned. She opened her mouth to say hello and blinked when nobody greeted her. Then she lowered her gaze and found Steph and Louis with a rope in their mouths, one that was connected to the door handle.

'Hey!' Ana called. The border collies dropped the rope, their tails wagging and tongues lolling out of their mouths.

Natalia cleared her throat. 'Your dogs answer the door.'

'Yep! Liam taught Steph how to do that and Louis' learned to copy her. Isn't it cute?'

Natalia grinned as she rubbed Steph and Louis' heads. 'Absolutely. You two are so clever.'

She'd always loved dogs, Louis especially, and would have had one herself if she hadn't worked night shifts and weekends. Perhaps that could be a perk to living in the country? She could get a pup who would be delighted to greet her every time she came home. Dogs loved unconditionally. A dog wouldn't hurt her.

'They are,' Ana said as she grabbed her keys. 'Ready to go shopping?'

'Always.'

With the wedding approaching, they had no time to waste, and Ana still hadn't bought a dress. Today's plan was to rectify that, so when Lucy and Meg arrived, the four of them drove to Cairns. Natalia may have only been in Elizadale for a few days, but she already longed for a shopping fix as she hadn't brought all her things from Sydney and could do with some more homewares.

'Have you seen the dresses Ana ordered?' Lucy asked Natalia as they sat in the bridal store sipping sparkling water. Ana had chosen four dresses online to try today, hoping that one would be the dress. If not, many more sparkling white gowns lined the pink-painted walls.

'No, I haven't,' Natalia replied.

'I hope she's picked something nice for us.' Lucy grimaced. 'It's going to be weird. I never wear dresses.'

'You can't wear jeans to a wedding,' Meg said.

Natalia glanced at Lucy. 'You've never been in a wedding?'

'Nah, Liam's the first person close to me to get married. Meg's the one who's been in all the weddings.'

'How many?'

'Four,' she muttered bitterly. 'This is my fifth time walking down the aisle and I'm still not the one wearing white.'

Natalia bit her tongue, not sure how to respond. Before

arriving in Elizadale, Ana had told her so much about Meg
and Jack that it had surprised Natalia to learn they weren't a
couple. Now, they weren't even speaking, which was
ridiculous when even Natalia could see they clearly adored
each other. And she'd only been in town for three days.

But she knew better to ask Meg about it as Ana had tried
and failed.

Lucy placed her hand on Meg's arm. 'I promise not to get
married before you,' she said as Ana called out from behind
the curtain.

'You guys ready?'

Natalia straightened. 'Yep!'

The store manager, Mary, pulled back the curtain and Ana
emerged in a beautiful sheath dress of white chiffon. A crystal
broach sat in the centre of the V-neckline and sparkling straps
adorned her shoulders.

'Wow ...' Meg breathed. 'You look so beautiful.'

'I know, right?' Ana's eyes glistened. 'It's not my favourite,
but it's pretty.'

'Beautiful,' Natalia agreed. 'Eight out of ten.'

'Eight,' Lucy whispered.

Meg frowned. 'Are you going to cry?'

'No.' Lucy averted her gaze and sipped her water.

Natalia studied Lucy, but since it wasn't unusual to get
teary at weddings, she turned her attention back to Ana.
Knowing her sister, Natalia agreed that the dress was too
simple, and Ana returned to the dressing room.

'Why so many weddings, Meg?' Natalia asked.

'I was a bridesmaid at my sister's wedding, both of my
cousins, and Emma Knight's, who's a good friend. But I don't
mind because I love weddings.'

'Have you come close to marriage yourself?' When direct

questions didn't work, there were other ways to uncover information. They may have just met, but Natalia liked Meg and Lucy and wanted to get to know them.

'Not really.' Meg sipped her water and eyed Natalia. 'What about you?'

'That would mean I'd have to date someone longer than a few weeks, which unfortunately has never happened. It's difficult when you work most days of the week. I may have been a little career focused …'

It might not be the main reason she'd never had a serious, steady relationship, but it wasn't untrue either.

'As a doctor, you'd have to be,' Lucy said. 'First with university and then internship. The learning never stops, does it?'

Natalia shook her head. 'Nope. But that's the beauty of science, it keeps developing and changing.'

'That's true.' Lucy crossed her legs and leaned forward on her elbows. 'Even in horse training there are new articles and techniques being developed.'

'So, what do you do at the retreat exactly?' She knew Lucy worked at Shadow Creek's retreat, High Ridge, with her aunt, but Natalia hadn't managed to ask Lucy more about it when everyone had been more focused on getting to know her.

'I'm the live-in host, so I'm there for anything the guests need. I help Wendy in the kitchen a lot, but I mainly work with the horses and run the tours.'

Natalia had never been near a horse but was intrigued by their beauty. And wary of their size. 'Ana said you used to do show jumping.'

'Yeah. My cousin Lily took it further and is quite the champion.'

'How does she find time while at uni?' Lily was the

youngest of the Maguires and currently studying veterinary science in Townsville.

'She makes time, trust me. But while I enjoy jumping, I prefer dressage. Now, I spend most of my time training horses and taking people for adventure rides through the National Park.'

'So, I know who to ask when I want to go riding then?'

Lucy grinned. 'Any time.'

'I'm ready!'

Ana emerged in a one-shoulder sheath dress made of lace over shining satin. Crystals embellished her waistline and decorated the shoulder strap with a pretty sparkle, but something about the fall of the skirt wasn't right.

'I think I like the other one better,' Natalia confessed. 'I know you like the lace style, but not this one.'

'It's nice,' Meg said, 'but I give it a seven.'

Shrugging, Ana returned to the dressing room. The next dress was a strapless, slim, A-line gown with a sweetheart neckline and lace draped over luminous satin.

Meg beamed. 'It's my favourite.'

'You look more and more beautiful in every dress,' Lucy said, sniffling.

'If you cry, I'm going to cry,' Meg warned.

'There are tissues on the front counter,' Mary said, and Lucy went to fetch them.

Ana studied herself in the mirror. 'It's nice, but I don't know if I want strapless. Do you think I can keep it up?'

'We can take it in. As long as you don't gain any weight before the wedding.'

Natalia swallowed a snort as Ana gave Mary a blank stare.

'I won't be gaining any weight,' Ana said dryly. 'What do you think, Luce?'

Lucy dabbed her eyes. 'You should try the next one so we can get out of here.'

Natalia took Lucy's hand. 'Are you okay?'

'Ahuh.' She folded her tissue. 'Just overwhelmed. You know, my brother is getting married and all. Ana looks so beautiful.'

Natalia sighed. 'Give us the last one, then.'

This time when Ana emerged, Natalia pressed her hand to her mouth and teared up too. 'Oh my God.'

Meg's face softened. 'You look so beautiful ...'

'Ten,' Lucy managed, grabbing more tissues and burying her face in her hands.

'I know ...' Beaming, Ana turned to Natalia. 'This is it, right?'

Biting her bottom lip, Natalia's breath caught. Her little sister ... all grown up and looking like a princess. Ana was so lucky.

'Yeah. That is The Dress.'

It was exquisite. Lace layered over satin and tulle in an A-line cut. The dress had beaded cap-sleeves, a sweetheart neckline, and the tiniest train. The corset back closure was a stunning touch and gave the dress a vintage gleam.

'Yeah ...' Ana melted as she stared at her reflection. 'I liked the others, but this one is perfect.'

'It is,' Meg agreed, reaching for a tissue herself as she rubbed Lucy's back.

With the dress chosen, they tried on a few veils before Mary brought out the bridesmaid dresses. They were pretty but simple, made of purple matte satin with thin straps and a pleated bodice. But as Natalia admired herself in the mirror with Meg and Lucy, they agreed they looked beautiful.

There were a few adjustments to be made to Ana's gown,

so they booked an appointment for the final fitting, then left for shopping at Cairns Central. Apparently, when the country girls came to town it was time to go crazy on both the practical and impractical. Natalia bought everything on her list—a rice cooker, new sheets, towels, exercise equipment, and other kitchen items. She stocked up on her dry goods at Woolworths—nuts, seeds, legumes, and nutritional yeast. Then she spoiled herself in the shoe and lingerie stores because a woman always deserved a treat. They'd brought Lucy's LandCruiser for a reason and had successfully filled it by the time they left for Elizadale.

Lucy turned up The McClymonts—who Natalia had quickly grown to love on the drive down—and they sang all the way home.

* * *

Monday dawned bright and early as Natalia ran laps around Elizadale, energised for her first day as a rural doctor. She arrived in her black pants and mahogany blouse, ready for whatever the day brought, which wasn't much as she learned the software, completed aged driving assessments, and diagnosed a young boy with tonsillitis. By five o'clock, she was quite in the mood for a lively chat when she joined Ana for drinks at the Royal, which she and her friends traditionally held every Monday afternoon. A crazy part of her was also keen to see Adam again, but since mechanical failure in the packing sheds had kept Adam and Jack on the farm, she thankfully didn't need to analyse those desires. Instead, she and the ladies talked about wedding plans while Liam and Michael gave little input over their beers.

On Wednesday, Natalia ran the consults while Joanne dealt

with some business matters. Her next appointment was Elanora Campbell. Natalia recognised the name, but it took her a moment to place Elanora as a teacher who worked with Ana.

'I heard you were joining us,' Elanora said as she sat in the consult room. 'Ana was so excited she couldn't stop talking about it.'

'I'm sure she was, and it has been fun.' Natalia opened the chart on the computer. 'So, what can I do for you today?'

'I've been trying to get pregnant for two years and am here for my monthly check-up. Joanne recommended I come in regularly because I'm agitated and depressed. I apologise if I start crying.'

'That's all right.' Natalia browsed Elanora's history and the notes from her last preconception counselling consultation. 'I understand it's difficult.'

'It's bloody torture. Shane and I did things casually for the first year, and nothing happened. I don't think my body liked coming off the pill. I never had regular periods before and I was on it for eight years, so I think everything's screwed up. It has to be else I'd be pregnant by now!' Frustration flared in Elanora's tone. Natalia offered her an empathetic smile and clicked on the results tab. 'I've been counting days and taking temperatures and sex isn't fun anymore. I mean, we still do it for fun, but I think Shane's getting as pissed off as I am.'

Natalia nodded as she read Elanora's fertility studies. Anything over a year was too long for making babies, but Elanora's hormones and blood work were all within normal range.

Natalia frowned at the screen, then glanced at Elanora. 'Yes, it can be difficult on the marriage.' She picked up the blood pressure cuff and Elanora extended her arm.

'If there was a medical reason, then I would understand, but there isn't. I should be able to have a baby.'

Natalia recorded Elanora's blood pressure. 'We'll work something out. You still have time and there are options.'

'But I'm thirty now and it isn't easy when I'm around kids all day. I'm the prep teacher.'

'I recognised your name.' Natalia reached for the infrared thermometer and held it to Elanora's forehead. 'Have you considered IVF?'

'Yeah, I'd do it, but Shane says we don't have the money.'

Natalia swallowed a sigh. Men. 'Do you have private health insurance?'

'Yep.'

'That'll cover the cost of day surgery, which is what usually makes it expensive. And the Medicare rebate is quite substantial.'

'I know. I do want to try, so I'll talk to Shane again.'

'I will warn you, though, IVF can be brutal.'

'Yeah, but at this point, I'll do anything to have a baby.'

Natalia completed her examination, counselling, then wrote a request for more blood tests.

'Thanks, Natalia,' Elanora said. 'I'll see you next week for the results.'

'Sounds good. Until then, try to relax, okay?'

'I will.'

As Elanora left, Natalia crossed her arms over her chest and tried to suppress the compassion rising inside her. As a professional, she couldn't get emotionally invested in her patients, but sometimes it was hard not to. The small-town vibe didn't help either. Elanora's struggle was heartbreaking and if there was a way Natalia could help her, then she longed to try.

Chapter Seven

Adam would usually complain about Jack dragging him to another damn workshop, but tonight, he'd rather be talking about soil testing, growth rates, and cyclone preparedness on Robbo's farm than sitting through another Friday Frenzy without flirting with Natalia. She'd been on his mind too much for comfort and fighting the urge to get to know her better was bloody torture.

They arrived in Innisfail, essentially the banana capital of Australia since the land between the coastal town and their southern neighbour Tully produced over ninety per cent of the country's bananas. They stopped to grab some food for the barbeque, then drove to Robbo's farm in South Johnstone. Robbo was a mate from way back and as they sat chatting on the back patio overlooking the banana trees, Jack's mood seemed to improve, which didn't surprise Adam. If anyone was invested in keeping up to date with the latest in everything banana farming, it was his brother.

But Adam enjoyed these events too, and he was better off spending his Saturday learning from colleagues than fantasising about a pretty woman, even though most of the information admittedly went in one ear and out the other. Thank God Jack was taking notes.

They were halfway home and about to grab dinner in Atherton when his phone pinged with a message. Jordan's name flashed.

Heading home. Meet me there?

Adam gritted his teeth. You'd think after all these weeks she'd get the bloody message. But even though there were things he longed to say, he thought it best to remain polite.

No thanks.

He tossed his phone on the dash and glanced at Jack. 'Want to skip the roadhouse and stop for a decent meal?'

'Suits me. No use hurrying home.'

Jack couldn't have spoken truer words, although the thought of having someone at home to welcome him brought a strange warmth to Adam's chest. He'd take her lean body into his arms and run his fingers through her long blonde—

He shook the image from his head. There was no use thinking such things. So, he indulged in a fine local steak and did his best to listen as his brother shared his thoughts about what they'd learned today and the best ways to implement the new techniques on Shadow Creek.

They didn't arrive home until late, but Adam was up with the dawn. He kept busy in the shed by sketching vases and organising the wood, anything to keep his mind off seeing Natalia at agility training this afternoon. Yet fate seemed hell bent on laughing at him when Jack called about a bloody pipe that had burst. Now, he was out in the field cold, wet, and miserable with an equally cranky Jack instead of running around the park with Rusty. He'd bathed the damn dog this morning and now the little bugger was having the time of his life rolling in the mud. His white and tan mate was black, and far happier than Adam was.

So he didn't make it to agility training, but his mood improved when he spoke to Liam and learned that Natalia and Ana had been in Mareeba visiting a wedding photographer. He hadn't missed the chance to see her after all.

But what was he trying to prove by suppressing his desire? Avoiding flirtation? Not being his usual happy and charming self? If he wasn't careful, he'd morph into Jack and he sure as shit didn't want that to happen.

He should simply be himself. Yeah, he wanted to shake his bad boy reputation, but that didn't mean he couldn't take risks. The main issue was the drinking. And flirting with too many women.

But wanting to *date* one woman? There was nothing dishonourable about that. It was just a stupid idea to try it with Natalia. She deserved a good man and he would only let her down.

That didn't mean he wouldn't try though. Shrugging into his motorbike jacket, Adam left the house for the regular Monday afternoon catchup. He revved the bike to life and rode to the Royal Hotel with steel in his spine and determination in his heart.

Stupid idea. Stupid idea. But how can showing a little interest hurt?

Natalia wasn't there when he arrived, but when she strode in, long-legged and gorgeous in her jeans, pink T-shirt, and white cardigan, he actually lowered his beer.

'Hey!' Ana cried as Natalia slid into the booth. 'How was your day?'

'Fantastic. I saw enough patients to keep me busy. People around here sure love Joanne though.'

Liam nodded. 'She's been with us for a while.'

'Longer than any of us have been alive,' Adam said. 'But if you stay, Nat, I'm sure everyone will love you too.'

Her mouth curved, eyes sparkled, and something twisted in Adam's gut.

Yep. Very stupid idea.

'Thank you. But I can't go anywhere for two years anyway.' She placed her hands on the table and glanced around. 'Who needs another drink? My shout.'

Natalia confirmed what they were drinking and slipped out of the booth. Adam seized the opportunity. 'I'll help you.'

He ignored the look exchanged between Ana and Liam while Natalia merely smiled and he followed her towards the bar. How did a woman get so … fit? Lean? She was stunning in every way with her athletic legs, beautiful face, and dazzling smile. An image of her stretching out at yoga flashed through his mind and he promptly tore his gaze away.

He had to stop with the fantasies, especially the physical ones. He didn't want that. The first step was to get to know her. She might be too intelligent for him, but just because she had brains didn't mean she couldn't be fun, despite what he'd once believed in high school.

Georgina, the owner of the Royal, smiled kindly at Natalia. Jordan, thankfully, wasn't working today. 'Another round?'

'Yes, thanks. Four Great Northerns and a soda water, please.'

As Georgina filled the order, Adam leaned his elbow on the bar. 'I'm glad you had a good day at work.'

'Thanks.' Natalia's glittering gaze met his and his blood heated so quickly it gave him a headrush. She flicked the lapel of his leather jacket and everything inside him tightened. 'You bring your bike to town?'

'Yeah, the ute was caked with mud. Almost got it bogged yesterday while fixing a busted pipe. Besides, I need to give the bike a run now and then.' He raised his eyebrows. 'You ever ridden?'

She stifled a laugh. 'A motorbike? No. I've never had a death wish.'

He grinned. Women. 'You think they're dangerous?'

'I worked in ED, Adam. You don't want to know what I've seen.'

'I'm sure there were plenty of car crash victims too, yet you still drive.'

'Not really.'

He frowned. 'You don't drive?'

'I do—' she handed her debit card to Georgina '—I just haven't had a car in a while.'

'You'll need to fix that.'

She raised her shapely blonde eyebrows. 'Why? I have feet. I could buy a pushbike though,' she mused, biting down on her bottom lip. Adam's gut clenched.

'I think you'll need a car.' He lifted the beers from the bar. 'Or a real bike.'

'A pushbike is much better than a motorbike.'

'Doesn't go as fast.'

'It's healthier. And I can ride pretty fast.'

It took all his control to keep a straight face. 'Really?'

Her cheeks pinked. 'What I *mean* is—'

'I know what you mean.' Laughing, he nudged her with his elbow. A shiver coursed through him and he took a shot. 'So, what do you say we blow this joint and go hang out? I can take you for a ride. Show you how fast I go. If you're up for it.'

Natalia stared at him. Time slowed and his pulse spiked. Shit. He'd taken it too far.

Idiot!

Then her head tilted, ponytail swished, and pretty lips curved. 'You think I want to climb aboard your motorbike?'

His shoulders relaxed. 'If you dare. Or we could dash across the road for a stroll by the creek. Have a chat.' He forced the cheekiness from his tone and aimed for gentle. 'I'd like to get to know you without this lot around.'

Her smiled widened. The swell in his chest threatened to burst through his jacket. 'You know what? That sounds nice. Except … I think Ana might try to stop us.'

'We need a quick escape, then.'

Her eyes dimmed. 'I guess so.'

'Then let's dump these drinks and get out of here.'

The musical sound of her laughter brought all sorts of warmth to his insides. 'Okay. Although one of these beers was yours.'

The last thing he gave a shit about was the loss of a beer. 'Jack'll drink it.'

Adam strolled back to the booth and handed out the drinks.

'Took you long enough, mate,' Jack muttered.

'Got distracted.'

Natalia placed her water on the table. 'We're going to go.'

Ana's eyebrows shot up. 'What?'

Adam grabbed Natalia's hand. 'Run.'

They dashed out of the pub. Natalia couldn't stop laughing as he led her towards his bike. His mouth curved until it felt like his face would crack.

Natalia? A good girl? He wasn't so sure.

'You cool with this?' he asked, handing her the spare helmet.

She nodded. 'Just don't go fast. Or kill me.'

'Hey.' He touched his fingers to her shoulder. 'I promise. But you're right about needing a quick escape 'cause they're coming.'

Jack, Liam, and Ana exited the pub. Adam threw his leg over the bike and turned the key.

'Nat!' Ana called.

Natalia slipped the helmet over her head, then took his offered hand. She swung onto the bike behind him, her thighs cradling his hips as she wrapped her arms around his waist and held on tight.

Shit. Perhaps this wasn't a good idea after all.

But it was too late. Heart thumping, Adam sped away from the pub.

* * *

She was mad. Natalia didn't dare ask herself what she'd been thinking. Yes, she'd sworn off men, but she couldn't get Adam out of her head. And then there he'd been, leaning on the bar hot as all hell flirting with her. Not affronting. Not creepy. Flattering. Fun. Did she want to ditch their friends and hang out with him? Hell yes!

A thrill shot up Natalia's spine. She sat flush to Adam's hard back as the bike vibrated beneath her, his firm body the perfect support as they cruised out of town. She wasn't sure if she liked the bike, but with her arms around his warm torso, she could stay there forever. And knowing that Ana didn't approve made Natalia feel slightly wild. She'd never felt wild in her life! But something about Adam had unleashed a demon inside her and Natalia wanted to roll with it. She might be foolish, but this sensation of her blood pumping and the inability to stop smiling … it was glorious.

Before long, Adam slowed and pulled onto the side of the road. He flipped his visor up and turned to her, his dark eyes gleaming. 'How was that?'

Natalia lifted her visor too. 'You're right. It's better than a pushbike.'

His deep rumbling laugh turned her insides to mush. 'Told you. Faster and a lot more fun.' He nodded across the road. 'Thought I'd bring you here. That's Shadow Creek.'

She turned her head and smiled. Finally, banana trees! A road led off the highway towards closed gates that boasted warning signs. *Keep out. Controlled zone.*

'I thought the entrance was behind town.'

'That's the residential entrance, which leads to the houses, High Ridge, and some of our other orchards. But we need a dedicated entrance for the banana farm.'

'Why?'

'Quarantine. We farm bananas under strict restrictions to prevent disease.'

Now the signs made sense. 'Right. So you only permit certain people on the farm?'

'Yeah, it's all about stopping the spread of dirt. The farm vehicles stay in the farming zone and we have rules about cleaning boots. Anything that leaves the farming zone needs to be sanitised before going back in.' Their gazes met again. 'I guess you probably get how that works.'

'Doesn't sound much different from medicine. But you'll have to tell me more about it, Adam. I know nothing about farms.'

'I can do that. How about we head back to town for that stroll by the creek? Have you been there yet?'

'I jogged along there, but I didn't stop to admire the view.'

His eyebrows lifted beneath his helmet. 'You jog?'

'Every day without fail.'

'Good on you. Let's go.'

Natalia flipped her visor down as he turned to face forward. Tightening her grip around his waist, she inched closer. This time, she didn't look over his shoulder to watch where they were going, she simply enjoyed the ride and admired the beautiful rows of banana trees until they disappeared. Everything inside her warmed, fuzzed, and settled to overpower any nervous fear. She'd never imagined she'd end the day on the back of Adam's motorcycle and yes, charming men had hurt her before. But there was something warm about Adam's company that niggled at her heartstrings and made this adventure feel right.

They rode through town and arrived at a car park opposite the golf course. Switching off the bike, Adam held out his hand to help her off. Natalia's legs shook, tingling from the vibrations as she lifted her helmet.

'Not so scary, is it?' he asked, grinning.

'No. But I think I prefer cars.'

'Or pushbikes.'

'Or walking.'

Chuckling, Adam secured their helmets, then offered his hand. Natalia's skin heated as his large, calloused fingers intertwined with hers.

'Beats hanging around the pub with that lot, though.'

'Yeah, but I like your family. Everyone was lovely on Friday night.'

'I like to think we're a welcoming bunch,' he said as they started down the concrete path by the caravan park.

'Ana always said you were.'

'Yeah, I think you're right about her not being impressed by that stunt we just pulled. She's probably told you why though, right?'

Natalia drew her gaze from the sloping green lawn to meet his. 'She's talked about you a bit, told me about your feud with the Kelly brothers and your bad boy rep.'

Adam winced.

'But I honestly don't see why that should matter.' Shrugging, she offered him a smile. 'Unless you think we're just going to sleep together and then you can forget about me, because that's not going to happen.'

Adam laughed and shoved his hand through his mussed hair. 'Natalia …' Again, the way his tongue wrapped around her name sent shivers up her spine. 'Okay, I'll admit that whatever Ana's told you is probably true. I've always been rebellious and not cared about what I said or did. But I want to put that behind me.' His serious gaze returned to hers. 'I know it sounds like a stupid cliché, but I mean it. I had an experience I don't wish to repeat.'

He was right about the cliché. A man could easily use the 'I want to change' speech to make a woman think she could be the one to help him do it. But Natalia valued her own honesty and could recognise it in others. He'd been thinking this before they'd met, so why shouldn't she trust it?

'Waking up in the park?' she asked as the path emerged along the creek.

'You heard about that too?'

She laughed, trying to keep the mood light. 'I believe a lot of people know about that. I'll admit, you must have had a bit to drink. What did you do?'

'That's the thing. I have no idea. I don't know who I went to the park with because Jack, Michael, and my mate Cade, reckon they weren't there. I woke up alone and with a whooping headache. And I'll admit, it scared the shit out of me.'

Natalia pressed her lips together, sensing his embarrassment as he shoved his hand into his pocket and fixated his gaze on the footpath.

'That sounds frightening,' she said gently. 'And you don't remember much?'

'Nope. And that's what scares me the most because … I think someone may have spiked me.'

Natalia exhaled, relieved that he'd recognised that possibility. It was the first thing she'd thought of when Ana had mentioned it all those weeks ago. But not having known the man, she hadn't said anything.

'Memory loss is often a sign of that. You didn't get checked out or—'

'Stupid me left it too late. So no, I won't try to seduce you and then screw you over, Natalia. If I was, taking a stroll in the late afternoon isn't how I'd do it. But I …'

His mouth twisted and she followed his gaze as he glanced out at the creek with its leaf-littered ground, gum trees spearing into the sky, and the soft trickle of flowing water. When Adam remained silent for too long, Natalia prompted, 'You …?'

His gaze shot back to hers. 'I like you. I don't know how to explain it, but since I met you the other day …' He lifted his shoulders and held them high for a moment before dropping them. 'I dunno. I just like you. And if Ana's told you not to get involved with me, then I hope you don't listen to her.'

Natalia stared at him, her heart dancing, squeezing, and screaming. With joy? Fear? Both, probably. This hadn't been the plan. She'd come to Elizadale to work, not to lose her head over another man.

But he liked her, and she couldn't deny the authenticity of that statement. Except ... *Does he like me because—*

She shoved that thought away. 'Ana hasn't said much. She just mentioned you a few times.'

'I'm not worried anyway because she loves me,' he said as he led her off the path. 'You want to sit?'

She nodded and sat cross-legged. Adam stretched one leg out and rested his elbow on his bent knee as he twirled a dry leaf between his fingers.

Natalia glanced out over the creek. It wasn't the most beautiful view, but she'd always loved water. The beach, waterfalls, creeks, it didn't matter—the trickling sound and rippling image always soothed her.

'This is a lovely spot.'

'Yeah, especially now that we have the pathway. One of Liam's brilliant town planning ideas. In winter, it's great to fish in or kayak or have a swim if it's not too cold. After the rain though, it can rage like a beast.'

'I bet.'

'This path also joins the caravan park to the roadhouse and is part of the lap around town, which you know.' He turned and pointed in various directions as he explained. 'There are playgrounds and barbeques up in the parkland and this is where we have our New Year's Eve fireworks.'

'I always enjoy fireworks.' She glanced back at the water. 'So where does this creek run?'

He tossed his crumpled leaf away. 'This is the actual Shadow Creek. Although the property was named first. Sort of. Or they named them together. Anyway, it starts up on the mountain behind the farm, where we have what we call Maguire Falls.'

Natalia grinned. 'I love waterfalls.'

'Then I'll take you there. It's nice in the summer and is a great swimming spot. The creek runs through our farm and forms the barrier between the farming and residential zones. Then it crosses the highway, turns down here and runs by other farms before it meets up with the Mitchell River.'

Natalia shook her head, lost. 'How many farms are around here?'

'Lots. There are a few little farms heading west, but the big ones are ours, the Kellys, Tropic Sun, and White Peaks. We all started out as cattle stations in the eighteen hundreds but have since diversified. Except for the White's. They still do cattle.'

Natalia resisted a grimace. Poor cows. 'What do the Kellys farm?'

'Coffee, and apparently not bad stuff either. Dunno though as I'm not a coffee drinker.'

'Me either. And they're north of you?'

'Yep, next door. Separated by the highway.'

'Right. It's a lot to remember, but I'll work it out eventually.'

His eyebrows lifted. 'Would you like a tour? I can show you around tomorrow if you like?'

Another afternoon with Adam? It might be foolish, but her fearless heart didn't hesitate. 'That would be lovely.'

'I'll pick you up from work, then.' He took her hand, his thumb brushing over the back of her knuckles. Her blood stirred. 'But don't worry, I'll bring the ute. Might even hose it down.'

'I'd appreciate it. The ute, even if it is muddy. The bike was fun, but not good for conversation.'

'Unless I get communication helmets. And you some safety gear.'

She nodded, not having a clue what had come over her. Even though she didn't like motorcycles, the ride had been fun and with her arms wrapped around Adam's muscular body … yeah, she could do that again. 'Sounds good.'

'Then maybe we could have dinner? Jack's always telling me to buy a woman dinner.'

'Yeah?'

'Yeah. But I'm not clueless, Nat. I *have* been in relationships. And despite what some people might think, I've always been a one-woman-at-a-time bloke.'

Her pulse spiked as his grip tightened around her hand. All he did was look at her, yet Natalia couldn't move, caught by the glint in his dark eyes. What was she doing? Sure, this afternoon had been fun and she liked Adam. She couldn't deny her attraction or that she enjoyed the sensation of his rough hand around hers, but could she risk dating him?

Tightness filled her chest and Natalia turned her gaze back to the creek, withdrawing her hand from his. 'Good to know. Because I don't care what you've done in the past, Adam, but I won't be just another random girl.' Then, before she could do anything foolish, Natalia pushed to her feet. 'I'd love to have dinner tomorrow. But I think we should go now. It's getting dark.'

Chapter Eight

Adam cursed the winter and its earlier sunsets as he dropped Natalia at Jackson Villas, then he rode through Shadow Creek with a foolish grin on his face. At home, he kicked off his boots and flung his jacket on the lounge. His phone rang and he snatched it from his pocket, hope filling him at the thought of Natalia calling to chat.

Except Jordan's name flashed on the screen and the bubble inside him popped. Fuck. What did she want? He probably knew. Should he answer? If he didn't, she'd more than likely turn up at his door.

Swearing, he pressed the green circle. 'Jordan?'

'Hey, sexy,' she purred, and Adam grimaced as he strode into the kitchen. 'You busy? It's cold tonight and perhaps we could warm each other up?'

Adam wrenched open the fridge. 'Sorry, Jordan. I'm settling in for an early night and like I told you, I'm not interested anymore.'

She laughed. 'Oh, Adam. You're always interested.'

'No, I mean it. I'm done fooling around.'

This time, her laugh had a harder edge to it. 'You're not serious.'

'Yes.' He snatched out a couple of potatoes. 'I am. Goodbye, Jordan.'

Hanging up, he dropped the potatoes onto the bench, but hell if he knew what he wanted to do with them. Why did Jordan seem to think the idea of him changing was so ridiculous?

Adam grabbed a pot from the cupboard. It didn't matter what she thought, he *could* change. He already had. He could be the man Natalia deserved because he'd never wanted anything more.

If only Jordan's irritating laugh would stop echoing inside his head.

* * *

The next morning, Adam was tempted to whistle while he worked, but he knew it'd annoy Jack. Sure, that tempted him more, but he didn't want to piss his brother off when Jack was dropping fifty kilos of bananas onto his shoulder.

He hadn't stopped thinking about Natalia. She sure was a surprising woman, chatty, kind, and he liked women with spirit. One second she had been giving him beef about motorbikes, the next she'd been climbing aboard. He still couldn't shake the memory of her body pressed against his and was counting the hours until he could escape Jack and see her again.

'Stop fucking daydreaming,' Jack snapped. 'I'm sick of needing to get your attention every time I have something to say. Seriously, mate. You're freakin' me out.'

'I'm freaking myself out! Is this what happens when you find a woman you could actually fall for?'

'How should I know? Does it look like I've got a woman?'

'No, but you damn well could if you wanted to,' he muttered, although he had no intention of being unheard.

Jack's eyes flashed as he reached up to hack off the next bunch of bananas. Usually, Jack and Adam supervised the fields more than worked them, as they had plenty of humpers—banana pickers—on the roster, but Shadow Creek was a massive farm and they enjoyed doing the heavy lifting. There'd be plenty of time for paperwork, management, and supervision when their father and Uncle Cliff were no longer around to do it.

Adam passed the bananas to Ed, who tied them onto the trailer, then returned to Jack. 'I mean, I didn't feel this way about Grace. I liked her, but … what about your serious girlfriends? Like Rebecca Hall? Before she married Jason Taylor over you.'

'She didn't marry Jase over me. We were young and she got with him years after we were through.'

Adam settled the next bunch onto his shoulder with a grimace. 'Maybe I should have this conversation with Liam.'

'Maybe you should.'

Resisting the urge to flip his brother the finger—which he would if he had one spare—Adam headed back to the trailer. Bloody happy bastard, that one.

For the rest of the afternoon, he continued to muse over Natalia. She was a woman who knew what she wanted and he liked that. He wanted to get to know her better and enjoy her smiles. Learn about her interests and explore them with her. Even thinking her name did stupid things to his head. But the most attractive thing about Natalia was her honesty. She was straight up and wasn't afraid to share her feelings.

Unless you think we're just going to sleep together and then you can forget about me because that's not going to happen.

Adam supressed a chuckle. She was right about that. Sure, he wanted her in his bed eventually, but right now, it was her company he longed for. To talk and laugh with her until he was no longer afraid. Sex? Yeah, one day.

He returned to Jack with pride surging through his chest. Change was possible. This was the new Adam, the twenty-eight-year-old with a missing night of his life. So he was happy to take things slow and casual, as he couldn't let anything ruin his chances with Natalia. The last thing he wanted was to be grumpy and alone like Jack.

But Adam wouldn't follow Liam's example any time soon either. Marriage? The thought almost made his knees buckle as he took the weight of the next bunch of bananas. He'd need a shit load of training before he'd be capable of that kind of commitment.

* * *

Jordan left the cold room, stock order in hand, and was shrugging off the oversized coat when she heard Hayley the kitchen waitress's voice drift from the bar.

'And then Adam whisked her away on the back of his motorbike.'

Hayley's friend laughed. 'Adam Maguire and the new doctor? Wow, he's got his work cut out for him there.'

Jordan frowned. Adam and *who*?

'No, I think she'll be good for him. Plus, have you seen her? She's super pretty.'

'Not surprised if she's Ana's sister. It'll be good having another doctor though.'

Then the girls began talking about an upcoming music event and Jordan tuned out. Tossing the stock order onto the bench, she paced the room. What the hell was going on with that man? He said he wasn't interested in fooling around, wanted to 'change', and then he takes the new doctor for a ride?

'Fuck!' Jordan kicked a pile of empty beer cartons. This wasn't part of her plan. Adam was *hers*, dammit, whether he knew it or not. Sure, she didn't always want him, but humans weren't meant to be monogamous and she had the right to have fun and enjoy her freedom. So did he. But if she was going to have any chance of a happy future, then she couldn't lose him. Not now. And she sure as hell wouldn't be replaced by some woman from the city who thought she was all class and propriety just because she was a doctor. Jordan had seen the blonde sitting in the booth on Friday night giggling with the Maguire clan and drinking fucking soda water. What was with that? She couldn't have poorer taste if she tried! How could Adam possibly be interested in her?

Snatching up the stock order, Jordan stomped back to the bar. She knew why he was interested. Blonde. Thin. Pretty in a way that couldn't be natural. Any man would want to fuck that.

Not that Jordan was worried. She was far sexier and probably more willing to please than Doctor Natalia Hamilton. The woman had 'prude' written all over her with her high necklines, ironed pants, and sensible shoes. When Adam found himself on the receiving end of 'no', he'd come running back to her. A man could only hold out for so long.

But that didn't mean Jordan would sit around and wait for

him. She had the trump card. So placing the stock order in Georgina's office, she grabbed her phone and called Elizadale Medical.

'Hey, Grace. It's Jordan Kelly. Can I book an appointment tomorrow?'

Chapter Nine

Adam parked his sparkling clean Hilux and strolled into Elizadale Medical, smiling as Grace glanced up from the computer. 'Hey, Gracie.'

'Fancy seeing you here. Then again, I guess it's no surprise considering you and Natalia sped off into the sunset yesterday.'

He laughed at the tease in her voice. 'You heard about that?'

'You *did* run out of the Royal Hotel and gossip spreads like wildfire. But I also asked Nat why she'd been smiling all day, so she may have mentioned something.'

A ball of heat mounted inside his belly. 'She's been smiling?'

'Don't flatter yourself, Adam. Natalia smiles a lot. And she's lovely, so if you are serious about ditching that dangerous reputation of yours, she could be a good woman for you.'

The door behind him opened and Natalia exited the consultation room with Joanne. Her eyes lit up, but she remained professional while they closed the surgery.

When they stepped outside, Adam took her hand. 'How was your day?'

'Good. I had one difficult case, but hopefully my plan will help her. How was yours?'

'Better now.' He flashed her a smile as he admired how pretty she looked in her slim black pants, flat shoes, and purple shirt he was sure city folk would call a blouse. 'You look gorgeous in your doctor clothes. I think this is the most I've seen you dressed up.'

Natalia's mouth thinned as she glanced down at her outfit. 'Yeah, I don't … I mean, I wasn't aiming for gorgeous. I'm supposed to look professional.'

Adam frowned, noting the change in her tone and the shadow that passed over her face. She *did* look professional, but that's what made her beautiful. And after only seeing her in jeans and shirts …

It clicked. 'Don't you like compliments, Natalia?'

'It's not that. I just …' Sighing, she met his gaze, her eyes warm. 'I'm sorry. Thank you, Adam. You look good too.'

Unsure what had happened there, Adam rounded to his side of the ute. Yeah, some women took compliments better than others, but he wouldn't be surprised if Natalia was sick of it. She probably received them all the time.

But that was a mystery to solve later as he settled behind the wheel. 'Righto. You ready for your tour?'

'Absolutely. Let's go.'

She clipped on her seatbelt as Adam started the ute.

'I'm sure by now you've seen everything in town,' he said. 'This is Riley Road, our main street, named after Stuart Riley, the guy who settled this place. I don't know much about it, but he was Meg's ancestor and if you want a history lesson, she'd be more than happy to provide it.'

'Meg bursts with town pride. Ana would talk about you guys all the time, so when I came here, it was as though I already knew you all.'

'Yeah, like those stories about me punching Kelly,' he muttered, adjusting his hands on the wheel.

'She said good things too. But I heard about how none of you like the Kellys. She wasn't sure why though. Is there a reason?'

Because Harrison Kelly was a fuckhead? And his brother was no better? But Adam didn't think Natalia would accept that as an excuse. And even though he wanted to be honest with her, he didn't want to tell her the Kellys hated him mainly because of his casual hook-ups with their sister. Some things didn't need to be said.

But their dislike for each other had begun long before Jordan had lured him in.

'Our parents are best friends, but our generation stopped getting along when Liz Kelly's father died. Stan had been close with Dad and a grandfather figure to us all, the only grandparent we and the Kellys ever knew. Harry and I had just started school when he died and Harry basically said we had no right to be upset. That Stan hadn't been our grandfather.'

'That's not fair.'

Adam shrugged. 'Yeah, but it was so long ago now. I barely remember Stan, but I remember Harry turning into a real bully. He always seemed to be on my back and sometimes, I felt the urge to piss him off because it was fun. Now, we all despise each other on principle.'

'Fair enough.' Natalia glanced out the window. 'Where are we going?'

He turned right onto the highway. 'We'll go north and I'll show you the farms.'

'Okay. I'd like to know more about who's who as it's important for me as a doctor to know the family connections. I've learned that the hard way.'

They drove past the sporting fields and into the bushland. 'Well, the Taylors operate Tropic Sun, the banana farm across the highway from us heading south. They're good people. Jack and I are mates with Jason Taylor. His sister Leanne runs their packing sheds and Claire's the hairdresser in town. And you know Grace is from White Peaks. Her brother's still out there. He's all right, but not really a mate. He and Jason Taylor married sisters, which is weird for them. Their wives, Zoe and Rebecca, are Meg's cousins.'

Natalia gave a quick shake of her head. 'God, I'll never keep that straight.'

'Their mum runs the bakery and is the sister of Meg's dad, Ron. He owns a hell of a lot of property, including the Riley Road shopping complex, roadhouse, and Jackson Villas. But Meg's mum is from Jade Farm, one of the biggest avocado growers in the north.'

Natalia exhaled softly. 'Wow.'

'Yeah.' Adam gave a lazy shrug. 'They originally made their money on tobacco, but that industry died in the nineties and they got out early. Either way, Meg's set to inherit a lot, but her grandparents aren't sure what they're going to do about the farm. Her cousin Chaz was the front runner to inherit, but he became a country music star and wants nothing to do with the farm. Neither does Meg or her sister, who lives out of town.'

But Adam knew exactly what would happen to Jade Farm if a certain couple would pull their finger out. The rumour was that if Meg and Jack were to stop mucking about and bloody well marry, then her grandparents wouldn't sell and Meg would inherit under some kind of merger with Shadow Creek. But such a thing would only be a rumour while his brother remained a stubborn bastard.

'That's unfortunate,' Natalia said. 'Ana told me about Chaz and his band. The Charlie Boys. I've listened to their music and they're quite good. So is Meg.'

'She sure is. Beats me why she stopped singing, but she wrote The Charlie Boys a couple of hits.' Adam nodded outside his window. 'Anyway. Here's the actual Shadow Creek again.' He didn't bother stopping as there wasn't much to look at, just the one-way, rail-less concrete bridge. Before long, he pulled onto the shoulder of the highway by the turnoff to Mossman that separated Shadow Creek from the Kellys. 'Out your window are more farms and eventually, White Peaks. The road ahead will take us to Cooktown.'

'Anything interesting up there?'

'Just farms and National Parks.'

'Have you ever been to the top of Queensland?'

'Once. Not worth it unless you like four-wheel-driving, dirt roads, and camping.'

Her nose wrinkled. 'Yeah, not really my thing.'

'Thought not.' He laughed lightly and pointed to the road on the right. 'That's the highway to Port Douglas.'

'Now *that* sounds good. I'm sure the beaches are beautiful.'

'Nowhere better than North Queensland for beaches.'

'I've heard that.'

'Maybe we could go one day?'

Her pink lips curved. 'Maybe we could.'

He held her gaze for a few pounding heartbeats, then glanced out the windscreen. Any longer and he'd be pulling her close and begging to whisk her away to a flash Palm Cove resort for the weekend, but it was far too soon for that.

Adam shoved the ute into gear. 'Do you want to get out and have a quick look at the farm?'

Her eyes brightened. 'Yes, please.'

* * *

A few minutes later, Natalia climbed out of Adam's ute by the entrance to Shadow Creek. Taking her hand, he led her towards the tin shack by the gate.

'Are those good shoes?'

She glanced down at her plain black loafers. 'Not particularly. Why?'

'Would you mind if the soles got wet? Otherwise, we'll have to stay on this side of the fence.'

She raised her eyebrows. 'We're actually going in? I thought visitors weren't allowed.'

'Random people aren't, but I can take you as long as your shoes are clean.'

'Oh. Well, no I don't mind if they get wet.'

'Excellent.' He led her inside the shack with a bench seat and a shelf lined with boots. Adam toed off his clean boots and replaced them with a pair a little more worn before checking the small walkway of water. 'Foot wash,' he explained, sloshing through it.

Natalia followed him, rubbing her shoes on the submerged rubber mat for good measure before stepping onto the farm. He plucked two boot covers out of the box on the wall and handed them to her. 'Just because your shoes have been elsewhere.'

Natalia smiled as she slipped them on. 'Feels like I'm going into surgery.'

He took her hand. 'You've been into surgeries?'

'Of course. I had fantastic placements at university and we must do a surgical rotation in the first year of internship. My favourite was cardiothoracic as there's nothing like having your hands on a beating heart.'

Adam blew out his breath. 'I think I'd faint, but I can see where you'd like it. Must feel pretty special to do that.'

'It is quite a privilege,' she agreed as they strode through the long grass and into the shade of the farm. 'Now, tell me about bananas.'

'Well ... bananas are the largest herbaceous flowering plant,' he said. 'They're not trees because trees have wooden trunks. Rather, we call these pseudostems.' Adam placed his hand on the large 'treelike' stem of the banana plant. 'They grow from a corm and take about twelve to eighteen months to grow, depending on weather, soil, and conditions. When the plant is mature, the corm stops producing new leaves and forms the inflorescence. Or flower.'

Natalia glanced up at the towering banana plants, their leaves fanning in arches over the grassy walkways. 'I knew they weren't trees. How many bananas do they produce?'

'Each plant produces one flower. After fruiting, the pseudostem dies, but offshoots develop from the base, which makes the plants perennials. See here?'

Adam pointed out the cut stumps and offshoots by those currently carrying bunches. 'So, they just keep popping up?'

'Yep. That's why they grow like weeds when people plant them in their backyards. But you need to cut the pseudostem so that the offshoot can harness enough energy from the soil to grow and produce fruit.'

'Huh.' Natalia peered through the bottom of the bright blue bag at the bunch of dark green bananas. The science behind farming didn't surprise her as it would take a lot of planning and agricultural engineering to maintain production in a large commercial operation. 'And why the bags?'

'To protect the bananas from the sun, leaf rub, insects, and other damage,' he said, stepping up beside her. 'We also colour coordinate so that we know which bunches need to be harvested. This week, we're checking the red bags.'

'It's all very interesting.' She loved to learn new things, so she wasn't lying as she wandered beneath the shady plants. 'Did you study at all or learn on the job?'

'I knew everything about bananas by the time I was ten, I reckon.' Chuckling, Adam slid his hands into his pockets. 'But I spent a year in Toowoomba doing my diploma in agriculture because Dad made me.'

'Is it hard work?'

'Harder than other types of farm work.' Dry leaves crunched beneath his boots as he walked beside her. 'Bananas require a lot of physical labour as we pick them by hand. The bunches can weigh up to fifty kilos and we carry them over our shoulder.'

Natalia imagined him with a bunch of bananas tossed over his shoulder, his muscles tense and working. Heat coiled inside her belly and she glanced upward again. 'Sounds tough.'

'Yeah, but I like it. I don't always work in the fields as we employ lots of people, but until Jack and I take over, we do the labour. It's our farm, after all.'

'You never wanted to do anything else?'

He shrugged. 'Not really. Dad and Uncle Cliff have run Shadow Creek together for thirty-odd years and Jack and I want to do the same. We each have our separate interests and such, but I honestly couldn't imagine leaving this place.'

After witnessing his passion for farming, Natalia couldn't imagine it either. He might be wearing his good jeans and a button-up shirt she wouldn't expect him to wear to work, but Adam belonged there among these plants.

A strange tightness filled Natalia's chest. 'It sure is beautiful …'

'I'm glad you think so,' he breathed as he wrapped his arm around her waist. Natalia lowered her gaze from the overarching leaves, her pulse spiking as his fingers splayed over her hip. All he did was look at her, but as his dark gaze roamed over her face, Natalia couldn't move. Thoughts vanished and everything inside her tingled. Then his gaze landed on her mouth. Her breath fell short. He could kiss her. Oh, she wanted him to kiss her. It was a terrible idea. Terrible! But what was the harm? Her lips parted to allow her breath to escape. She'd already taken a few risks, so placing her hand on his shoulder, Natalia lifted onto her toes and took the kiss for herself.

Common sense vanished as Adam's warm mouth moulded with hers. If he was surprised, he didn't show it as his arms wrapped around her and pulled her close. His lips drove hers apart and everything feminine inside her ignited and danced as he nibbled at her lips and took the lower one between his.

Adam drew away and lifted his hand to cup her cheek. Then his mouth was back on hers, softer this time. Slipping her arms up around his neck, a shiver coursed through Natalia until her loins ached. Damn, he tasted good. He sure was one hell of a man and nothing like those groomed and uptight city folk she'd dated before. No, Adam Maguire was so much more. Tough, strong, and all natural—a testament to a lifetime of cutting, planting, and harvesting the plants surrounding her. Utterly consumed, she never wanted to let go.

But she recovered some sense when she could no longer breathe. Slowly, she pulled away.

His dark, hooded eyes snapped to hers. 'You only beat me to that by a second.'

'I'd been thinking about it …'

'So had I. Constantly. For days.' He drew in a deep breath, then let it out slowly. 'I can't stop thinking about you.'

Her heart resumed its newfound arrythmia. 'Strangely enough, I can't get you off my mind either.'

* * *

The words were music to Adam's ears, music he hadn't realised he was missing but had always wanted to hear as he resisted the grin that longed to break free. She was going to give him a chance! How he felt about that he didn't know, apart from hot as hell after that kiss. But deep down, he felt good about this. Felt good about *her*. He might be punching above his weight, but nevertheless, Natalia was in his arms and she'd been thinking about him.

That was enough.

'I think you're quite unforgettable, Nat. And I'm glad we're doing this.'

'Me too. But I meant what I said yesterday, Adam. I won't be a random girl.'

Her eyes darkened and Adam couldn't help but grin. He loved women when they were honest. They always seemed to make a point of what they were saying.

But despite the hope inside him, his chest tightened as he ran his hand down her golden ponytail. He wanted to give Natalia something he'd never given a woman before, and even though he'd never mean to hurt her, he was taking a massive risk. He was in over his head and when that happened, he always fucked it up.

He cleared his throat. *One day at a time.* 'There's nothing random about you, Natalia.'

She smiled and with that settled, Adam lowered his mouth back to hers. Her lips parted and he kissed her softly, savouring her taste as everything inside him settled. Would he ever get enough of her?

She drew away first, an odd smile on her lips. 'You know, you're quite charming, Adam.'

He chuckled as she moved back a step. 'So, they tell me,' he said, taking her hand and strolling back the way they'd come. 'Do you have any more questions about bananas?'

'Yes, why the quarantine? What disease are you controlling?'

'Panama Tropical Race 4. It's a fungus that kills the banana plant and the Department of Agriculture detected it in Tully about seven years ago. Two years later, they found it again and biosecurity imposed quarantine to prevent accidental movement of the disease.'

'Better to be safe than sorry,' Natalia said as they stepped back into the sunshine. 'But thank you, Adam, I enjoyed that and would love to learn more.'

'Sure. Next time, I'll take you to the packing sheds.'

'Sounds good,' she said as they returned to the entrance. Adam switched out his boots and she tore the covers off her shoes. 'Can I have a farm fresh banana?'

'If you like. There are plenty of bananas around here.' They strode back to the ute. 'So, how about we head back for dinner?'

'Okay. But I have to say, I am kind of particular about what I eat.'

He glanced at her as they climbed into their seats. 'Are you a vegetarian like Ana? 'Cause that's all right. She's not a big fan of the Royal, but she has the cook onside and he makes her vegetarian dishes.'

'Yeah, she was very impressed when Liam organised that for her. But no.' Natalia shook her head. 'I'm entirely plant-based.'

He frowned and switched on the ignition. 'Plant-based?'

'What you might call vegan.'

He'd heard about vegans, but plant-based? 'There's a difference?'

'Depends. You can eat a plant-based diet for health and nutrition reasons, but not be vegan by buying other products, like wool or makeup that's not cruelty-free. I started out with the diet only when I got serious about my health, but quickly became vegan all-around when I learned what happens to the animals.'

Adam nodded and pulled back onto the road. If eating a plant-based diet is what she wanted to do, then that was fine. He might not want to think about life without chicken or barramundi, but they weren't talking about him. And it made sense that she was health conscious since she enjoyed running and looked bloody fantastic.

'I can work with that. Should take you to Smithy's then. I haven't had a good look at their new menu, but by the way Ana goes on about it, I'm sure they'll have something for you. If you're okay with that. Otherwise, we could … I dunno. Skip dinner?'

'No. If nothing else, there's always a garden salad I'm happy to eat. But if we could check out Smithy's, that'd be great.'

'Righto. But you have to tell me … what *is* "plant-based"?'

She laughed. 'Exactly what it sounds like. Eating food that's grown from the ground. Wholegrains, fruit, veggies, nuts, seeds. Very little processed foods. It might sound limited, but it's not. There's nothing more delicious.'

'I'll admit, Ana cooks good food. They invited me to dinner once and we had black bean burritos. Bloody delish.'

'Beans are awesome. You can do heaps with them.'

'I'm sure you can. So, was there a reason for this health kick? Or did you do it because you're a doctor, learned about it, and it made sense?'

Natalia chuckled. 'I certainly didn't learn about it as a doctor. And I don't think anyone needs a reason to prioritise their health. But yes, there was a turning point for me.' Her gaze lingered out the window for a moment before returning to his. 'Has Ana told you about our dad?'

'I know he died when you were little.'

'Sudden cardiac death. By all appearances, he'd been healthy, but his heart had been seriously compromised and he died at thirty-seven.'

Adam winced. 'That's tough. So, are you afraid the same thing will happen to you?'

She blew out her breath. 'I *was*. Mum was aware of the genetic risk, so she made sure Ana and I stayed active and ate well. I ran cross-country throughout school and did various activities. I thought I had a handle on it.'

His gut clenched. 'But?'

'I had blood tests at nineteen and my cholesterol was elevated.'

His eyebrows shot up. 'At nineteen?'

'Yep. It terrified me. I'd done everything I'd been told to do by health authorities, but it was no good. I realised then that nothing I'd learned would help. Short of Lipitor. So, I looked elsewhere, and that's when I discovered the power of plant-based nutrition, one of the best kept health secrets. For decades, doctors who trust it have been reversing heart disease with wholefood plant-based diets. It's fascinating stuff. So, I gave up all animal protein, my blood work is fantastic, and I feel great every day.'

Adam's forehead tightened as he stared out the windscreen. He'd admit, he rarely thought about health or food. He understood the basics that his mother and Doctor Brennan had bashed into his head, which was all he'd thought he needed. But he'd never had a problem with people giving themselves a little extra care. Grace White was health conscious and Lucy exercised regularly. But Natalia …

He parked outside Smithy's and turned to face her. 'And it worked?'

'Yep. So, no, I'm not scared. I don't want to die young, Adam, but I *am* my father's daughter. I can't escape that. I believe I have his heart, so I do everything possible to look after it. At least then, if I die young, I'll know it hadn't been my fault.'

Passion sparked in her eyes and Adam admired her resolve, strangely proud of her as he reached across the console and took her delicate hand. 'I don't want you dying young either, Natalia.'

She smiled softly. 'Thank you, Adam.'

Chapter Ten

Natalia's pulse raced as she climbed out of the ute. What was Adam doing to her? She'd met many people who understood her vegan lifestyle, but she'd also had men she'd dated turn up their noses, ask why she bothered, and take her to a steakhouse and tell her to order the salad.

But after spending time with Adam yesterday, it didn't surprise Natalia that he understood.

She squeezed his hand as he led her around the cream-rendered building to the bistro entrance of the Smithfield Hotel. Adam grabbed the laminated menu off the first table he saw and handed it to her.

'Tell me what you think.'

She glanced at the menu. In Sydney, being vegan wasn't too difficult as there were plenty of food options throughout the city, even though she rarely dined out. Natalia preferred cooking for herself, but she wasn't about to reject dinner with Adam.

Her gaze fell to the salads and her eyebrows shot up. The chef's salad was better than she'd seen in a while—based on spinach with quinoa and chickpeas. She read the description of the roast pumpkin and walnut salad and her mouth watered.

'Yeah, this is—ooh, they have a veggie burger!' Then she noticed they'd marked the vegan dishes with the VG label.

'They do?' Adam picked up a menu himself. 'Huh. This really has changed.'

'When was the last time you ate here?'

'Hell if I know. I rarely come to Smithy's.'

'Only when Georgina kicks you out of the Royal,' she teased as she glanced back at the mains. 'Ooh, an Asian stir-fry on brown rice. Wow. Not only are there options, but they're not lacking nutrition either.'

'Luke's a health nut. I believe he revamped the menu to give Elizadale better eating out options. And he threw out the deep fryers.'

She blinked. 'Really?'

'That's the rumour.'

Natalia scanned the rest of the menu. The steaks came with baked potatoes and veggies. 'Wow. Luke certainly has it all together. No wonder Grace likes him.'

'I guess. So, you're happy to eat here?'

She broke into a grin. 'Happy? You'll be bringing me back!'

'Excellent.' Adam led her towards a table for two but didn't sit. 'Is it sparkling water you'd like?'

'Yes, thank you.'

Natalia relaxed into her chair as Adam strolled towards the bar. She'd spent all day going back and forth in her worry about getting involved with him. He seemed to be the type of man she should avoid and if things went wrong, not only would she hurt herself, but possibly Ana, Liam, and the Maguires too.

Then again, it was only one dinner and what was life if she didn't have fun? The bigger problem was what she was going to order. There were too many choices!

Adam returned to their table with their drinks, his phone vibrating as he slipped into his chair. He took it out and frowned.

'Everything okay?' she asked.

'Yeah, nothing important.' He put his phone away and picked up his beer, but she didn't miss the flash of irritation in his eyes.

She placed her menu down. 'So, what did you do today?'

'Spent the morning harvesting. Then turned wood this afternoon.'

'Turned wood?'

He took a swig of his beer. 'Yeah. You know, making wooden bowls and such.'

Natalia raised her eyebrows. She thought she knew what he meant, but the only wooden bowls she was familiar with came from Myer. 'Is that a hobby of yours?'

'It used to be. I got into it during woodwork in high school and would make many things for my family and friends. After graduation, my parents bought me my first lathe and I've been experimenting ever since. I've entered comps at the Show, but everyone's been telling me I should take it seriously and start my own business.'

'And sell your work?' She had to admit, she was impressed.

'Yep. Whenever I've been in the mood and made a lot of things, I'd give them to Sue and Heather at Elizadale Homewares. They've always asked that I do it more regularly, but you know …' He sighed and shoved his hand through his hair. 'I was too lazy for that.'

She could imagine. Supplying a steady stream of goods took commitment. 'But now you've changed your mind?'

'All part of the new life I'm trying to build, I suppose. I'll always have the farm, but it would be nice to have something that's just mine. So, I've started the business and sworn off partying and women. Well—' his mouth curved '—I had, until you arrived in town.'

Natalia's heart pounded as she returned his smile. Adam Maguire had left her speechless once again. He honestly was trying to better himself and if going into business didn't show growth, she didn't know what did.

But while the woodturning sounded interesting, that wasn't the change of his that made her throat close over. Keeping their gazes locked, she reached across the table and took his hands. 'Adam, what are you looking for?'

'What do you mean?'

'Yesterday you whisked me out of the Royal. Now we're having dinner and I want to know before this goes any further … what are you looking for?'

Adam remained silent. His eyes darkened and anxiety clawed at her belly. She liked him and he liked her. He was attentive, understanding, and the last thing she'd call him was a bad boy. In fact, Adam Maguire was quickly becoming the most interesting man she'd ever met.

'I just want to be with you, Natalia. I don't know what I'm looking for, but I hope I can get to know you while I figure it out. Is that okay?'

Her shoulders relaxed. 'Yes, Adam. That's okay.'

His thumb stroked the back of her hand. 'So … are *you* looking for anything?'

'No. In fact, I'd sworn off men as dating has never gone well for me. *But* I am glad I met you.'

He grinned. 'So, you want to come back here tomorrow?'

Squeezing his hand, Natalia ignored the doubt that niggled inside her. 'Yes, Adam. Tomorrow.'

* * *

'This sure is a place that makes you happy,' Natalia said, waltzing through the house the next morning after letting Ana inside.

'You're happy?'

'I am. I don't know what you really think of Adam, but we had a lovely evening last night and he's more than what people make him out to be.' Natalia took the jug of water from the fridge and grabbed two glasses. 'So what if he has a past that makes people think he's some sort of rebel? Sure, he may have given people reason to think that, but I don't think he's lying about wanting to change.'

Ana sat at the dining table. 'Me either. And I know he's a decent man, Nat. I've always liked Adam, but I don't want to see you get hurt. He's still known as the bad boy and Adam has heartbreaker written all over him. Just ask Grace.'

'Grace?'

'They dated once, and Liam says despite the claim they split amicably, Adam still broke her heart.'

Natalia sank into her chair. Grace had dated Adam? Who else had dated Adam?

No. She wouldn't go there. This was a small town and she didn't need to know those things. There were enough intimacies she'd become aware of as a doctor and honestly, it didn't matter. She wasn't a woman who became intimidated by a man's ex. 'They seemed friendly enough when he picked me up this afternoon.'

'Look, I don't know the whole story. But if you want to date Adam, then please be careful. I don't know him well enough to be sure he won't hurt you. But I know *you*. I'm afraid people might talk and I know how that makes you uncomfortable.'

Natalia covered her grimace with a sip of water. Ana was right. She hated gossip. But she couldn't deny that what she felt for Adam was different. She couldn't spend her time in Elizadale resisting him. And deep down, she longed to see where things went.

Ana reached for Natalia's hand. 'But I'm glad you're happy, Nat. Honestly.'

'Thanks. Anyway, it's just casual. And with the changes he's making, I'm sure people will see he's a good man. Are all the Maguire men so funny and charming?'

'Jack's more the silent type, but yes, they are.'

'How were they all single before you arrived?'

'I don't know, but I snagged Liam. And we posted our wedding invitations yesterday, so make sure you collect your mail!'

Natalia laughed. 'I'll go straight after work.'

* * *

Adam sang along to The Wolfe Brothers over the mechanical whir of the lathe. He couldn't help it, he was happy. It wasn't an unusual feeling as he'd always considered himself an easy-going bloke, but right now, he couldn't remember ever feeling so bloody fantastic. So, he held his spindle gouge steady to add the curve he desired to the bowl and thought about Natalia.

Fuck, he was screwed. She filled his head, his heart, and

did things to him he'd never thought a woman could with her glittering smile, soft touch, and perfect kisses. It had been impossible to turn wood all afternoon and not make her something. Yeah, he'd promised Sue and Heather to deliver ten goods by Monday, but he had time. Right now, the most important thing was that he made a gift for Natalia, and he'd chosen his precious piece of redwood to do it. He'd considered making her a vase, but the redwood was flat and the perfect shape to fashion into a shallow bowl. She could keep it in the kitchen as a fruit bowl, in her bathroom for soaps, or in her bedroom for trinkets. He didn't care, as long as she had it.

'What do you think, mate?' Adam switched off the lathe and looked for his dog. Rusty was convinced he had a rat and was busy sniffing under the workbench, his white bum in the air and tail wagging. Adam had chosen a Jack Russell for their hunting abilities and Rusty was the best rat catcher around, so he was usually right about these things. He was also a fabulous snake alarm, but Adam knew it was a rat Rusty was chasing. Rats required silent hunting. He barked at snakes.

Tossing his safety glasses aside, he strode towards Rusty. The little dog scurried back, his tongue hanging out and eyes gleaming. Adam grabbed the torch. 'Got anything?'

Dropping to his hands and knees, he shone the light beneath the bench, finding nothing but cobwebs and wood shavings. 'You're dreamin', mate.'

But Rusty remained convinced as he stuck his head between the piles of wood. Adam returned to the lathe and stared at the bowl. He could add a decorative groove ... but no. Best to leave it. Maybe he'd throw in a few bananas and present it as a fruit bowl. Pity the lychees weren't in season, but there were guavas around. Did she like lychees and guavas? Surely if she was keen on nutrition, she would try any fruit.

It'd sure be different dating a vegan, or 'plant-based' eater, especially since all his culinary skills centred around grilling or roasting various cuts of meat. But he'd still like to cook for her at some point. It wasn't a skill he boasted about, but when in the mood, he enjoyed whipping up a hearty meal. And women were often impressed with a man who could cook. At least, that's what his mum had told him when he'd refused to learn. After that, he'd entered the kitchen with enthusiasm.

But he wouldn't consider Natalia's choices a negative thing and he'd cook her something tasty when the time came. At least Smithy's new menu had come to the rescue and he looked forward to trying their coconut chicken breast on pineapple rice. He might be a man who loved his meat, but he loved fruit more. Pineapple on pizza? Fuck yes!

Satisfied, he took the bowl off the lathe and scratched the itch at the back of his neck. He was keen to see how things developed with Natalia. After yesterday, it no longer seemed like such a stupid idea, despite it making him uneasy. He wanted to grow and mature, so dating a serious woman was a positive step to take.

But if there was one thing he'd always known, it was that if the right woman came along, he wouldn't let her go. If he were to marry, it would be forever. And Natalia—

Wood crashed. Rusty shot across the floor in chase of a black flash. High-pitched squeaking sounded over the music, then stopped. Dropping the dead rat, Rusty looked at Adam, his tail wagging.

'Good boy, mate. Proved me wrong yet again.'

Chapter Eleven

Work kept Natalia busy as she vaccinated a baby, diagnosed gout, and endured a long, tedious discussion about diabetes management with a man who 'couldn't help' all the soft drink he consumed. Her debrief with Joanne ended in Natalia reminding herself there was only so much she could do for people who were in denial about their health risks, then she reviewed results. It was approaching the end of the day when Natalia called in her next patient.

'Jordan Kelly?'

The woman in the corner stood. She was tallish and slim with long dark hair hanging loose over her shoulders.

'Hi, I'm Natalia, the new doctor.' She gestured Jordan inside.

'Hey.' Jordan sat and crossed her bare legs. 'So, are you missing the big city?'

'Not particularly. Elizadale's a nice town and I'm enjoying it.' Natalia opened Jordan's chart. 'What can I do for you?'

'I'm pregnant,' Jordan said matter-of-factly, the corners of her mouth curving.

'Congratulations.'

'Thanks. I'm a little along, but I thought I better get checked out.'

'Good idea.' Natalia turned to the computer and opened a new antenatal record. 'So, when was your last period?'

'Twelfth of May. Dunno how this happened, though. I mean, I *had* been a little lazy with the pill, but no one's perfect.'

Natalia resisted a frown. 'So, this wasn't planned?'

'Not really. But I thought I'd keep it.'

Natalia's gaze darted towards the two previous antenatal records, ones she had ignored before but were marked 'ended by termination'. Of course, she was pro-choice, but Jordan's tone …

'And you're okay with that?'

'Yeah.' Jordan gave an easy shrug. 'I mean, I've had abortions before and they made sense at the time. But I can't keep having them and I … sorta want this baby.'

Nodding slowly, Natalia studied Jordan as something strange flashed through her pale eyes. Pride? Joy? Determination? Natalia didn't know. 'Did you do a home pregnancy test?'

'Yep. I was in denial, so I only found out three weeks ago. But I'm fine.'

Jordan certainly seemed fine with her steeled spine and hard attitude, but her foot constantly tapping on the floor suggested that beneath her tough veneer, anxiety lingered.

'What about the father? Is he in the picture?'

Her lips quirked. 'Not yet. I'll tell him eventually.'

It took all of Natalia's strength not to comment. She hated to judge her patients, but sometimes she couldn't understand them.

'All right.' She reached for the blood pressure cuff. 'We'll take some baseline measures and I'll give you a pathology referral to make sure you're healthy. I'll also do a HCG to date the pregnancy for you.'

Jordan stuck out her arm. 'Do whatever you need. I mean, I know I had to come in, but I'm not worried. I've always been healthy.'

'Antenatal appointments are important, Jordan,' Natalia said gently as they waited for the blood pressure reading.

'Yeah, I know. And I guess I should make sure everything's okay before I share the news. I still need to tell my parents, but my brothers will be pissed that I got knocked up, especially if I don't make things right. Although I don't know why I should tell Adam when the bloody bastard doesn't talk to me anymore.'

Natalia froze. Her hands tightened around the arms of her chair and her heart began to race. Adam? Adam who? *Okay, think rationally, Natalia. Almost two thousand people in this town, there was bound to be more than one Adam.*

Taking a deep breath, she turned back to the computer. She needed to print a pathology form. And respond.

'I don't know how you tell him,' she muttered for lack of better words. Her hands shook as she selected the blood tests she wanted and searched for the dating HCG. She was being stupid. Absolutely stupid.

'He won't be happy. He's wanted nothing to do with me since his birthday. The guy gets off his face and then changes all his fucking values.'

Natalia's curser hovered over the print button. The world shut down around her. She couldn't move. Couldn't breathe. Her fingers numbed. Her heart thudded … broke.

It was him. Her Adam. The man she had …

The pain inside her coiled hot and tight.

She clicked print.

'Yes, well … people can do that.' Natalia snatched the form from the printer and hastily signed it. Blinking back tears, she held her composure. She was a professional, dammit, and she was going to remain that way.

She handed Jordan the form, then the part of her brain she couldn't control said, 'But it's probably best you tell him sooner rather than later.'

Jordan's eyes hardened again. 'I dunno. I might wait. And if he doesn't talk to me anymore, why should I bother? Besides, I'm only eleven weeks. Aren't you supposed to wait until twelve? When the danger period is over?'

Natalia clenched her teeth. *To tell other people maybe, not the bloody father! And you* should *bother because it's* his *baby!*

'That's up to you.' Needing Jordan to leave, she stood, not caring that she hadn't asked if there was anything else she could do for her. 'Come in on Monday and Grace will take your blood.'

'Thanks. I will.'

Natalia wrenched open the door. Jordan left and lifted her hand in farewell. Somehow, Natalia lifted her own, then quietly shut the door.

She took a deep, calming breath. This could *not* be happening. No. Not …

'Dammit!' Exhaling, she paced the room. She needed to shake this off, and to get through the rest of her day. She only had one more consultation, so Natalia forced herself to smile as she called the man in. Thankfully, he was seeking a hypertension review, so she did her check-ups, wrote the scripts, and shoved Jordan's situation from her mind.

But she couldn't remove it from her heart. For once, Natalia wished the agonising ache inside her chest *was* ischemia. A heart attack she could manage. But a secret?

Oh, God. Jordan has to tell him. She has to!

Farewelling her patient, Natalia closed the door and crumpled into her chair. Of course, a person could do as they chose, but surely Jordan wouldn't be so selfish. Would she?

Natalia's belly clenched. While she could never imagine not telling the father if she was pregnant, she knew some women didn't. And if Jordan …

Groaning, she dropped her head into her hands. What was she going to do? She should never have gone out with Adam Maguire. She'd known better. Two weeks, that's all it'd taken. Initial attraction, agonising desire, and the romance she'd always wished for had beckoned. She'd longed to seize it.

But unless Jordan spoke up, Natalia's newfound hope would wither and die. Because she couldn't keep this secret.

Yet, she had no choice.

Chapter Twelve

Natalia shut down the computer and helped Emma close the surgery. After waving goodbye, she hurried to the corner and was about to turn right for home when she remembered Ana's wedding invitation. She should collect it. So, since a short walk and distraction wouldn't hurt, she turned left towards the shops, gazing at the grand old Queenslander, Riley House.

But Elizadale wasn't as beautiful as it had been yesterday. Adam desperately wanted to change and yet fate thought he deserved this? It might be hard for Jordan not to reveal who the father was in a small town, but Natalia didn't know the social dynamics and Jordan could keep it a secret. And if she never said anything, then Natalia was bound by law to remain silent.

Forever.

The vice around her heart turned and locked tight. Dammit, why had she thought she could be a doctor in a small town? If Adam never found out, she wouldn't be able to stay. And if Jordan told him, then what would that mean for Natalia? Would Adam want to be with Jordan?

Inhaling, Natalia steeled her spine and strode into the small post office. With forced cheer, she collected the lone purple envelope and headed home.

She didn't know what had happened between Adam and Jordan, and she didn't want to. But if he wanted to be with Jordan, then Natalia couldn't condemn him for that. She couldn't compete with the mother of his child. She'd get over their short romance. Their three-day fling. And in time, she would be happy for him.

Natalia blew out her breath. She had to stop thinking about it. Just wait and see what happened when he found out.

If he found out.

Oh God.

Returning home, Natalia kicked off her shoes, dumped her handbag, and sank onto the lounge. She switched her thoughts to the wedding and forced a smile as she opened the invitation. Weddings were happy occasions and she couldn't wait for her sister's big day. But as she ran her finger over the gold embossed writing, there was nothing inside her but misery. Anxiety. Pain.

Nope, she refused to feel that way. Jumping to her feet, Natalia stuck the invitation on the fridge. She couldn't talk to anyone, but she had to settle her erratic thoughts. So, she changed her clothes, tied up her joggers, and ran to Ana's house. Her feet pounded the pavement until she arrived at the sprawling acreage, climbed the stairs, and knocked.

'Hey, Nat!' Pushing open the screen door, Liam's smile dropped into a frown. 'What's wrong?'

Apparently, she wasn't doing as good a job of holding herself together as she'd thought. 'Is Ana home?'

'Of course. Ana! Nat's here!'

They entered the kitchen and Ana appeared from the hallway. 'Hey, what's up?'

'Can I talk to you?'

Ana frowned, glancing at Liam and Natalia before holding out her hand. She led Natalia onto the back deck and as they sat, Louis wandered over and rested his head on Natalia's knees. Stroking his soft ears, she drew comfort from his adoring eyes.

Eventually, Ana broke the silence. 'What is it?'

Natalia shook her head, unsure of what to say. She couldn't ask about Adam and Jordan as that could get her into trouble. Somehow, she needed Ana to give the information freely.

'Whatever it is, Nat, just ask. Did something happen?'

Maybe she should go with the simple question? It might sound ridiculous after yesterday's conversation, but at least it wouldn't breach confidentiality.

'Please don't read into this because I don't really care … but what do you know about Adam's exes?'

Ana raised her eyebrows. 'Are you sure you don't care?'

'Just answer the question.'

'Well … I told you about Grace, and he had a fling with Claire Taylor once. Then there's Jordan Kelly, but they've been on and off for years.'

Natalia's belly clenched. 'Were they together recently?'

'They were on again before I started dating Liam, but they probably haven't been since his blackout because a few weeks ago he was complaining about how she doesn't like being rejected.'

Natalia frowned. 'Rejected?'

'Yeah. He'd turned her down for what I suspect was a booty-call. But anyway, I thought you didn't want to know any of this?'

Natalia stared out at the palm fronds blowing in the breeze. She still didn't like the idea of Adam and Jordan, but she'd promised herself not to care about his past and she would stick by that.

'I don't. But ...' She met her sister's gaze. 'You're saying they haven't been together since February?'

'As far as I know.'

There should be comfort in that, but there wasn't. It took less than five minutes to make a baby and you didn't need to tell your friends about it.

'Thanks, Ana.' Natalia stood. She needed to go. To run. To think.

She fled down the stairs and rounded the house with the border collies at her heels, throwing all her energy into her run. It was the only way to clear her head.

* * *

But it didn't work. Natalia collapsed onto her bed, a mix of sweat and tears. Rage filled her as she curled her fist over the blankets. She hated her job. Hated being a doctor. It had brought her nothing but misery and vexation. It had lowered her self-confidence and esteem. And now, it had broken her heart.

But why did it hurt this much? A thousand knives punctured her body, twisting and jabbing to worsen the unrelenting pain as she curled into herself. Whatever she felt for Adam couldn't be that strong. She'd just met him. It was physical attraction, that's all. She shivered under his dark gaze, warmed at the curve of his lips, and the sensation of his hand around hers had her longing for him to touch her elsewhere. Everywhere.

That was all physical. It wasn't the beginning of anything more. It couldn't be.

Except she *did* enjoy his company, and they'd had a wonderful date last night. Adam was kind, understanding, and considerate. He was charming, funny, and he made her smile. He made her feel like a woman. A person. He *respected* her. Adam could be the unexpected man she'd been waiting for. Which was why the rage she felt was for him.

It was unfair. No matter what Adam wanted, the decision had been made. He was going to be a father. She knew it, Jordan knew it, but only Jordan could tell him. And until she did, Natalia couldn't face him. How could she sit across from him and—

She bolted upright. He was picking her up in less than an hour! She couldn't go to dinner. She would never break confidentiality, but she couldn't pretend that nothing was wrong either.

Natalia reached for her phone. She should send him a text, but that didn't seem fair, and she wanted to be polite. Calling, she prayed for voicemail, and found her wish granted.

'Hey.' She forced her voice to remain steady. 'Um … I can't do dinner tonight. I'm not feeling well and it's best that I stay here. I'm sorry. Please … don't call me. I'll see you later. Bye.'

Everything inside her throbbed, but she didn't know what else to do. Lying back, she considered what little she knew about the situation as night closed in. Ana thought Adam wasn't keen on Jordan anymore, so was Adam really the father?

She slapped her hand over her eyes. *Stop it!* The only people who would know if they'd been together were Adam and Jordan, and it wouldn't do Natalia any good to torture herself.

But there had obviously been something between them, even if it had been casual sex. And now, Natalia was caught up in their mess.

Sighing, she sat up. She wouldn't get answers until Adam knew Jordan was pregnant and right now, she needed to eat.

Easing herself off the bed, Natalia dragged her feet downstairs. She hadn't prepared anything since she'd planned to go out, but she had beans soaking for tomorrow's lunch, so teriyaki stir-fry it would be.

She was setting the pots on the stove when a knock sounded on the door. She turned. They knocked again and curiosity had her inching out of the kitchen.

'Nat!' Adam called, and she froze. 'Natalia, please open up. I know you're there.'

No, you don't.

'You wouldn't leave the lights on if you weren't home. Please open the door.'

Dammit. How could he already know her so well? She would *never* leave the lights on.

But she couldn't face him. Seeing his broad silhouette through the kookaburra-gazed windowpane was hard enough. Talking to him would only cause more heartbreak. More anger.

Before she could stop herself though, Natalia pulled back the chain and opened the door, grateful that the locked screen separated them.

'I'm sorry,' he said, his hands braced on the doorframe, biceps bulging in his short-sleeved black T-shirt. 'I know you said not to call, but you sounded upset and I couldn't …' He shook his head, dark hair swishing over his forehead. Natalia pressed her lips together. 'Are you okay?'

The worry on his handsome face made her chest ache. He cared about her and yet there was nothing she could say that would put him at ease.

'No, Adam, I'm not okay. But I can't talk to you about it. I'm sorry I cancelled on you. I didn't want to, but you have to go.'

He frowned. She tightened her grip on the doorhandle and took a deep breath.

'What did I do wrong?' he asked, and she crumpled against the doorframe. 'I thought … we were … Natalia, please. Talk to me.'

Leaning her head on the screen, she broke their gaze as tears streamed down her cheeks. She couldn't bear the pain in his eyes, but she couldn't pretend she wasn't hurting. One day, he would understand.

'You did nothing wrong, Adam. You were … perfect. Oh God.' She straightened. 'I need you to go.'

'Are we over? Or did something today upset you?'

Lifting her gaze back to his, she'd expected to see hurt or anger, which she would've preferred. But the emotion she witnessed was something closer to panic.

'I don't want it to be over.' She drew another breath and forced strength into her voice. 'I hope that one day you'll find out what happened, but I can't tell you. Please go.'

It was too much. Any longer and she'd break. She couldn't hold it in. Yet she couldn't bear to close the door.

'Tell me, Natalia,' he whispered, and her knees weakened. 'Tell me what's wrong and I'll go.'

'I can't.' Humiliation washed over her as tears erupted in full flood. 'I can't tell you. Please, Adam. If you care about me, just go!'

His jaw tightened. Hesitation swept over his face. He didn't want to leave and she wished he didn't have to. She wished she could tell him everything and they could work it out. She wished she could pretend she knew nothing.

Finally, Adam's shoulders sagged. 'Okay. I'll go. But … you know you can tell me anything, Nat.'

She dropped her gaze. 'I know.' *She* could, but Doctor Hamilton couldn't.

He stepped away from the door. 'Then … I'll talk to you soon?'

'You will.' She just didn't know when. 'Goodbye, Adam.'

She couldn't bear to risk another glance as she closed the door. Sliding to the floor, she wrapped her arms around her knees and sat among the pieces of her shattered heart.

Chapter Thirteen

Adam's chest tightened until he could barely breathe. What just happened? Was she upset with *him*? *Were* they over? No. They couldn't be!

He leaned his forehead against the screen door, his fist curling at the sound of Natalia's tears. Crying women were his weakness and his fear, and it killed him to know that something had upset her.

Especially if it *had* been him.

Cursing under his breath, Adam stepped away. Where had it gone wrong? She'd been happy when he'd dropped her home last night. There'd been plenty of kissing and promises of tomorrow.

Now tomorrow had arrived and there was nothing but heartbreak. And he didn't know why!

Shoving his hand through his hair, Adam stalked to the ute. Natalia wanted to be alone and he'd respect that. But if he had to grovel every day for the rest of his life for doing fuck-knows-what, he would do it. He couldn't let her go.

He slammed into the ute, shoved it into gear, and drove to Ana and Liam's. If anyone knew what had upset Natalia, it'd be her sister.

'Okay, put some clothes on,' he called as he strode inside, never bothering to knock with family. 'Ana?'

'We're in here,' Liam called from the living room. 'Fully clothed.'

Ana laughed. 'Disappointing, but true.'

'Whatever.' Adam fell onto the lounge next to theirs. 'Ana, what's up with your sister? She cancelled dinner, won't talk to me, and is upset about something. I fucking left her crying. Do you know how that makes me feel? Like shit! She won't tell me what's wrong and I swear I didn't do anything. But you're her sister so you have to know what happened!'

He didn't care that he sounded desperate, not when Natalia's happiness was at stake. The image of her tear-stained face swarmed into his consciousness and he shuddered.

Ana glanced at Liam, then Adam. 'I don't know what's wrong.'

His hands lifted in frustration. 'But you're women! You tell each other everything! Why is she upset? Why won't she see me? I don't like it!'

'That she won't see you?'

'No! That she's crying!'

A slow grin spread across Ana's face and Adam's jaw clenched. What the fuck was so funny?

'Look at you, all worked up over a woman you're afraid to lose.'

Adam took a deep breath and counted to three. 'Ana, I'm in no mood.'

Liam narrowed his eyes. 'You kill my fiancée, I kill you.'

Ana sobered. 'Okay, I'm sorry. So, you really like her?'

Like. Adore. Want to worship for the rest of my life. He exhaled. Fuck. 'I *really* like her.'

Liam stood. 'Beer?'

'Please.' Adam sank onto the lounge and strove for calm as he studied Ana. 'Come on, what do you know?'

She sighed and scooted across her lounge closer to him. 'I don't know much, but yes, she stopped by asking questions about you.'

Adam's gut churned. 'What questions?'

Ana dropped her gaze as she tucked loose hair behind her ear. 'Um …'

'Ana.'

'Well, it's hard because she's my sister. But … she asked about … your exes.'

Adam blinked, his hand tightening over the chair. 'She said she didn't care.'

'I know, and don't worry, I didn't say much. I just told her you'd dated Grace once and about Jordan.'

Adam jolted. 'What did you tell her about Jordan?'

'The truth.'

'The truth!' His heart leapt. 'You told her the truth?'

'I probably don't even know the truth!' Ana cried as Liam returned with the beers. Adam took one gratefully. 'But she's my sister and that's what I told her. I said there was a history between you and Jordan but that as far as I'm aware, you haven't been with her since the month I came to town. And that you turned her down the other weekend.'

Adam sculled half his beer. Fuck. What did Jordan matter? Natalia had accepted his desire to change and had granted him a clean slate. All she'd asked was that he didn't hurt her or let his past affect their relationship.

Yet it had. She'd cried, so he must have hurt her. And that only made him feel *worse* than a bad boy. Worse than the devil. Worse than the time he and Cade had covered up the disappearance of Lily's guinea pig and he'd endured his sister's crying for three days. *That* was the worst thing he'd ever done. He hadn't been able to fix it. But this …

Could he fix what had hurt Natalia? Something must have spurred her to question Ana. Maybe he should visit Jordan and ask what her problem was.

Hell, he didn't know what was worse, Natalia's pain or a conversation with Jordan. He wasn't proud of his relationship with her. It'd never bothered him before, but things between them hadn't been meaningful and she'd quickly take up with someone else without notice. When she did, he got out of there. That's how shit got complicated and he'd had no interest in being one man in a bunch.

It hadn't always been like that though. When they'd been younger, she'd been funny and easy to talk to. But as the years had passed, Jordan's attitude had grown harder while her boundaries had stretched further and further. He should have ended their arrangement long ago and had found great satisfaction in finally doing so.

The last thing he wanted to do was turn to her now.

Sighing, he ran his hand down his face. 'Then why is Natalia so upset?'

'I don't know, Adam. But I hope you work it out because I don't like seeing her like this.'

'Neither do I. And you can't disapprove of us because you owe me.'

She quirked an eyebrow. 'Owe you?'

'Yes. You said when I was carrying you out of those trees that you hoped you could do something for me one day. So, I'm cashing in. I don't want you to disapprove or tell Natalia she shouldn't see me because I'm crazy about her.'

'I thought you said I didn't owe you anything.'

'Yeah, but now the stakes are too high. And I'm going to fix this because I need her.'

Ana smiled. 'I don't disapprove, Adam. I know Nat likes you, so yes, please fix whatever this is.'

He nodded, then frowned as Natalia's words crept through his head. *I hope you find out what happened.*

So even though she couldn't tell him, did that mean he might be able to discover what it was?

Adam took a swig of his beer. It was a mission, all right. One he'd accept because the image of Natalia's tears would haunt him until he discovered how he'd hurt her.

* * *

Jordan wasn't home or working at the Royal Hotel. Adam climbed into his ute, his heart a lead weight inside his chest. He didn't doubt Jordan was the reason Natalia was upset. It wouldn't be the first time she'd interfered with his love life. Anytime he'd found himself in an actual relationship, she'd tried to steal him away. Jordan was predatory like that and he wouldn't put it past her to make a scene.

But since he didn't know where else to look for her, Adam drove home.

Had he hurt Natalia? She'd said he'd done nothing wrong, but that couldn't be true. She'd been devastated and if it was his fault, he'd never forgive himself.

Swearing, he slammed his fist on the steering wheel. It couldn't be over. Not now. He didn't want to have one perfect week with her only to have it end over something stupid. And it was stupid because he didn't know what it was. If he didn't have any respect for her, he'd sit outside her door until she spoke to him.

But such a thing was pointless. And mean.

Crushed beyond comprehension, he returned home. Adam slammed the door and tossed his keys onto the lounge. Striding through the dining room, he entered the kitchen, which overlooked the open-planned family area. Three bedrooms were at the back of the house while his was at the front, which was just the way he liked it.

The dog flap rattled as Rusty raced inside.

'Hey, mate.' Adam bent to rub his head. 'Fucked up big time.'

Rusty smiled, tongue hanging out as his tail wagged. Silly dog was hardly any comfort when he couldn't possibly understand such pain.

Adam kicked off his boots, not caring where they landed, and headed for the fridge. So much for coconut chicken at Smithy's, he'd settle for leftovers. Finding roast beef and mashed potato from High Ridge, he tossed it in the microwave, ate, then left the dishes in the sink. He wasn't in the mood to clean up.

Entering his bedroom, Adam dropped his clothes onto the floor and fell into bed. Fatigue took over and he escaped his torment.

But when he woke with the dawn, the pain hadn't vanished. Misery consumed him. He threw on the first clothes he found and headed for the kitchen. Rusty was snoozing on the lounge with his legs in the air but sprang awake at the sound of the fridge opening. Adam fed him, then fed himself, spreading peanut butter onto toast until it melted down his fingers. He took a large drink of milk straight from the bottle, then snatched up a banana on the way out.

He'd settle this bullshit today. He'd get through work with cranky Jack, then find Jordan and demand to know what she'd said to Natalia. The possibilities terrified him. If anyone knew a bad thing about him, it was Jordan Kelly.

But why would she do such a thing?

Chapter Fourteen

Adam tried not to think about Jordan and headed to work. The day dragged, but Jack wasn't quite as cranky.

'We've got our camping trip coming up this week.'

Having forgotten about that, Adam blew out a long breath. Freedom! He could escape for a few days with Jack, Jason Taylor, and their young workers to teach them crucial farm safety lessons while spending the nights under the stars. It'd be cold, but that would be a blessing when he'd spend most of his time thinking about Natalia.

He sent her a text at lunch time. **Hope you're feeling better. Thinking about you.** He didn't know what else to say.

She replied with, **Thanks. Hope you're having a good day.**

Sighing, he got back to work. He wouldn't give up without a fight, so at four o'clock, he jumped into his ute and headed into town. He loathed facing Jordan as he never knew what mood she'd be in, but he needed answers and Natalia wouldn't have asked Ana about his exes unless she'd had reason to.

But no matter what Jordan said, he'd tell her—*again*—to leave him alone. He'd had enough. He pulled up outside her unit on Forbes Street, marched up the driveway, and knocked on the door. Her car was there, but it took her a while to answer.

'Adam!' Jordan's mouth curved, the all too familiar glisten filling her eyes. 'I knew you'd come back. Changed your mind?'

He gritted his teeth. 'No. Can I come in?'

'Sure.' She stood back. 'I just changed my sheets.'

Taking a deep breath, he stepped inside. He'd get through this. 'And like I keep telling you, it's not happening.'

'Aww, stud …' She pursed her lips and wrapped her arms around his waist, pressing her large breasts against his chest. 'You're very tense. Do you want me to loosen you up?'

Calmly, he took her hands from where they were creeping beneath the waistband of his jeans and dropped them at her side.

'I'm good. Thanks.' Jordan pouted. Recognising the moves, Adam sighed. 'Don't play with me, Jordan. I'm not in the mood.'

She huffed out a breath and placed her hand on her hip. 'Fine. Then what do you want?'

His eyebrows shot up. 'You don't know?'

'You only ever want sex, so no, I don't.'

'Fine. What did you tell Natalia that made her not want to talk to me?'

'What do you mean?'

'Did you speak to her?'

Jordan scoffed. 'Why would I?'

'Well, she's not talking to me.'

'And she said that was because of me?'

'She didn't say anything. But Ana told Natalia about ... us. So, why would that have upset her, Jordan?'

She raised her eyebrows. 'So the rumours are true. You're sleeping with the new doctor?'

He blew out his breath. 'No. I'm thinking about dating her, but it doesn't help when she isn't talking to me!'

Jordan stared at him. He wanted to kick something. Then the corners of her mouth curved and she placed her hand to her lips.

'Don't laugh, Jordan.' He crossed his arms over his chest to hide his curling fists.

'I can't picture it. You, dating the doctor. You're a bit ... you're not the Adam I know.'

'I don't want to be the Adam you know anymore. I told you that. So, just tell me if there's anything I need to know so I can fix things with Natalia.'

Biting down on her lip, her eyes flashed. With what? Panic? He wasn't sure. Time ticked away. Then an odd smile curved Jordan's lips. 'Maybe you should forget about Natalia.'

His teeth clenched. 'Why?'

'Because I'm pregnant. I think it's yours.'

Adam blinked. She said it coolly, like she was telling him how fine a day it was. But the moment the words settled, everything blanked. 'You *think*?'

Jordan shrugged. 'Fine. I know.'

'You're sure?'

Her smile vanished as she popped her hands onto her hips. 'What are you saying? That I sleep around and therefore wouldn't know?'

'No, I did *not* say that.'

'You're no better than me,' she spat. 'Do you really think that a man like you could make things work with Natalia? I can't believe a self-respecting woman like her would even consider "dating" you.'

As Jordan's fingers curled with air quotes, his blood boiled, her words reminding Adam of every fear that simmered inside him. But he didn't want to discuss Natalia with Jordan, so he leaned back against her ugly brown lounge and focused on the other matter.

He cleared his throat. Words. He needed words. 'Then tell me. How far along are you?'

'A few weeks,' she replied, shrugging dismissively.

'Jordan.' He darkened his tone. He wouldn't call himself an academic man, but he was damn good at math and judging by her slim-as-usual figure, something didn't add up. 'How far?'

'Fine. Eleven weeks today.'

Adam frowned, his mind whirring. It was relatively simple logic, so he must be right in that …

The tightness in his chest evaporated and air filled his lungs. What did she think he was, stupid? They hadn't been together in much longer than eleven weeks. The last time had been March and, bloody hell, it was July!

'Ah … we haven't been together for about four months. I believe the last time was when you turned up at my place drenched.'

'Yeah …' A smile curved the corner of her mouth and bile rose in his throat. Nothing about that night had been amusing, pleasant, or even memorable. 'But no, Adam. We have.'

Even though he knew he was right, Adam wracked his brain, confused. He hadn't been with Jordan since then. He hadn't been with anyone.

'Fine. When?'

Her smile widened. 'Your birthday.'

Adam's blood ran cold. That night. The night that remained a blur. Had he had sex with Jordan? Would he have? He faintly remembered a woman being there. He'd kissed someone for sure. But ... that hadn't been Jordan. He knew Jordan, and that woman ...

Jordan exhaled and thrust out her hip. 'Adam?'

'I didn't sleep with you on my birthday.'

'Yes, you did!'

'I was too drunk.'

She snorted. 'You were certainly plastered, but I remember it well. We headed to the park and had a *really* good time. Remember, you woke with no shirt or shoes? I know because I woke before you. You were out of it though, so I left you there.'

His brain fuzzed. That was right about his clothes, but it didn't prove anything. Everyone had heard the story. And if what she was saying was true ... 'I wasn't drunk, Jordan. Someone had spiked me.'

She released a puff of air and averted her gaze.

Adam stilled. 'You don't believe me?'

'Hey, it's not my problem if you took shit—'

'I didn't *take* anything!'

'—but I *am* pregnant and figured I better tell you.'

'Well, thank you for giving me that courtesy.' He slipped his hands into his pockets and straightened. 'But we didn't have sex.'

'Yes, we did.'

'No.' His control snapped, fury surged. With her, himself, the world. 'We didn't!'

Not wanting to hear another word, he stormed out of the unit.

* * *

Adam kicked the front tyre of his ute until the pain in his foot dulled that inside his chest. Fuck. Fuck, fuck, *fuck*!

He sank against the bonnet and raked his hands down his face. This couldn't be happening. The one night he didn't remember couldn't have resulted in an unexpected pregnancy. He'd been drunk. Drugged. He hadn't a clue what had happened and his chances with Natalia …

Shit! Natalia!

Adam leapt into his ute. Natalia must have known. Jordan must have seen her at work and mentioned he was responsible for this. And she hadn't been able to say anything because doctors weren't allowed. No wonder she'd been upset!

Heart pounding, he pulled up outside Jackson Villas. She wouldn't be home yet, so he sat by her front door, leaned his head against the screen, and stared at the concrete driveway, his mind whirring.

He'd been vulnerable. Out of control. But who had drugged him? And why? Jordan's claims couldn't be true. He wouldn't have slept with her. He hadn't wanted her for weeks and with the amount of alcohol he'd consumed mixed with whatever fucked-up substance that had been in his system, surely sex wouldn't have been possible. Adam had experienced that inability before, and that had been a night he *could* remember.

Fuck, he was a bloody idiot. He should have got himself tested. Natalia would certainly agree. What would she think of him now?

Thankfully, he didn't need to agonise over that question for long. He glanced up at the sound of footsteps and Natalia halted in her tracks.

Adam scrambled to his feet. 'Nat, it's not true.'

Her shoulders sagged and the tightness inside him loosened. But her eyes remained dull as she approached. 'Really?'

'It can't be. We haven't ... yes, Jordan and I used to ... get together. But I haven't been with her since March. Can you tell me she's four months pregnant?'

'Then why is she saying it's yours?' she asked calmly, but Adam heard the hurt lingering beneath her words.

'She reckons we slept together the night of my birthday.'

Closing her eyes, Natalia shook her head. 'She's claiming she slept with you on a night you don't remember.'

'Exactly! It's incredibly convenient, don't you think?'

Her adorable nose crinkled. 'Yeah. But ...'

Adam stepped forward, careful to keep a respectable distance. 'Look, I might be in some sort of shock or denial, but I know I didn't sleep with her. I couldn't have.'

'Oh, Adam. I know this must be hard, but ...' Natalia's eyes flashed. 'Was Jordan sober?'

'She said she remembered, but what does that matter? Jordan's not known for her honesty, Nat, and I'm a bloody fool—'

'No, you're not. You wanted a new path and you took it.'

'But I left it too late!' Adam's chest tightened. 'This blackout ... it's not me, Nat. I don't do that sort of shit.'

'I know, but it wasn't your fault. The drugs people use are nasty and in hindsight—'

'In hindsight, I was a fucking idiot.' He took her hands and closed the space between them. 'But I know what I did and didn't do, Nat. I didn't sleep with Jordan. And I need you on my side. I can't lose you.'

'Adam ...' Pain etched her face as she drew out of his

grasp, stepped back, and placed her hand on his shoulder. 'I want to be on your side. I hate that this has happened to you. Honestly. But I need some time to think. And you need to find out who spiked you. Because if Jordan did have sex with you, then …'

Her eyes darkened. When she didn't continue, Adam frowned. 'Nat?'

She shook her head. 'Sorry. My mind is racing. But you need to decide what you want.'

'I want you.'

Her breath hitched. 'But you might be having a baby with another woman.'

Adam blinked. Her words rattled around inside his head. *Shit.* He didn't want to think about it, feared to acknowledge it, but Natalia was right.

He swallowed hard. 'And if I am … you wouldn't be able to do that?'

Natalia pressed her beautiful lips together and shrugged. 'I don't know.'

His shoulders sank. 'Oh, Nat. I'm sorry.'

'Adam, don't.' Her eyes glistened and before he humiliated himself by shedding tears too, Adam pulled Natalia into his arms and held her tight. She buried her face into his shoulder and he kissed the top of her head, inhaling her strawberry scent.

'It's okay,' he whispered. He wouldn't blame her if she didn't want to get mixed up in his mess. 'I'm sorry, Natalia.'

'Me too, Adam. I'm sorry this happened to you.'

He continued to place kisses in her hair and along the top of her forehead. She didn't stop him. 'Damn, Natalia. I'm seriously falling for you.'

'Me too, Adam. But I'm afraid …'

Again, she didn't finish her sentence. He rubbed his hand up and down her back. 'Don't give up on me, okay? I'll figure it out.'

She lifted her head. He wasn't sure if it was a true spark of hope in her eyes or just his wishful thinking, but it was enough to keep his heart beating. He wanted her more than he'd ever wanted anyone, but if she wanted space, he'd give it to her. And hope like hell she chose to stand beside him.

Natalia pulled out of his embrace. 'You should go. I want to go to yoga tonight.'

'Okay.' He tucked loose hair behind her ear. 'But I'll see you soon, yeah?'

'Of course. I'll let you know when I figure stuff out.' She moved past him and unlocked the door, stepping inside before turning back. 'But remember, there'll be someone out there who knows what happened that night. And if it wasn't you, then someone else got Jordan pregnant. If you ask around, maybe you'll figure out what happened.'

Adam nodded. She was right—someone must remember. It wasn't his brothers or friends, but there were other people in this town.

He slipped his hands into his pockets. 'Thanks, Natalia.'

With a sad smile, she closed the door.

Chapter Fifteen

Natalia sank onto the lounge. What was she supposed to believe? Was Adam right? Had he not slept with Jordan? God, she hoped not because if they had, then Adam was facing more than an unwanted pregnancy. Coupled with the drink spiking, Natalia was now more concerned about how that pregnancy had come about.

But Adam seemed to be too busy battling with regret and disbelief to make that connection, so the last thing Natalia wanted was to add to his burden. It was hard enough to feel vulnerable, let alone fully comprehend the consequences of your actions and those of others. To hear about the pregnancy would have been a shock and he had every right to hesitate.

But why would Jordan lie? Wouldn't she want to create a story that *didn't* call her own actions into question?

Natalia's stomach roiled as she walked to yoga. She wasn't in the mood, but she'd promised Grace and hoped that yoga would help settle her inner turmoil. Meeting Ana outside the hall, Natalia brushed off her sister's concerns with assurances that she was fine. She made it through the breathing exercises, core work, and many poses. But despite her effort to enjoy the distraction, she continued to worry about Adam.

'What did you think?' Ana asked as they rolled up their mats.

'I enjoyed it. Grace is a great teacher.'

'I'm so glad she started it,' Meg said. 'I'm feeling much stronger since January.'

Natalia smiled. 'Yoga's amazing like that.'

It took a while to leave as Ana played the social butterfly and introduced Natalia around the room. She did her best to be polite, but it was hard to smile.

Finally, Ana drove Natalia home, where she dropped her mat by the door and dragged her feet upstairs. What was she going to do? All day, she'd been worrying about Jordan withholding the information from Adam for weeks, months, or never telling him at all, so she was glad that he knew. But she hadn't expected the revelation to open another can of worms.

Natalia stepped into the shower and snatched up her mango shower gel. Could Jordan have spiked him? Was she capable of drugging and taking advantage of a man like that? Or did Adam have a point? His blackout could be a convenient opportunity for Jordan to lie and Natalia had heard many stories about women claiming men to be the father of their baby because it was easy or got them out of trouble.

But the incidents of some women trapping men into babies continued to play at the forefront of her mind. They tricked them to get what they wanted. And then there were the women who took advantage of men and the subconscious erections they couldn't control. She'd met and consulted victims of both situations, and the men always found their stories difficult to share.

Natalia rubbed Surge Duck's yellow head. It'd certainly be easier if Adam's claim was correct. She didn't want their brewing romance to be over, but she'd followed her heart last week and now it was aching. If she was going to pursue her feelings, then she needed to use her head.

She would never hold it against Adam if this was his baby, but Jordan would be a different story. Whether or not she'd drugged him, she'd taken advantage. And as the baby's mother, she would become a permanent fixture in Adam's life.

Could Natalia handle that? Could Adam?

Exhaling, she shut off the shower. She should let him go. Shouldn't get involved. She didn't need such a mess in her life.

But even though it'd only been a few kisses and dates, what she felt for Adam was real. And she didn't want to lose that.

* * *

'Fuck.' Cade Wilson blinked as he, Adam, and Darren Hudson sat around the crackling fire pit out the back of Cade's place.

'Tell me about it.' Adam popped open his third beer in forty minutes. He didn't want to contemplate Jordan's news and Natalia's uncertainty had made everything inside him shrivel, so he'd called his mates for an emergency beer as what else was a man to do? 'But I couldn't have been with her, right? You guys were there.'

'At one point, yeah.' Cade rested his elbows on his knees. 'We went with you to Smithy's.'

'Where Cade flirted with Jessica,' Darren said. 'She found your drunken arse very amusing until she knocked off and took us home. She offered to take you too, Adam, but you insisted on staying.'

Adam knew the story up to arriving at Smithy's. Jack and Michael hadn't joined them, but Liam had enjoyed one drink before leaving Adam with Cade and Darren. Which meant that by the time he'd arrived in the park, he'd been with people he rarely partied with.

He downed a gulp of beer. 'Fucking fantastic.'

'Sorry, mate.' Cade clapped his hand on Adam's shoulder, empathy in his eyes. He truly was the best mate a bloke could ask for. Back in their school days, the two of them had wreaked havoc, but a few months after high school, they'd been bumming around on the farm and Cade's father, the town sergeant, had given him an ultimatum—find a job or go to the police academy. Too lazy to consider other options, Cade had gone to the academy and when Adam had visited him in Townsville, they'd wreaked havoc over that city too. Cade had become somewhat less of a rebel by the time he'd returned to Elizadale, but nothing had changed where women were concerned. Cade enjoyed them maybe more than Adam.

'I'm sorry too, mate,' Darren said. He hadn't been as wild and had been the good influence in their quartet with Liam. There'd been no doubt that Darren would become a mechanic like his father and join him at the workshop by the roadhouse.

Adam downed more beer. He wouldn't make it home until the morning and that would piss Jack off, but he didn't give a shit. Not about Jack. Not about anything.

'I dunno what I'm gonna do. I just hope I still have a shot with Natalia. She didn't say it was over, but she can't be impressed. I know I only met her a week ago, but she's the best fucking thing to ever happen to me.'

'She just needs time to process,' Darren said kindly.

'Won't blame her if she doesn't want to be involved,' Adam admitted. 'It fucking sucks. But I swear I didn't sleep with Jordan!'

Darren nodded. 'Then we need to find out who did.'

'And if she was the one who spiked you,' Cade said. 'Seriously, mate, I can't believe you—'

'Don't start on me again.' Adam had already received the third degree from Cade when he'd failed to get tested after the fact. Not that it mattered since whatever had been in his system had likely already left. 'I know I fucked up. And I don't doubt Jordan was involved if I'd gone back to the Royal, but surely we didn't do it in the fucking park with other people around!'

'Well … I wouldn't put it past her,' Darren said.

Adam groaned again. Shit. Could Jordan be telling the truth? Yes, she was a liar. Jordan had lied to him before. She connived and stole and tricked people. She'd made condescending remarks about Grace when Adam had dated her, had spread nasty rumours about Claire once, and always seemed to be in a one-sided war against her sister. But none of that meant she wasn't capable of honesty. Adam just hoped this wasn't one of those times. It couldn't be. It was entirely *too* convenient. That's what bugged him the most.

And the possibility of fatherhood? This wasn't how he'd imagined it. He'd always thought that if he met the right woman and married, he'd have children. But while kiddos were cute, he'd done his best to prevent having them prematurely. He may have been bad, but he wasn't stupid. Adam had kissed more women than he'd slept with and he'd never, not once, forgone the condom. He always asked about contraception and even though he rarely did long relationships, he never did nameless one-night stands. He didn't venture outside the local area, so usually saw women again. That way, if he had a one-nighter like Claire Taylor, he'd been sure there had been no repercussions.

Adam downed the last of his beer. He may not like the situation, but he couldn't pretend it hadn't happened. Elizadale was a small town and he'd see the child all the time. He would do right by it, and Jordan. He might not like her much anymore, but she'd been part of his life since forever.

He was a bloody idiot for not getting himself checked out after his birthday though. Cade had asked him that morning if he suspected spiking, but Adam had waved the notion away. It hadn't been until later that night when he'd still felt sick that he'd honestly considered it as a possibility.

His hands tightened around the beer bottle. Bloody pride had got the better of him and now he would need to live with that regret. But hurting Natalia? He couldn't live with that. He'd broken her heart with no intention of doing so and it tore him to shreds. If he was going to prove himself worthy of her, then he couldn't brush that night aside again. Couldn't deny it.

He glanced at his friends. 'Either of you know anything about paternity tests?'

'Nope, but I'd be asking for one if I were you.'

'You'll have to wait until the baby's born,' Cade said. 'I hear it's possible beforehand, but it'd require the mother's consent because it's her body.'

Adam's shoulders sagged. 'Shit.'

'I know.' Cade squeezed Adam's forearm. 'But I've had pregnancy scares myself, mate, so I'll sit here as long as you want and get drunk with you.'

Adam managed a smile. 'Thanks, mate.'

Chapter Sixteen

Jordan nibbled on her lower lip as she stretched out on Paul's front verandah, eyeing her brothers' beers with longing. She'd known Adam wouldn't have taken her news well and that he'd need to stew over it for a while, but once he'd finished kicking himself, he'd accept her story. He'd take responsibility and she'd never need to reveal the truth.

But what if he questions the pregnancy? The party? What if Natalia has already turned his eye?

Jordan shook the thoughts away and bit into another potato chip. Now wasn't the time as she had a bigger problem to face. She glanced at Paul and Harrison as they muttered about the status of the coffee plants. As brothers went, they weren't so bad. They may be overprotective, but that's because they were loyal to a fault. They'd have her back. And if she was going into battle, then she'd need to deploy her army.

So, she threw back more potato courage and said, 'I'm pregnant.'

Her brothers stopped mid-sentence. Paul's eyebrows shot up while Harrison's mouth remained open. Jordan ate more chips and wished Paul had something other than beer or water to drink.

'You're what?' Harrison asked.

'Please tell me you're joking.'

Jordan shook her head. 'Nope.'

Exhaling, Paul took a long swig of his beer. 'Shit, okay. What are you going to do?'

Jordan shrugged. 'Have it, I suppose.'

'You always said you don't want kids.' Harrison raised his eyebrows. 'What changed?'

Jordan stared into the empty chip packet, her heart pounding. 'What does it matter? I'm having this baby because I want to.'

'Who's the father?' Paul asked. 'Please tell me that you know.'

Her gaze darted to his. 'What the hell does that mean?'

'Exactly what I said. That you know so you can get his help.'

'And we can punch him if he refuses,' Harrison added.

Jordan didn't know whether to laugh or roll her eyes. She settled for a bit of both. 'Of course, I know who the father is, but I don't think you'll be pleased.' With the truth or her lie, but she'd settle for the lesser of two evils.

Harrison tapped his fist into his hand. 'Who do we have to thump?'

This time, Jordan did snicker. 'Who do you think?'

Paul's eyes darkened. 'Don't tell me it's Maguire.'

She shrugged. 'Better him than some random one-night stand. You got any more chips?'

Her brothers swore.

'That bloody bastard,' Harrison said, snatching up his beer. 'Does he know?'

'Told him today.'

'When the fuck did this happen?' Paul asked. 'How far along are you?'

'Happened the night of his birthday, so almost three months.'

Paul shook his head and ran his hands down his face. 'Shit. Are you serious?'

Jordan swallowed, then nodded. This was the riskiest part of her plan. 'Ahuh.'

'And what did he say?' Harrison asked. 'Is he going to do the right thing or do we really have to kick his arse?'

Exhaling, Jordan crossed her arms over her chest. 'Well, he's busy at the moment trying to get into the new doctor's pants, but I'm sure he'll come around. Once the shock wears off. He doesn't believe me because he doesn't remember that night.'

'Of course he doesn't,' Paul muttered.

Harrison glanced from Paul back to Jordan. 'You said he was off his face.'

'Oh, he was out of it, all right. But yeah, it happened.' She didn't need to add to that story as her brothers wouldn't want to hear it. 'So, you got any more chips or what?'

Paul shook his head. 'No. But let me get this straight. Maguire gets high and knocks you up, then wants nothing to do with you?'

'While he chases after the new doctor?'

Jordan nodded. 'Pretty much.'

Harrison's eyes flashed as he exchanged glances with Paul. 'We can't let that happen.'

'No.' Paul's jaw tightened. 'And after what Maguire did to me, he has another thing coming if he thinks he can do this to Jordan.'

She grabbed her water, drinking it only to hide her grin.

'On the other hand, though,' Paul said, 'what are you going to tell our sister?'

Jordan continued to drink. When there was no water left, she lowered her glass and sighed. 'What can I tell her? She'll just have to accept it, won't she?'

'Yeah, but ...' Paul's eyes softened. 'Go easy on her, okay? She's been struggling lately and to hear that you're pregnant ... I don't want it to break her.'

Jordan nodded, avoiding her brothers' gazes as she placed her glass down. 'I'll tell Elanora tonight.'

* * *

Seeing Elanora's name in the appointment book, Natalia hoped that consulting with her might be the distraction she needed. Work was all that kept her going today, and even though Elanora's situation wasn't easy, Natalia wanted to help her. But the moment Elanora sat down, she burst into tears and dropped her pretty face into her hands.

Reaching for the tissue box, Natalia placed it on the desk between them. Patients breaking down wasn't unusual, but Natalia couldn't stop her heart from going to her. 'It's okay, Elanora. You tell me when you're ready.'

Natalia sat close for comfort but remained a polite distance away despite the overwhelming temptation to pull the other woman into a hug.

After a moment, Elanora peeked her pale eyes over her fingertips. 'My sister's having a baby.'

Natalia blinked. That was the last thing Elanora needed right now. 'Oh. I'm sorry, Elanora. I understand that it must be difficult for you.'

'It is.' Exhaling, Elanora dropped her hands and reached for the tissues. 'Especially when she wasn't even trying. She doesn't even want kids! But my stupid, immature, pain-in-the-arse little sister sleeps around and gets knocked up. On the pill! I mean ... God hates me.'

'I'm sure he doesn't.'

Elanora dabbed her eyes. 'I'm sorry. And I probably shouldn't have broken down like that in front of you.'

'It's part of my job.'

'Yeah, but ...' Elanora folded the tissue in half. 'I'm sorry, you probably don't even know. Jordan is my sister.'

Natalia couldn't stop her eyes from widening. 'You're a Kelly.'

'Don't hold that against me.' Elanora leaned back in her chair. 'But yes, I'm the oldest and I'm sure you've heard all about my siblings.'

Natalia waved her hand, dismissing it. 'That's irrelevant. And so is my ...' She winced, unsure how to explain it. 'Personal connection, I suppose.'

'I heard about you and Adam.' Elanora shook her head. 'I'm sorry. Maybe I should go back to seeing Joanne.'

'No.' Natalia placed her hand on Elanora's forearm. 'Please don't. Unless you're uncomfortable, because I'm not. I'm here if you want to talk about it.'

Elanora smiled softly. 'Thank you, Natalia.'

Exhaling, Natalia pulled back and turned to the computer, having not yet opened Elanora's chart. She didn't know how she hadn't made the connection between Elanora and Jordan, especially as they looked quite similar. Yet the small-town conflict suddenly grew clearer.

'So, did your sister just tell you she's pregnant, did she?'

'Yep. Last night. I don't see her much because we don't get along. So, she sent me a text message. A *text*, Natalia! "Hey, just letting you know I'm pregnant." I honestly thought she was joking. I actually texted my brother Paul to see what he knew about it. He wouldn't lie to me, so when he called me back to confirm, I couldn't believe it.'

Natalia nodded slowly and resisted a frown. 'Why didn't you believe her straight away?'

'You don't know her, Natalia, but Jordan's never been truthful.' Elanora's eyes darkened. 'I mean, she's my sister and because of that, I care about her. I would never wish her ill. But half the things that come out of her mouth are lies.'

That's what Adam had said. 'Does she lie to you often?'

'I wouldn't say often, but I don't trust her. And she's always seemed to resent me, ever since we were kids. I'm six years older than her, but that didn't stop her from stealing my clothes and makeup. She ruined a new top of mine once and didn't care because it would "one day be hers anyway" as though all she ever got were my hand-me-downs.'

Natalia listened, curious to hear Elanora's point of view as it said a lot about Jordan. If her own sister didn't trust her, then did Adam also have a reason not to?

Elanora shook her head. 'But anyway. I guess I was just shocked. Shane was hardly any comfort, but my mum called to make sure I was okay. And I will be.'

'You will,' Natalia agreed, smiling softly. 'It may be Jordan's turn now, but you and Shane will have a baby of your own, El. You need to believe that.'

She exhaled. 'I do. At least, I'm trying to.'

Chapter Seventeen

Adam texted Jordan. After the way he'd stormed out yesterday, it was the least he could do, as he didn't want to appear to be a total bastard. They'd been friendly once and he couldn't completely deny that she might be carrying his baby, even though the thought made him want to throw up. He had to keep her onside.

Sorry about yesterday. It was a shock. I'm sure you understand.

It'd probably been a shock for her too, which was something else that didn't make sense. Jordan had always said she didn't want kids because they would 'ruin her life', and she did everything she could to avoid it short of abstinence. So why had she chosen to have this baby?

He shook his head and continued typing.

It's hard for me when I don't remember what happened that night. So if you could give me some time to think. Or fill me in?

He considered asking after her health or how she felt about the pregnancy, then decided it was best to keep it simple. So, he added a simple **thanks**, sent the message, and headed to the shed. He wasn't in the mood to work, but hopefully the feel of wood beneath his hands would distract him and he needed to make two more vases for Sue and Heather.

Jordan's reply came an hour later.

Take your time. But if you want to come over tonight, feel free. Pregnancy is making me horny.

Adam's lip curled. *Really?*

He didn't reply. Turning the music up, he blasted Travis Collins through the shed and resumed work.

He didn't go to Friday Frenzy. Cade called asking where he was, but Adam hadn't been able to face it when he was still hungover from last night. Nor did he want to see Jordan, who worked Fridays. Natalia hadn't gone either, so Adam told Cade to send his apologies and tell their friends what was going on. It was cowardly, but at least he wouldn't have to witness Jack's murderous face and everyone else's disappointment. He couldn't worry about them when he was at a loss as to what to do himself.

But it didn't take long for Jack, Michael, and Liam to arrive at his door. Michael carried a carton of beer and Jack drew him into a tight hug.

'We don't need to talk about it,' Jack said. 'But Cade reckons you don't think you're responsible.'

Adam hugged Jack tighter than usual. 'I wouldn't know, but I bloody well hope not.'

'We'll figure it out, mate. But until then, let's throw some steaks on the barbie and talk about something else.'

Damn, his brothers were good blokes. Adam's shoulders relaxed as he threw some frozen steaks into the microwave to defrost. Liam found potatoes while Michael fired up the barbie and Jack cranked up the music. Adam welcomed the company and the night passed with ease.

But Natalia still hadn't called.

On Saturday, he sat on the lounge with Rusty snoozing beside him, his house clean and smelling of lemony freshness after his mother had dropped by. Bless her.

Wendy Maguire had arrived after a phone call from Liz Kelly, greeting him with a well-practised mother-of-a-rebel look before asking for his side of the story.

'I don't know, Mum. Jordan's pregnant, but I haven't slept with her in months, more than she claims to be. I'm over that bullshit.'

'Well, you know I'm glad to hear that. And I'm so proud that you want to sell your beautiful crafts.' She eyed him shrewdly as she scrubbed his dirty dishes. 'But I'm not happy about this. And I have to take it out on you because I have no right to tell Jordan what I think. But I don't trust that woman as far as I could throw her.'

Adam leaned against the bench. 'I don't either. And I'm sorry, Mum. Really.'

'She's claiming it happened the night of your birthday, right?' Wendy's voice hardened as she tossed a pile of cutlery into the washing up stand.

'Yeah.'

'The night you don't remember?'

'Exactly. It creates the perfect opportunity to lie.'

'I can certainly see that.' She scrubbed the plate with vigour. 'And I know you don't want to hear this, but you need to talk to the police.'

Adam exhaled. 'But what can they do about it now?'

'Ask questions. Access cameras at the Royal to see who spiked you. I don't know, but it's better than nothing.' She pulled the plug and turned from the sink, wiping her hands on a tea-towel. 'Please do it. For me.'

He sank back against the kitchen counter. He couldn't say no to that. 'Fine.'

'Good. And you're not alone as I believe you have reason to hesitate in accepting Jordan's story. And so does Liz.'

Adam raised his eyebrows. 'Really?'

'Liz didn't say that in so many words, but she's my best friend and I know her. However—' she tossed the tea-towel on the bench '—you're not taking any legal or financial responsibility for that child until you have biological proof.'

He swallowed a smile. 'Yes, Mum.'

'Good. Come here, darling.' She held out her arms and Adam went to her. His mum needed the hug. Maybe he did too. 'I'm on your side, okay?'

He hadn't doubted that for a second, but it was comforting to hear. 'Thank you.'

'And I'm sorry this has happened.' Wendy squeezed him tight. 'But she'll come back to you if she cares for you.'

Adam prised his mother away. 'What?'

She smiled, grabbed the dishcloth, and wiped down his bench tops. 'Deborah said you're interested in Ana's sister.'

He slipped his hands into his pockets. 'Oh. Well … maybe. But I don't want to talk about it.'

His mother did though as she continued to clean his house. It wasn't messy, things had just got away from him these past few days. Besides, it wasn't his fault that Rusty shed so much hair or that he'd escaped to the creek and returned with muddy footprints. But his mum hounded him about being neat again, told him to use his laundry basket and dust more often, then said she loved him no matter what before leaving Adam to brood.

On the lounge, he dropped his head into his hands. He would keep his word to his mum and talk to the police, but damn, he wished he remembered. He'd retraced his steps this morning from the Royal to the park and sat there for an hour, but it hadn't helped. His only memory of the park was singing badly and kissing a woman. Maybe two? Even having to ask that question made him sick.

He shook his head, anger rising inside him. At himself, at the world.

Fuck it all.

Later that afternoon, he'd just finished reassuring his sister Lily, who'd called from Townsville after hearing the news, when there was a knock on his door. Just wanting to be left alone, he ignored it. But the knocking persisted, and Rusty wouldn't stop barking, so Adam unfolded himself from the lounge to find the wrong Hamilton sister on his doorstep.

Ana offered him a small smile and held out a plate of chocolate chip biscuits. 'I thought I'd come and see how you're doing. I brought bickies.'

He accepted the plate as food sounded pretty good right now. 'Did you make them?'

'Of course.' She stepped inside and closed the door.

He bit into a biscuit and moaned. 'These are great. Thanks, cuz.'

'So, how are you doing?' she asked, sitting and patting her knees for Rusty to jump up for cuddles. The little dog looked at her, turned, then leapt onto the other lounge. Ana shrugged and returned her gaze to his. 'Cade told us what happened. I spoke to Nat last night and she said you're not taking it well.'

'I'm taking it fine,' he said, his mouth full as he sat beside her. 'I couldn't have slept with Jordan so I have nothing to worry about.'

'Adam ...'

'What? I'm telling you, Ana.' He swallowed the biscuit and

reached for another. 'I hadn't wanted her for weeks and we were in the bloody park! All I can come up with is that she's got herself into some serious trouble and has chosen me to take the fall. And yes, I don't *want* to have slept with her, but surely you see why I'm suspicious.'

'I do, Adam.' She placed her hand on his arm. 'And I hope she's lying too.'

His heart warmed. 'Thanks. But what I want is for Nat to stand by me. I know she can't take my word for it, but dammit, Ana, it kills me that she's hurting.'

'Yes, but you understand why she was upset, right? Jordan gave her the impression she might not even tell you, so Nat was in an impossible situation.'

'I get that.'

'Good. And she was worried you would leave her for Jordan.'

'I told her I wouldn't!'

'Before that. Now, she's more concerned about what really happened to you that night.'

He gritted his teeth and snatched up another biscuit. 'Yeah, me too. And I'll work it out, but I want Natalia back.' He sank into the lounge and ran a crumby hand down his face. 'Jeez, Ana, she'll still go out with me, won't she?'

Ana smiled, her blue eyes so much like her sister's it tortured him. 'Adam, Nat's so taken by you. I've never seen her like this about anyone. And what hurts her most is that this happened to *you*. Not to her. So yes, I'm sure she'll still date you.'

'I hope so. Your sister is amazing, Ana. She's spirited and fun. Passionate. Smart. Honest too. And she's bloody beautiful.'

'Yeah, she's all those things. But I'm happy to hear you say it.' Ana stood. 'I should probably get back to town. I am sorry, Adam.'

He shoved the biscuit into his mouth and pushed to his feet. 'Thanks, cuz.'

Ana glanced down at the plate. 'Um … Adam, you ate all those biscuits.'

He looked at the empty plate, then back at her. 'Wasn't I supposed to?'

'You could have saved some for later! But anyway, just know I'm on your side because in Kelly verse Maguire, I have to take Maguire.'

Smiling, Adam pulled her into a hug. 'You're one in a million, Ana. And please tell Natalia that I'm working on it.'

'I will.'

He walked her to the door. She stepped outside, then spun around. 'I almost forgot. Next weekend, you guys are going to Cairns for suit fittings. You need to tell Jack and Michael.'

'Why?'

'You're the best man, Adam. You have things to do.'

He groaned. If he'd known that, he'd never have agreed to it. 'Can't I just stand beside Liam at the altar, plan the bucks night, and embarrass him at the reception? Jack's better at organising crap than me. And—'

Ana's eyes narrowed in a don't-mess-with-the-bride look and Adam shut up. 'You are the best man. You get everyone to Cairns. It's not hard. Then you can stand by Liam at the altar, plan a reasonable bucks night, and *not* embarrass him at the reception. Your speech can be funny, but heartfelt and nice. Tell embarrassing stories at the bucks night. Do *not* ruin my wedding, Adam Maguire.'

He laughed. 'I won't. And I promise to give the greatest best man speech ever.'

Chapter Eighteen

When exercise didn't help Natalia regain her equilibrium, she thought nothing would. After lunch, she'd lain on the floor to complete a series of crunches, clams, planks, and various Pilates exercises, but her anguish lingered. Sitting in lotus position and completing rounds of alternate nostril breathing did nothing to calm her mind either.

She didn't know what to do. As a knock sounded on the door, every muscle in her body tensed, then relaxed when Ana called out. Scrambling to her feet, Natalia let her sister in, desperate to talk to her even though they'd only spoken that morning.

'I went to see Adam.'

Natalia's heart leapt as she closed the door behind Ana and followed her through the unit. 'How is he?'

Sitting on the lounge, Natalia folded her hands in her lap and waited for Ana to say something that would vaporise the uncertainty inside her.

'The man's a wreck, Nat. He misses you and what he said about you was lovely. You would have approved.'

Her eyebrows rose. 'What do you mean?'

'He rattled off many qualities that he liked about you, said you were smart and fun and spirited. Only as an afterthought did he say you were beautiful.' Ana quirked her eyebrows. 'Isn't that what you want to hear?'

The knots in her shoulders loosened a smidge. 'It's certainly nice.'

'I thought so. And I'll admit, the whole situation is unfortunate. Adam has changed, Nat. It just seems like it might have happened a little too late. But I hope he's right about Jordan lying because I'd hate to think that woman took advantage of him.'

'I know. It makes me mad.'

'But he'd have to remember something about that night, surely? You're a doctor, Nat. Don't you know how memory works?'

Natalia fiddled with the end of her ponytail. 'It'd be helpful if we knew what he'd been drugged with because those sorts of substances can have awful effects on the body. He's lucky he wasn't sicker. Amnesia is bad enough.'

'True. But I think what he wants most right now is your support, and I think you should help him figure out what happened, Nat. It'll be good for you because I think it's what you want.'

Natalia dropped her head in her hands and stared at the floor. She could deny her growing feelings, and she'd have to if she wanted to protect herself. Fearlessness had made her reckless and hadn't led to anything good. But even though it'd be easier to run in the opposite direction, she wanted to support Adam because she couldn't leave him to face this on his own.

'But, Ana, what if Jordan's the one who spiked him? What if she took advantage of him and is right about the baby?'

'If she is, will it change your feelings for Adam?'

Natalia's head shot up. 'Of course not.'

'Then you have your answer.' Ana's mouth curved. 'I know you're scared, Nat, but give this a chance. Be there for him.'

'I want to be ...'

'You can do it.' Ana reached for Natalia's hand. Her sister was right. The situation terrified her and people would undoubtedly talk, but whether or not Jordan had a hidden agenda, Adam was in serious trouble.

She couldn't turn her back on him.

* * *

Natalia drove her sister's Toyota Yaris through Shadow Creek, following Ana's directions along the road that stretched forever through the bush. How did Adam live out here? Granted, there were powerlines and she'd passed one fruit orchard, but other than that, there was nothing. She'd taken her first drive on a dirt road through the scrub to nowhere and couldn't fathom the appeal of such isolation.

Finally, she arrived at the intersection. One sign pointed ahead to High Ridge Retreat and the other right to the main house.

Natalia turned left. A wallaby leapt into the bush, which made her smile as the tree-lined creek drew closer. Then a dark brick house came into view. There was a small garden out the front, a large shed to the right, and a four-foot wooden backyard fence that separated the house from the sloping lawn down to the creek.

Breath catching, she lifted her sunglasses. She'd expected some sort of shack or a bit of disarray, but Adam's house was a home. *A family home?*

Shaking her head, she parked beside his Hilux and stepped out into the cool breeze. She approached the verandah on leaden feet, took a deep breath, and knocked. A dog started barking and the door opened.

The relief on Adam's face brought warmth to her heart. 'Natalia.'

'Hey.'

He pushed open the screen door and stepped aside to let her in. Natalia glanced around the spacious living room where an old rug lay between two adjacent blue lounges. White curtains hung over the windows and the cream walls stood bare. While it could do with some sprucing up, she liked it.

But she hadn't come to check out the house. As the little dog scratched at her leg, she bent over and rubbed his head, smiling at the delight in his big brown eyes. 'You must be Rusty.'

Rusty was adorable with his reddish-brown ears, markings around his eyes, and spot on his back. His white body shook as his tail wagged furiously. He was the sort of dog she'd always loved, little and cute, but as she went to pick him up, he scurried out of reach. 'Well, I hope you've been giving your daddy plenty of cuddles.'

'I'm not his daddy.'

Natalia frowned. 'Then what do you call yourself?'

He shrugged. 'Rusty's my dog. My little mate. I love him, but I don't call myself his daddy.'

'Oh. All right, then.' She glanced up into Adam's dark eyes and everything inside her settled. Smiling softly, Natalia stepped towards him, wrapped her arms around his neck, and buried her face into his shoulder. His body relaxed against hers as his cheek dropped to her hair. 'I'm sorry, Adam.'

'It's okay.'

'I'm here for you. You may not know what happened that night, but I'll support you and help you figure it out.'

His arms tightened around her. 'I swear, Nat, there are smidges of memories and none of them involve me having sex with anyone.'

She looked into his eyes, those of a man who was hurting and didn't want to lie to her. 'How about you tell me what happened?'

His gaze darkened. 'Can I kiss you first?'

Longing clenched in her belly. She wanted to make up for what they'd lost, to revel in it, but she had to remain careful. 'Let's not get distracted,' she suggested. 'Talk first, then we'll see.'

Adam nodded and brushed his fingers down her cheek. 'I'm glad you're here.'

'Me too.' Her heart skipped a beat as she moved to sit on the lounge.

'You want a drink while we talk?' he asked, shifting his feet.

'No, I'm fine.' She smiled softly, hoping to put him at ease as she crossed her legs and leaned her elbow on the arm of the chair. 'Just tell me, Adam. I won't judge.'

Rusty jumped up beside her and stretched out in his own space. Adam lowered himself onto the lounge next to hers. He blew out his breath, then dived right in. The further he got into the story, the more he seemed to relax. He'd had dinner with his friends and a few beers before turning the night into a party.

'Cade and I were already wasted when Ana dropped us at Smithy's. We did some shots, then Jess took Darren and Cade home.'

'They left you there?'

'Apparently, I insisted on staying. They said other farmers were around, but I don't know who.'

'What about Jordan?'

'She'd have been working, but I don't remember going back to the Royal. Only snippets of the park ...' He dropped his gaze.

Natalia waited a moment, then asked, 'What do you remember, Adam?'

'Darkness. Being outside. There were women there, I'm sure. And what's worse, I think I kissed one or two of them. But if Jordan was there, I swear that's all we did.'

She nodded slowly. 'Okay. Then I'd say that you most likely had a fragmentary blackout.'

Adam frowned. 'And that means?'

'That part of your memory is still there and that it's less likely you'd have blacked out having sex with Jordan. Or at least part of it.' She forced a smile. 'It's a good thing.'

'If you say so. Does that help tell you what they spiked me with?'

'Not really.' She'd done a lot of reading about drink spiking over the past few days. 'Did you experience any other symptoms? Nausea? Rage? Were you sick at all?'

His gaze dropped back to the floor. 'I did feel sick. Was confused and tired. But I mainly had a whopping headache, worse than I've ever had before.'

None of that surprised Natalia. 'Both stimulants and sedatives could have caused amnesia. Mixed with alcohol, most drugs are dangerous, whether prescription or illegal. Have there been other spiking incidents in town?'

'Not that I've heard of. And I'm not sure who'd have done such a thing. There have been drugs around town, for sure. Not sure what kind, but even though I enjoy having a good time, Nat, alcohol's enough for me. I've never touched that other shit.'

'Has Jordan?'

Adam blinked. He opened his mouth to speak, then shoved his hand through his hair. 'Shit. Do you think *she* spiked me?'

Natalia's hands curled over the arm of the lounge. 'Do you think she would?'

'I've heard of her doing some wild things, Nat, but I've only ever seen her drink. Besides, why would she? Jordan ...' Adam shook his head, brow furrowing. 'No. She's many things, but I don't think she'd drug me.'

Natalia wasn't so sure. She didn't want to cast blame, but Adam had been rejecting Jordan's advances and, as the barmaid, she'd had the opportunity. Stranger things had happened.

'Well, you know her better than I do. But without drug tests or witnesses, it's hard to know what happened.'

'I'm going to go talk to the police. I doubt they can do anything now, but—'

'You can lodge your concerns and they could make some enquiries. Drink spiking is a crime, Adam, so you need to report it.'

'Yeah. And tell me, how do we go about doing a paternity test?'

'You'll need to wait until the baby's born. You *can* do it beforehand, but it's complicated. The invasive tests involve taking tissue from the baby and that carries risks. Most women don't go for it. And the non-invasive tests based on blood cost a fortune. I know it sucks, but you're better off waiting. You may have to take Jordan to court if she doesn't agree, but once the baby's born, she can't stop you.'

Adam grimaced. 'Bloody sucks.'

'I know. And I hope you're right about her lying.' Natalia cleared her throat. 'Because if you two did have sex—'

'How could we have?' Adam threw his hands in the air. 'We were in the park and … I dunno. Maybe she doesn't even know who the father is?'

Natalia stared at him. That could be possible, but did he not see what may have happened if Jordan *was* telling the truth? That he wasn't only a victim of drink-spiking but of assault too?

'I mean, she has no limits,' Adam continued. 'Younger men, older men, married men. It doesn't matter to her. As long as she's got someone in her bed, she's good. So, you see why I'm firm on how she could use this blackout of mine to peg me for this?'

Natalia sighed. Perhaps the scenario of Jordan telling the truth needed to be left for another day when his shock had worn off. 'Yes, Adam. I do see. So, what are we going to do?'

'I think the first thing we should do is have that dinner we missed on Wednesday.' A flirtatious gleam replaced the seriousness in his eyes. 'Do you want to go to dinner with me, Nat?'

That wasn't what she'd meant, but even though she wanted to continue their discussion, she understood why he didn't. Maybe just for tonight, they could put their worries aside and enjoy some time together to recapture what they'd been building.

'Yes, Adam. Dinner would be lovely.'

Extending his hand, he inclined his head and grinned his sexy grin that she hoped would always have a touch of dangerous. 'Can I kiss you now?'

She hesitated, but he *had* talked so she could give him that kiss. Nodding, she took his hand and Adam yanked her towards him. Natalia laughed as she collapsed onto his lap and he crushed his mouth to hers. Yep, denial was fun. Her body trembled as she kissed him back, his hand grazing down the side of her cotton T-shirt and almost kicking in her ticklish reflex.

'I missed you, Nat,' he whispered, drawing her lip between his. Nipping lightly, he lathed her lip with his tongue before diving back in. She swallowed a moan and pressed her hand to his stubbly cheek.

'I missed you too,' she breathed, the air clogging inside her throat. As his tongue brushed hers, she shivered and tightened her grip on him. She couldn't get enough. Natalia had had good kisses before, but no one kissed like Adam. She wanted him to kiss her all over, to trail his lips down her body until his mouth sent her into a crazier state of euphoria.

But she wouldn't rush it, so drew away. 'I've enjoyed our time together, Adam. And I want to continue to hang out, date, whatever you want to call it. But we'll need to take it slow until we work out this thing with Jordan.'

He nodded. 'Fair call.'

'Right. I should go. If you're taking me out to dinner, then I want to dress up and look pretty.'

His mouth curved. 'Shouldn't take much. You're damn pretty right now.'

She blushed. 'Adam …'

'Why don't you like compliments?' His dark eyes turned serious. 'I know they embarrass you, but they shouldn't.'

Natalia bit down on her lower lip. She'd brushed him off when he'd asked the other day, but she needed to tell him eventually. In fact, could doing so help him come to terms with what Jordan may have done?

'I'm not embarrassed. It's just … I've experienced a lot of sexual harassment.'

His eyes narrowed. 'Really?'

'Yes.' She swallowed nervously. 'For most of my life, actually. Then …'

His thumb stroked down her spine. 'You don't need to talk about it right now if you don't want to.'

The tension eased from her shoulders. Now they were both avoiding the tough subjects. Of course, she'd tell him, but right now, she'd rather keep the mood light.

'Thanks. It got out of control at one of my workplaces and I stopped putting an effort into my appearance. I thought looking plain might reduce the innuendos, judgement, and people viewing me as just a pretty face.'

Adam's eyes flashed. 'I'm sorry that happened to you, Natalia. But you know … you *are* beautiful. And you should be proud of the fact that you look after yourself.' His gaze followed his hands as they roamed down the sides of her body, bringing warmth to her belly. 'You do yoga and running and everything else to make yourself feel good.'

'I know.'

'But I understand that it would have been frustrating for you.' His gaze returned to hers. 'And if you don't want me to compliment you, then I'll try my best. But I'm afraid—'

She pressed her finger to his lips, her eyes widening. 'No, I don't want that. You and I are dating, Adam, so compliment me all you want.'

'Oh, thank God.'

His shoulders relaxed as he captured her mouth again, smothering her laugh. Random strangers and colleagues commenting on her looks weren't appreciated, but she wanted Adam to call her beautiful. And tonight, she'd make sure she was. It'd been far too long since she'd worn heels, a pretty dress, and makeup. Ages since she'd felt sexy, treasured, or empowered. Recognising that, Natalia pulled herself closer and kissed Adam with everything she had.

He tore away first and loosened his grip around her. 'Yeah, you need to go. Else I won't want to do slow.'

Laughing, she untangled herself and stood. 'Okay. So, what time should I be ready?'

'How's seven? I'm not sure I'll be all that hungry though. I just ate a whole plate of Ana's chocolate chip cookies.'

'You liked them?' she asked as they walked to the door.

'Bloody delish.'

Natalia smirked. 'I know. They're the best.'

He opened the door. 'You ate them?'

'Of course. They were vegan, Adam.'

She had the pleasure of seeing his eyebrows shoot up. 'Blow me down. I'd never have thought.'

'No one ever does.' She stepped outside. 'And if you like, we can go to the Royal tonight. I still want to try some food at Smithy's, but I had a lot of pasta for lunch and a few of those bickies, so I'm happy to try the salad at the Royal.'

He shrugged. 'I don't mind either way.'

'Might be nice to have a bit of comfort tonight at your regular watering hole, that's all. Then we can go to my place for dessert. *Only*—' she poked him in the chest '—dessert. *Food.*'

Adam laughed and rested his forearm on the door jam. 'Food dessert sounds good.'

'I love desserts and make many yummy things. You'll see.' Grinning, she patted his arm, then turned and strode towards

Ana's car, but not without a cheeky backward glance. 'See you later.'

He watched her with a strained expression of desire on his handsome face and something inside her warmed.

God, she'd forgotten how much fun flirting could be.

Chapter Nineteen

Adam almost dropped the fruit bowl when Natalia opened the door. Since seeing her on his verandah that afternoon, the world had almost righted itself and he could breathe easier. He had her support and couldn't ask for more.

Except perhaps the right to deserve her.

His gaze swept down her glorious figure. She hadn't been kidding about dressing up. Her long-sleeved, high-cut, dark blue dress wrapped around every inch of her athletic body and hugged her thighs to her knees. Her hair cascaded over her shoulders in long golden waves, she'd darkened her eyelashes, and he longed to taste her pink, glossy lips.

Bloody hell, she wanted to take it slow? It'd be torture, but he'd do it because he didn't want to rush into unknown territory and stuff it up.

He swallowed the lump in his throat. 'Hey.'

'Hey. You look nice.'

He wore his best jeans and a plain red shirt, but whatever. 'Thanks. I think you outdid pretty. You're absolutely beautiful.'

She didn't blush. Instead, her eyes shone. 'Thank you, Adam. You brought me fruit?'

He'd almost forgotten about the bowl. Chest swelling, he held it out. 'I made this for you. Just thought fruit would be nice in it.'

Her eyebrows shot up as she accepted the gift. 'It's beautiful.'

Adam slipped his hands into his pockets. 'Thanks. It's simple compared to some things I can do, but I whipped it up on Wednesday 'cause I wanted you to have something.'

Her smile wrapped around his heart and squeezed. 'Aww, thank you. Come in.'

She turned and strode towards the kitchen, her sexy hips swaying. Adam kept his hands in his pockets and followed. She placed the bowl on the bench and unloaded the fruit to better examine his craftsmanship. 'I don't know much about this sort of work, but I love it.'

His shoulders relaxed. 'I'm glad.'

She placed the bowl down and picked up the bananas. 'Did you grow these?'

'Yep. It's all from home. Bananas may be our primary business, but we grow other fruit, both commercially and for ourselves.'

'Well, I enjoy passionfruit,' she said, placing it back in the bowl. 'And lemons. What's this?'

He grinned as she held up a small green fruit. 'Guava.'

'I don't think I've had fresh guava, so that'll be nice.' She moved in for an embrace. 'Thank you.'

'You're welcome.' He wrapped his arms around her and dropped a kiss to her glossy lips, resisting a moan at her taste. Strawberry. The sensual minx. How had she known he had a weakness for strawberries?

Her hands snaked up his back and he shivered. Shit. Better get to the pub and put a table between them.

But when they strode into the Royal, he saw Jordan behind the bar and his chest tightened. Beside him, Natalia hesitated. Unease passed through her eyes and he swallowed.

'Do you want to go to Smithy's?'

Natalia bit down on her lower lip. After one agonising moment, she shook her head. 'We can't avoid the Royal, Adam.' She inhaled, then flashed him a smile and placed her hand on his chest. 'I'll grab the booth and you get the drinks.'

Watching her weave through the crowd, the pressure inside him eased. Damn, she was wonderful. Natalia had no reason to feel intimidated or threatened by Jordan Kelly. And neither did he.

But he approached the opposite end of the bar from where she was serving and went light tonight with the soda water Natalia loved so much. It'd do him good to have something other than beer.

He joined her at the table and they fell into light conversation, neither of them hungry enough to place a meal order yet.

'You're a dancer?' He raised his eyebrows, ignoring the sudden fire in his belly.

'I *was* a dancer. I gave up ballet after uni and ballroom a few years ago because I didn't have the time anymore.'

'But still. Dancing. Pilates. Yoga …'

She stifled a laugh. 'You're thinking dirty, aren't you?'

'Yeah, I am.' He shrugged, not ashamed to admit it. 'Sorry, but you have to expect that.'

Shaking her head, she placed her glass down and crossed her forearms over the table. 'Oh, Adam. And yes—' her wicked eyes gleamed '—I can put my leg over my head.'

He stared at her. *Don't picture it, don't picture it.* But his mind went there and the thought of what they could get up to …

He swallowed hard. 'Tease me much more, Nat, and you'll find out just how much control a twenty-eight-year-old does *not* have.'

She laughed. 'I'll find out in October, but until then, twenty-seven-year-olds have a lot more, so I'll tease you all I like.'

'Then you can forget slow,' he muttered, taking a gulp of his drink. He could seduce her into needing him within a matter of seconds, but he wouldn't. 'Did you do anything else besides dance?'

'Just running.'

'How far do you like to run?'

'I go for forty minutes, which usually gives me eight or nine kilometres. Occasionally I go for longer, but only when I'm training for a marathon.'

He blinked. 'You've run a marathon?'

'I've run a few. I did the Sydney Marathon again last September and was thinking I might try the Cairns one next year. But for now, forty minutes is enough.'

Adam blew out his breath, tired just thinking about it. Sure, he'd hump bananas, saw wood, and do any sort of manual labour, but running ten kilometres? Or a bloody marathon?

'What?' she asked, her smile far too cheeky.

'I understand the obvious health benefits, but I don't think I could do it. I'd get bored.'

'You never did sporting activities at school?'

'I enjoyed PE and sports days. I excelled at sprinting and throwing stuff and liked touch footy. We weren't allowed to tackle—not in class, anyway. But no one was better than me at the ultimate school activity of all.'

'What was that?'

'Truanting.'

Natalia laughed. 'Wagging school was an activity? Oh, Adam …'

'Hey, there was a lot of skill involved. You had to be sneaky and run fast.'

'Why did you wag school?'

'Because it was fun. And I hated English. Cade and I had more fun in primary school when it was Aunty Deb handing out the punishment. We still ditched in high school, but it wasn't as easy in Mareeba. The principal suspended us once and Dad put us to heavy work on the farm for the week. After that, we preferred school.'

'You stopped ditching?'

'No. Just did it less often.'

Natalia shook her head. 'You sure were a rule breaker, weren't you?'

He grinned. 'You know it. So, you never did anything rebellious?'

A sly smile crept across her beautiful face. 'Well … you're not the only one who ever wagged school.'

Adam actually felt his jaw hit the floor. Her grin widened. 'Natalia Hamilton! I thought you were a good girl!'

She laughed and reached across the table to grab his hand. 'I am. But you will learn that if I choose, I can be very, *very* bad.'

He dug his fingers into her palm. 'You're teasing me again.'

'You make it so easy. But you must *never* tell Ana about this. Nobody knows.'

'In that case, I'm honoured. Now tell me why you did it.'

'Okay. It was grade twelve and I'd finished my final exams, so my friends and I thought we'd do something wild before graduation. We brought a change of clothes, got on the train, and went shopping in the city. I bought the cutest pair of shoes.'

Adam's smile had vanished. 'That doesn't count.'

'It does too!'

'No, it doesn't. School was practically over. Who would care?'

'Um, the teachers and my mother. And it was scary, okay? Don't take this away from me!'

He sighed. 'Fine. Sorry, Nat. It totally counts.'

She grinned. 'Thank you.'

'I see now what you mean about being a very bad girl.'

They both laughed.

'Ha. You wish. Now, should we order because I'm getting hungry?'

Nodding, Adam slid out of the booth. Locals filled the Royal Hotel as they dined, drank, and chatted over the music blasting from the jukebox. He ordered their meals and returned with fresh drinks. Soda water sucked, so he'd chosen a Coke instead. He and Natalia resumed their discussion, moving on from their high school days to her time at university.

'So, what are your plans for this week? More "humping" bananas?'

'Actually, we're going camping on Monday. Me, Jack, and Jason Taylor, along with a few young farm hands. It's something we do every few months.'

'Sounds like fun. Where are you going?'

'To this spot we have out west.'

'Is it a campground?'

'No. We roll out the swags and dig a hole.'

Her eyebrows lifted. 'Right. So, you're going to spend, what, a few nights in the middle of nowhere for no reason?'

'It's to teach the young blokes about farm safety.'

'Oh, okay. Why not do that on the farm?'

'We do, but it's not as fun. This way, we can escape to the bush and do it with beers around the campfire.'

'And sleep with the bugs.'

'And the snakes.'

She visibly shuddered. 'Don't say that word.'

'What? Snakes?'

'Seriously, don't!' Her shoulders straightened and eyes widened with genuine fear. 'I hate them.'

Adam grinned. Ah, city girls. He hadn't known many, but they sure were fun to tease about country living. 'But they're just innocent little animals. They don't mean any harm.'

'They're poisonous and they slither! Seriously, I can't bear the name or even look at pictures.'

Since she honestly seemed afraid, he let it go as a waitress arrived with their dinner. Hungry, he shoved a chip into his mouth while Natalia mixed her salad.

But he had to ask, 'Did you know Ana and Meg found a taipan in the kitchen?'

'What?' Her fork dropped to the ground with an audible clutter. 'A taipan?'

Unwrapping his fork, he handed it to her and tried not to laugh as he reached down to collect hers. 'She didn't tell you?'

'No, she knew I'd freak out. Are you going to eat with that fork?'

'I wouldn't expect you to,' he said, wiping it off on a napkin before piercing his Spanish mackerel.

'Oh my God. Was it in her kitchen?'

'No, Meg's. Jack and I found them huddled on the counter with knives in their hands in case Mr Taipan wanted to eat them.'

Natalia's knuckles whitened around her cutlery. 'You took the taipan away?'

'Yeah.'

'You touched it?'

He rolled his eyes and chewed. 'We're not that stupid. We have snake tongs.'

'But … you still go near them and pick them up?'

'Sure. Why not?'

'Are you crazy? It could kill you!'

Adam laughed. Damn, she was adorable, freaking out about something as harmless as a little taipan. 'Don't worry, I know what I'm doing. And I won't sleep with any snakes while I'm camping. They're more scared of us, you know?'

'Yeah.' Taking a deep breath, she loaded salad stuff onto her fork. 'So, they say.'

'I'll think about you though.'

The glitter returned to her eyes. 'I'm sure you will while you're out there in the middle of nowhere lying on the hard ground and I'm warm in my soft bed.'

'Swags are comfy. I've got a double one. Come camping with me and see for yourself?'

She laughed. 'Yeah. Right. I'm not going camping with you.'

'Why not?'

'In the bush with the taipans? Do you want to kill me?'

'I haven't slept with a taipan yet.'

'Hmm … maybe I could do the backyard one day, but I'm just too city to go without a running toilet.'

'I'll hold you to that,' he said, accepting it as a win. Camping with her in the backyard would be as good as anywhere else. Maybe one day they could move down to the creek?

'But you know, they made walls centuries ago so that people no longer had to sleep outside. And before then, they found caves and other shelter.'

'Point taken. How's your salad?'

'Good. It's missing legumes, but I'll happily eat it again.'

'I'm glad. Mine's good too,' he said, scooping some of the lettuce and tomato off the side of his plate. 'Although I'm still not a fan of this fancy lettuce stuff. What's wrong with iceberg?'

'Nothing if you're having a sandwich or Mexican. I still like iceberg lettuce on my tacos. But leaf mix is much better in a salad.'

'If you say so,' he muttered, munching on his. Thankfully, the sweet tomato masked the bitter taste of the purply lettuce. 'I still prefer iceberg.'

'Spinach is much better than this stuff. God, I miss spinach.'

Frowning, Adam bit into a chip. 'You don't have spinach?'

'They don't sell it at the produce store. I have frozen spinach, so I can use that in curries and pasta, but I'll have to drive to Mareeba to buy the fresh stuff.'

'You like it that much?'

'It's a staple,' she said, reaching for her drink. 'So yeah, I've had to resort to iceberg lettuce too, which is no substitute.'

'No, probably not.' He didn't know much about spinach and was only familiar with the frozen kind, but he realised there was a big difference. Besides, spinach was supposed to

be more nutritious, which was important to Natalia. So …
'Why don't we grow it?'

She blinked, pausing with her fork halfway to her mouth.
'What?'

'Assuming we can.' He abandoned his dinner and reached
for his phone. 'Let me see … Ah! Suitable for all climates.
Excellent! Should be able to figure it out.'

He placed his phone down and met her gaze. She was still
staring at him, her fork lowered.

'You want to grow me spinach?'

Adam's heart swelled. He'd hit a soft spot. The good kind
that made her all mushy. But what else would he do? Growing
food was what he did. It'd been his idea to plant the lemon
trees and he had a passionfruit vine in his backyard. Why not
spinach?

He reached across the table and took her hand. 'Yeah. I
want to grow you spinach. Hell, you can have a whole veggie
patch.' His blood pumped at the prospect of a new project.
He'd dig out a patch of dirt and plant her any damn thing she
wanted.

Natalia laughed. 'Are you serious?'

'Nat, I like to grow things, and we've grown many different
foods on Shadow Creek. Mum has her own veggie garden at
High Ridge and we've always had tomatoes growing outside
the homestead. So, if you want spinach, I'll plant you some
spinach.'

'Oh, Adam.' Her eyes glittered. 'You sure know how to
woo a girl.'

He laughed. 'So, we'll do it, hey? This weekend? I'll go to
Mareeba and get some seedlings.'

'I thought you guys were going for suit fittings this
weekend?'

'Right.' Nodding, he resumed his dinner. 'Leave it with me. I'll work it out. And if there's anything else you want, let me know and I'll see if we can grow it.'

'Cherry tomatoes might be nice.'

'No worries. Tomatoes grow anywhere.'

By the time they'd finished eating, they had quite a list of what she'd like in her veggie garden. There were some foods that were too difficult, like strawberries, and he talked her out of carrots because she was better off buying them. But they'd try sweet potatoes, cabbage, capsicums, and plant a few herbs too.

They were sitting cosy in the booth, delighted by their new venture, when their friends arrived unexpectedly. Adam wasn't sure if he was happy or annoyed to see them.

'Hey. What are you lot doing here?'

Ana slipped into the booth. 'Liam and I felt like going out. We did message you.'

Adam had seen her text come through but had been too busy reading about how to grow cauliflower.

'We were having dinner,' Natalia said.

'Good. I'm glad you guys sorted things out. Meg and Jack did too.'

Adam exhaled. 'Finally.'

Meg beamed. 'He apologised and admitted he was wrong.'

'I wasn't wrong. You agreed I was right.'

'Yeah, about Scott and I not being right for each other, not that I shouldn't have dated him.'

Jack rolled his eyes. Adam smothered his grin with a sip of Coke, exchanging an amused look with Lucy.

'I'm glad I ran into you guys,' Ana said. 'Liam and I can't choose a wedding song.'

'*You* can't choose. There are plenty of great songs.'

Ana shot Liam her bride-look and he shut up.

'How about Meg, Lucy, and I come over tomorrow to help?' Natalia suggested.

'Yeah?' Ana's eyes brightened. 'That'd be great. We need a buffer.'

'That's what we're here for,' Meg agreed as her eyes locked on the pub's door. 'Uh-oh.'

'What?' Jack looked up. 'Fuck.'

'Ah, Adam,' Lucy said. 'Fuckhead and his even bigger fuckhead of a brother just walked in and they have their eyes on you.'

Chapter Twenty

Natalia was still reeling with the thought of her own vegetable garden, unsure whether her heart would ever recover from Adam's offer to grow her spinach. But her excitement evaporated at the mention of the Kelly brothers. Adam's arm tightened around her shoulders.

'Luce, stop staring,' he hissed as Natalia turned to look. 'Nat!'

'Which ones are they?'

'You'll find out.' He placed a kiss on her temple. 'I apologise in advance for my behaviour.'

'What?'

'Maguire!'

Natalia glanced up as two men arrived at their table.

'Fuck, I wish I'd had a beer,' Adam muttered, staring at his empty glass of Coke before glancing at the brothers. 'Harry.'

'What's this we hear about you knocking up our sister and then saying you want nothing to do with her?'

'I never said that. But I can't be sure I did knock her up.'

Natalia studied the Kellys. The one doing the talking, Harrison, was shorter than his brother but stocky, with wide shoulders and thick arms. Paul was lankier, but just as broad. They looked similar to Elanora, but Natalia wouldn't have considered them to be related if she hadn't known. She could never imagine Elanora's face curling in a horrible snarl or seeing such anger in her eyes.

'Of course you can't,' Paul said. 'You were off your face.'

Lucy's eyes narrowed. 'How do you know how drunk he was, Paul?'

'Everyone knows! He can't even remember the bloody night!'

Adam unwrapped his arm from Natalia. 'Exactly. So, how can I take Jordan's word for it?'

Harrison folded his thick arms. 'Are you saying Jordan's lying?'

'No. I'm saying I want to know what happened that night.'

Anger flashed through Harrison's eyes. Natalia drew in a breath.

'Piss off, Kelly,' Jack snapped. 'Unless you want to see this get ugly, we'll talk about it later.'

Harrison lifted his chin. 'Yeah. I want to see it get ugly.'

'Right.' Jack downed the last of his beer and began to slide out of the booth.

'No!' Meg grabbed his arm. 'No one's fighting tonight.'

'Shut up, Riley,' Harrison spat.

'Don't talk to me like that!' she cried as Jack escaped her hold and stood.

Everyone else scrambled out of the booth. Natalia reluctantly followed Ana to let Adam out. The last thing she wanted was anyone fighting, but what could she do?

'Now, you listen,' Adam said, facing Harrison with Jack standing beside him. 'Stay out of my business. I don't know what happened that night, so until I do—'

'It's fucking simple. You got drunk and knocked up our sister.' Harrison's fists clenched at his side. Natalia tried to reach for Adam, but Ana grabbed her hand and pulled her back.

'What proof have you got?' Adam asked.

'We believe our sister.'

'That's your problem, but I'm going to need more than just her word—'

Harrison threw the punch. Natalia shrieked as Adam stumbled backwards, and Ana dragged Natalia back a few steps. A stool crashed as Adam tackled Harrison into the bar and Jack grabbed Paul in some sort of headlock.

Liam's shoulders heaved, relaxed, then he stepped forward. Natalia watched in stunned silence as he pulled Jack away from Paul and palmed him off to Meg.

But Adam and Harrison were still at each other. Natalia didn't want to watch, but she couldn't tear her eyes away.

'Oi!' Georgina rounded the bar in a five-foot-rage of fury. 'Kelly! Maguire! Get your brothers off each other!'

They needed both of them to pull the fuming men apart.

'Find someone else to pin your lies on, 'cause I'm not taking it!' Adam yelled as Jack and Liam held him back.

'Fuck off, Maguire!' Harrison shouted as Paul pushed him away. 'Own up to your mistakes. You think you can trade in my sister for this new hot piece of arse?'

Natalia gasped. Ana grabbed her hand.

Jack and Liam grunted but managed to stop Adam from charging at Harrison. 'Don't talk about Natalia like that!'

'Enough!' Georgina shrieked, and the whole pub fell silent. Heat rose in Natalia's cheeks. Everyone was staring at them.

Harrison snarled. 'What? You're dating her for her brain? She mustn't have one if she's interested in you.'

Natalia winced. Couldn't Harrison think of anything more original?

Adam didn't hold back. 'Let me at him, Jack. Let me fucking go!'

'For fuck's sake,' Jack grunted, his feet shifting as he struggled to restrain Adam. Jack glared at the Kellys. 'Adam has every right to ask for proof he's the father of that child, and if he is, I think you'll find you have a bigger problem. Take a look at your own family before you insult mine.'

Georgina snapped her tea-towel against the table. 'I said enough!'

Everyone shut up. Adam stopped struggling, and they all turned to the tiny blonde woman.

'You two—' she pointed her finger at the Kellys '—keep your bullshit out of my pub! And Maguires!' She rounded on all seven of them. 'I don't care what you lot think either but take it outside. I don't want to see any of you for the rest of the week!'

Meg raised her eyebrows. 'You're kicking us all out?'

'Yes. Get these two cleaned up.'

Georgina turned on her heel and marched away. Jack and Liam released Adam and Natalia went to him, gripping his forearms as she assessed the damage. His lip swelled and a bruise would probably form around his left eye.

'I'm sorry, Nat.' His hands brushed up her arms to her shoulders. 'I'll fucking kill him for saying that about you.'

'I've had worse,' she muttered, reaching for her handbag. 'Let's just go.'

Outside, Meg fussed over Jack while Liam stood with his arm around Ana. Lucy paced with her arms crossed.

Natalia turned to Adam, unsure of what to say. Should she tell him they should have settled their anger in another way?

That he shouldn't let Harrison get to him? That he looked kind of hot with battle wounds?

She hated to admit it, but she would have punched Harrison too.

Adam placed his hand on her shoulder. 'Are you okay?'

'I'll be fine. Take me home and I'll put some ice on that face.'

'Nah, it's not that bad.'

Her jaw tightened. 'Don't argue with me, Adam Maguire. You just got me kicked out of the pub and that face needs some ice.'

He nodded, and after saying their goodbyes, they climbed into Adam's ute. Natalia stared out the window the two blocks home. She hadn't liked Adam fighting and for a split second there, she'd been terrified. Most of the time, bar fights only ended with bruises and lacerations, and she'd stitched up many lips and eyes in ED. But people had died in the bloody things too. Did he not realise that?

She rolled her eyes as they pulled up outside her unit. Men.

Adam cleared his throat as they strolled to the door. 'Nat, I'm sorry. That's not how I wanted our date to end.'

She slid the key into the lock. 'The date hasn't ended, Adam. Sit down and I'll get you some ice.'

She grabbed a bag of frozen peas, wrapped it in a tea-towel, then joined him on the lounge. He'd have a shiner tomorrow, but she'd check him out to make sure he hadn't broken anything.

'Lie down,' she said softly, and Adam obliged. She moved with him, twisting her legs between his. Propping herself onto her elbows, she placed the peas on his bruised cheek. He'd shaved before picking her up but still looked devilishly handsome as she brushed dark hair from his forehead. Her heart pounded against his and moments passed locked in each other's gaze.

'Are you mad at me?'

Natalia sighed. She didn't approve, but mad? He'd only been defending himself. And her. 'Not really. He punched you first.'

His eyes darkened as he slipped his hand into her hair. 'I'm glad you noticed that.'

'Yeah, but don't do it again. You could get seriously hurt.'

'I know.' He ran his hands down her shoulders and caressed her arms. 'Fighting doesn't go well with the whole self-improvement thing. But I can't make any promises if he insults you again.'

'Don't worry about that. I'll get him back for it one day.'

'Not if I do first.'

Unable to resist a smile, she moved the ice to his swollen lip. 'Hold that, would you? Tell me if this hurts.' He released her arm and held the peas so that she could assess his eye orbit. She poked and prodded. He winced, but she didn't suspect any damage other than bruising. 'You should be fine.'

'I usually am, doc.'

'But you know—' she moved the peas up again '—I have to wonder why Jordan hasn't been trying to win you back.' She frowned. 'Or has she?'

Adam's eyes darkened. 'I texted her yesterday, apologising for not taking the news well. She invited me over for a booty-call.'

Natalia stilled. 'Really?'

He nodded, his hands resuming their gentle massage of her biceps. 'I ignored her. Didn't know what to say.'

Natalia didn't know what to say either, but as Adam wrapped his arms around her waist, her body curved against the ridged planes of his chest, torso, and thighs, and any thoughts about Jordan vanished.

'We'll figure this out,' he said, his voice deep and determined, his gaze boring into hers. 'Trust me.'

She swallowed and tried to recover her breath. Natalia wanted to trust him. She did in some respects. But her fears lingered. 'I'm sure we will.'

His hands resumed their gentle massage. Seconds, possibly minutes, ticked by and his eyes never left hers.

'Can I ask you something?' he whispered.

'Okay.'

'What do you think of Ana and Liam falling in love so quickly?'

She shrugged. 'I'm happy for them, of course. Although, I'll admit, it was fast.' Not that she had any doubts about Ana and Liam's relationship.

'Yeah … it certainly made me think. I always thought that love was something you could fall in and out of. But now, I'm not so sure …'

Something in his eyes changed and Natalia froze. Her heart pinged, zapped, and squeezed. Hook her up to an ECG and she'd have no clue what was going on. 'Do you think about this often?'

'Sometimes.'

Nodding slowly, she tried to find some words. Any words. 'You're not afraid of love? Commitment?' She'd thought a man like Adam would run for the hills at the mere thought.

'I'm afraid I'll suck at it.'

Exhaling, she broke their gaze and trailed her fingers down his chest to fiddle with the logo on his shirt. Why was he even thinking about such a thing? It might explain why he'd turned a new leaf, but right now … the light in his eyes terrified her.

'Nat? Are you okay?'

She nodded, although she wasn't sure. Silence filled the room. She fiddled with his buttons and he stroked her back.

Again, Adam broke first. 'Have you been in love?'

She shook her head, the tightness in her chest easing. 'I guess I've always thought about love differently. When you're in it, there's no turning back.'

'Yeah, I'd agree with that.'

Her gaze shot back to his. 'But you just said you can fall in and out!'

His smile lit up his face. 'I said I'd *thought* you could.'

'Right …' She swallowed. 'Well, I always thought it'd be a one off for me. Like my mum.' She moved her fingers to fiddle with the button at his throat. 'Mama loved my father. He's been gone twenty years and she still loves him.'

Adam's hand brushed through her hair. 'I reckon my parents would feel the same way.'

'And I've always wanted that. But I guess I'm …' She took a deep breath. 'I'm scared, Adam.'

'Of what?'

'Lots of things. I've never been with anyone long-term and I've had terrible dates in the past. And I'm insecure.'

'Maybe about some things, but mostly, I find you very secure indeed.'

She blinked, speechless. Was he right? Sure, others had treated her poorly, but at least she knew who she was. And she was fighting to get that person back.

But she wouldn't be ready for love until those insecurities at the back of her head were silenced. Even if she did have the sexiest man she'd ever met lying beneath her.

'Thank you, Adam. I am trying, but I guess we all have little things we can't shake.'

'We do. But until then, I'm happy to take things between us one day at a time.'

'Good,' she whispered before silencing his dangerous mouth by pressing her lips to his. Stupid idea though since his passionate kiss only increased the threat upon her heart. He tightened his grip and pulled her closer, brushing his tongue against hers. Desire shot through her so hot that she forced herself to pull away.

Adam grinned. 'Not slow?'

'No, it's fine. I just …' Shaking her head, she picked up the peas from where they'd dropped onto the lounge. 'Let's not do this here.'

His eyes brightened. 'Too hot?'

'Dangerous. Enticing.' She managed a smile. 'It may make me want to forget slow and let you stay over.'

He laughed. 'I wouldn't say no, but I don't want to stay over.' He drew her close and kissed her again. 'I want to bid you goodnight—' she almost moaned as he sucked in her bottom lip '—and see you tomorrow.'

She joined in his laughter. 'Okay. But trust me, we won't hold out for long, Adam.'

The wicked gleam returned to his eyes. She pulled out of his grasp and let her knees slip to either side of his thighs. Her dress rode up, but not enough to be indecent. The peas lay abandoned as he followed her to a seated position.

'I hope not.' His hands caressed her hips, temping her to surrender. 'I want to be with you, Nat. I want to taste your skin, feel your body, and make unbelievable love with you like nothing we've ever experienced.'

Natalia trembled as his hands brushed down her hips and settled on her thighs.

'You have high expectations, don't you?' She flashed him

her most seductive smile, then leaned close to whisper in his ear. 'I'll let you in on a little secret. I like sex, Adam. And I'm good at it.' She had the pleasure of hearing him groan as she placed a kiss on his bruised jaw. Her grin widened. 'Too bad we won't experience it tonight.'

He pulled her close until her breasts pressed to his hard chest. She shivered. 'The teasing must stop, Natalia. Seriously.'

'You love it. Besides, I thought you were going to bid me goodnight—' she brushed her lips over his, yearning for him '—and see me tomorrow?'

He swallowed hard. 'I am. But first, you promised me dessert. And I'm in the mood for something sweet.'

Still laughing, Natalia untangled herself from him and stood. 'Okay. One citrus tart coming right up.' She paused halfway to the kitchen and tossed a look over her shoulder. 'Pity I don't do whipped cream.'

Chapter Twenty-One

After the most delicious tart he'd ever eaten, Adam kissed Natalia senseless and made his escape. It was perhaps the hardest thing he'd ever done, leaving her waving at the door while he drove away into the night. Being a gentleman was not easy.

Warmth filled his chest and he cranked up the music. Despite the unfortunate punch-up with Harry, he'd never had a better evening. Every time he learned something new about Natalia, she surprised him even more. Because somehow, he, the rebellious bad boy trying to make good, was dating a beautiful, prim, and proper bad girl.

He blew out his breath. Natalia was damn perfect, but hell if he knew why she was standing by him. He was grateful though, and as the tempting woman had laid her warm body alongside his and nursed his wounds, a strange hot sensation had filled him from head to toe.

How would he ever be worthy of her? He wanted to be. He never wanted to let her go. But he wanted to move slowly, and it was obviously what Natalia needed too. Because even though she had a good sense of who she was and what she wanted, the insecurities and vulnerability she hid so well continued to lurk. The sexual harassment she'd experienced had not been kind on her soul.

His hand tightened around the wheel as he recalled the insult that had come out of Harry's mouth. *Hot piece of arse. Not dating her for her brain.* If Jack and Liam hadn't been holding him back, he'd have punched Harrison again. No wonder Natalia was sensitive about her looks when that's the type of talk she'd experienced. She may have shrugged it off on the outside, but he'd seen the hurt in her eyes.

What had Natalia been through? Sure, he understood why she hadn't wanted to talk about it when they'd been warm and cosy on his lounge that afternoon. Hopefully, when the time was right, she'd share her story.

* * *

The next morning, Adam headed for the shed to do a final check on his woodwork. He examined the bowls and vases with a satisfied nod. They weren't works of art, but each piece was unique and exactly what people wanted when shopping for local handcrafted homewares.

He packed them up to deliver to Heather, then prepared for the camping trip. Falling off the grid with the boys for a few days was just what he needed to put his head on straight. He could eat, drink, and fish while teaching the young blokes about farm safety, which was something the Maguires and the Taylors were passionate about since farm accidents had traumatised both of their families.

Adam threw his swag and a change of clothes into the ute as his phone rang. He pulled it from his pocket and groaned at Jordan's name on the screen. He didn't want to answer, but what else could he do?

'Hi, Adam. How you doing?'

Grimacing at her flirtatious tone, he leaned over the tailgate and stared into the tray. 'I'd be doing better if you told me what happened.'

'I already have. Do you want to get together?'

'To talk about that night?'

'No, to talk about what we're going to do about the baby. Then maybe you could keep my bed warm as I've been kinda lonely.'

He squeezed his eyes shut and fought for control. Which of those suggestions should he even respond to? 'I can't, Jordan. I'm going camping tomorrow.'

'When you get back then?' Frustration rose in her tone. 'I need to know if you're going to be involved or ignore us. Of course, I hope you choose us. There's nothing your new squeeze can give you that I can't.'

His jaw clenched. 'Don't talk about Natalia like that.'

'I wouldn't have thought you'd be the type to ignore your family.'

Adam turned and raked his hand down his face, guilt swarming in his gut. Of course, he wouldn't turn his back on family. It was the most important thing in the world to him. 'You know I won't, Jordan. I'll do the right thing by you, but we both know we'd never be happy together. And I *am* going to need proof I'm the father before I take responsibility.'

She gasped. 'My word's not good enough?'

'Come on, any man has the right to ask. If I'd remembered sleeping with you, it'd be a different story. But like I told you, someone spiked me—'

'This shit again?'

The anger in her tone drew him to a halt. She'd known him long enough to know he'd never used drugs, so why didn't she believe him? Could Natalia be right in her concerns? Could Jordan have been the one to spike him? Because if she had, then—

He shook his head. No. Jordan may be a liar, but she didn't need to drug a man to screw him.

'Yes, this shit again. You claim you were there, Jordan. Did I appear just drunk to you? Because blacking out rarely happens on alcohol alone.'

'So because you got shit-faced on some drug, I have to be subjected to this crap?' Her voice hitched into a familiar sound—hysteria. 'Why would I lie to you, Adam?'

He kicked a pebble with his toe. He could rattle off many reasons, but he didn't. 'Jordan, calm down. I'm not being unreasonable. I just want answers. If the kid is mine, then I'll do what I need to do. And if you know you're right, then you shouldn't have a problem agreeing to a paternity test.'

Exhaling, he glanced down at the creek. He hadn't thought about it like that, but if she had nothing to hide, she'd agree. If she wanted him to accept the paternity, she'd agree. But if—

'Fuck off, Adam.'

She hung up and he lowered his phone, frowning. Fuck, he hated this. Why did *he* have to be the one to come off as a bastard? He was right to ask.

So, was she pissed that he had? Or did Jordan have something to hide?

* * *

Natalia had not yet made it to agility training after spending her first Sunday meeting the wedding photographer and then needing to stitch up a child who'd come off his skateboard last week. But after the way Ana had raved about the dog sport, she was keen to see Steph and Louis in action. As well as Rusty. Grinning, she scooped the little dog into her arms. He wasn't impressed and wriggled about, but she didn't care.

'Don't I get a cuddle?' Adam asked.

'My arms are full, but you can have a kiss.' She lifted her chin and Adam obliged, pulling her close and squishing Rusty between them.

'You look nice,' he said.

'Thank you.'

'But I'm afraid your shirt's going to be covered in little white hairs now.'

She glanced down at Rusty's white and tan face, his eyes meeting hers. 'It's worth it. He'll learn to love cuddles.'

'Doubt it.' He rubbed Rusty's head. 'I dropped the goods off with Heather.'

'Did she like them?'

'She made quite a fuss, but Heather does that.'

Natalia quirked her eyebrow. 'Or you're actually more talented than you believe.'

Adam rolled his eyes, and she sighed. How could he not appreciate his own work after the way he'd proudly given her that fruit bowl, her now dearest possession? Did he really lack faith in himself?

She didn't get the chance to ask though as claws scratched her leg. Gasping, she glanced down to find a little dog identical to Rusty jumping up at her, his eyes shining, mouth open, and white tail wagging. 'Oh, hello.'

Adam laughed. 'You better put Rusty down.'

Rusty squirmed so much that Natalia didn't have a choice, and the two Jack Russells jumped at each other.

'Sorry about that. Freddy has no manners.'

Natalia glanced up at the voice to find a tall, attractive man striding towards them.

'He would if you trained him,' Adam said, reaching out to slap him on the shoulder. 'Meet, Nat. Nat, this is Cade, my best mate.'

Cade grinned and extended his hand. 'So, you're the woman he doesn't deserve.'

Natalia laughed as Adam elbowed Cade in the ribs. 'I guess so. Nice to meet you.' She shook Cade's hand and glanced between the two men. Adam was sexy with his muscular build and unruly dark hair, but Cade was a different kind of hot entirely. They certainly made a pair. 'You two even have the same dogs?'

'Blame him.' Cade jerked his thumb in Adam's direction before crossing his arms over his wide chest. 'He wanted a rat catcher so found a litter of Jack Russells, asked if I'd go for a drive, and before I knew it, I had a dog too.'

'I didn't make you do anything and you know it. You just can't say no to a big pair of needy eyes.'

'He was the last one left! He didn't have a home! What was I supposed to do?'

Natalia stifled a laugh. And these two called themselves rebellious bad boys? Please. 'I wouldn't have left him either. Besides, it's nice they got to stay together. They're brothers.'

'And don't they know it. Trust me, Nat—' Adam touched her arm '—you can try to win Rusty's affections all you want, but he loves no one more than Freddy.'

Natalia watched Rusty and Freddy sniff the bushes, their brown ears perked, white tails wagging, and faces happy. She loved Louis, of course, but if she had a dog of her own, she would want a little one who would curl up on her lap and she could tuck under her arm. So, she'd convince Rusty he wanted to be a lapdog despite Adam's claims that such a thing was impossible. But since she wouldn't sniff bushes and roll in the dirt with him, Freddy could remain his best friend.

'We'll see.'

Adam wrapped his arm around her waist. 'He might come around. So, how did the wedding meeting go? I tried working on my speech, but I don't know what I'm supposed to say. I've never been good at writing that sort of stuff.'

'I'm sure you'll figure it out. You just need to say nice things about Liam and how happy you are he married Ana. But yeah, I had a good afternoon. We worked on the playlist and I warn you now, Adam—' she poked him in the shoulder '—you will dance with me.'

Natalia expected a groan, a wince, or some sort of excuse. Instead, he smiled. 'Isn't it traditional we do so as best man and maid of honour?'

'Yeah, but dancing at weddings seems to be going out of fashion, based on those I've been to. Everyone just seems to drink and eat these days.'

Cade laughed. 'This is the country, Nat. We'll do both.'

She glanced up at Adam. 'So you'll dance with me?'

A wicked gleam filled his eyes. 'If I must.'

But he hardly made it seem like a hardship as Liam called the group to attention. Adam and Cade went to wrestle their dogs away from the bushes and Natalia joined Isabella Brennan on the park bench beneath the massive ficus. She smiled softly at the younger woman and patted the King Charles Cavalier on Isabella's lap.

'Doesn't Evie do agility?'

Isabella shook her head. 'No. We come to socialise and watch, which is just as fun.'

And fun it was. Natalia watched as Ana and Liam ran their border collies through tunnels and over hurdles, both dogs quick and agile. Lucy did just as well with her German Shepherd and Meg encouraged her fluffy Pomeranian over what Isabella described as practice obstacles—tiny seesaws and dog walks.

But mainly, Natalia focused her attention on Adam and Rusty. The little dog's dark eyes shone with such delight and trust, waiting for the next treat out of Adam's hand as he ran up and over the dog walk, through tunnels, and leapt over the hurdles. Not that Natalia blamed Rusty as she'd do anything to put that smile on Adam's face too.

But while he might look like a different man from yesterday—easy going and relaxed—Natalia only wished it would be that easy to eradicate the demons that plagued him.

Chapter Twenty-Two

The surgery was quiet for a Monday and with a break in patients, Natalia planned to catch up on some study. She strode across the staffroom with a mug of peppermint tea as a voice drifted in from reception.

'No, I cannot see that woman. When is Joanne available?'

Natalia halted. On the other side of the ajar door, Emma sighed. 'Joanne could see you this afternoon, but Natalia can easily—'

'No. What sort of self-respecting doctor goes gallivanting around with that man-whore? Claiming he was spiked and shirking his responsibility to that poor woman. Please.'

Natalia's hands tightened around her mug at the woman's repugnant tone. Had she heard that right?

'I'm not sure that's actually the case,' Emma replied flatly.

'Either way, I'll come back to see Joanne. What time?'

'Two-thirty. In the meantime, if you wish to continue attending here, please consider how you speak about our staff.'

Natalia blinked. There were no more words from the rude woman, but she waited for the front door to close before exiting the staffroom. Emma spun around in her chair and winced.

'How much did you hear?'

'Everything. Who was that?'

'Sonia Mansfield.' Emma's lip curled. 'Not someone worth getting upset over.'

Natalia sipped her tea so that she couldn't reply.

'I'm sorry, Natalia. I'll speak to Joanne, but I—'

'It's okay. I've been called worse. But is that what she really thinks of Adam?'

'I'm afraid she's not the only one.'

Natalia's belly clenched. 'Perfect. Thank you for sticking up for us though.'

Grateful more than she could say, Natalia forced herself to smile, but Sonia's words continued to gnaw at her as she sat at her desk.

Would other locals think along the same lines? Despite his efforts, was Adam's reputation not that easily squashed? Would *other* people not wish to seek her professional help based on who she dated?

Groaning, Natalia dropped her head into her hands. Why did everyone always want to judge her? She may be a doctor, but she was still a person.

She'd never be a rural doctor if she didn't study though, so Natalia shoved Sonia from her mind and began reading. She consulted with a young woman about ongoing contraception and had another break until her next appointment. But she could barely focus. Why? She'd moved on from her initial devastation and Adam knew about the pregnancy. But that didn't stop Natalia from wanting to wring Jordan's neck. She'd obviously spread the word that Adam hesitated in accepting responsibility for her. Or flat out refused, more like. And after Sonia's comment, would locals label Jordan as the victim?

Probably, and that's what was absurd about the whole situation. Whatever else had happened that night, Adam was a victim too.

Maybe she could speak to Jordan and …

Natalia slouched in her chair. No, she couldn't overstep by confronting Jordan.

A knock sounded on the door and Natalia jumped. 'Yes?'

Joanne poked her head in. 'Are you busy? I want to show you something.'

Natalia exhaled. At least Joanne remembered she was there to practise medicine. She followed Joanne into the neighbouring consult room, where she examined a dark mole beneath the dermatoscope. With discontorted edges and the patch of black in the middle of the deeply pigmented brown lesion, Natalia agreed it had the characteristics of a melanoma.

'Do you want to take it out?' Joanne asked.

Natalia smiled and contained her excitement with a simple nod. 'Absolutely.'

'There you go, Mark.' Joanne placed her hand on the patient's shoulder. 'Let's take you out the back and get this done before the pathology courier arrives.'

Natalia strode into the treatment room and washed her hands, her pulse now racing for an entirely different reason. She was in Elizadale to learn, to improve her skills and to become a better doctor. Could she do that and date the bad boy?

Her teeth clenched as she gloved up. All she wanted to do was support him through this difficult time. And while he might put a fire in her blood like she'd never felt before, it was still casual. Neither of them was looking for anything more than that. And while she was in town, she planned to enjoy herself. People could just keep their noses out of her business.

'Okay, Mark. We're going to do the local anaesthetic now.' Natalia attached the needle and drew up the lignocaine and adrenaline. She applied the local, then under Joanne's guidance, excised the lesion. Natalia popped the skin ellipse into the formalin, cauterised the bleeders, then stitched Mark up and remained on a high for the rest of the day.

She spent Tuesday evening wedding planning with Ana. During lunch on Wednesday, received a text from Adam.

Returned to civilisation with reception. Still alive. No need for antivenom.

Warmth filled her belly and she laughed, glad he was on his way home. She'd missed him and had worried about how he was doing out God-knows-where with the bugs and snakes in this cold weather while she'd lain in bed cosy and warm.

As she filed results, Natalia's heart sank as she read Elanora's fertility studies. Elanora was healthy with all her hormones in range. Even her iron levels were good. And yet, she still couldn't conceive while her sister ...

Sighing, Natalia closed the results file. Life was cruel.

That afternoon, Grace showed Natalia how to operate the x-ray machine. Then, after a few more patients, she left work early and strolled down to Elizadale Homewares, hoping to find her mother a gift for her birthday in a few weeks.

She would definitely buy something of Adam's, even though he would probably tell her she shouldn't have wasted her money. But while he might be able to make her something special and convince her it was a gift, Natalia wanted to support his business. So, after marvelling over everything on the display and wondering how he did it, Natalia chose a tall vase, then continued to browse.

There was far too much to choose from. Apparently, Sue and Heather created most of the items in the shop—the knitted throw blankets and tea cosies, doilies and table runners, quilts, and cushion covers. Meg had said she wished she had a morsel of her mother's skill as Sue and Heather were the most talented sewers and knitters in town. Yet there were many locals who sold through this store and Natalia thought it wonderful they had the opportunity.

She was admiring soy candles made my Rebecca Taylor when voices drifted from across the store.

'I don't know why a woman would get herself caught up in a situation like that. If she were my daughter, I'd have told her to leave him quick smart.'

'I like this bowl and it's nice to think he wants to make something of himself, but I wouldn't have thought he'd ignore his responsibilities. Even if it is Jordan Kelly.'

Heart pounding, Natalia peered around the candle stand to where two middle-aged women she didn't know browsed Adam's display.

'Jordan may be many things, but she doesn't deserve this,' the blonde woman said. 'That boy's always been a wild one and is just chasing tail. So, are you going to buy that bowl?'

The other woman shook her head and placed it back on the shelf. 'Leave it for the tourists who don't know who they're buying from.' They walked away. 'Pity though, 'cause it'd have been good to have two doctors. But he'll break her heart and she'll be gone.'

'I wouldn't want to see her anyway. Traipsing around with the bad boy is no way for a doctor to behave.'

The women were almost out the door, but Natalia heard those last words as clearly as if they'd been said to her face. Her chest constricted and hand tightened around a candle.

Was that honestly what people thought about her? About Adam? What exactly was Jordan saying about them?

Exhaling, Natalia glanced at the candles and chose the eucalyptus one at random. Her mother would like that. Then she chose a banana scented candle for herself, made her purchases, and hurried home.

She hated gossip. People talking about her, about them, making judgements and thinking they could tell her how she should act, think, and feel. She didn't want to think about it, so returning home, she grabbed an apple from her beautiful fruit bowl and planned to lose herself in a book Isabella had recommended. Natalia rarely read regency romance, but she had to admit, society sure had class back then and she was hooked.

Two pages later, a knock sounded on the door. She lifted herself from the lounge with a groan. Whoever was interrupting her evening in a fantasy world of a passionate love affairs with a duke was not appreciated.

But a passionate love affair became reality when she found Adam on her doorstep.

'Hey there, you.' He stepped inside, wrapped his arms around her waist, and swooped in for a kiss. Natalia didn't even have a chance to smile, let alone greet him. Instead, she welcomed his kiss as he gripped her hips and she ran her hands down his hard body. His muscles rippled beneath her fingers and as his thumbs slipped beneath her blouse to brush her bare skin, she shivered and pressed herself closer. It may only be a simple touch, but damn it was tantalising. Sinful. She wanted him to touch her more.

But not today.

A moment later, he drew away. 'I think I missed you more than I expected.'

Heart fluttering, she ran her hands up his hard biceps and gripped his shoulders. 'Thought about me, huh?'

'Constantly.' His dark eyes gleamed. 'I've been longing to kiss you.'

Smiling, she looped her arms around his neck. 'You can kiss me any time you like.'

'Deal.' He swooped in for a quick peck. 'So, how was your day?'

'Better now. When did you get back?'

'About one o'clock. Then I went to Mareeba to get what we need for your veggie garden.'

Her eyebrows shot up. 'Already?'

'Yep. I've got it all worked out, but it'd be best I have a week to prepare the soil, so next weekend works out well. They had all the seedlings we wanted though. The cherry tomatoes will be easy, but your spinach won't last through summer.'

Her nose crinkled. That's when she'd want it for salads.

'But I got various herbs, broccoli, cauliflower, eggplant, and got beetroot too because I like it.'

'Beetroot's good.' She reached onto her toes and kissed him. 'Thanks, Adam.'

'No worries. We can dig out the garden next Sunday.'

'We?' She raised her eyebrows. She had no problem helping but had never wielded a shovel, except maybe on the beach when she was a kid building sandcastles.

Adam laughed and pulled her an inch closer. '*I'll* dig. I don't expect you to swing the mattock. You can stand there and—'

Natalia stilled. *Look pretty?* She'd heard that one plenty of times.

'—help.'

She inwardly scolded herself. Adam would never say that.

'I'll definitely help,' she said. 'I'm just so thrilled you want to do this for me.'

'It's not a problem.' He ran his hands up her back. 'So, what did you get up to while I was gone?'

'I did an excision! It was awesome. It was my first one in ages and something I want to do more of.'

'Well, I'm glad it made you happy,' he said with a smile. 'Just keep your scalpels away from me.'

She laughed. 'Will do. So, did you sleep with any taipans?'

'Nah, but we saw a red belly black.' She shuddered. 'It was cold though. Next time, come and keep me warm?'

'Yeah, right.'

'Oh, well. I had to try. You want to go out to dinner?'

Natalia paused. She had chickpeas soaking, crushed tomatoes to use, and had been looking forward to her tikka masala. 'How about we stay in? Do you like curry?'

He grinned. 'As long as it's hot.'

'Oh, Adam.' She shook her head. 'So, you don't mind? I've been eating out too much lately and I don't enjoy doing that.'

'No worries. I bet whatever you're making will beat anything at Smithy's.'

'Chickpea tikka masala.' She raised her eyebrows. 'Do you like chickpeas?'

'I don't see how I won't.'

'Good. Then let me go and I'll get it started as it'll take some time to cook.'

Stepping back, he looked her up and down as she straightened her shirt. 'You are beautiful, Natalia.'

Her insides buzzed. 'Thanks. But you know, these are only work clothes. Just wait until I bring it.'

His mouth curved slowly. 'Bring it?'

'Oh, I'll bring it.' She hooked her fingers through his belt loops and urged him a step closer. 'You won't know what hit you.'

Adam took two controlled breaths before he spoke. 'Next time you say something seductive, Natalia Hamilton, I'll have no choice but to show you how much of a naughty girl you are.'

She pressed her body closer to his. 'Oh, yeah?'

'Yeah. You get one more chance.'

'Then I'll have to pick my moment wisely. Because you know I can be a very, very bad girl.'

On a groan, he reclaimed her mouth. Natalia grinned into the kiss, her heart swelling with the power she wielded over Adam Maguire. Whether or not it was something he was used to, it sure would make the final game more fun. But until she could smother the idea that everything would crumble around them, she didn't want to rush things. And the thought that Jordan had drugged and assaulted him was tearing her to shreds, so she needed to talk to him.

Later though. Right now, all she wanted was to cook Adam her favourite tikka masala and talk veggie gardens.

'You're a seductive woman, Natalia.'

She grinned and patted his cheek. 'Baby, you don't know what powers I possess. Now, let me get you a cool drink.'

Chapter Twenty-Three

Adam followed Natalia to the kitchen and leaned his hip on the bench. His hands tingled from her velvety skin and her sweet taste lingered on his lips. Camping had almost subdued his worries about Jordan, but he hadn't stopped thinking about Natalia.

'I'm sorry I don't have beer,' she said, taking a bottle of soda water from the fridge. 'I'll pick some up though. What do you usually drink?'

'Great Northern, but you don't need to do that.' He'd rather not have the ability to lower his inhibitions at Natalia's house.

'Having a six-pack won't hurt. Would you like soda water or plain? Or a herbal infusion?'

'I'll have whatever you're having.'

'You won't be sorry.' Grabbing two teabags, she made their drinks and handed him a glass of slowly-turning-pink water. 'Hibiscus tea. Mango and strawberry flavoured.'

'Two of my favourite fruits.'

'You can brew hibiscus tea, but I use it as an infusion. It comes in many flavours and makes water less boring. Also proven to help lower blood pressure.'

Swirling the glass to mix in the flavour, he recalled her concerns about her heart and cholesterol. 'Is your blood pressure high too?'

'Of course not.' Natalia took a bag of rice from the pantry.

'Anything I can do to help?'

'No, I've got it.'

Adam lowered himself onto a stool and sipped his drink. He'd never considered drinking flowers before, but the sweetness the tea added to the water was rather refreshing.

'Nice?' she asked, setting the pot on the stove.

'Yeah. Better than plain soda water.'

She smiled. 'Good. Now, tell me about your camping trip.'

He did as she cut up carrots, then she sat beside him at the bench while they waited for the rice and chickpeas to cook. When she stood to make the curry sauce, he downed the last of his drink, his gut churning. He loathed to bring it up, but he didn't want to hide anything from Natalia. 'When I got service back, I had messages from Jordan.'

She glanced over from the stove. 'Yeah?'

'She called me on Sunday and I mentioned the paternity test.'

'How'd she take it?'

'Told me to fuck off and hung up.'

Natalia snatched bottles of herbs and spices from the rack. Lots of them. 'You have every right to ask, even if you remembered that night. Too many men take a woman's word for it only to end up being cheated.'

'I know.' He stood to refill his glass. 'You got any more of that tea?'

She gestured towards the box. 'Help yourself.'

He flipped through the labels, chose blackcurrant and blueberry, then resumed his seat with a dark red drink.

Natalia uncapped the turmeric. 'What did the messages say?'

'That I should take her word for it. Like I told her on Sunday though, if she has nothing to hide, she shouldn't object to a paternity test.'

'Exactly.'

'She doesn't believe I was spiked either, but I'll go talk to Cade and see if he can do anything. Doubt it'll be much.' He sipped his water, enjoying this flavour too. 'I know Jordan may be right and I'm prepared to deal with that. But I know her and my gut's telling me she's hiding something.'

'It sure sounds like it,' Natalia said, her tone clipped as she shook various spices into the curry.

Exhaling, Adam stood and wrapped his arms around her waist, glancing over her shoulder into the bubbling, tomatoey sauce. 'I'm sorry, Nat.'

'Don't be. It's an unfortunate situation, but we can't avoid it.'

'I wish we didn't have to wait so long to find out.'

'Yeah, but if Jordan's refusing to cooperate, then there's not much you can do. Besides, I think ...'

He frowned as she trailed off and stirred the curry. 'What do you think, Nat?'

Her spine tensed, but she remained silent. Adam didn't move and waited patiently.

Eventually, she sighed and turned her head to meet his gaze. 'Adam, I know you want it to be a lie, but what if she did drug you? Or even if she didn't, how do you feel about having a sexual encounter that you don't remember?'

Adam watched the clouds storm in Natalia's pretty eyes. He'd considered the possibility since their discussion on Saturday, but Jordan spiking him still made little sense.

Yet someone *had* spiked him. And if he and Jordan had had sex, then that was all sorts of fucked up.

'If she's telling the truth I'm going to be bloody pissed.'

Natalia spun around and wrapped her arms around his neck, drawing him close. 'I know. And you'll have every right to be. But it's okay.'

He shook his head. 'It won't be, Nat. Not if I'm having a baby with her that … hell, she could have planned the whole thing! Drugged me. Used me. Not worried about protection …'

He tightened his grip around Natalia and laid his forehead against hers, fury raging inside him. They couldn't have had sex. He'd been *far* too drunk and if whatever else had been in his system had fucked with his memory, then surely he wouldn't have managed an erection.

But if he had, and he'd wanted Jordan in his alcohol-fuelled haze, then he had no one to blame but his own stupid self.

'I'm so sorry, Natalia.'

'You have nothing to be sorry for. It wasn't your fault.'

'Yes, it was.' He drew back to meet her gaze. 'It's not like I was careful with my drinks, Nat. I'm the idiot who put myself in this situation, partying with people I don't know. If I hadn't, then I'd be able to accept responsibility for Jordan, or she'd never have been able to pin this on me.' And he'd regret it for the rest of his days, knowing he could never make it up to this beautiful woman in his arms.

Natalia stared at him, and the storm in her eyes deepened.

He sensed there was more she wanted to say, but she turned back to the stove and reached for another spice bottle.

To make himself feel better and ease her tension, he placed a kiss on Natalia's neck. 'Food smells delicious.'

'Thanks. It's one of my favourites.' She exhaled deeply and cheekiness returned to her voice when she asked, 'Now, how hot do you want it?'

'Whatever you're having.'

She met his gaze and he was relieved to see those clouds had disappeared. 'I like it hot.'

His arms tightened around her. 'Bring it on.'

Smiling, Natalia reached for the chilli and shook it over the pot. He released her as she grabbed the chickpeas draining on the sink. Soon, they were at ease again as they sat with steaming bowls of chickpea tikka masala and fresh glasses of hibiscus tea. Adam would admit it was different from his usual meat, veggies, and beer for dinner, but he didn't mind.

'Shit, this is good.'

She laughed, pressing her fingers to her full mouth. 'Thanks. Chickpeas are my favourite legume. It's not too hot?'

'Nah.' He scooped more curry onto his fork. 'So, how do chickpeas reduce heart disease?'

'They don't reduce heart disease on their own. It's a plant-based diet with the absence of saturated fat in animal products that prevents the body from developing significant atherosclerosis. Plaque in the arteries.'

'Hmm …' He stared thoughtfully at the saucy chickpea, then popped it in his mouth. 'I guess it's never too early to prevent such things.'

'Nope. The sad thing is, no one seems to think that taking care of themselves matters until they end up with chronic disease. But I'm a big believer in preventative health.'

'I've noticed. Do you suggest plant-based diets to patients?'

'Absolutely. Everyone deserves the information, so I like to talk about nutrition, plant-based or not, and try to get people to change their lifestyles before trying medications. I approach every person differently, but I've had some who've gone plant-based with success. One patient avoided blood pressure pills. Another came off most of his medications. And I'd just started on a diabetic when ...' She paused, her mouth tightening around her fork as she dropped her gaze. 'When I left that practice.'

Adam's heart clenched. They'd stumbled across that other issue, one he desperately wanted to know more about. 'You left?'

'Yeah, but it was okay.' She waved it off with her hand, moving her food around in her bowl. 'I wanted to leave. That place was ...'

She shook her head. The light had disappeared from her eyes and even though it might not be easy to hear—and she wouldn't find it easy to tell—he had to know.

Placing his fork down, Adam took her hand. 'Nat, it's okay. And I know it must be hard, but if you're willing to talk about it, I'd like to know what you've been through.'

It took a moment, but eventually, she looked up. 'All I've ever wanted was to be a doctor, Adam, but it's given me nothing but grief.'

'I'm sure it hasn't been easy, but I bet you've helped many people along the way.'

'Yes. And deep down, I love what I do. But I worked my butt off so I could become a GP and I was so happy when I finally got there, only to have my ideals shattered by Doctor Mason Canning.'

Adam's jaw tightened. 'Is he the one who harassed you?'

She nodded and glanced back at her dinner. Adam let go of her hand to finish his own, giving her a moment to continue. 'He wasn't the first man to do so. It took me a while to realise it, but I've been sexually harassed for most of my life. It seemed harmless at first, brief comments from guys that I always passed off as normal, you know?'

He nodded and pushed his empty bowl aside.

'I didn't realise how big a problem it was until I started working. People commented on my appearance every day and I was sick of it. It wasn't funny and half the time I wondered if they even remembered I was a doctor and there to learn. The supervisors didn't do anything and passed it off as workplace teasing. Nearly all the women were subjected to it, and a few good-looking male doctors.'

She placed her bowl aside and Adam took her hand again. 'Doesn't sound like a nice environment to work in.'

'It wasn't. But I did my time at the hospital and moved on, where I became Doctor Canning's registrar.'

She exhaled deeply. Adam took his own steadying breath, unsure if he was ready to hear what happened next.

'Mason was a well-respected doctor with a prestigious medical practice on Castlereagh Street. Everyone seemed to like him and at my interview, he was nice and professional. But a week after I started, the sexual comments began. I was the "pretty new registrar" and the "good-looking one" and the "sexy blonde doc." By then, I'd been through so much that I decided I wouldn't take it anymore.'

Adam's mouth curved. 'Good for you.'

'I told him I didn't appreciate comments about my looks.' She quirked her eyebrow. 'You know what he said?'

'What?'

'That he hired me because I'd be pretty to look at.'

Adam blew out his breath. 'Bastard.'

'Yep. From then on, I was vigilant, but it only got worse. He complimented me every day on what I wore or how I looked. I hardly noticed when I started dressing down. One day, I looked at myself in a loose blouse and baggy pants and realised how far I'd fallen. I simply didn't want to look nice anymore.'

Her head dropped and Adam's hand went to her shoulder. 'I'm sorry, Nat.'

'I hated it, Adam, but I felt like it was my only choice. I stopped wearing makeup and always wore my hair in a ponytail. But it didn't work.'

Adam hadn't doubted that. Natalia was stunning without the bells and whistles. When men started harassing women like that, dressing down wouldn't stop them.

'There wasn't anyone at work to tell. Mason was the practice owner. There was no one above him. The manager didn't seem concerned and when I started digging around, I realised Mason was screwing one of the receptionists.'

Adam's eyebrows shot up. 'And this guy was a respected doctor?'

Natalia scoffed. 'Please. Doctors can be as flawed as anyone. Bottom line was, he had all the power and could do anything he wanted.'

'How long did you stay?'

'I was there for six months. At first, I wanted to stand up for myself and I managed that for a while before the touching began. He'd stand close to me, brush against me and leer. I'll admit, I should have got out sooner. I'd asked my training provider to find me a new job, but it took them a few weeks. And despite it being an awful place to work, I didn't want to give Mason the satisfaction of walking out.'

'Fair enough.' It was brave. Risky, but brave. Because standing up to a predator like that could also lead to … 'Did he ever physically assault you?'

'He tried,' she said, and his jaw clenched. 'I used to say he didn't, but that only downplayed the incident. He grabbed me by the hips, tried to kiss me, and asked me to go home with him. I shoved him away. The next day, he fired me.'

Adam straightened. 'That can't be legal.'

'Of course, it's not! But that wasn't the reason he gave. He dismissed me based on "professional differences" because he didn't like me talking nutrition instead of medication with patients.'

Bile rose in Adam's throat. How dare this Doctor Canning think he could act in such a way? There was a line when it came to physical attraction and it needed to be fucking respected. He'd spent much of his life flirting with women, but the moment they'd expressed their disinterest, he'd shrugged it off and looked elsewhere. 'So, you got another job?'

'Within a week, I'd been relocated. But once bitten, twice shy. I was wary of men and it took me a while to trust my next supervisor, but he proved his worth. My new workplace took harassment seriously, so it wasn't much of a problem and I completed my training.'

Adam smiled as the light returned to her eyes. 'I'm glad. Then you came here?'

'Yes. And I'll admit, having a female supervisor was a major drawcard.'

'I'm sure. But … I need to know. What happened to Doctor Canning?'

Natalia grinned. 'After I settled into my new job, I reported him. The receptionist saw it as her opportunity too and came forward. The medical board had a lot of questions and it was quite a stressful time for me, but after the court found him guilty and charged him, Mason was deregistered.'

Adam's eyebrows shot up. 'Oh, Nat. Well done you.'

'Thanks. It certainly helped me breathe easier, but it took me a while to regain my confidence.' She relaxed into her chair and sighed. 'I'm still working on it because I want to walk down the street with my head held high. I want to dress up without the fear of lewd looks and unwelcome invites.'

His chest constricted at the pain and frustration in her eyes. 'And you should be able to.'

'Exactly. And I know physical attraction is a thing. You can't look at a person and think they're funny or smart or kind. It's something physical that catches your eye first. But that doesn't mean you have to say it.'

'No. Especially not to a colleague or someone you don't know.'

Her eyes clouded and her shoulders sank. 'I just want to love being beautiful again.'

Adam hated that she'd experienced such abuse, and that she'd never been able to escape it. No wonder her soul was crushed.

'Nat, don't be afraid. You are a beautiful woman and work hard to be so. And I'm sorry, but whether you dress up or down, that will never change. So, embrace it. Because if anyone so much as looks at you the wrong way, they'll have me to deal with.'

His body steeled as he tightened his hand around hers. He'd never been more serious. Deep down, he knew Natalia was strong and confident, if the far-too-sexy flirtation they had going on was any indication. But until she overcame her other demons, she remained fragile, and God help anyone who hurt her.

'Thank you, Adam, but you don't need to protect me.'

'Sure, I do. It's in the handbook.' The theoretical handbook of how-to-keep-a-woman-forever that he needed to read. 'You can't expect me to do anything less.'

The brightness returned to her eyes. 'All right. If it makes you happy, I can accept that.'

She touched her lips to his and Adam cupped her face, easing into the kiss. Control. He needed to practise control. Because damn, he wanted her.

She drew away. 'Tell me something? What was the first thing you thought when we met?'

He frowned. 'You want the truth or …'

'Yes.'

Sitting back, he raked his hand through his hair. 'Well, I thought you were bloody hot.'

Her eyes sparkled. 'But you didn't say it.'

'Course not.'

'Exactly. And you know what? I thought you were bloody hot too.'

Grinning, he leaned forward again and rested his elbows on his knees. 'Oh, yeah?'

'Yep.' She brushed her lips over his, her mouth warm and tender. Something deep inside him quivered and he loosened the reins on control, diving into her and reawakening the passion he'd sparked earlier at the front door. Natalia's arms wrapped around his neck and with a gentle tug at her hips, she practically leapt into his lap.

Everything inside Adam fired. His hands hardened on her back as she pressed her body close to his, her kisses hungry. Trouble had never been more fun, and he wanted more. He wanted Natalia with every fibre of his being, but that wouldn't be slow. And he liked this slow business because he still didn't know what the fuck he was doing.

Savouring one more taste of her, he lowered his hands and drew away. 'Thank you for telling me that, Natalia.'

'Thank you for listening. It helps. And I wanted to tell you.'

'It's just hard to talk about.'

She nodded and that cloud from earlier returned to her eyes. 'It is.'

'I can imagine,' he said, rubbing her shoulders. 'And I think I get it. I'd like to think I've always been careful when chatting up women because I don't like unwelcome advances either.'

Natalia pressed her lips together as she gently cupped his face. 'Nobody does. Which is why I think we need to talk about what's going on with you.'

Adam frowned. 'What about me?'

'Adam … men are sexually harassed too.'

'Well, I don't know about harassed 'cause I've never minded if a woman chats me up. But it's certainly pissed me off when I've been in a relationship. Like now, with Jordan sending me those texts and suggesting we hook up. But that's Jordan for you, always wanting what she can't have.'

Natalia's eyes steeled. 'No, Adam. That's harassment.'

Adam resisted a frown. Yeah, he didn't like it. Jordan's booty-calls were inappropriate and his whole body tightened with dread whenever she contacted him. Those messages today had sent anger coursing through his veins and all he wanted was for her to leave him the hell alone.

But just because it was Jordan being Jordan, that didn't mean …

Shit.

Bile rose in his throat, his guts churning until he thought he'd be sick. 'I suppose I've never thought about it like that. She did the same thing when I was with Grace.'

Natalia loosened her grip around his shoulders. 'It can be hard to acknowledge, Adam. It's easy to pass it off as nothing and hard to see when you're close to the situation. But what Jordan's doing isn't right, which is why I think she was capable of spiking you on your birthday.'

He stilled. 'You do?'

'Yes, Adam. I know it's difficult to come to terms with and it took me forever to realise what was happening to me wasn't right. But Jordan's a predator and you had been rejecting her advances. To her, that isn't normal.'

Time seemed to halt as Natalia's words rattled around inside his head. She was right. He'd been too close to see it, but of course Jordan was capable of such a crime. She'd handled their drinks and he *had* told her no.

She hated 'no'.

'I … I just …' He dropped his gaze from hers and pressed his hand to his forehead. 'Fuck.'

That's what Natalia had meant about a sexual encounter he didn't remember. If he *was* the father of Jordan's child, then not only had she spiked him, she'd sexually assaulted him too.

'Adam, it's okay.'

'No, it's not.' He lifted his gaze back to hers. 'But, Nat … how do I know I didn't want her? What if—'

'It doesn't matter.' Natalia gripped his shoulders, her face patient. 'You were vulnerable and in no state of mind to agree to sex.'

'Yeah, but I can't bloody prove that, can I?' Adam blew out his breath through gritted teeth and Natalia drew him close.

'It's okay …'

No, it fucking wasn't. Nothing about this was okay. A woman he'd grown up with and he'd once liked may have drugged him. Assaulted him. And he'd been helpless to stop it.

'Fuck, Natalia, I hope she's lying.'

'Me too.'

He tightened his grip around her and breathed her in, taking comfort in the sensation of her fingers brushing up and down his back. What was he going to do? Before dinner, he'd seriously considered seducing Natalia. Not all the way, but fooling around on the lounge and playing with intimacy had been an appealing way to spend the evening.

But now, that was the last thing he wanted to do. Rage bubbled through his veins and his skin prickled with the sordid sense of violation. He couldn't comprehend it. Didn't want to. Denial worked.

Adam straightened. 'I think I need dessert.'

Smiling softly, Natalia climbed out of his lap. 'I'll see what I can do.'

Heart plummeting, he watched her as she strode into the kitchen. He didn't deserve Natalia. She was too kind. Too caring. He was in one hell of a mess and shouldn't be dragging her into it.

Lowering his gaze, he clenched his fists in his lap. He should thank Natalia for her understanding and tell her to forget about him, but he didn't want to because fuck-knows how he was going to face this without her support. And he couldn't bear the thought of confronting Jordan any time soon.

How dare she do this to him? She was the fucking barmaid! He and thousands of others trusted her to serve them drinks!

But now that he thought about it—

'What do you say to banana pancakes?'

Adam's head snapped up. 'Oh, Nat, now you've found my weakness.'

Chapter Twenty-Four

Adam arrived at the police station on Friday afternoon just as Cade pulled up in the cruiser. Taking a deep breath, he shot his friend a wave. He didn't really want to talk to his best mate about making enquiries into Jordan, but even though he had the option to talk to Brett or Jim, if anyone would understand, it was Cade.

'You been patrolling the highways again?' Adam asked, slipping his hands into his pockets.

'Always. People need to learn they can't speed on my roads.' They fell into step. 'So, are you here to see me?'

'Kinda.'

Cade pulled open the door. 'Officially?'

'I guess.'

'Come in then.' Cade waved to the receptionist and led Adam into the office, tossing his police cap on the desk. 'What can I do for you, mate?'

Adam's lips quirked. 'You can give me one of those hats.'

'You don't give up, do you?' Cade snatched the hat back up and placed it on the shelf behind the desk. 'You only get one if you're a police officer.'

Adam sighed and leaned back in his seat. He'd been asking for a police hat ever since Cade had returned to Elizadale from his various rural postings. But despite their misspent youth, Cade was strangely proud of his job and protective of his damn hats.

'Fine. Then could you look into the night of my birthday? Because even though I can't prove the spiking, it happened. And I think it might have been Jordan.'

To Cade's credit, his face remained impassive as he nodded and grabbed a notepad. His friend had warned him a few times over the years about Jordan, but Adam had always waved it off. So what if he'd helped her out with a few things around the house? He enjoyed doing that sort of thing. Although it sure seemed convenient that she'd always want to hook up when there was something wrong with her car or the taps were leaking.

'All right,' Cade said. 'Tell me what you suspect, for the record.'

Adam expressed his concerns and answered Cade's official questions, determined to remain calm even though he couldn't shake the vile distaste that filled his mouth. Dread consumed him every time he imagined what may have happened in the park that night. What if he had managed an erection? Fuck, he'd had many erections he couldn't control, ones he didn't want to use. It was a bloody natural thing. But it was entirely possible, so he couldn't deny the truth. If he was the father of Jordan's baby, then he was also a victim of sexual assault, which was difficult to wrap his head around. But the more he thought about it, the more he believed Jordan was capable of it because once, there had been a time she'd gone too far. He hadn't realised it then, but on a subconscious level, he must have felt uneasy because it had stuck with him.

He didn't tell Cade that bit, but that night in the park? Yeah, she had it in her to commit such a crime to get what she wanted.

'Don't worry, mate. I'll look into it,' Cade said, laying down his pen a few minutes later.

'Thanks. I didn't know what else to do. Jordan's being evasive. She laughed at the thought of spiking and won't even discuss a paternity test.'

'Of course not. Either way, she'd lose. She'd prove herself a liar or guilty of assault.'

'Which makes no sense. If she's making it up, it's a fucked up lie.'

'Agreed. But if she won't tell us who else was in the park, I can ask some questions and see if I can find out. Meanwhile, try not to worry about it too much. You guys are heading to Cairns this weekend, right?'

'Yeah. Tomorrow.' He'd done as Ana had asked and organised Liam and his brothers. Ana had arranged the fittings, so all they had to do was turn up, try on what he expected would be ridiculously formal suits, then have a beer at a seaside bar before driving home again.

'Cool. And Meg said we're going to her house for a potluck dinner tonight?'

Adam raised his eyebrows. 'You're going?'

'Why not?'

'Thought you'd be at Smithy's with Jessica.'

'Yeah …' Cade leaned back in his chair. 'I dunno …'

Adam frowned. 'Not keen on her anymore?' His mate had been beating around the bush with his attraction for Jessica Smithfield for the better part of a year now and it was driving Adam nuts. Why didn't he just ask the woman out?

'Nah, I am. It's just …'

'Someone else caught your eye?'

'Forget it.' Cade straightened and shook his head. 'I'll lodge this report and if there's nothing else you want to tell me, I'll see you at Meg's.'

* * *

I can't believe you still think I spiked you! Where's the trust, Adam? Now Georgina's questioning me too. What if I lose my job? Are you going to support us both? You'll have to if you get me fired.

The text message came through when Adam arrived home from Monday afternoon drinks. Thankfully, Jordan hadn't been working as he wasn't sure he could face her. The thought of being near her and seeing her come-hither grin quaked on his soul.

Fuck, he dreaded Friday night. The bloody woman would ruin the Royal for him.

Tossing his phone onto the lounge, Adam tore off his shirt and headed for the shower. Cade had called him earlier to say he'd visited the Royal this morning but hadn't uncovered much. Jordan had denied all allegations and there had been no sign of drink spiking on the cameras overlooking the tills. But that didn't mean it couldn't have occurred in the store cupboard or anywhere else she might have prepared his drinks. Or in the park, of course.

He banged his fist on the shower wall. Dammit, someone had to know the truth. His memory hadn't improved, but he knew another woman had been around. One that hadn't been Jordan. He'd kissed someone and partied hard with a mate, singing drinking songs until they'd drunk themselves blind.

But which mate? A random bloke from the pub? A local or worker he wasn't close with?

And who was the woman?

Exhaling, Adam turned off the taps and shook his head. He had to stop thinking about it. His worry was already putting a damper on his relationship with Natalia as he'd made an excuse not to see her on Saturday night after returning from Cairns and had spent Sunday woodturning. She didn't deserve that. Natalia was the only light in this nightmare and he didn't want to push her away. But he couldn't help but feel he'd already let her down, so he needed to find out what happened because he'd never be worthy of Natalia until he did.

Chapter Twenty-Five

Adam was in the fields on Friday morning fitting bags onto new banana bunches when his mother called, suggesting that everyone come over for a barbeque.

'You know you're hijacking our Friday night drinks.'

'It's just the once. Jack and Michael have agreed and Meg's bringing her mudcake.'

Adam's mouth watered. Meg's mudcake was pure sin. 'Can I bring Natalia?'

Wendy sighed in that mum way she was so good at. 'Adam, why do you think I'm having a barbeque? Of course you have to bring her!'

'And people wonder where I get it from. Fine, we'll be there. But you know, Nat's vegan.'

'Deborah told me and I've got it sorted. I'll see you tonight.'

They said their goodbyes, then he called Natalia.

'A barbeque with your family?' He didn't miss the surprise in her tone.

'It's not as scary as it sounds. The usual crowd will be there and the food's always good. Mum knows you're vegan.'

'Well … okay.'

'I'll pick you up at six.'

He was there on the dot and when she opened the door, everything stilled. Would he ever be able to breathe normally around her again? She looked gorgeous. Dark skinny jeans moulded to her athletic legs, and she wore a canary yellow top beneath a black trench coat that brushed her thighs. A black headband held her hair back, her lips were pink, and her eyes were shadowy.

Adam swallowed. Right. Words. 'You look beautiful.'

'Thank you.' She reached onto her toes and kissed him. 'I'm wearing makeup.'

'I noticed. I hope you have a stash of that strawberry lip gloss.'

'Why?'

''Cause it tastes good.'

Laughing, she locked the screen door. 'Let's go, hey?'

He employed a strange act of chivalry as he opened her door and helped her into the ute. By the time he slipped behind the wheel, she was jiggling her leg. 'You okay?'

'Yeah. It's just … I'm nervous.'

Glad he wasn't the only uneasy one, Adam frowned. 'Why's that?'

'I've never met a man's parents before.'

Smiling softly, he reached for her hand. 'Oh, Nat, there's no reason to be nervous. My mum invited you, so she wants to meet you.'

'Really? What have you told her?'

'I think Aunty Deb and Lucy have done most of the talking. But I told her I was falling for you and she seemed to like the idea because you're the best thing that's ever happened to me.'

Natalia smiled, but he wasn't sure if he had put her at ease as they drove along the dark dirt road. Soon, he pulled up outside the homestead, a long, single-level brick house with a wide verandah and lush flower gardens. It was lit up like a beacon as he rounded the ute to join Natalia.

'This is it, our main living quarters. Over there—' he pointed over her shoulder '—is Aunty Deb's house. She and Uncle Cliff built it a year after this homestead was complete.'

'Your parents built it? I thought farmhouses were old and filled with family history.'

'Yeah, but the old one was crumbling around Dad's ears and he wanted something new to raise his family in.'

'Well—' she glanced around at the playground, family orchard, and the stables '—it looks lovely. It must have been fun growing up here.'

'Yeah, there was always something to do.' He squeezed her hand and took a deep breath. 'Come on.'

He led her inside, through the hallway and into the open-planned living and kitchen area where his mum, Lucy, and aunt were chopping vegetables.

'Adam!' Wendy smiled, wiping her hands on a tea-towel before hugging him. 'How are you, my boy?'

'Good, Mum.' He squeezed her gently before pulling away. 'Food smells great, as always.'

'I wouldn't have it any other way.'

He placed his hand on Natalia's back. 'Mum, let me introduce Natalia.'

'Hello! It's lovely to meet you.'

'You too, Mrs Maguire. Thank you for inviting me.'

'It's our pleasure. Now, I believe you've already met Deborah.'

His mum took Natalia's arm and led her into the kitchen. As Adam filled her a glass of water, a strange buoyancy filled his chest. Joy? Pride? Both? It wasn't the first time he'd brought a woman to a family dinner, but as he watched Natalia chat with the ladies in the kitchen of his childhood home, his head spun. Clearing his throat, he handed her the glass, then left her in the safe hands of his mother.

He needed a beer.

* * *

It didn't surprise Natalia that Adam left her alone. She was fine. Wendy hadn't given her a scrutinising eye and seemed positively excited to meet her.

'How are you enjoying Elizadale?'

Natalia leaned her hip against the bench as Wendy resumed her food preparation. 'It's a beautiful town. I've enjoyed how quiet it is, although there is still a lot to do.'

'It's a different lifestyle from the city, I'll admit,' Wendy said. 'Elizadale's changed a lot in the thirty years I've been here, but it has its charm. Have you settled into work?'

'Yes, it's a wonderful practice.' Apart from another old biddy calling her 'Adam Maguire's latest floozy' today and two more patients refusing to see her this week. She'd overheard Nikki's end of the phone calls to understand that their refusal wasn't based on preferring to see Joanne. But while it hurt, people had every right to choose their doctor and feel comfortable. It wasn't her fault if they carried certain prejudices.

Swallowing her feelings down, Natalia placed her glass aside. 'Can I help?'

'We've got it under control. I made you and Ana red lentil burgers because that's what I had in the cupboard. I hope that's okay?'

'Sounds delicious.'

Maybe a night like this was just what Natalia needed. She'd been nervous at the thought of meeting Adam's parents, but it was hardly avoidable in a small town. Falling into easy conversation with Wendy, Deborah, and Lucy, Natalia arranged bread rolls onto a tray, surprised to learn that Wendy had baked them. But that was what country women did, wasn't it? Especially ones like Wendy. Natalia liked Deborah, but Adam's mother was cheerful, energetic, and seemed like a woman that everyone in town would be friends with. She didn't look old enough to have three almost thirty-year-old sons and a daughter with her bright eyes and long dark ponytail, but she was down-to-earth and welcoming. When Adam returned to the kitchen with his father, it was Wendy who jumped at the chance to introduce her.

'Nice to meet you.' Henry smiled warmly and shook Natalia's hand. 'I believe my son has spoken of nothing else since you came to town.'

'Why would I when she's all I've thought about?' Adam snatched carrot sticks from the tray Lucy was preparing and received a well-deserved swat.

Soon, they moved outside and Natalia found herself in a foldout chair beside Adam. Sipping her water, she watched the Maguires in awe as chatter, laughter, and gentle teasing filled the patio.

So, this was what it was like to be part of a big family. Henry and Cliff manned the barbeque while Wendy cooked the lentil burgers in the kitchen. Deborah, Lucy, Meg, and Ana arranged the food while Jack, Michael, and Liam got the firepit going. They were a curious and mesmerising bunch who loved fiercely and were loyal. Family was family and nothing would change that.

Natalia smiled as she watched Ana, who slotted in easily and talked a million conversations at once. It had never bothered her she'd only had her mum and Ana while growing up, but surrounded by these rowdy, welcoming people, it brought a strange sense of comfort. And longing.

The homestead was also a beautiful reflection of the family with bits and bobs she guessed could be as old as the house. After using the bathroom, Natalia made her way down the long hallway, brushing her fingers along the picture frames. Did Adam know how lucky he was to have had one place to call home? Not only this house, but Shadow Creek itself?

Natalia paused at a family photo. Lily was a baby, so Adam would be seven and the Maguires looked so happy sitting on the homestead verandah. Natalia couldn't fathom such a history. She and Ana had moved from rental to rental after their father had died, never staying in one place longer than three years. It hadn't been until Ana was at university that their mum had bought her own house, so to have had one place to call home …

Heat blossomed inside Natalia's chest until her heart ached. That's what she wanted. She'd never given home or family much thought, but she wanted what Ana had found— roots, love, and a sense of belonging. And as she slipped back into her chair beside Adam, that heat turned to fire.

He was special.

'You okay?' he asked, quirking his sexy eyebrow.

'Yep. Fantastic.'

'Good. Let's grab some food. I'm starving.'

Wendy stepped outside and handed Natalia and Ana their burger patties. 'I hope they taste good.'

'I'm sure they'll be delicious.'

Natalia slipped the patty between two slices of bread with lettuce, tomato, and grilled pineapple, spoiled herself with tomato sauce, then loaded her plate with the crisp garden salad. Back in her chair, she bit into the burger and moaned.

'Good?' Adam asked.

'Delicious. Your mum's a wonderful cook.'

'Yeah, she's a professional chef,' he said, and Natalia's eyebrows shot up. 'Didn't you know that?'

'No.'

'Mum was about to become a sous chef at a fancy restaurant in Brisbane. Then she came to visit Aunty Deb, who'd just started dating Uncle Cliff. She and Dad had what she describes as a whirlwind romance and she didn't look back. Jack was born within a year and they're still as mad as ever about each other.'

Natalia smiled at the awe in his casual tone. 'That's such a sweet story. Yet it sounds awfully familiar …'

Adam grinned as he cut into his steak. 'I know. Gives me hope.'

A gleam filled his eyes and his foot bounced happily where it rested on his knee. He may have been a little subdued earlier in the week, but tonight, Adam seemed like his charming and confident self again. Biting into the burger, everything inside Natalia hummed and yearned.

'So … you want to come over for dinner again tomorrow?' she asked.

He nodded, then paused. 'How about you come to my house? You've cooked for me, so it's my turn.'

Natalia almost choked. 'You can cook?'

'You're surprised.'

She shook her head, but she was. The hormones that had been doing a happy dance a second ago broke into an all-out rave. Could Adam get any hotter? She hardly knew anyone who could cook with the tendency these days being takeaway, dining out, and convenient processed foods.

His dark eyes gleamed. 'Yes, you are.'

'Fine. Maybe a little. I've never dated a man who could cook.'

'Well, I need to eat. And Mum insisted we learn. Probably thought it'd get her out of the job, but whenever we're too lazy, we rock up to High Ridge and she feeds us.'

'I guess if I was a chef, I'd teach my children to cook too. But yes.' She squeezed his thigh and flashed him her wickedest smile. 'I'd love to come over for dinner. And dessert.'

His eyebrow quirked as he hastily swallowed his salad. 'You're very naughty with your dessert.'

'Dessert isn't naughty. Overindulgence is naughty. Although …' She leaned towards him. 'I wouldn't mind some naughty dessert. If you like?'

She held his gaze, her heart pounding and hand tightening around his thigh. Heat flashed through his dark eyes.

After what felt like an age, he cleared his throat. 'In that case, I'll make something saucy.'

Chapter Twenty-Six

Adam spent Saturday morning kicking himself. What had he been thinking offering to cook Natalia dinner? He wanted to, but usually he'd try to impress a woman with his delicious lemon chicken or pineapple glazed beef. How could he substitute that? Pineapple chickpeas?

Mmm … chickpeas. Damn, that curry had been good. Could he make something with chickpeas?

At a loss, he glanced at Rusty curled up on the lounge. Damn dog wasn't helpful, but Google was. After a lot of scrolling and scratching his head, Adam found inspiration, snatched up his keys, and headed into town.

At the supermarket, he grabbed a bag of chickpeas and was browsing the nut milks when he heard his name. He glanced up and smiled as Susan Riley pushed her trolley towards him.

'I was going to call you this afternoon. Most of your stock has sold!' His eyebrows shot up and she beamed. 'We only have a vase and two bowls left.'

'Out of ten?'

'Yes!' She clapped her hands together, then sighed. 'Why aren't you more excited? This is good news.'

Adam blew out a long breath. Within a fortnight, she'd sold most of his products? Really? People had actually bought them? 'I'm just surprised, is all.'

'Why? You know you do excellent work.'

So everyone told him. Of course, he liked the things he made and took pride in his woodwork as having the ability to make homewares he needed, or to give someone a gift, was useful. But they were still only lumps of wood elegantly carved.

Susan frowned. 'Adam?'

He shook his head. 'Sorry. You're right, this is good news. I didn't think they'd sell so quickly.'

'Why wouldn't they? I told you you're a talented man.' Her tone turned smug as she poked him in the arm. 'Why don't you believe in yourself?'

It's not that he didn't believe in himself, it's just that everything he did ended up going downhill. He'd thought this would too.

Except people have bought my stuff.

Susan smiled and placed her hand on his arm. 'Adam Maguire, you have more going for you than you realise. And you will be a successful craftsman.'

He quirked an eyebrow. 'You think so?'

'I know so. You didn't win those Elizadale and Mareeba Shows for nothing.'

His shoulders relaxed. That was true. And she was right. Many people wanted his work. Not just his mother and Liam, who'd both insisted he make tables for their restaurants. Not just Lucy, who'd wanted vases to place wildflowers in around High Ridge. And not just Natalia, who still raved about her fruit bowl. People in Elizadale had been telling him for years to get his arse into gear, so why the hell was he surprised?

Knowing people wanted his work was why he'd started the business.

Warmth filled Adam's chest and a smile broke free. Maybe he wouldn't be a failure after all?

'Now that's the reaction I was looking for,' Susan said with a laugh. 'Be proud of yourself. And maybe you could deliver us a few more goods by next weekend?'

'Sure, I can do that. Thanks, Sue.'

After saying their goodbyes, Adam completed the rest of his shopping with an added spring in his step.

It seemed he had more woodturning to do.

* * *

'It's beautiful, Mama,' Natalia said, her phone on speaker while she packed an overnight bag. Nadia had called after Ana had refused to tell her about the wedding dress they'd collected from Cairns today. 'But if Ana doesn't want to tell you what it looks like, then I can't either.'

'You two are awful daughters,' Nadia pouted.

'I'm sure Ana just wants to surprise you.'

'Only four weeks now and I'll be there with you girls.'

Natalia's heart ached as she searched for clothes suitable for gardening. 'I can't wait. I miss you.'

'I miss you too. How are you, Nat?'

She grabbed one of her oldest T-shirts and shoved it into her bag, along with her oldest jeans. 'I'm fine.' She tried to keep her tone casual, but her mother's instincts were too sharp for nonchalance.

'You don't sound fine. You sound happy. What are you up to, Natalia?'

Busted, she eased onto the edge of her bed. She'd never been one to keep things from her mum. 'Okay, I am happy. I'm so glad I came here. It's everything Ana said it'd be. And I met Liam's cousin …'

'Oh, Natalia. Tell me. But first—' her tone sharpened '—has he been good to you?'

'He's been the perfect gentleman.' Sort of a gentleman, anyway, considering his many risqué suggestions. Not that she had been any better. 'And I know it's only been a few weeks, but he's funny and gorgeous and so damn sexy. We have a great time together.'

'Oh no. You're going to stay there too.'

Natalia laughed. 'I don't know about that, but I do like it here. Elizadale's beautiful and welcoming.' Apart from that arrogant Kelly, his troublesome sister, and the gossip in town, but Natalia didn't tell her mother that. She'd only worry. 'Plus, I'm feeling confident again. I'm wearing my pretty things and putting an effort into looking nice without feeling anxious about it.'

'Good. I'm glad that you have a little romance going on. But which cousin is this? Doesn't Liam have a few?'

Praying that whatever Ana had shared about the Maguire men with their mother had been favourable, Natalia told her.

'Oh, Adam's the one who helped rescue Ana!'

Natalia grinned. 'Yes, exactly!'

'But isn't he also the bad one?'

Dammit. 'No, he's not. Maybe he was a little wild when he was younger, but he's a good man, Mama. He's thoughtful and is trying to start his own business. He does woodturning and he made me the most beautiful fruit bowl.'

'That does sound lovely.'

'It was. And tomorrow, we're planting a vegetable garden all because I mentioned how I missed spinach.'

'I'd say he sounds like a keeper.'

She swallowed nervously. 'Yeah … he could be.' Then she changed the subject to Nadia's jewellery making, talking for a while longer before noticing the time.

They said their goodbyes and Natalia dashed to the bathroom, excitement shimmering through her. In the shower, she rubbed Surge Duck's head as she puzzled over which scented shower gel to use. Mango? Strawberry? Moringa? It was an important decision as for the first time in years, she felt in control. She wanted to take that bad country man and help him regain anything he felt he'd lost. She wanted to show him exactly what power she possessed above any other woman he'd had an inkling of attraction towards.

Showered and dry, Natalia's skin warmed as she applied her body butter. Then she slipped into her lingerie and zipped up the dress she'd carefully selected for this evening. Smiling, she added the strawberry lip gloss Adam loved and fluffed her hair in the mirror.

A thrill shot down her spine as she spun a quick turn, oozing confidence.

This was it. And as promised, she was bringing it.

* * *

After returning from the shops, Adam switched off the sprinkler soaking the soil for the vegetable garden, then set about preparing for tonight. A strange sense of pride overcame him as he vacuumed every inch of the house, used the duster his mum had left, and scrubbed the bathroom he never used. Then, realising he was missing things to make tonight perfect, he escaped to the homestead where his mum was all too happy to load him up with spare homewares.

He set two placemats on the table, then puzzled over how the scent diffuser worked. Did he just put the sticks in the bottle? Yes, that looked right. Maybe he should even fan them out? There. Now the house smelled of lemon floor cleaner and lavender, which was better than the usual scent of Rusty and old socks. The poor dog had endured another bath and was glaring at Adam from where he sat at the locked doggy door, begging to go roll in the dirt.

'Get over it. If Natalia wants to cuddle you, you can't stink.'

Rusty lay down and placed his head on his paws.

Resisting the urge to laugh at himself, Adam strode into the kitchen. Natalia sure was making him act strangely, yet there he was in his tidy house that smelled weird with a clean dog, no meat to cook, and his favourite country music playing. His woodturning business hadn't died within a month, and he had a woman he was crazy about.

Yeah, this change thing was good. Casual, meaningless, and boring relationships? Why had he ever thought that was fun? *Natalia* was fun. The thought of having her around long-term grew less frightening every day. And when he'd been vacuuming those empty bedrooms, he'd actually thought ...

Adam shook his head, snapping out of those ridiculous fantasies as he took the pears off the boil. He left the kitchen to shower and dress, then returned and began slicing vegetables. Not long later, Rusty let out a bark, leapt off the lounge, and raced through the house. Adam followed, holding Rusty back with his foot as he pushed open the screen door. He glanced up and stilled.

Natalia strolled towards the verandah, long blonde waves

falling sensually over her shoulders. She'd done something to her eyes to make them brighter, her lips shone with lip gloss, but her dress …

His blood heated and swirled inside his head. The sexiest black dress he'd ever seen hugged her athletic body, highlighting her slender shoulders, tight torso, and sensual hips like a mould. For the first time since he'd known her, she displayed a hint of cleavage.

And with one pull of that zipper teasing him down the front of her dress, he could have her out of it.

Natalia beamed. 'Hey!'

'Dammit, Nat.' His mouth dried as she stepped inside. Rusty sniffed her feet as Adam let his gaze roam from her pretty face, down to her hot pink toenails, and back up again. 'That dress …'

Her blue eyes sparkled. 'I thought you'd like it.'

'You're trying to tempt me again, aren't you?' Wrapping his arms around her waist, he pulled her close.

She laughed. 'Not at all.'

Pressing his lips to hers, Adam lost himself in her intoxicating taste. Her wicked mouth returned the kiss as she pressed her long body against every hot plane of his.

When they drew apart, her eyes gleamed. 'You like the zipper, don't you?'

'I do.'

'Then check this out.' Slowly, she wrapped his fingers around the golden zipper dangling at her chest and gave a gentle tug. All the blood drained from his head as it zipped down … down …

Two inches later, she pulled his hand away. Their gazes met. 'It works.'

Adam almost boiled over. She was good. Really good. Taking a breath, he tried desperately not to throw her over his shoulder and take the two steps into the bedroom where he could have her beneath him with that dress where it belonged—on the damn floor.

But he'd promised her dinner, and dinner first was the gentlemanly thing to do. Then they'd finish this game as his control was hanging by a thread.

'Yeah.' He cleared his throat. 'It works.'

'So, something smells great.' Her hair swirled as she turned on her heel and strolled into the dining room. Adam raked his hands down his face, then slipped them into his pockets before following.

Chapter Twenty-Seven

'Oh my God, I love your table! Where did you get that?'

Adam's chest expanded as Natalia placed her hands on the edge of the mango wood and stared wide-eyed at the massive table. 'I made it.'

Her gaze shot to his. 'You *made* it?'

'Yeah.' He brushed his finger along the raw, natural edge. 'It won first prize at the Mareeba show a few years ago and is one of my favourites.'

'Wow. All of my furniture has come from Ikea. To pay for something like this … it'd cost a fortune!'

'Probably. Have you seen the big bastard at The Bent Banana?'

Her eyebrows shot up. 'You made that too? It's gorgeous.'

The tightness inside him loosened. 'I made all The Bent Banana's tables.'

'Wow. So, why don't you do more? You know, to sell?'

'That's the plan. I was just starting small. But guess what?' He grinned. 'Sue and Heather have already sold most of my stuff.'

'That's fantastic! You must be thrilled.'

'I was shocked at first, but yeah, I'm pretty happy. I have a piece of cedar in the shed that I thought I'd fashion into a coffee table, so I might start on that.'

'Sounds exciting, Adam. I'm so happy for you.'

And that, he thought as he took her hand and led her into the kitchen, was the best thing he'd heard all day. 'Thanks, Nat. Would you like a drink? I bought hibiscus tea.'

'You did?'

'Yep.' He'd already infused the tea and had it waiting in a jug. He poured them both a glass. 'It's growing on me.'

'I bought a of variety of teas in Cairns today, so I can give you some more. There's a berry one I think you'll like.'

'If you want. Did you have a good day?'

'Yeah, we picked up Ana's dress in Cairns, then stopped by Barron Falls on the way home. It was a beautiful walk and such a stunning view. I'd love to see it flow in the wet season.'

'Barron Falls can be quite spectacular.'

'I also liked the rainforest around Kuranda.' Natalia slipped onto a stool on the other side of the counter as he grabbed a pot from the cupboard. 'So, what are you cooking?'

'Risotto.' He flashed her a smile over his shoulder. 'I'll admit, I didn't know what I was going to make, but I have this chicken and mushroom risotto I love, so I figured I'd use chickpeas instead.'

'Sounds delicious. And thank you.'

He scooped rice into the pot. 'For what?'

'Cooking for me even though it's not the food you're used to.'

He set the pot on the stove with a shrug. 'It's still risotto, whether there's chicken in it or not. Besides, you know what?'

She quirked her eyebrows and sipped her drink. 'What?'

'It turns out I *love* chickpeas.'

Hastily swallowing, she laughed. 'Really?'

'Yeah. They're yum, nutty, and there's a lot you can do with them. I read a lot of chickpea recipes today.'

'They go great in salads.'

'I bet. Besides—' he leaned his elbows on the bench to face her '—it's one of my favourite things about you.'

'That I like chickpeas?'

'No, that you're dedicated to your health.'

Her eyebrows shot up. 'Really? Some people can't stand that about me.'

'And they're the people who don't care about you.'

'That's true. You never batted an eye and your mum was very kind. I haven't even had many jokes about it while I've been here.'

'People teased you about that too?'

'Sometimes. It doesn't happen as much anymore, but I rarely take offence because the way I live isn't anyone's business.'

'No, it's not. But that's what I like, that you stick to your guns and don't care what anyone else thinks. It's hot.'

She squeezed his hand. 'So, you won't mind if I go for a run in the morning?'

His mouth curved. 'Oh, what? You're staying over?'

'Aren't I?'

'I won't object.' He swirled his finger around on the inside of her wrist, watching her eyes warm and glitter.

'Well, you can't expect me to drive home in the dark. I could hit a kangaroo and smash Ana's car.'

'And hurt yourself. Roos are nasty creatures.'

'Exactly.'

'Then, if it's a matter of your safety, how can I refuse?' He straightened and released her hand. 'I gotta stir the risotto.'

And break the sizzle between them. Not that it was any cooler by the stove, but this heat he could handle.

'But no, I don't mind if you go for a run. In fact, I thought maybe you'd like to go up to High Ridge? It's a fair distance and we graded the road recently.'

'Never mind that. I'm used to cross-country.'

'Good to know. You'll find the campground at the bottom of the hill, but there's a road that leads up to the lodge or the goat track if you want to take in the view.'

He wasn't sure if she liked hills as part of her run, but everyone enjoyed a good view.

'Thank you, Adam. That sounds lovely.'

'It'll be dark, but just stick to the middle of the road and keep your eyes on the ground for sn ... things that slither.'

'I will.' She sipped her drink and gazed around the room. 'I do like your house. I didn't say that the last time I was here. When did you build it?'

'Three years ago. Michael and his mentor Graham built it, but we all pitched in. We did this one first, then Liam's. Michael's currently building his own. Before that, we all lived in the shack Jack's in now. With the four of us out of the homestead, they were the best years of our lives.'

'I bet, hanging out in your bachelor pad. I'll admit, I was curious about how you could build out here, but after seeing this place and the homestead, it doesn't seem like it was too hard.'

'Yeah, we've always had town power, but we've got solar now too and mainly use that. Dad's always been keen about sustainability.'

She smiled. 'I'm glad to hear it.'

'Water, however, is a different issue. I pump from the creek for irrigation and rely heavily on rainwater.'

'Makes sense. I just think you're lucky to have all of this. Your own home and land.'

He smiled and stirred the pot as the rice fluffed. 'I suppose. There are a few parts of the property not suitable for planting anything, so Mum and Dad said we could all pick a spot and build.'

'Like I said. Lucky.' Wistfulness filled her tone, but he didn't get a chance to comment when she said, 'I'm going to buy a car.'

'You are?' With the rice absorbing, he lowered the heat and began on the next pot, pouring in the vegetables he prepared earlier. 'What kind?'

'I don't know. But I think I'll need one because I can't keep borrowing Ana's.'

'Yeah. Will you buy something new?'

'I don't think so. Even though I'd like to spoil myself, I can't justify the cost. I'll get something less than five years old, but I'm not sure if I want a little car to zip around in or something more practical.'

'How about a ute?'

Her nose wrinkled. 'I don't need a ute.'

'They're practical,' he said, adding coconut milk to the mushroom and chickpea mix. 'You can move stuff.'

'I don't have much to move. Besides, you have a ute.'

'So, if you ever need to move anything, you think I'll help?'

'Wouldn't you?'

She grinned and his heart flipped. Adam turned back to the pots. 'You don't need a ute.'

They continued to discuss other car options while the rich aroma filling the kitchen made his stomach rumble. Even with the change to coconut milk and chickpeas, he had no doubt the risotto would be delicious.

By the time he served their dinner, he'd convinced Natalia to buy a Toyota.

'They are good cars,' she agreed, grabbing the jug of hibiscus tea. 'I'll call the dealers and see what they have. There's a car dealer in Mareeba, isn't there?'

'Yeah, give the guys in Mareeba and Atherton a call, but you'll probably find something you want in Cairns.'

'I have no problem shopping around. Do you want to come with me?'

'Sure. And if we go to Cairns, we could come home via a scenic route through Port Douglas or Atherton.' And maybe stay the night somewhere, but he wouldn't mention that yet. Just looking at her now with her dress partly unzipped sent his brain fuzzy. He ached to taste her body, but his empty stomach reminded him to satisfy one appetite before the other.

'I hear they're both beautiful places,' she said as he followed her into the dining room. He placed her meal before her, then sat adjacent. 'This looks fantastic, Adam. Thank you.'

'You're welcome. I hope you like it.'

With one bite of rice, chickpea, and mushroom, Adam's worry faded. It tasted as delicious as he was used to, but even better with the coconut milk.

Natalia moaned. 'I can safely say that you can cook.'

'Did you doubt it?'

'Absolutely not. But I'll admit, it's impressive.'

'That's how Mum convinced me to learn.'

'I can imagine.' Laughing, she scooped up another forkful. 'It's nice though because I've never had anyone cook for me. But then, I guess it's different in the country, isn't it?'

'We don't have many other options, but I'm sure there are

plenty of people around here who can't cook. Cade's hopeless in the kitchen.'

'Well, I'm glad you're not one of them. I prefer homecooked meals.'

'I'm happy to stay in more often. We can take turns cooking.'

'And also …' She paused to chew. 'Don't feel like you can't have meat when we're here. But the vegan in me can't bring myself to cook it for you.'

'And I wouldn't ask you to.' He'd rather not eat meat around her anyway, especially when he planned on kissing her. Something about avoiding it for her just felt right. 'But we'll take things one day at a time.'

He had more on his mind right now as his gaze strayed towards her lowered zipper and the distracting view beyond. The blasted winter and her conservative clothes had kept her arms and shoulders covered since he'd known her, but as their bowls continued to clear, all Adam could think about was dessert.

And *not* the food kind.

Having him lower that zipper earlier had been a cruel seduction and welcome invitation. Yet as she scooped up the last of her risotto, for the first time in his life, Adam was at a loss. How the hell was he going to move things into the bedroom? Suddenly, it all felt new to him.

His heart lodged in his throat. Fuck.

'That was definitely the best mushroom risotto I've ever had.'

He swallowed. 'Really?'

'Yep.' She reached for his limp hand and smiled. 'So, what's for dessert?'

He interlocked their fingers and everything inside him

coiled tight. Did his anxieties linger because a woman had never been more important? Sure, it'd been a long time since sex had meant anything to him and his interest had waned with the mysteries surrounding his birthday. But he couldn't let that stop him. He needed to feel in control again. Needed to find the spark. Natalia deserved nothing less.

Yet it took him a moment to find his voice. 'Poached pears with a berry sauce.'

'Sounds delicious.' She pulled her hand away and gathered their plates. Adam didn't move, watching her as she stood. 'But can I let you in on a secret?'

Cautiously, he nodded. With a wicked grin, Natalia leaned down and brushed her mouth along his jaw. 'I lathered myself in strawberry body butter.'

Then she turned on her heel and strolled into the kitchen. Adam's hand fisted against the table. His jaw tightened and heat coursed through him like a virus.

Control snapped.

His chair scraped along the tiles as he stood and strode into the kitchen. Wrapping his arms around Natalia's waist, Adam pulled her against him and their dishes clattered into the sink. Her body melted against his as he pressed his lips to her scented neck.

Fuck. She actually did taste like strawberries.

'Strawberry always wins,' he whispered, and the fear inside him eased as she turned, threw her arms around his neck, and crushed her mouth to his.

Adam gripped her hips and pushed her against the sink, deepening the kiss and relishing her delicious lip gloss. She was addictive. Intoxicating. Her hands hardened on his back as he moved her over to the bare bench. She fired, kissing him with heat equal to his own as she reached for the buttons of his shirt. Wasting no time, he helped her, untucking his shirt from jeans that were quickly growing too tight.

Her hands met his, then lifted to splay over his chest. Adam shivered. Her fingers danced across his skin and pushed his shirt off. Then she tore her mouth from his, gripped his shoulders, and pushed him away, her wide eyes roaming. 'Damn, you look hot in just jeans.'

He grinned and *finally* pulled down that damn zipper. Her dress fell open to reveal Natalia's taut body encased in cobalt blue satin underwear unlike any he'd ever seen. He drowned.

'Natalia …' Wrapping his arm around her waist, he lifted her onto the bench and pulled her against him. 'I seriously don't deserve you.'

She moaned her response as he reclaimed her mouth. Skin to almost-skin, their bodies burned. Her breasts were tender, nipples hard through the thin fabric of her bra. Adam's mind emptied until there was nothing left but a deep need for her. Only her.

She drew away, breathless, and he set up camp in her neck, aching to taste every inch of her delicious body and kiss all the way down to her little toe. Natalia quivered as his thumbs rubbed the satiny underwire of her bra.

'Why?' she breathed.

He pressed his lips against her pounding throat. 'Huh?'

'Why don't you deserve me?'

'You're too beautiful.' He didn't know how he managed to get words out as he sucked gently at her collarbone. His body felt like a furnace, raging with desire unlike any he'd ever known. But damn, it felt good. 'Spirited. Special. And I've done things not to deserve you.'

'Oh, Adam.' She cupped his chin and lifted his face back to hers. 'Don't. You can have me.'

His throat tightened. All he could do was nod.

'But …' She drew on his lower lip. 'You can't have me on the kitchen bench.'

'Not tonight, anyway.'

She laughed as he pushed the dress from her shoulders. Her legs wrapped around his hips and he carried her through to the dining room, where he placed her on the edge of the mango wood and ran his mouth down her throat. She arched back as he continued to lower, kissing her shoulders and into the swell of her perfect satin-and-gauze-encased breasts. Her breath turned raspy as he took his time to devour her on his prized table.

He sucked at her nipple through the fabric and she gasped. Her hands raked up into his hair and held him in place, not that he needed the encouragement. Her body grew hotter until sweat dampened her spine. He moved to give the same attention to her other breast.

His name escaped her throat on a moan as he continued down, running his tongue along the inside line of her rib cage before pressing a kiss deep into her belly. Her back arched and legs loosened, allowing him to move to the waistline of her tiny scrap of underwear.

His heart hitched. Mouth watered. He wanted to savour this moment, wanted to send her crazy. So, he kissed the lowest point of her belly before giving a teasing pull on the elastic, snapping it back against her hip with his teeth. Natalia's nails dug deeper into his shoulders. Damn, he liked a woman with claws. He needed to get them to the bedroom. Fast. Placing a kiss between her breasts, he brought his mouth back to hers and plundered.

She was panting when he drew them both upright. 'I needed to taste you.'

'I'm glad you did.' Her hands ran down his biceps and dropped to his quivering belly. He pulled her to the edge of the table, trailed his fingers up her spine, and flicked open her bra. Natalia let the straps fall down her arms, then tossed it away, gripping his hips as he filled his hands with the weight of her. Adam's blood surged. Her breath caught as his fingers roamed her delicate skin.

How could anyone be so stunning?

He pulled her close, skin to skin for real this time as she wrapped her strong legs around him. Natalia grew limper and his knees weakened as he carted her through the next doorway and placed her on the back of the lounge. He didn't know why he had to stop. She was far from heavy and the bedroom was only a few feet away. But first, he needed to remove the remaining barriers.

He held her tight, afraid she'd fall backwards onto the lounge as he hooked a finger under her knickers and pulled them down her slender legs. Then he found her, wet and ready for him. Her grip around his shoulders tightened.

'Adam …'

He slipped his finger inside her and she shattered, her head falling back as her nails clawed at his skin. Overcome, he slid in another. She cried out as pleasure ploughed through her, her gorgeous body tightening around him.

'Oh, Natalia …' Adam raced his lips over her damp, trembling shoulders. He needed her. Needed to be inside her. Needed it more than his next breath.

He supported her in the precarious position as she met his gaze and unclasped his straining jeans. Then she had him in her hand and he lost it. The ache in his chest stretched until he was certain he'd never breathe again.

'Adam …'

'Nat …' Desire tortured his soul as she stroked him and his forehead fell to hers.

'One more room to go,' she breathed and he kicked his jeans away, lifted her up, and made it those last few steps.

Kneeling onto the mattress, he lowered her gently, her mouth finding his again as he scooted her up onto the pillows.

She blew out her breath. 'We made it.'

'We did.' Gazing into her seductive eyes, everything inside him tightened. He couldn't describe what he felt for her. All he knew was that he wanted to feel every tight inch of her around him and make love with her until dawn. Or longer. 'So, you …'

'Now. I want you now.'

He switched on the bedside lamp and dug in the drawer for the fresh box of condoms. He rolled one on and she pulled him towards her, caging him with her knees. Pressing his mouth to hers, he kissed her softly, relishing the passion that continued to pulse. Then, looping his arm under her leg, he dug his knees into the mattress and slid inside her.

Her lips left his on a gasp. He moved deeper and her legs wrapped around his hips, her ankles locking as she pulled him home. Damn, she was good. She had him exactly where she wanted as she matched her movements with his.

'Oh, Natalia …' Her hand fell from his shoulder and he clutched it tightly.

'Don't stop,' she breathed.

'Never.'

She tightened her grip around him—her legs, her fingers, her. Adam built and built but wanted to prolong this moment. He nipped at her lips and held her close. Fire coursed through them both. She met his soft kisses until he was on the verge of shattering. Her nails dug at his back until he swore she drew blood as their worlds collided in earth-shattering orgasms. Working through it, it seemed like hours before they stilled, chests heaving. Sweat dampened the bedspread around her, her golden locks in disarray. His body softened and her arms lifted, welcoming him into her embrace. His face found her scented hair as her legs loosened.

They held each other for what felt like an eternity until she spoke. 'Fuck, that was amazing.'

He grinned, delighted to hear her swear. 'You were amazing.'

Her chest continued to heave beneath him. He tried to move, but her thighs tightened, not allowing him to go. She needed air though, so he put his superior strength to use and rolled onto his back, pulling Natalia's limp body into his side. Her leg draped over his belly and she pillowed her head on his shoulder. Adam closed his eyes and savoured the moment as emotions he'd never felt before rose to overwhelm him.

Shit. He might not deserve her and she might yet give up on him. But right now, he was one lucky bastard.

Chapter Twenty-Eight

Despite getting little sleep, Natalia's internal runner's alarm woke her before dawn. Stretching her aching body, warmth overpowered her until she relaxed in contentment. Adam's arms tightened around her as he dropped his mouth to her shoulder. She didn't want to get out of bed. She wanted to stay there and not move. Forever.

But habit had her feet itching, rearing her legs to go, and if she didn't run, she'd be mad at herself later. Once she got it over and done with, she could spend the rest of the day in bed with Adam, guilt free.

'You going?'

Rolling over, Natalia lay over his warm, hard body, grinning as he pulled the doona up over her shoulders. Damn, he was sexy. Hard chest, strong arms, and the tightest arse. Every inch of him was perfect. *Every. Damn. Inch.*

'I don't want to, but I—'

'Go.' He gripped her hips and gently urged her away. 'If you stay, I'll never get back to sleep. You kept me up all night.'

'Me?' Laughing, she climbed out of bed and reached for her clothes, dressing quickly to battle the chill. 'What about you?'

He hugged her pillow to his chest but didn't take his eyes off her. 'Not my fault you're addictive. Now go. I'll keep the bed warm.'

She slipped on her shoes, then swooped down to kiss his cheek. 'I'll run fast.'

She could keep that promise. Leaving the house, adrenaline surged as her feet pounded the dirt. Before too long, she reached the corner and turned left towards High Ridge. She hadn't explored this part of Shadow Creek yet, but always enjoyed running a new track, especially when a view was involved.

The sky lightened and she kept her gaze to the ground as sounds of the bush waking whistled through the air. Leaves rustled, birds called, and Natalia's heart swelled. God, this place was beautiful. And last night had been fantastic. Nothing had held them back and she was grateful for that. Adam had impressed her with dinner, dessert had been delicious, and the sex had been incomparable. Mind-blowing. Worth sacrificing sleep for.

The memories kept her entertained until she found herself at the campground. The fact Adam had suggested this route had touched her deeper than she could say. No other man had kicked her out of bed and considered her wishes like that before.

Grinning, Natalia followed the wooden signs until she found the stairs to the lodge and hastened up the uneven, rocky path. Dawn seeped through the towering trees and within minutes, she emerged at the top. The double-storey brick building of the High Ridge lodge remained in darkness, as did the surrounding cabins nestled onto the hillside while garden lights lined the pathways through the lush landscaping.

Then Natalia turned to the view and stilled. Her breath caught. The sun rose behind her, casting a golden glow over Shadow Creek towards the west. Bush spread towards the tree-lined creek and the endless rows of banana trees beyond. She could almost identify the highway that led to Port Douglas and what must be Kelly Coffee past that. On her left were the guava and lychee orchards and the glowing lights of Elizadale.

She'd never seen a more beautiful sight. Natalia breathed in the cool, fresh air as her gaze darted towards Adam's house. The roof peaked past a cluster of trees and her chest expanded with longing.

One day, all of this would be his. And Jack's. He'd been born here and would die here. Shadow Creek was where he belonged.

Natalia pressed her lips together. Knowing that she could live anywhere and be content had helped her leave Sydney. A house was just a house. A suburb just a suburb. And while she'd been happy to stay in Elizadale for her contract, she hadn't considered what she'd do beyond that. She'd wanted the fellowship and the challenge of being a rural doctor. But for what? So that she could return to city life with yet another qualification on her resume?

Natalia pressed her hands to her forehead. She'd wanted to escape. She'd wanted to find a purpose. And she'd done that here. Yes, people were talking, but the gossip wouldn't last once they uncovered the truth about Jordan. Elanora had continued consulting with her and other locals booked appointments with her too, so she could stay and help them. Become part of the community. Ana had stayed and her sister's happiness was palpable. Could she find that too?

Wouldn't it be glorious to feel grounded and rooted in one place?

Natalia dropped her hands and smiled out over the beautiful land. She could certainly try. She could grow her own vegetables, run through the bush, and go swimming in the creek. There was a sense of freedom here that she'd never had in Sydney. She wanted to embrace it. To enjoy her newfound country life for however long it lasted.

And she had just the man to help her with that.

With newfound delight, Natalia hurried down the stairs. There was movement at the campground, but nothing could distract her as she raced back down the road. It seemed to stretch endlessly in the pale light, but the vastness didn't scare her. A wallaby hopped past and she grinned. After taking the turn for Adam's place, she broke into a sprint and didn't stop until she leapt onto the front verandah and pulled open the door.

'Adam!'

He appeared in the kitchen doorway wearing nothing but black satin boxers and Rusty came barrelling from behind him to greet her. Breathless, she raced towards Adam and threw her arms around his neck. He held her tight and chuckled.

'Must have been a good run.'

'Amazing. Running always gives me time to think.'

'You think anything interesting today?'

'Yep.' Drawing away, she lowered her hands to splay her fingers over his chest. She gazed into his dark eyes and something niggled around her heart. Something that made her belly clench, but she promptly ignored it as she said, 'I want a tour of Shadow Creek.'

He frowned. 'That's your big revelation?'

'No.' Laughing, she tightened her grip around him. 'But

while I'm living here, I may as well embrace it, don't you think? Become more of a country girl?'

He smiled and dropped a kiss to her lips. 'If that's what you want. And yeah, I can give you a tour. But what about the veggie garden?'

'Don't we have all day?'

He laughed. 'I guess we do.'

* * *

They had priorities though and returned to bed, so it wasn't until later when Natalia and Adam entered the kitchen showered and dressed. 'What do you usually do for breakfast?' she asked, her stomach rumbling.

'I'll admit, I'm lazy. I'm a toast guy.'

'I can work with toast. What do you have on it?'

'Whatever.' He opened the fridge and gestured. 'I have jams galore and more spreads in the cupboard.'

'You're not an egg man?'

'Nah, never liked bumnuts. Peanut butter's my fav.'

Laughing, she examined his range of jams. 'Peanut butter is good. Where did you get this pineapple jam?'

'People jam everything around here, Nat,' he said, popping bread into the toaster. 'All small business. Even Mum sells jam at High Ridge.'

She grabbed another with the High Ridge label. 'Red papaya?'

'That one's good. And the banana, of course.'

She certainly wouldn't have a problem having breakfast at Adam's house. Placing the pineapple back, she grabbed Wendy's two jams and had one of each. The red papaya was deliciously sweet and she enjoyed the banana.

'I might need to buy some of this.'

'Then perhaps High Ridge will be our first stop today.'

They finished breakfast, then climbed into the ute. Everything inside Natalia continued to glow as they drove up to the retreat and Lucy greeted them from the verandah of the lodge. It was difficult to tell the gardens from the bush as Adam showed her around the hillside cabins and pergolas while pointing out the various trails leading into the National Park. But with the variety of flora, endless birdcalls, and the chance of spotting Australia's beautiful wildlife, the land was stunning.

Why had she been so worried about life in the bush?

'The trails are good for walking, but some are better explored by horseback.'

'That's something I'd love to do.'

His eyebrows lifted. 'You want to go riding?'

'Yeah. I mean, I find horses big and scary, but I'm keen to try it. Lucy said she'd take me riding one day, but—'

'Nah, I can take you. Do you want to meet the horses? My gelding, Vendetta, would love to meet you.'

She smiled. 'I'd like to meet him too.'

Natalia bought various jams, politely declining Lucy's insistence about not needing to pay as she handed over her debit card, then she and Adam left the retreat. At the homestead, Natalia followed him towards the paddock where the horses were grazing. She took a few deep breaths but couldn't stop her knees from shaking. Adam slipped through the wire fence and she halted.

'I thought we were staying on this side.'

Chuckling, he held out his hand. 'Come on. They won't hurt you.'

Her palpitations continued as she followed him. Natalia

held his hand tight as the golden horse with a white mane and tail approached.

'This is Lightning, my sister Lily's mare.' Adam rubbed her nose. 'She's got attitude, but she's friendly. Like Lily.'

Swallowing, Natalia reached up to pat her. Lightning's nose was velvety soft, her snout hard. 'Hello.'

'Lily does show jumping and Lightning sometimes lives in Townsville, but Dad brought her back last week now that the show season has ended.'

'Fair enough.' Then a shadow fell over them and a warm breath blew against her neck. Turning, Natalia jumped as she came face-to-face with a large dark horse.

'This is Vendetta.'

'He's massive!'

'But friendly. And like me—' she stilled as Vendetta's nose brushed her shoulder '—he likes to flirt with the pretty ladies.'

Vendetta sure did. Natalia tried to relax as he sniffed and studied her. He was much bigger than Lightning, but she forced a smile and placed her hand over his dark cheek.

Vendetta exhaled, his ears twitching.

'Hey, boy. You're beautiful, aren't you?'

'Come around here and rub his neck. He likes that.'

Vendetta turned to follow her but halted at Adam's command. As Natalia stroked the gelding's neck and brushed her fingers through his dark mane, the tension in her spine eased. She could do this. It might take some getting used to, but she'd always longed for new experiences.

It wasn't until late afternoon that they began work on the vegetable garden. Natalia had to stop herself from skipping as she helped Adam gather various tools. He'd fenced off a spot outside the yard to keep wildlife away and had prepared the soil, explaining that the position would give the vegetables plenty of sunlight but ample shade at certain times of the day. Natalia simply nodded along, trusting his judgement.

He picked up the mattock. 'Righto. Let's get started.'

Adam strode to the edge of the garden, spread his legs, and swung the mattock into the ground, over and over until they had a trench. And for once, Natalia didn't mind standing there looking pretty because she could watch him all day. Her breath caught as sweat pooled at his chest and into his singlet, his arms bulging beneath the sleeves of his open denim shirt. Before long, his jeans were caked in dirt and her body hummed with pleasure.

Could they get down and dirty in the garden?

Natalia shook her head. *Control yourself!*

He was almost finished when a phone beeped. Reaching into her back pockets, she grabbed both their phones and swiped the screens. 'Adam, you have a message.'

'Who is it?'

Natalia pressed the icon and swallowed. 'Jordan.'

'Shit. What does it say?'

She raised her eyebrows. 'You want me to—'

'Just read it,' he said, leaning his forearms on the mattock.

Natalia's stomach churned as she opened the message. **It doesn't matter. Enough is enough. Just dump your new slut already and come back to me.**

Natalia's throat tightened as she read it aloud. Adam swore. He swung the mattock and dirt flew into the air.

'I'm sorry. She has no right to call you that. And I don't know why she can't answer my bloody questions!'

Natalia read the message he'd sent yesterday. **Why can't you tell me who else we partied with?**

'I mean ...' He paused, his chest heaving. 'It's not hard. We weren't alone. I partied with *people*. I just want to know who.'

'Cade couldn't find out?'

'Nope. Seems no one fucking knows anything.'

He kicked a pile of dirt as he strolled towards her to begin the last row. Natalia placed her hand on his sweaty arm. She knew he didn't want to do anything until he had proof of paternity, but she had to ask. 'Adam, what will you do about the baby if Jordan's telling the truth?'

His gaze remained low. 'If she was telling the truth, she wouldn't be hiding things from me.'

'Yes, but I think you need to prepare yourself for if ...'

His shoulders slumped as he leaned the mattock against a star picket. 'I know. And honestly, Nat, I think Jordan might have ...' He stared down at the creek, hands on his hips. Seconds passed before he turned back and drew her close. Natalia wrapped her arms around his sweaty waist and as he tilted her hat back, the hollow expression in his eyes broke her heart.

He hadn't wanted this and the fact that Jordan may have used or tricked or assaulted him into fatherhood still weighed heavily on him. But what could she do to comfort him other than be there? Hold Jordan down, withdraw blood, and go to prison for assault herself?

If only.

Adam's chest expanded, then relaxed. 'I won't forgive her, but I will accept the kid, Natalia. I couldn't ...'

She gave him a moment to continue, the vice inside her tightening as she waited. But he remained silent.

'Do … do you want children?' she asked.

His eyes dimmed. 'Haven't had much to do with them. But I find kiddos cute, so I thought I'd have them when the right person came along. I always tried to be careful and if it happened, it happened. But I never thought it'd be like this.'

She nodded slowly. Neither of them spoke as he brushed his fingers up and down her spine. She'd considered having children one day too, but she'd hoped to welcome them with joy. The thought of court orders and custody arrangements and Jordan manipulating Adam for the rest of his life made Natalia want to scream.

Eventually, he exhaled. 'It won't be too bad, right? Having the kid around?'

'No, it'll be fine.' She meant it, yet her heart still sank, her throat tightening until she feared she might cry. Lowering her gaze, she studied where her fingers rested on the sweaty V of his chest. 'You are a good man, Adam. An honourable one.'

'I'm trying. And I am sorry, Nat. I wish I'd never been involved with her, but—'

'It's difficult, but I understand.' What she didn't understand was the tension building low in her belly. 'We do need to figure out what happened though because I can't handle the gossip forever.' Tears sprang unwillingly to her eyes and Adam pulled her close. Thankfully, they didn't fall. 'I'm still on your side, Adam, but I've worked so hard to be a doctor and I want to be approachable. I know that it's stupid and that it shouldn't matter that I'm dating you, but—'

'People don't see past my party history and blame me for dumping Jordan.'

'Which is wrong.'

'Yeah.' He exhaled with a whoosh. 'But … you don't blame me for not wanting to be with her, right?'

'Hell no.' Natalia ran her hands up his sweaty back, her tears drying. 'Kids need parents, Adam, but those parents need to be happy. And single parents can raise happy kids. I'm proof of that.'

'You are, Nat. So, I promise—' he drew away and caught her chin between his thumb and forefinger '—I will sort this out. Okay?'

She nodded.

'Good.' He brushed his lips over hers, then stroked her cheek. 'Now, let's plant our veggies.'

Taking a deep breath, Natalia pushed her pain aside. This had been a good day and she couldn't let a text from Jordan ruin that. So, she forced a smile and turned to the seedlings at her feet. 'Okay. You said herbs along the fence, right?'

'Yeah, then they'll get partial shade.'

She picked up the oregano and rosemary and headed towards the first row to kneel in the dirt. Adam joined her with the rest of the herbs and they dug, planted, and stroked soil on each other's faces. When they finished, he wrapped his arm around her shoulders as they gazed over their garden.

She leaned into him. 'I love it, Adam. Thank you.'

His hand tightened on her shoulder. Hard. Possessively. Like he never wanted to let go. 'You're welcome, Natalia.'

Chapter Twenty-Nine

August grew cooler, but Adam found his mood improved as he spent the next few days working the fields in the morning and turning wood in the afternoon. He dined with Natalia of an evening and they moved from one day to the next battling the cold in the warmth of each other's arms.

'What the hell are you drinking?' Jack asked as they supervised the humpers on Wednesday morning.

Adam smacked his water bottle closed with a grin. 'Hibiscus tea.'

'It's pink.'

'And delicious. You should try it, it's good for you. Reduces stress.' Hell, his brother needed it.

Jack grunted as he tied the next bunch of bananas onto the trailer. 'I'll stick with water.'

Adam was peeling off his farm boots when his phone pinged with a message. His pulse spiked as he reached into his pocket. Yep, it was Jordan.

I know it's early but I found some nice baby furniture online. Here's a link to the cot I want but I'll need help

buying it. Come over tonight after I finish work and we can have a look together.

Adam shoved his farm boots onto the shelf a little harder than necessary. Come by after work? Ten o'clock? Yeah, because she'd really want to talk at that time of night.

He grabbed his regular boots and tugged them on before replying.

I can't come over. If you want to talk, you can tell me why I have no memory of my birthday.

He almost wanted to say he wasn't having any financial input until he had proof of paternity—and that no kid of his would sleep in a cot he hadn't built himself—but he wasn't in the mood to reopen that discussion.

Her reply came as he slipped into his ute. **I could come to your house. I like your bed better anyway.**

It took all his strength not to throw his phone and break it. Thank fuck he'd bought a new bed. **No, you can't come over. I'm dating someone as you know. Please leave us alone.**

He tossed his phone onto the passenger seat and drove home, seething. What the hell was going on with Jordan? Why couldn't she stop suggesting that they hook up? He was taken, dammit. *Taken.*

Had she always been this way?

The answer to that made his gut clench tighter. Yes, she had been. She harassed and abused in a way that was so subtle it was considered normal. He'd never realised it until Natalia had explained it to him and, even though it was a bitter pill to swallow, he could now see the truth about Jordan Kelly.

Exhaling, he ran his hand down his face. Thank God for Natalia. For four nights now, she'd been insatiable. An angel by day, devil by night. He'd never experienced anything like it. Hell if he knew how he found such passion with her among the chaos that raged inside his head, but the power she wielded anchored him. And during those moments where they talked, laughed, and loved, he found genuine happiness.

Yet he hadn't been able to return the question she'd asked him. What would Natalia do if Jordan was right about the baby? She didn't seem to be going anywhere, but that didn't mean she would stay. The idea of Natalia getting caught in Jordan's clutches because of him made Adam's teeth clench. If he didn't fix this soon, she might have no choice but to move on, and he couldn't bear the thought of that. The sight of Natalia making herself at home in his house these past few days brought a warmth to his heart that both terrified and thrilled him. She cooked, tended the garden, and was relentless in her mission to soften up Rusty. She forced him to cuddle, constantly kissed him, and referred to Adam as Rusty's 'daddy' after stating, 'Well, what else can you be called?' When she wouldn't accept 'Adam', he'd kept his mouth shut and let her have her way. He'd give her everything she ever wanted.

So, when another message pinged from Jordan, he couldn't leave it until he got home and pulled over by the footy grounds.

Oh, stud, are you still deluding yourself? I have much more experience in keeping you satisfied.

His phone smacked against the dash and landed on the floor. Satisfied? More like controlled. The woman just took charge.

Raking his hand through his hair, he retrieved his phone. He couldn't let this shit continue.

Jordan, this is harassment. I've asked you to leave me

alone and won't ask again. Tell me who else was in the park or give me proof of paternity, then we can talk.

Shoving the ute into gear, he drove home.

Jordan didn't reply, but Natalia was proud of him when he shared the messages with her over dinner. She was on-call, so they were staying at her place where Rusty enjoyed hunting in the garden.

'I know it's hard, Adam, but you need to stand up to her.'

'I'm trying,' he muttered. 'It's easy to do by text. But after all the reading I've done about sexual abuse, I have started to see …'

Blowing out his breath, he shook his head and shoved more pasta into his mouth. The stories he'd read online had been enlightening as many men had revealed how they had been pressured to have sex or woken to find women taking advantage of their sleeping erections. But just because he wasn't alone didn't make it any easier to talk about.

'Adam, it's okay,' Natalia said. 'You can tell me.'

He stared at his dinner, steeling himself before slowly lifting his gaze to hers. 'I think Jordan might be telling the truth.'

Natalia's expression didn't change. 'You do?'

'Yeah.' He swallowed, but the lump didn't dislodge from his throat. 'There have been a few times I can think of that I now see weren't right. She could never take no for an answer. One time … Jeez, Nat.' Exhaling, he slammed his elbow onto the table and dropped his head into his hand, keeping his eyes on hers. 'I hadn't seen her in weeks, but she came over and I wasn't in the mood. I asked her to leave, but she joined me on the lounge and … you know?' He didn't want to go into details, but she'd get the idea. 'I found it easier to give in, but I really didn't want to.'

'She should have left when you asked her to,' Natalia said softly, her eyes dulling.

'I see that now. So, I think that if it was possible on my end, then ...' He took Natalia's hand and squeezed. 'I'm sorry.'

'You don't have to be sorry,' she said, leaning forward and resting her forehead against his.

'I just wish I'd recognised Jordan taking things too far earlier. But I passed it off as normal. As Jordan having fun. But these texts and what she's doing now ... how nasty she was to Grace when we were dating ... it's all wrong.'

'It is.' Her arms came around him. 'And I wish I could help you, Adam. I wish I could confront her and demand that she gives you answers. And I will if you want me to, but I don't think it's my place.'

His heart lightened as he looked into her steeled eyes. 'Thanks, but I can handle her.' He'd try to anyway. Apart from a few glimpses of her at the Royal on crowded Friday nights, he still loathed to face Jordan directly. 'I don't want her to go after you.'

Her mouth twisted. 'Yeah, the rumours are bad enough and while some people have become regular patients, there are still those who want to run me out of town. Sonia Mansfield was in again this week and called us both some terrible things.'

Adam relaxed into his chair. 'I wouldn't pay attention to what the Mansfields think. They recently got done for animal abuse.'

'I know. Grace told me. Those poor horses ...' Natalia shook her head, not wanting to think about the neglect they'd inflicted on the innocent creatures. 'I know you don't like

Paul, but it was good of him and his mother to find them new homes.'

'Liz Kelly would care for every injured, sick, or neglected horse in the world if she could. And Paul's just like her. But Sonia's only talking to take the heat off her.'

'As gossipers usually do.'

'Yeah. But, Nat—' he took her hand again '—there are answers. And I will find them. The night is growing a little clearer, and one day I may put faces to who I was with. Just don't give up on me, okay?'

She smiled softly. 'I won't, Adam. And the truth will come out when the baby's born.'

He managed a nod and cleared his throat. 'It will. But are you ... how do you feel about it being true?'

She sighed and he clenched her hand tighter. 'I've been prepared for it to be true ever since I found out. I hope it's not, but it won't change how I feel about you.'

He should feel good about that, but the dullness in her eyes suppressed any hope that longed to rise. He wasn't sure if he was ready for parenthood himself, so he couldn't expect to ask it of her.

'You're sure?'

'Why should it?'

'Oh, Nat ...' He brushed his mouth against hers. 'I seriously don't deserve you.'

She smiled softly. 'No, Adam. You don't deserve the crap you're going through, but me ... we'll make it work. Now, let's finish our dinner because it's getting cold.'

* * *

A week later, Elanora Campbell took a deep breath as she sat in Natalia's consult room. 'I want to try IVF.'

Natalia grinned. 'Has Shane come around?'

'No, but I thought if I had more information, he might. If it hasn't happened by now, it's not going to naturally.'

'After a year, it's not unreasonable to consider other options. Are you still trying?'

Elanora's shoulders slumped. 'Only during those few days a month when he does it to please me. Otherwise, he doesn't seem interested. I almost have to make him and—' Elanora burst into tears. 'Oh, Nat, it's awful! Last week I was ovulating and he refused to touch me! We had this massive fight and he stormed off. Then he came back and he ...'

Natalia's eyebrows shot up. 'Did he hurt you?'

'No, but it felt like we were mating. There was no pleasure and I felt so disgusting. Afterwards, he apologised for getting mad and we tried to talk about it, but he still wasn't on board with IVF. He says that now might not be the right time. But if not now, then when?'

'I understand it must be difficult ...'

'It's awful! And I feel terrible because I can't give the man I love what I should be able to. I just want one baby, Natalia.' She held up a finger, gesturing desperately. 'Just one. Is it too much to ask?'

Natalia shook her head, unable to imagine Elanora's pain. If she ever wanted a baby, it should be as simple as removing her implanon and having plenty of fun. But to reach the point of frustration with no intimacy and sex out of necessity? No couple should have to endure that.

'It's not too much at all and I'm happy to help you with IVF. Let's write a referral and see what the specialist has to say.'

Elanora managed a soft smile. 'Yeah, okay.'

Natalia patted Elanora's hand, then turned to the computer. 'It can happen for you, El.'

'I hope so. How does it work?'

Determination hardened Elanora's pretty features and Natalia's heart clenched. She knew she shouldn't become personally invested, but if there was one thing she'd learned during her time in Elizadale, it was that there was no avoiding intimacy in small-town general practice. She was on Elanora's side and this woman needed to have a baby, especially considering her sister had beaten her to it.

Natalia took the time to explain IVF in as much detail as possible. 'It's costly, but the rebates will help.'

'I'll pay it off. People go into larger debts for cars.'

'So true,' Natalia said, laughing as she thought about her newly purchased Rav-4. She'd only taken out a small loan as she'd had considerable savings, and she and Adam had picked up her car in Cairns on the weekend. As promised, they'd taken the scenic route home through the Atherton Tablelands, where he'd shown her the famous fig trees and crater lakes.

'Is IVF risky?'

'No, it's perfectly safe. The biggest issue is the emotional stress. It's not an easy process, especially if it doesn't work.'

Elanora shrugged. 'I'll manage. And if it doesn't work, I'll get myself a dog.'

Natalia began writing the referral. 'Have faith, El. You're healthy, so I think your chances with IVF are good. But when you start treatment, I'd like to see you weekly for a mental health check in. And if it works, then you'll be the happiest woman alive.'

Hope filled Elanora's eyes. 'I will be.'

'And I'm glad you want to try.'

'Me too.' Elanora's gaze lowered while Natalia continued to type. 'I have to because I can't … I can't watch …'

Natalia paused. She gave Elanora a moment to continue before saying, 'It's okay, El. This is a safe space.'

'I can't watch Jordan have a baby when I feel like this! So helpless and un … unwomanly.'

Natalia clicked print and turned to Elanora. She held out her hands and Elanora took them. 'It's okay to be upset, El.'

'I still think it's unfair and I'm working on suppressing my jealousy. But I am happy for her.' Elanora exhaled. 'Sort of. We may not be close and most of the time I can't stand her because she's so friggin' mean, but she is my sister. I always wished we could be friends and you never know, becoming a mother might help her grow up. Besides, it'll be fun to be an aunty, right?'

Natalia nodded, glad to see the light back in her patient's eyes. 'Of course. You can buy cute clothes and toys and you never know? It might bring you and Jordan closer. Because honestly, I believe you will get your chance to be a mum.'

Elanora reached for the tissues. 'Hopefully. But you know, I think she's lying about Adam being the father.'

Natalia froze. 'Did she say something?'

'No. She's not talking to me, but I know my sister and even though she treated him like trash, Adam was the only decent guy she regularly hooked up with. If she wanted to choose a father, it'd be him.'

Natalia understood that too as she signed the referral. 'Thank you, El. He is a good man.'

'He is.' Smiling, she took her paperwork. 'Thank you, Nat.'

'You're welcome.'

But as Natalia waved her off, unease prickled at the base of her spine. She wasn't sure if Elanora knew the whole story about that night, but the fact that she found Jordan suspicious was a positive sign. Even if they weren't close, they were sisters and no one knew you better than flesh and blood. But life *was* unfair, so she hoped everything would work out for Elanora. She deserved it.

* * *

Inspiration had struck since his conversation with Sue, so on Saturday, Adam took Natalia to visit his timber supplier. He was keen to craft furniture and she insisted on helping in any way she could, which apparently meant asking a million bloody questions about wood on the drive to Yungaburra. Her willingness to learn floored him and she sure put his knowledge to the test, but they rescued a jarrah that had fallen in a recent storm, plus some mango and eucalyptus.

'I was hoping to get some of this soon,' he said, tossing the chunks of eucalyptus into the ute. 'This is the best wood to make a kettle or pot stand out of. You know why?'

Natalia shook her head. 'No, but I bet it smells good.'

'Exactly. The wood holds its smell, so when you put a hot kettle from the stove on there, the scent will travel and the house smells like eucalyptus.'

'Wow. You'll make me one of those, right?'

Adam tossed the last chunk in and pressed a kiss to her forehead. 'You can have the first one.'

He secured the wood in the Hilux's tray, then they began their drive home.

'Jarrah is a pretty wood,' Natalia mused.

'Yeah, it's strong and durable. They used it a lot in construction back in the day for wharfs and railways. Despite its strength though, it's easy to turn.'

'And that mango would make a beautiful coffee table. You could slice off that top end and do whatever you do to make it flat.'

'Sand it down?'

'Yeah. What do you think?'

'Sounds doable.' He'd been thinking about it himself. 'It'll be nice with the bark edges.'

'Yes, you need to keep the natural edges.' She turned in her seat. 'That's what I love most about your table. But to compliment that, you could create round legs and carve roses in them or something.'

Adam frowned. 'Carve roses?'

Her blonde ponytail swished as she tilted her head. 'Can you carve?'

Wincing, Adam adjusted his hands on the wheel. 'I'm a craftsman, Nat, not an artist.'

'Don't you want to challenge yourself?' she asked, her eyes curious rather than challenging.

Adam sighed. 'I should just turn something simple. If we want the rough, country look, then I shouldn't do anything fancy. Save that for candlesticks and vases.'

'Yeah, okay. How about a large round top that tapers into a smaller foot? With a few grooves, of course.'

'All right. Do you want to draw it?'

Her eyes brightened. 'Okay! And I can help?'

Adam chuckled. 'What? You want to work the lathe?'

'Hmm … maybe not. But I could do something.'

Smiling, Adam reached for her hand and squeezed. 'How about you help with the oiling?'

That delighted her, so they returned home and on Sunday, hunkered down in the shed to get started. He gave her a few easy things to do, then began the heavy work of sawing wood while she wandered around, inspecting and asking questions about every tool in the shed. Only when he switched on the sander did her curious mind ease and she settled down to read a book while he worked.

'You know what?' Natalia said later, standing at the entrance of the shed and gazing out over his front yard while he cleaned up. 'I think you need a frangipani tree.'

Adam frowned. 'Why?'

'Because they're pretty.'

'They're messy and drop flowers everywhere.'

'But I like frangipanis.'

He gathered his tools. 'I'll think about it.'

On Tuesday, he'd finished turning the fourth table leg when he checked his phone for Natalia's regular 'almost finished work' message. Instead, he found a text from Jordan. Guts churning, he ran his dusty hand through his hair as he strode out of the shed into the fresh air. He didn't want to read it. Didn't want to engage. But he had to because until he knew the truth, he had no choice but to keep Jordan onside.

Then he'd change his phone number.

Steeling himself, he opened the message. **Had my ultrasound today. Everything's okay. Wanna come over tonight to see photos?**

No, he didn't want to see the fucking photos. They'd screw with his head and emotions until he was even more messed up. Besides, if she wanted to share, she could easily send them to him. This was just another ploy as, once again, she was ignoring what was important.

He wanted proof before he grew attached to photos because if it was his kid—

The phone vibrated again and he exhaled. Natalia. **Will finish on time. Can't wait to see the table!**

Smiling, he messaged back. **Finished the legs. We can put it together later.**

Natalia sent a smiley face, then he replied to Jordan's message. **I'm glad everything's okay. Can't come over. Unless you wanna tell me who we partied with?**

Shoving his phone into his pocket, he strode towards the ute. He was bloody sick of asking. Why wouldn't she answer him?

Adam started the engine, then let it idle as he slumped in his seat. He felt so powerless. Lost. Why was Jordan doing this to him? Was she trying to avoid sexual assault charges or lying to coverup some horrible truth? He'd asked every worker on Shadow Creek if they'd partied with him, only to receive a constant stream of 'no, boss'. He'd tried desperately to uncover his lost memory through dedicated focus, but apart from drinking and singing with his hazy mate, all he could remember were ridiculously hot and hungry kisses. Kisses of a woman who'd been looking for a good time. He still didn't think that woman had been Jordan, but perhaps his denial was fucking with his mind there too as who else could she be?

Groaning, he pressed the heels of his palms to his eyes. Six more months of not knowing would be fucking torture, but what else could he do? Natalia had suggested hypnotherapy, but the last thing he wanted was to take regular trips to Cairns.

So, perhaps patience was a virtue and he should focus on the positive things. His business was growing and his relationship was as hot as ever with his beautiful keen assistant. So, shoving the ute into gear, he went to pick up Natalia so that she could help assemble her coffee table.

Chapter Thirty

The pub was quiet for a Thursday night as Jordan poured Shane Campbell another bourbon and Coke. He'd asked for a single, but she gave him a double because she was nice and her brother-in-law needed it.

'You're beginning to show.'

Jordan resisted a smile, avoiding Shane's gaze as she glanced down at her growing belly. 'Yeah, I'm gonna blow up like a balloon.'

Shane sipped his drink. 'I'm sorry you're doing this alone. I never took Maguire to be such a wanker.'

'Neither did I.' Heart pounding, she grabbed a cloth and began wiping down the bar. 'He doesn't give a shit about many things, but he does about family.'

'Yeah. Family.' Shane sighed miserably. 'Sometimes I wonder if it's worth it.'

'Is Elanora still driving you bonkers?'

'She's trying crazy herbal remedies now and has changed her diet. This obsession with yoga is out of control. Now she wants to spend thousands of dollars on IVF, which may not even work. Some days, I wish she'd give up.'

Jordan snorted. 'She should. If sex didn't work for her, then I doubt IVF will.'

'Bloody waste of money if you ask me. Especially for something that should come naturally.' Shane tossed back most of his drink as his mate Keith strode in and plopped down beside him.

'Hey. The missus tying herself in knots again?'

'As long as she's not tying herself around me.'

'Yeah, but I tell ya, this new yoga craze sure is shaping some fine booty. Not that you need to be there, Jords.'

He winked and Jordan flashed him a smile. 'I wouldn't stretch out with that lot for a million bucks.'

'Yeah, it's bloody stupid,' Keith agreed. 'How's the bub?'

'Good.' She placed his preferred beer in front of him. 'Still fatherless.'

'Bastard.'

'Yep. He's too busy hiding out on the farm with his new skank.' As infuriating as that was. Jordan hadn't expected Natalia to be a worthy opponent, but a month had passed and Adam was still with her. He should have grown bored by now and granted, there was still time. But Jordan had heard about the vegetable garden he'd built Natalia and she seemed to be adjusting to life in the bush. Adam would never give up the idea of a paternity test and accept her story while Natalia was still around.

'Yeah, I don't blame him,' Keith sniggered. 'She sure is one sexy babe. Sorry, Jords.'

A strange heat surged through Jordan as she snatched up her cloth. 'She's not that pretty, you know,' she said, attacking the counter with vigour. 'It's all a mirage. Hair, makeup, clothes … anyone can do it. And those looks? They're nothing that can't be achieved without a bit of plastic surgery.'

Shane's eyebrows lifted. 'You think?'

'Oh, please.' Jordan's lip curled as she stopped scrubbing. 'She's probably had it all. Eyebrow lift, tummy tuck. With a bit of Botox and a good boob job, anyone can look like that. She's got nothing I don't have.'

'Except a heart.'

Jordan froze, her gaze shooting towards the door where Elanora stood with a bunch of lycra-clad ladies.

One of them was Natalia Hamilton.

* * *

Jaw clenching, Natalia stared at the horrid woman as Jordan's words swirled inside her head. Botox? Tummy tuck? Didn't Jordan have anything more original? Probably not since the woman was incapable of a unique thought, but that didn't stop the hurt from rising to clog her throat.

Ana reached for her hand. Natalia squeezed while Meg rubbed her shoulder in support.

Jordan broke into a grin—fake if Natalia had ever seen one. 'Hey, sis! What can I get you?'

'Nothing.' Elanora placed her hand on Shane's shoulder. 'Babe, I was going to have a drink with the girls. But now, I think we may take our business elsewhere. After Jordan apologises to Natalia.'

Jordan rolled her eyes. 'Please. Tell me I'm wrong.'

Meg exhaled. 'Oh, for—'

'Seriously?' Ana breathed.

Natalia stepped out of their supportive hold and approached the bar. Despite the insult, a hint of confidence wormed its way up her spine. Jordan's behaviour didn't surprise her. The woman had no shame. And while she may have promised Adam not to engage with Jordan, this situation had nothing to do with him. Jordan had no right to make Natalia feel any less than what she was. Spreading horrid rumours was merely weakness, jealousy perhaps that Jordan hadn't got her own way. So, even though her knees shook, Natalia held her head high.

'You *are* wrong, Jordan. I don't need to resort to lies or manipulation to get what I want. There is nothing fake about me.' She placed her hand to her pounding chest. 'Everything I have achieved is the result of hard work and discipline. Something you clearly know nothing about.'

Shane snorted. Elanora glared at him.

Jordan simply leaned her hip against the bar. 'You don't know me.'

'And you don't know me! So please, keep your opinions to yourself.'

'Yeah, but I'm allowed to be pissed. You stole the father of my baby.'

Natalia's cheeks heated as everything inside her squeezed. Words failed her and a gleam passed through Jordan's eyes.

No. Don't let her get to you. You've done nothing wrong.

And neither had Adam. Jordan had lost him by treating him like a toy, discarding and beckoning him at her whim.

'I didn't steal him, Jordan. Adam can make his own decisions.'

'Oh, yeah? Then who put the idea of a paternity test in his head?'

'He was smart enough to ask for that himself.'

Jordan rolled her eyes with a snarl. 'Whatever. He never would have if you hadn't come to town. But since it's none of your fucking business, do you want one of your boring soda waters or not?'

'No, thank you.' Natalia turned to Elanora. 'Thanks for inviting us out, El, but I think we'll go.'

She nodded, her eyes dull and apologetic. 'No worries. Shane and I will be going too. After I have a word with my sister.'

Happy to leave that to Elanora, Natalia strolled out of the Royal. When they reached the car, she paused and ran her hands down her face as Ana's arm came around her shoulders.

'Are you okay?'

'I will be. But what the hell is wrong with that woman?'

'She's always been nasty,' Meg muttered. 'Do you two still want to get a drink or—'

Natalia shook her head. 'I want to go home.'

Ana nodded and they climbed into Meg's Astra. 'I'm sorry, Nat. I promised you'd love living here and now—'

'I do love it. Elizadale's everything you promised, Ana. It's just … Jordan Kelly …'

'I know,' Meg sighed. 'She needs to be brought down a peg.'

'Don't let her get to you, Nat.'

Natalia gritted her teeth as Meg turned into Jackson Villas. 'I won't. But I'm okay. Really.'

After more reassurances and goodbyes, Natalia alighted and forced her smile in place as she waved her friends away. Then, closing the door, she blew out her breath and leaned her forehead against the kookaburra windowpane.

Why were people so cruel? She'd hoped to have escaped this. Bullying. Harassment. But no matter what, it seemed to follow her everywhere.

She grabbed her phone to message Adam, saying she was home early and that he was welcome to come over. Then she sank onto the bottom step and dropped her chin into her hands. It took a few minutes for her pulse to steady and her strength to return. She'd come so far since escaping Mason Canning in regaining her confidence. Adam had helped unleash the flirtatious woman who'd been afraid to play and she was learning so much from Joanne. For the first time in ages, Natalia almost felt like she knew who she was.

She couldn't let Jordan Kelly destroy that. Jordan could spread all the lies in the world, but Natalia wouldn't allow her to manipulate her feelings. There was nothing that Jordan had that she …

Except the swell in her belly.

Natalia covered her eyes as pain warped through her.

* * *

Peeling the not-so-perfect banana, Natalia smiled. Adam called them 'doubles', but she preferred to think of them as Siamese bananas as they hadn't split properly on the plant. Commercial buyers deemed them unsellable, but Natalia had never seen anything cooler.

'I sure love it here,' she said, biting into her extra thick banana as she relaxed into Adam's warm hold on the picnic blanket.

'I'm glad. You're turning out to be quite the country girl, you know.'

'I am trying,' Natalia said, meeting Adam's dark eyes. Her heart swelled until she feared it would burst. Two months ago, she'd never thought it possible, but life in the country? It wasn't so bad.

She glanced at Rusty, watching him pounce as he hunted in the scrub along the creek. Yesterday, she'd tried teaching him to beg, but after sitting, he looked at her as though saying,

'Well, I did it, give me my treat,' and had refused to lift onto his back legs. She'd rewarded him anyway because he was too cute to say no to and Adam had laughingly accused her of spoiling him. But the little dog was softening. Twice now when she'd sat on the lounge, he'd jumped up and curled onto her lap.

But Rusty still loved hunting and it took some convincing for him to abandon the creek and return to the house.

'You want to help me varnish that hall table after agility?' Adam asked as they slipped through the gate into the backyard.

'Absolutely.' Watching Adam's muscles flex while he worked wood or seeing him stand behind the lathe with sawdust in his hair was Natalia's new favourite pastime. 'I'm glad your things are selling too. You've done so well.'

'Yeah. I still can't believe it, but I think I can keep it up,' he said as they stepped inside.

She patted his cheek. 'You should be proud of yourself.'

'I am.' He dropped a kiss to her throat. 'But we still have some time before agility. Any ideas?'

'I think we could find something to do on that lounge over there.'

'Gotcha.' His arms came around her and he hoisted her over his shoulder. Natalia laughed, smacking his sexy butt as he carted her to the lounge. This wasn't the first time he'd treated her like a bunch of bananas.

She landed on her back and he lay over her, crushing his mouth to hers as he snuck his hands under her T-shirt. Flames coursed through her body and her thoughts faded. There was nothing but Adam and the way his fingers danced across her skin. No sound other than their clothes rustling, the lounge squishing, and Rusty barking outside.

Adam lifted his head and glanced at the back door. 'Rusty's got a snake.'

Natalia froze. Arousal turned to fear. Her nails dug into her palms. 'How do you know?'

'That's his snake bark.' Adam stood. 'Stay there. I need to see what he's got.'

She scrambled upright. 'You're going out there?'

'Don't worry, I know what I'm doing.' He kissed her quickly, then slipped out the sliding door.

Heart thumping, Natalia took a deep breath. And another. She feared to move but found strength in her shaking legs to walk to the screen door. Adam approached Rusty who stood with his tail up, barking in a way that certainly sounded different.

'Ooh, good boy.' Adam peered at the ground. 'Got a nice big brown there, haven't you?'

Natalia's hand flew to her chest. Tears sprang to her eyes before she could stop them. A brown snake was in the yard. And the man she loved was going near the damn thing! And Rusty ... Oh God, don't let it kill Rusty!

Wait. The man she what?

'Nat! Run to the shed and grab my snake tongs and a bag. They're on the shelf by the door.'

'What?' she squeaked.

'Whatever you find is good. Or do you want to watch the snake?'

'I'm going!' She bolted through the house and out to the shed. Natalia had no idea what she was looking for, but there was a thick bag on a hoop stick and another tong-like contraption which she supposed could pick up a snake. She grabbed them both.

When she returned, Natalia saw Rusty tucked under

Adam's arm and she almost crumpled against the door. Her doggy was safe. But now, she needed to be brave. How could she call herself a country girl if she couldn't help Adam catch a damn snake? Otherwise, he may get himself killed, the idiot. And she couldn't have that when she loved—

Inhaling, Natalia stepped outside. Now wasn't the time for stupid thoughts. She had to stay focused. How long would he have if he got bitten?

'Come this way, he's over there.' Adam pointed. Natalia tiptoed towards him, shaking as she kept her eyes on the ground in case Mr Brown had any buddies.

Then she saw the snake and froze. A soft cry escaped her throat as her hands tightened around the equipment. It was long. Thick and long. Its tongue flickered and she shivered violently. Air clogged in her lungs.

It was a real snake.

'Hey, it's okay.' Adam placed his steady hand over hers. 'Give me the stuff, take Rusty, and go inside. Slowly.'

Natalia exchanged the equipment for Rusty, squeezing the little dog to her chest as he continued to growl and bark. Fear tightened everything inside her as she watched Adam step towards the snake. But before she could say anything foolish, she turned and crept out of the danger zone.

Burying her face into Rusty's soft fur, she told him instead. 'I love you, boy. Don't scare me like that again.'

She shut him inside the house and turned in time to see Adam twist the bag closed. Natalia collapsed into a chair and dropped her head into her hands. Rusty rattled the screen door, barking to be let out. Natalia stared at the ground.

Shit. Those feelings sure had snuck up on her. But what had she expected? She'd chosen to believe in him because he was a decent man. A kind, funny, and generous man. When she'd stood on that hill gazing out over Shadow Creek, she hadn't been longing for home. She'd wanted him. To stay on the farm with him. Because her foolish, fun-loving heart had gone and fallen in love with him.

But as Adam's boots filled the spot she was staring at, there was no way she was telling him that. He ran his hand over her hair and her pulse slowed. Standing, she wrapped her arms around him and held him tight.

'I know you think I'm irrational, but I can't stand those.'

'It's okay. I knew what I was doing and you did good.'

She loosened her grip. 'I don't get why you don't kill them.'

He snorted. 'I thought you were vegan.'

'Yeah, but that doesn't mean you let an animal kill you!'

'He wasn't going to kill me. He's just lost. We'll go put him out in the bush and let him roam free. You want to go for a drive?'

Her head shot up. 'With a snake?'

'He'll be in the back, locked in the bag where he can't get to us.'

She blew out her breath. Yeah, right. Adam mustn't have seen *Snakes on a Plane*. She hadn't either, but she knew the concept. Those bastards could get through anything.

'Okay, I'll come.' She kissed him softly, revelling in it before drawing away and touching her finger to his mouth. His dark eyes bored into hers until he sent her heart into an arrythmia. She couldn't deny it. He was everything she never knew she'd always wanted. There was no turning back.

She dropped her hand and stepped away. 'Just ... don't get bitten.'

'They only bite if provoked, Nat. It's no big deal. I've been bitten before.'

She startled. 'What?'

Laughing, Adam drew her back into his arms. 'It was just a little python. I was fourteen and it was awesome showing off my bite at school.'

'I'm sure you'd have thought so,' she said dryly. 'Don't get bitten by a venomous one.'

'I won't. Now, let's go.'

Nodding, Natalia went inside and gathered Rusty into her arms. 'Good thing I'm getting used to the bush, little one,' she said, grabbing her phone and keys. 'Because apparently, I love your silly daddy.'

Chapter Thirty-One

'The upside is we don't see the Kellys at the pub on Friday nights,' Jack said, leaning against a doorframe in Michael's half-built house. The roof was on and the outer brick walls were complete, but Michael still had a way to go with his masterpiece. He hadn't started on the electrical and plumbing systems yet, but that didn't stop the Maguire men from having a beer in what would be the rumpus room after they finished installing some plasterboard on Monday afternoon.

'True,' Adam agreed, taking a swig of his beer.

'Are you any closer to figuring out what happened?' Liam asked.

'Nope. But I swear at the end of the night, it was only me and my mysterious mate left standing. I just wish whichever mate it was would bloody well own up.'

'Makes me think it wasn't a mate at all,' Jack said, taking a swig of his beer.

Adam scoffed. 'Yeah, a mate wouldn't have left me alone passed out in the park.'

'Not a good one,' Jack agreed.

Michael nodded. 'It's fucked up, I'll give you that. I had a go at some bloke the other day who said you'd had it coming. But you know we're on your side, right? Even if we are to become uncles.'

'Yeah,' Jack sighed, leaning back against the doorframe. 'It'll be all right.'

'We'll love the kid, even if it is a Kelly,' Liam agreed.

Adam managed a half-smile. 'Thanks, guys.'

'How's Nat coping?' Liam asked.

'She's putting on a brave face, but the situation does hurt her and is affecting her work.'

'Yeah, that sucks,' Michael said. 'But I can't believe you found yourself a girlfriend first. Out of all of us, I'd have expected Lucy to be next.'

Liam winced. 'Why?'

'Well, Lily still has uni, Jack's taking forever, and I need to finish this place first. Adam was never going to settle down, so that only left Luce.'

Adam sipped his beer. 'I never said I wouldn't settle down, but I see your point. Jack could have been done by now, but he's too stubborn. You lot just shouldn't have always teased me about never finding the right person.'

Jack blinked. 'What? You're going to marry Natalia?'

Adam froze. Why did that word still cause his heart to clench? All he wanted was to be with Natalia. They were having all sorts of cheeky, playful, and super-hot fun. He didn't want to imagine life without her.

But it *had* only been six weeks since things had grown serious, so he couldn't be ready to make a commitment and promise to love and honour and cherish her until the day he died. He could be a boyfriend, but a husband? That meant something to him. Husbands had to be sturdy and reliable, and he didn't feel like either when he didn't know if he was having a lovechild with the woman who might have assaulted him.

Wincing, Adam ran his hand through his hair. Fuck it, he couldn't let this go on. There was only one thing left he could do, even though the thought made his stomach churn.

He glanced at his brothers. 'I don't plan to let her go.'

Michael laughed. Adam would have kicked him if he were close enough. 'Shut up.'

'On ya, mate,' Jack said, downing the last of his beer. 'Now, let's pack up and head to the pub. The ladies will be waiting.'

They did a quick tidy up, and half an hour later, Adam was in their regular booth with Natalia beside him. He held her hand as he gathered the strength for what needed to be done. But first, he enjoyed the distraction of wedding talk.

'Have you written your speech yet?' Ana asked Adam.

'When is it again?'

'Three weeks!'

'Plenty of time.' He dismissed it with a wave of his hand, but the look on Ana's face made him reconsider. 'Fine, I'll start on it this week.'

He wouldn't as he didn't have a clue what to include in the bloody thing, but he would say anything to make her happy.

'Did you talk to my aunt about the cake?' Meg asked.

'Yep.'

'And we've done the flowers,' Natalia said. 'Now, we just need Mama.'

Ana nodded. 'Is it still okay she stays with you?'

'Of course. And Joanne's given me the afternoon off so I can come with you to pick her up.'

'She's arriving two weeks before the wedding?' Adam asked, resisting a frown. Two weeks without making love with Natalia on the lounge? What were they going to do?

She patted his thigh, easily reading his mind. 'We'll be fine.'

'I still can't believe you two,' Meg said with a laugh. 'You're so cute together, but it's weird seeing Adam with a girlfriend.'

'Don't tell him it's weird,' Jack warned her. 'He'll throw it back in your face.'

'I'll throw it in yours, not Meggy's. But I surprised you all, didn't I? Wouldn't have happened if Nat hadn't come to town.' Grinning, he kissed her cheek. Then he took a deep breath and glanced around the table. 'I'm going to the bar. Anyone want anything?'

Adam confirmed orders and Natalia squeezed his hand as he slid out of the booth. Anxiety threatened, but he smothered the dark thoughts as he leaned his forearms on the bar where Jordan was serving. She could avoid his messages, but she couldn't escape a direct question. If he kept his temper, he might get somewhere.

But their conversation would depend on Jordan's mood. Would he get cold and distant or was the seductress out to play?

Her eyes landed on his and gleamed. The corners of her mouth curved as she slid along the bar towards him. 'Hey, sexy. What would you like?'

Adam's fists clenched. *Stick to the plan.* 'What I've been wanting for weeks. Answers. Who else was in the park that night, Jordan?'

'Come on, that's not what you want.' She laughed and placed her hand on his arm. His skin crawled and it took all his effort not to pull away.

'Why can't you just tell me? I know there were a few of us.'

'Why does it matter? You were with me.'

'Exactly, and you're trying to hide the truth!'

Her eyes flashed as she leaned her exposed hip on the bar.

'I am not. You either believe this kid is yours or you don't. Nothing else matters.'

'It does because I want to know who spiked me.'

'You weren't spiked, Adam. You were just drunk.'

Fury bottled in his throat as his fists clenched. 'And you know that because …?'

Exhaling, she adjusted her stance. 'Look, you can't prove it either way, so simply accept the fact that you were out of control.'

'But were you?' It was an effort to keep his voice low and steady.

'I'd had a few beers …'

'But you were of sound mind. So, if we had sex, then I don't know how you see nothing wrong with that.'

His heart pounded as Jordan stared at him. Her eyes steeled and mouth twisted in thought. His hope of a lie and fear of the truth battled inside him until everything tightened and his vision fuzzed.

Then she exhaled and crossed her arms over her chest. 'Fine, there were a few of us. You and me. Some Norwegian backpacker who worked on the Taylor farm. Never knew his name. But it was so long ago I don't remember anything else. Now, are you satisfied enough to come back to me?'

His hands gripped the bar until he was afraid he'd snap the timber in half. 'No. I will be there for the baby if it's mine, Jordan, but I am *not* coming back to you. And if you and I had sex that night, I will take legal action. I *was* spiked and I'm sure you damn well know how.'

Jordan sniggered. 'You'll never be able to prove that.'

Words died on Adam's tongue. Was that a confession? He wasn't sure, but it was clear that she didn't understand what she may have done. He could see how it would have unfolded.

It didn't matter whether he'd wanted to in his intoxicated state or not, she could have led him behind the bushes and taken—

'For fuck's sake, forget it.' Unable to look at her, Adam pushed away from the bar. Everyone could get their own fucking drinks.

* * *

Natalia took deep breaths as she stared into the basin, her hands tight around the porcelain edges. But before she could do something stupid like cry, the door opened and Ana stepped inside the ladies restroom.

She placed her hand on Natalia's shoulder. 'You okay?'

'No.' She squeezed her eyes closed, but the pain inside her refused to ease. Watching Jordan flirt with, touch, and harass Adam had been unbearable. Bile rose in Natalia's throat. She wanted to slap that woman into next week. How many times did Adam have to tell Jordan that he wasn't interested and to leave him alone?

Before Natalia could stop it, the truth escaped her in a whisper. 'I love Adam, Ana.'

Ana rubbed her back. 'I know …'

'How?' She glanced at her sister to find her smiling. 'I only realised yesterday.'

'You may have, but I knew you'd fall for him. How could you not?'

'I should have known better. Now, I love him so much it freaking hurts and that woman …' Her hands tightened around the basin. After a few more breaths, the urge to march into the bar and cause a scene subsided.

'I know, Nat. She's not being kind and it must hurt.'

'It's torture. I still don't know why she'd lie, which scares me to bits. And I'm bloody sick of her harassing him. She's still sending him booty-calls!'

Ana's nose crinkled. 'Oh, God.'

'I know.' Natalia reached for the paper towel to dry her eyes. 'I mean, I'm glad he's recognised that how she treated him was wrong, but I hate seeing him go through this.'

'Yeah, but if there's one thing I know about Adam, it's that he's a determined man. The truth will come out.'

'But we're going to look like fools if it is his baby.'

'And if that's the case, you'll both handle it.'

'I guess …'

Ana gave Natalia a moment as she fixed herself up. It was difficult, but she wouldn't let Jordan bring her down. *She* was in control. She chose how she felt.

But as she slipped into the booth beside Adam, Natalia's belly continued to churn. How much longer could this go on?

* * *

Jordan sped out of town, her hands tight on the wheel. She couldn't believe Adam was still with that slut. She'd tried all the old tricks to make him see he still desired her, but nothing had worked. He wasn't coming back. He wouldn't leave Natalia or sign a birth certificate.

Legal action? Her throat closed over, sweat trickling between her breasts as she drove home. She'd never seen fire like that in Adam's eyes before. It was like what had been between them had never existed. Yeah, it'd just been meaningless fun, but that's all she'd wanted. And so had he!

Then something had changed. She didn't know what, but she'd stripped down and waited for him that afternoon, hoping to entice him back, and he hadn't even blinked an eye!

Not even her lie about being pregnant with his child was enough to keep him.

Jordan thumped the wheel. She was fucking screwed. Six months ago, Adam would have fallen for the con. But now, she was going to be stuck with the brat alone.

Pulling into her driveway, she slammed the door and headed inside. What was she going to do? She couldn't change what happened. And it wasn't her fault. She'd only done what the man had asked and she enjoyed giving men what they wanted. She delighted in fulfilling their fantasies. She had little else going for her, but she knew how to have fun. Deep down, she probably should regret what she'd done, but she didn't.

Besides, lately, things had been different between them. So maybe she could tell him the truth? Maybe he'd want her? It might be a risk, but why shouldn't a baby have both of its parents? She wanted it, so consequences be damned. Her mother might be devastated at first, but Liz Kelly had a heart of gold and would never cut her own daughter out of her life, let alone her grandchild. Jordan could take the disappointment for however long it took her mother to forgive her if it meant she wouldn't be alone.

The thought almost made her smile. But as for Adam …

Jordan's hands shook. Adam wouldn't back down from wanting answers. But *he'd* left *her* and she'd be damned if he got to be happy when she might lose everything.

So, if Adam wouldn't leave Natalia for her, Jordan had no choice but to get rid of the uptight city doctor herself.

Chapter Thirty-Two

Natalia's hand froze on the mouse as she stared at the email. She couldn't move. Couldn't breathe. All thoughts disappeared, except one.

That bloody bitch!

Her hands flew to her mouth as she reread the horrifying words from the Australian Health Practitioners Register.

Received notification ... submitted by Miss Jordan Kelly about you under the Health Practitioner Regulation ... What you need to do ... Provide a written response ... Whether you shared confidential medical information about Miss Jordan Kelly ... Whether you disclosed your conflict of interest ...

Natalia dropped her elbows on the desk and covered her face. Her shoulders shook. Her pulse raced. This couldn't be happening.

Jordan had gone to the Health Ombudsmen and Natalia had two weeks to respond. But with what? This wasn't a medical complaint. She kept thorough notes to protect herself from those. This would be her word against Jordan's.

She'd done nothing wrong. Natalia hadn't said a single word about Jordan or her pregnancy. She'd simply asked Ana what she knew about Adam. *Jordan* had told him she was pregnant. Surely Adam and Ana could back her up on that. Except, wouldn't they be considered conflicts of interest too?

Pushing to her feet, Natalia paced. What was she going to do? Doctors had been deregistered for many things that were untrue. This spiteful bitch could end her short career.

'Okay.' Taking a deep breath, Natalia gripped the edge of her desk and fought for calm. 'Don't panic, Nat.'

She would talk to Joanne, phone her insurance company, and draft her response. Because she was no longer staying out of this. If Jordan wanted a war, she had one.

* * *

'That bitch!' Grace shoved her lunch into the microwave. 'I can't believe it.'

Emma raised her eyebrows as she sat at the table. 'Can't you?'

'Well, yeah, Jordan's known to make a scene. But still! I'm so sorry, Nat. You don't deserve this.'

'It is an unfortunate and serious situation,' Joanne said, 'but Natalia didn't breach confidentiality. We'll need to support her in this and respond effectively.'

'Absolutely.' Emma took Natalia's hand and squeezed. 'Don't worry, Nat. We're here for you.'

Natalia managed a smile as she mixed her salad. 'Thank you, ladies. I appreciate it.'

Joanne returned to her consults and Grace flopped into a chair opposite Natalia. 'I know what you're going through. I bloody hate that woman. Jordan Kelly doesn't care who she hurts as long as she gets her way. But she's the one who screwed up and she has no one to blame but herself.'

Natalia raised her eyebrows. 'You don't hold back, do you?'

'We've known Jordan all our lives, Nat,' Emma said. 'She's never been kind.'

'She's a bloody vulture!' Grace cried.

Natalia nodded and ate her salad, the red wine vinegar hitting the spot. 'I won't disagree.'

'She chatted up Ian once,' Emma said. 'We were engaged. But I'm the sergeant's daughter so Ian wouldn't dare stray.'

Grace smiled. 'He loves you too much. But I don't know what Jordan's thinking as she's certainly crossed a line. Does she think that if she gets Natalia deregistered that she'll leave town and Adam will take her back?'

Natalia rolled her eyes. 'Please. I'd stay just to spite her. It's not like I'll have anywhere to go without a job.'

Yet even though the words gave her strength, the pressure inside her didn't ease. Being a doctor was all she'd ever wanted. She couldn't lose that now. Not after she'd escaped those horrible intern years, the harassment, and Mason Canning to find herself here. She loved this job. She loved Elizadale and wanted to help the people who lived there.

If only small-town general practice hadn't turned into a bloody nightmare. In Sydney, work and home had always remained separate, but here, there was no escape. She'd always know everyone's business, always be Doctor Hamilton.

And she wasn't sure if she could live her life like that.

* * *

It had been less than three months since Natalia had seen her mum, but Nadia couldn't have chosen a better day to arrive. No matter how old you grew, mum cuddles always brought comfort. But Natalia let Ana and Liam greet Nadia first since this was the first time her mother was meeting him in person.

'You didn't bring your man, darling?' Nadia asked, drawing Natalia into a hug.

'No, you'll meet him tonight,' she said, squeezing her mum a little too tight.

'Deborah's arranged a barbeque on Shadow Creek so that everyone can meet you,' Ana said as they headed to baggage claim.

'How lovely. I'd like to see the banana farm, but I'm sure there are a lot of places you want to show me.'

'We'll take you to The Tablelands on the weekend,' Natalia said, 'but I'm sure Adam can show you around the farm. It's fascinating to learn how it all works and the fields are beautiful.'

Not that there was much time for sightseeing since both Ana and Natalia still had to work, but their mother didn't mind. These past nine months had been the longest they'd ever been separated, so being together was all that mattered.

Although Natalia doubted she'd have any fun over the next few days while she drafted and fretted over her response to the medical board. She would talk to her mum about it if she found a quiet moment before dinner, but Adam … God, he was going to lose it.

She would do what she had to though and tell her side of the story, then she'd put it out of mind because she was damned if she'd let Jordan ruin Ana's wedding for her.

Natalia settled into Liam's LandCruiser and engaged in happy conversation with her family as they left Cairns and drove the hour and half home.

'I certainly see what you girls love about this little town,' Nadia said when she and Natalia were alone at Jackson Villas after their brief tour of Elizadale. 'Ana has a lovely house like she's always wanted, and Liam's café is beautiful.'

'Yeah, it is.' Sighing, Natalia sank onto the lounge beside her mum. 'And I do love it here, although I'm not sure …' What? That she'd stay? That's what she'd been about to say, but was it true?

'Nat? Are you okay?'

'Yeah. It's just …' Part of her didn't want to tell her mum before she'd spoken to Adam, but now that Nadia was there and looking at her with eyes Natalia had trusted for twenty-seven years, the story spilled out. She withheld a few details, but summed up Jordan trying to trick Adam into fatherhood and the rumours she was spreading about them both.

When Natalia finished, Nadia took a moment before letting out a deep breath. 'Well, I don't like the sound of this Jordan woman one bit. She certainly has little grounds for the complaint.'

Natalia nodded, though that didn't stop terror from shimmying up her spine. 'Joanne thinks I'll easily defend myself and my insurance advisor is reviewing the case. I'll talk to her again tomorrow. But I did nothing wrong, Mama. Jordan has an agenda for reasons we don't know and I just got in the way. "Stole her man", apparently, even though he was already gone.'

'I can see why,' Nadia muttered. 'But don't you worry, sweetie. You will write a stellar response, I'm sure, and this is what you pay your insurers for. There's no use worrying until you have something to worry about.'

Natalia took a deep breath, then let it out slowly. 'Yeah. I know.'

'I'll be here for you though. And do you know what might cheer you up?'

'What?'

Nadia laughed and rose to her feet. 'What do you think? I thought you asked for new lingerie.'

Natalia shot to her feet, having forgotten about that. With her mum coming, she would have been a fool not to have put in an order and had spent up big. 'Yes, that's exactly what I need.'

* * *

Adam's heart pounded as he gripped Nadia Hamilton's hand. Joy? Terror? Probably both. But he forced the many reasons Nadia would disapprove of him aside and offered her a smile. 'So pleased to meet you, Mrs Hamilton. I can see why Natalia and Ana are so beautiful.'

Pink appeared in Nadia's cheeks. 'Oh, Adam. Ana said you were a charmer.'

'He tries to be,' Natalia said, slipping her arm around his waist and easing his nerves. He knew that the kindness he'd shown Ana after her assault had already put him in Nadia's good books, but he needed to maintain that favour since Natalia had told her mum about the rumours Jordan was spreading. Natalia had texted him shortly before she'd arrived, explaining it had come up in conversation. He hadn't minded as the subject had been bound to surface, but the last thing he needed was for Nadia to think her daughter could do better than him when he already knew that himself.

Adam gestured the ladies into the homestead. Finding his mother in the kitchen, Natalia beat him to make the introductions.

'So nice to meet you!' Wendy greeted Nadia with a hug.

'And you, Wendy. You have a lovely home.'

'Thank you. Come and meet everyone.'

Adam's arm tightened around Natalia as Wendy whisked Nadia away. He wasn't sure what to make of his mum, but for some strange reason, she'd been as excited about Nadia arriving as Aunty Deb.

'I like your mum.'

'I'm glad she's here,' Natalia said with a sigh. Frowning, Adam was about to ask her what was wrong when her eyes suddenly brightened. 'Guess what she brought me?'

'What?' he asked, leading her to the fridge.

'New lingerie. The new line is seriously sexy and I have some stunning pieces to model for you.'

Handing her a bottle of water, he twisted open a beer and took a long drink. Damn woman. Since being introduced to her coordinated city undergarments, he'd become quite the fan of lingerie.

'You tell me this when we're about to spend the next two weeks apart?' He took another swig of beer. 'What did you get?'

'Lots of things. A black sheer chemise, a pink set that has more straps than you can count. Suspenders …' Her grin widened as she stroked her finger down his belly. He quivered. Fuck, suspenders …

'I'm going to leave now before I seduce you on my mother's kitchen floor.'

He turned and walked away.

Vixen.

The night passed with ease as everyone talked and ate, but while the general mood remained cheerful, Adam couldn't help but sense that something was bothering Natalia. She didn't engage much and while she'd been keen to tease him, the spark inside her had diminished. He didn't get a chance to ask her about it though, and soon everyone began to leave. Natalia's eyes reflected his own despair as she turned to him on the verandah and he slipped his arms around her waist.

'I understand your reasons, but I hate your objection to letting me sleep over.'

She sighed. 'Me too.'

He quirked his eyebrow. 'So why don't you be a naughty girl and sneak me in?'

'I know you could probably convince me, but no. It'll be okay. I'll come over and we'll have all the sex we want.'

'It'd rather sleep beside you without sex than not sleep with you at all.' The words left his mouth without thought, but he meant them. He'd grown used to her companionship this past month and would miss waking to her jumping back into bed warm and sweaty.

Natalia stretched up onto her toes and kissed him. 'I know. I'll miss you too. But I'll say goodnight now before I cave.'

He tightened his arms around her, not ready to let go. What would he hold tonight? A pillow? That wouldn't work. Pressing his mouth to hers, he lingered in the kiss. It seemed she didn't want to go either, but eventually, she proved to be the strong one. Natalia slipped her hands into her pockets and backed away towards Liam's idling LandCruiser.

'Goodnight, Adam.'

He leaned his shoulder against the verandah post and forced a smile. ''Night, Nat.'

Adam watched as Liam drove her away and felt like something had ripped him in two, which was ridiculous since he'd spent many nights alone and content. Besides, it would be nice to spread out in his own bed without her being a total cover hog.

Behind him, the screen door opened and his mother

stepped onto the verandah, pulling a jacket around her. 'That was a nice evening.'

'Yeah. Aunty Deb and Nadia couldn't stop talking about the wedding.'

'It'll be lovely. Have you written your best man speech?'

Guilt prickled his spine. 'No. I can wing it, right?'

The same frustration passed through her eyes that had when he'd refused to do his homework. 'No, Adam, you can't wing it. This is Liam's wedding. Don't make me remind you every day.'

He resisted a smile, knowing she'd do it. 'Yeah, okay.'

'I see things are going well between you and Natalia.'

'Yeah.' He dropped his gaze to the ground and shifted his feet. 'I hope to keep her around.'

'I'm glad to hear it. She's a fantastic girl. Do you hope to keep her around forever?'

Puffing his cheeks, he let out a long breath. 'Mu-um …'

'What?' She blinked innocently. 'I just want to see you happy.'

'I know. And I am happy. Natalia … she's more than I deserve.'

'Oh, Adam, give yourself some credit. You're a wonderful man and worthy of Natalia. I can see how much she loves you.'

Adam scoffed. 'Don't say that.'

'Why not? Aren't you …?' His mum frowned. 'Don't you love her?'

Everything inside Adam tightened. 'Come on, Mum, it's only been two months! Love takes longer than that.'

Wendy rolled her eyes. 'That's not true, Adam Maguire, and you know it. I fell in love with your father the moment I laid eyes on him. Within two months, I was living here.'

Exhaling, Adam dropped his gaze to the ground. 'Yeah, yeah. I know.'

'But I can understand if you're not ready. Admitting you love someone can be scary.' She let that linger as she patted his arm. 'Now, I hate to change the subject, but have you got any answers out of Jordan?'

Adam leaned back against the post. Jordan had gone silent since their chat at the pub, and that was terrifying. She was never silent. What was worse, he'd called Jason Taylor only to learn that the Norwegian had left Tropic Sun in June to return to his homeland, leaving his Australian number disconnected.

How convenient.

'Nope. I still think she spiked me even though Cade found nothing suspicious on the cameras, but Georgina only has them over the tills. And Jordan refuses to talk about her pregnancy, so I don't know what to believe.'

Wendy's mouth thinned. 'Maybe I'll go. She'll damn well answer my questions.'

Adam straightened. 'No, Mum. Don't.'

'I won't.' The fire dimmed in her eyes. 'But I agree, that girl has got herself into serious trouble. Liz is worried. She says Jordan's not even speaking to her.'

'She must be in deep if she won't talk to her mother.' He wrapped his mum into a hug. 'But it'll be okay, I promise. I'm working it out.'

Yet every time he said that, he wondered if he ever would.

'Okay. So, when do I get my own wedding to get excited about?'

His heart lodged in his throat. 'Don't pester me, Mum. You know it'll never happen if you do.'

'True. But I think you answered my question anyway. Just remember that I love you, Adam.'

'I love you too.' He kissed her on the forehead. 'I better go.'

He said goodbye to the rest of the family, then headed home. Tossing his keys onto the kitchen bench, Adam glanced around the house with Rusty sitting at his feet. Natalia's fruity scent lingered and a pair of her glittery sandals sat at the door, but without her presence, the house seemed empty.

Picking up the little dog, Adam scratched his ears. 'Just you and me tonight, mate.'

Rusty licked his face. Adam winced. Damn woman had even changed the personality of his dog, teaching him to love cuddles, treats, and human attention.

Adam popped Rusty onto the floor and glanced around again. No wonder the place felt empty when it was so big. Why did one man need so much space?

He strode into the bathroom, his chest aching at the sight of Natalia's toothbrush on the bench. It looked strange, but also normal sitting on his sink. As did the two hair ties and the shampoo she'd left in his shower. Apparently, the cheap shampoo-and-conditioner-in-one that he used wasn't good enough for her hair. Or cruelty-free. Yet the fact she'd left these things lying around didn't bother him. He should get a toothbrush holder though, and a dish for the soap. It'd be better than leaving everything scattered on the bathroom bench. He'd kept a tidier house since she'd come along as he no longer left shaving cream or toothpaste in the sink. He even used the laundry basket rather than pile his clothes on the floor. They were only little changes, things he always should have done but hadn't bothered to when there was no one around to witness his laziness, but it made him feel good about himself.

And it was all because of Natalia. She was his angel in more ways than one. And dammit, he was in love with her.

The thought came out of nowhere. He braced his hand on the shower wall as his breath caught in his throat.

Shit. Thanks, Mum. Thanks a lot.

But his mother had rarely been wrong when it came to her children, as much as that irritated them. And everything about Natalia brought light into his life. He'd never have survived these past months without her. Not only had she opened his mind, but she'd helped inspire pieces for his business and because of her, he'd become the man he wanted to be. The thought of coming home to Natalia every day for the rest of his life …

Adam suppressed a smile as he rinsed his hair. He didn't mind that image. Six months ago, it would have terrified him. It still did. But that didn't make him want it any less.

Did she feel the same way? She'd stuck by him so far and his mum seemed to think so. But he wouldn't rush into telling her such a thing. Not when he still didn't have the answers he sought.

Besides, he couldn't shake the feeling that something tonight had been bothering her.

Turning off the taps, he dried and pulled on his boxers. When he found Rusty curled up on the pillows, Adam shook his head. That was Natalia's fault too as he now had to share the bed with his bloody dog. But there were worse things and he'd upgraded to a king-size for a reason, so he crawled beneath the covers and rubbed Rusty's ears.

'She'll be back, mate. Don't you worry.'

Chapter Thirty-Three

Natalia didn't mean to delay in telling Adam about the complaint, but with her full day of work and a ladies-only dinner with Ana and her mum, there was no opportunity on Tuesday. But when he stopped by the surgery on Wednesday on his way home from the farm—because he wanted to see her, kiss her, and drop off some double bananas 'for her mum'—guilt prickled her spine when she actively avoided the subject. It's not like it wasn't weighing on her mind when she'd spent the past two hours reviewing her response with Joanne, Grace, and Emma. She could easily take him aside and tell him.

But she didn't.

By that evening though, she could hardly bear it. Part of her wanted to call him and get it over with. She wanted him to hold her in his arms and tell her everything would be okay.

But neither of them could know that. While this might be another one of Jordan's lies to get what she wanted, that didn't mean she wouldn't win.

While Nadia prepared for bed, Natalia made a salad to accompany tomorrow's cashew pasta lunch. She'd send her response to her insurer tomorrow, yet she couldn't shake her fear.

Natalia bid her mother goodnight and headed into the bathroom. Flicking Surge Duck's beak, she did her best to shove thoughts about board reviews, peer assessment, and deregistration aside. There was no use in worrying. It might be her first complaint to the Health Ombudsman, but she'd get through it.

She was brushing her teeth when her phone pinged with a message from Adam.

Missing you. We haven't had a chance to talk and sorry if I'm wrong, but I have a feeling something might be bothering you. Hope you're okay. Let me know. Sweet dreams and dirty thoughts.

Natalia smiled sadly, not surprised he'd sensed her worry. But she didn't want to tell him over text when she couldn't stop him from going directly to Jordan and confronting her.

I'm fine. Just got out of the shower thinking dirty thoughts.

She switched off the light, crossed the upstairs landing, and kicked off her dachshund slippers before crawling into bed. She'd tell him. Tomorrow.

I miss you. Send your mum to Ana's tomorrow and come to my place for dinner.

Hmm, good idea. She could wear her new fuchsia babydoll. Then tell him.

Only if you make it hot, sweet, and a little spicy …

Desire stirred in her belly. She could imagine his 'don't think about it' face as he tried to suppress his arousal. Giggling, she curled up beneath her doona.

U bad girl. Wash those dirty fingers. Far too teasing. You like it …

Tired, she closed her eyes. Five minutes later …

Makes me want you.

That's the point.

Her heart full, sleep beckoned, and she was about to text him goodnight when her phone pinged.

Come downstairs.

She sat up, wide awake. He was here? Throwing back the doona, she crept out of the bedroom and checked on her mum. She seemed to be asleep, but Natalia pulled the door closed anyway before tiptoeing downstairs.

She opened the door to the chilly night air and unlocked the screen. 'What are you doing here?'

Adam grinned, far too sexy in his jeans and leather jacket as he shouldered past the screen, grabbed her hips, and covered her mouth with his. Natalia fell into it, her feet freezing as she wrapped her arms around his neck and drowned in his kiss.

He drew away, leaving her dizzy. 'Oh. That's why.'

His mouth trailed down her throat. 'I've missed you.'

Goosebumps prickled her skin. 'Me too. But you have to go.'

His mouth moved over her shoulder, pushing the sleeve of her pyjama shirt down. Desire swirled in her belly and sank to warm her thighs. 'I don't like your mum visiting.'

'Me either.' She kept her eyes open, not allowing herself to be seduced. 'But you can't come in.'

His hands ran up the outside of her shirt and cupped her breasts. 'Your mum asleep?'

She nodded.

'Don't you like to live dangerously, Natalia?' His mouth met hers and her body arched in response, her breasts aching to be kissed, body screaming to be pleasured. 'Feel the thrill? Be bad?'

'Yes.' She couldn't deny that as he laid his forehead against hers. 'But I can't do it. Makes me nervous.'

His mouth moved to her ear. 'You want me to ease those nerves?'

Her body fired. 'Yes, please.'

Chuckling, Adam stepped over the threshold, quietly closed the doors, then lifted Natalia off her feet. His mouth toyed with hers as he strode through the unit and laid her on the lounge.

'What if we get caught?' she whispered.

'Honestly? It'll be a very awkward moment.'

Natalia almost laughed. What the hell, right? He took her mouth back with his and she didn't think, only enjoyed. Adam lifted off her shirt and she unzipped his jacket. He shrugged it off and dropped it to the floor. Pulling off his shirt, Natalia welcomed the warmth of skin on skin, Adam's chest heavy on hers as he eased her long cotton pants down. Natalia relaxed, remembering to breathe quietly as he kissed down her body.

Once he was ready, her fingers brushed down his muscular back and over his fine butt as she lifted herself to him. Her blood ignited, overwhelmed by the passion that would burn forever for this man. Their quick spark had lit an eternal flame.

'Natalia ...' His lips moved back to hers as he eased into her. It was slow and romantic, the air chilly but their bodies warm. Their hands continued to caress, lips locking to drown each other's moans.

When they finished, they held each other tight. Natalia loved looking into his eyes, solid chocolate brown with no flecks of green or gold. 'I'm glad you came over.'

'I'm glad you let me in.'

'Me too ...' Her belly flipflopped. She had to tell him. She couldn't keep it in.

He was going to lose it.

As though reading her mind, he brushed his hand up her back. 'What is it, Nat?'

She bit down on her lower lip. 'Jordan made a complaint about me to the medical board.'

Adam shot upright. 'She what?'

'Shh!' She pressed her finger to his lips and pulled him back down. 'I know. I'm ... I'm terrified. She said I breached confidentiality and—'

'Fucking hell.' His jaw clenched. 'I can't believe ... Nat, I'm so sorry.'

He pressed his forehead to hers. Natalia closed her eyes, her pulse slowing. 'It's not your fault.'

'Could you lose your job?'

'I could be deregistered.'

'Surely I can make a statement.'

'My insurance company isn't sure right now. The board will review my response and we'll have to see how it goes.'

Adam sat up again. This time, Natalia followed. 'I'm going to have a word with Jordan—'

'No. Neither of us should speak to her. I've been talking to the advisor, Adam, and I have it sorted. It'll be okay.'

God, she hoped so.

Adam's eyes softened as he cupped her chin and brushed his mouth over hers. 'It will be. And I'm glad you let me in. I wish I could stay with you tonight.'

'I'd love you to, but you should go.' She let him hold her for a few minutes though, drawing comfort from his embrace. But it was late, so eventually, Natalia reached for her pyjamas while Adam pulled on his jeans. Once he'd dressed, she walked him to the door and kissed him goodbye.

'I promise, Nat ... Jordan won't get away with this.'

Natalia frowned. 'You won't do anything stupid, will you?'

'Like what?'

'I don't know ...'

He zipped up his jacket, eyes steeled. 'Me neither. But if something comes to me, I can't make any promises.'

Chapter Thirty-Four

Natalia sent her response to the insurance company, then focused on enjoying the weekend with her mum and sister as they visited the Atherton Tablelands. Adam and Liam acted as wonderful tour guides and as Natalia stood and admired the majestic Millaa Millaa Falls, she relaxed into Adam's embrace and felt her troubles ease away, if only for a moment.

By Wednesday, her insurance advisor had redrafted her response, so Natalia approved it, emailed it to the medical board, and woke on Saturday determined to put the complaint out of her mind.

Cockatoos squawked overhead as she jogged past the vibrant golf course thriving with early spring. At home, she showered, threw on her jeans and pink 'maid of honour' shirt, and had already started on breakfast with her mum when Ana arrived in her favourite white sundress.

'Happy wedding day!' Natalia wrapped her arms around her sister and squeezed.

'Thank you! Are those pancakes I smell?'

'Yep. Blackberry since purple is the official colour of the day.'

Ana laughed. 'I love it!'

After breakfast, Meg and Lucy arrived and they began the long process of beautifying themselves. Meg painted everyone's nails and Natalia administered the facials while they enjoyed cucumber smoothies. Claire Taylor had returned home from her beauty course that week, so she styled their hair into classic, low chignons, then Natalia and her mum helped Ana into her wedding gown.

'Oh, Anastasia ...' Tears filled Nadia's eyes as she clipped in Ana's veil. 'You look so beautiful.'

'I'm not going to cry.' Struggling to hold back tears, Ana studied herself in the mirror. The white lace cascaded down her long, lean body, making her the most stunning bride Natalia had ever seen. She dabbed her own eyes, but thankfully didn't have time to cry as Meg announced the photographer had arrived.

They had great fun taking both elegant and cheeky photos. Then it was time to leave.

'We'll meet you there, Ana,' Meg said after seeing Ana into the white Holden Commodore. 'Thanks for driving them, Dad.'

'No worries.'

Ron Riley slipped behind the wheel. In the passenger seat, Natalia resisted biting down on her lower lip, unsure why her belly was churning as Ron took the scenic route to the golf course. He helped Ana out of the car, then went to take his seat.

'Mum, it's fine,' Ana said as Nadia fussed with the veil and Natalia rechecked she had everything. Vows, rings, and the time—whoa, talk about fashionably late!

Grinning, Natalia turned to Ana. 'You ready?'

'Yep.' Gripping her bouquet, Ana took a deep breath, her

lovesick grin in place. 'Let's do this. Hold me tight so I don't run to him, Mama.'

Laughing, Natalia air-kissed Ana's cheek. Meg and Lucy did the same before they led the way around the hall. Natalia took a few deep breaths, but they didn't calm her racing pulse. Dammit, what was wrong with her?

Gripping her bouquet, she eyed the ceremony. Colourful guests filled the white chairs spread in rows on the lawn beneath the shady gum trees. Their musical cue played and Lucy started down the aisle. Natalia relaxed her shoulders, exhaled, and followed Meg. She smiled at the guests, grateful to see so many had come to celebrate her sister's big day.

Then her gaze strayed to the altar and locked onto Adam. He flashed her his wicked bad boy grin and her hormones spun until she felt dizzy. Damn, he looked good. His black suit stretched over his shoulders and his dark hair swept up and over his forehead oh-so-handsomely. Arriving at the altar, her knees shook. If he and Liam swapped places then—

The music changed and the guests shuffled to their feet. Natalia mentally slapped herself and turned to watch her sister.

Ana's smile lit up the gardens as she and Nadia walked down the aisle. Her cascading purple bouquet enhanced the sparkle of her dress as her veil fluttered in the light breeze. Natalia's belly tightened when Ana arrived at the altar and took Liam's hand.

'Friends, family …'

Natalia tried to focus as the minister gave a sweet and romantic service. But as she held Ana's bouquet so that she and Liam could join hands, her eyes met Adam's again and she almost dropped the flowers. Would she ever make these same promises to him? Would he want to? Despite everything, they still called their relationship casual. It's what they were both used to. But dammit, she wanted more. Whether she be a doctor or not, he a father or not, she wanted to live out her days on Shadow Creek with the man she loved.

Caught up in her fantasy, Natalia almost missed it as the minister announced Liam and Ana as husband and wife. The guests erupted into applause while Liam swept Ana into his arms and kissed her. Joy burst through Natalia and she exchanged smiles with Meg and Lucy.

Adam appeared at her side as they moved to sign the register. 'I saw you tearing up.'

'It's my sister's wedding. I'm allowed.'

Chuckling, he placed his hand on her lower back. When they sat together at the small table, she watched, mesmerised, as Adam signed his name on the marriage certificate. Her hand almost shook as she signed hers beside it.

* * *

Everyone loaded their plates and chatted happily beneath the white tulle and fairy lights. Starving after the photos, Natalia devoured her brown rice and vegetables.

'Did you enjoy your dinner?' she asked Adam as they lined up for dessert.

'Delicious. The curry was good and I think I ate too much roast beef. Probably making the most of it.'

'Do you have a weakness for buffets?'

'Doesn't everyone?'

Natalia shook her head. 'I had one serving, thank you very much.'

'I wish I had your discipline.' He loaded extra fruit onto his pavlova. 'But no, I was just taking advantage of the beef.'

'Well, I know you like it,' she said, scooping fruit salad into her bowl.

'Yeah, but soon I won't be eating it as much.'

'Why not?'

'Why do you think? When you move in, I'll probably only have meat when we go out.'

Natalia stared at him. He would *what*? Wait, *she* would what?

'Nat, you're holding up the line.' Grinning, he dumped more fruit salad into her bowl. 'Come on.'

Adam led her back to the table and took Meg's seat beside Natalia. Placing her bowl down, she cleared her throat. She didn't know which issue to address first, so went with the easier one. 'You'll stop buying meat? You don't have to, you know.' The fact he'd do that for her though made her heart waltz in time with the music.

But was he seriously thinking about moving in together?

'I know. But it was just a thought I had 'cause even though it's probably too soon, I ... I was thinking ...'

Natalia stared at him as he shrugged and ate his pavlova. Damn, she could pack her things and move into his house in an instant. But since it did seem too soon, she asked, 'It doesn't scare you?'

'Only a little. But I don't want you to be uncomfortable, so I can give you a meat-free household when the time comes. You've already shown me how it's not hard.'

'Oh, Adam.' She wrapped her arm around his waist and leaned close, struggling to find the right words. 'You are too much.'

'So, they say. But I don't mind. I can't eat differently to you every night.' He kissed her forehead as Meg arrived at his side.

'Um, that's my chair.'

Adam glanced up. 'Do you have a problem sitting next to Jack?'

Meg rolled her eyes and moved on without a word.

'Those two …' Natalia shook her head.

'They drive me nuts,' he muttered, wrapping his arm around her shoulders as he scooped up more pavlova. 'But I tell you, I'm sure going to miss merengue.'

Natalia patted his thigh. 'Don't worry. I can make vegan merengues.'

His eyebrows shot up. 'Seriously?'

'Yeah. With the water from cooked chickpeas.' She smiled wickedly. 'Don't worry, we vegans can still have all the good stuff.'

He laughed. 'Those chickpeas are amazing little buggers. But for now, I'm gonna enjoy my egg-white pavlova.'

With his mouth full, he stopped talking nonsense and left Natalia to catch her breath.

* * *

After he'd helped the guests clear the dessert buffet, Adam returned to his seat beside Liam to prepare for his speech. He'd quickly whipped it up two nights ago, annoyed with himself for the fuss he'd made. It hadn't been hard to put together a bunch of garbage about what a great man his cousin was.

Leaning back in his seat, Adam downed a mouthful of beer. The day had been a blast. He'd met Liam and his brothers for lunch at the Royal, then talked shit all afternoon. They'd thrown on their suits minutes before the photographer had arrived and he wasn't sure the ridiculous photos they'd taken would impress Ana, but they'd thrown in enough nice ones too. Then, after walking to the golf course and teasing Liam about tossing him into the lake, they'd grown serious and waited for the bride. Ana was, of course, stunning and the ceremony had been strangely moving. Although he'd almost forgotten to hand over Ana's ring, having been far too distracted by her sister.

Standing at the altar with Natalia … Adam had no words. Perhaps marriage wasn't so scary? Look at Liam! The smug bastard couldn't wipe the smile off his face. He'd managed to do it and Adam had no doubt that Liam and Ana would spend many happy years together.

But Adam … he was different to Liam. His cousin had always wanted the house, dog, and kids dream with the happily ever after. Whereas he …

His gut clenched. How was he different? He may have always considered himself and Liam opposites—Liam good while he was bad. Liam serious while he didn't care less. Liam knowing what he wanted while he hadn't a clue. But in the end, they were both men. Men in love with beautiful women. *Sisters*. And that …

Adam blew out his breath and forced the thoughts away. Weddings were not good places to be *thinking*.

He downed the last of his beer and stood. 'Good evening, everyone.' It took a moment for the room to quieten. 'It's great to be here tonight to celebrate the wedding of the lovely Anastasia to my best mate and cousin Liam. I'm sure this'll be my first and last crack at the best man gig 'cause I doubt my brothers here will marry any time soon, so I'm going to go out with a bang.'

Jack rolled his eyes and Adam resisted a grin as he glanced around the room. 'Now, there was once a time before I knew

Liam. For the first forty-one days of my life, the world completely revolved around me, until Aunty Deb brought Liam home and he stole my thunder.' Liam chuckled. 'But obviously, I got over that and we've shared our whole lives together. Not just as cousins, but as best mates. I'll never forget the day he told me he'd proposed. I told him to tell Ana he'd changed his mind.'

Liam shook his head while Ana laughed. Yep, he'd said it. Jokingly, of course, because after having rescued Ana only the day before, Adam couldn't have been happier for them. And had wondered why he wasn't seeking the same thing.

He avoided Natalia's gaze and turned back to the guests, telling his humorous version of their love story with anecdotes about Liam thrown in. 'And today we get to celebrate with them as they've joined their lives together. So, congratulations, Ana. Good luck, Liam. We wish you all the best.'

The guests applauded and Liam stood, his eyes shining as he wrapped Adam in a hug.

'Thanks, mate.'

'You're one lucky bastard.'

They sat and the speeches continued. Natalia said a few words, followed by Nadia then Cliff and Deborah. Liam stood to close, then asked Ana for their first dance and led her onto the dance floor.

Adam watched, sipping his water as Liam turned his bride around in a slow waltz. His foot tapped, but he gave the newlyweds ample time before standing and moving to Natalia's side.

'Would you like to dance, maid of honour?'

'Of course, best man.' Grinning, she took his hand and he led her to the dance floor. 'I didn't know Liam could waltz.'

He turned to her. 'And that's surprising?'

'A little. I haven't waltzed since my ballroom days and long to … anyway. I guess we're not supposed to outshine them.'

'No, I guess not.' He pressed his hand to her back, pulled her close, and took her into a strong waltz hold. Natalia's eyes widened. 'But you know me. I like to break the rules.'

Stepping into the next verse, Adam led her into a gentle waltz of their own. Natalia's gaze remained locked to his, until finally, she swallowed and blinked her long dark lashes. 'You can dance.'

He grinned. 'Of course. It was one school activity I'd actually show up for. I could hold girls and not get into trouble.'

Laughing, her body melted against his while her arms maintained her strong dance hold. 'Oh, Adam. And here I thought you couldn't continue to surprise me.'

Grinning, he turned her out, then drew her close. Turned her. They fell into the steps. He'd listened to this song a million times last night in preparation for sweeping her off her feet and he loved it when a plan paid off. She was clearly impressed as her eyes never left his.

'You look beautiful in purple.'

Her smile broadened. 'You look sexy in your suit.'

'You'd look beautiful in white too.'

Her eyebrows shot up. 'What?'

'Shh …' He brushed his lips against hers. 'We're dancing.'

Chapter Thirty-Five

Natalia's mind whirled. Adam could *waltz*. He was a banana farmer who rode horses and motorcycles, yet he held her like any of her former dance partners as he twirled her around the hall.

Had he just said she'd look beautiful in white?

No, he was teasing her. He was hardly sure he wanted to live with her and that would be a big enough step for them both.

'Look at all these people,' he mused. 'See? I told you country people would dance.'

Natalia nodded. Jack had Meg in his arms and Deborah and Cliff were swaying slowly. Even her mum had been asked to dance by Ed, a supervisor on Shadow Creek. Nearly everyone she knew was there—the Taylor family, Grace and Emma, the Brennans, all the staff from The Bent Banana and the school. Natalia frowned when she spotted Elanora dancing with the physical education teacher while her husband talked to some men at their table.

'I doubt Jack will dance with anyone else. And Mum and Dad won't stop until dawn.' Adam frowned. 'Why's Cade dancing with Lily?'

Natalia laughed as she watched the short, pretty Maguire dance with the far-too-tall police officer. She'd liked Lily and the Maguires were whole again by her arrival this week. Her brothers clearly adored her even though they teased her constantly, but Lily was impressive and could hold her own against three united men.

'Why can't he? She was dancing with Darren and Michael earlier.'

'Michael's her brother.'

'Oh, look at you. Is your sister allowed to dance with anyone?'

'Hmm …' His mouth thinned.

'I'd be more worried about what Lily gets up to back at uni, not that she's dancing with your best mate.'

'Shit, don't tell me that. She studies at uni and does nothing else.'

Natalia tightened her arms around his neck. 'I'm sure she does. But it is nice to see so many people here.'

'Yeah, small towns.' He glanced around the room again. 'We all know each other and Liam's …'

Natalia almost stumbled as Adam's steps slowed, his gaze fixed behind her head. His eyes darkened and grip tightened around her waist.

She glanced over her shoulder. 'What—'

'Nothing. It's …' He cleared his throat, but Natalia couldn't see what had caught his attention.

Then his hand dropped from his waist and he stopped dancing. His face paled.

'Adam? What is it?'

'Claire.'

'Claire?' She spun to locate the hairdresser, spotting her across the room in her pink bodycon dress.

'Yeah. I mean—' he shook his head '—not like ... fuck.'

Adam dragged Natalia off the dance floor. She blinked, confused as they intercepted Claire Taylor on her way back from the bar.

'Claire—'

'Hey, Adam! Oh my God, I've been meaning to tell you, I saw your things in the shop and just *had* to buy that round coffee table.'

A smile broke through Natalia's confusion. 'The jarrah? It's gorgeous, isn't it?'

'Absolutely.' Grinning, Claire gave Adam a friendly punch in the shoulder. 'You should be proud of yourself.'

Adam cleared his throat. 'I am. But Claire, what ... Were you with me on my birthday?'

Natalia stilled as Claire's carefree laugh drowned out the music. 'Of course, Adam. Why? Don't you remember?'

* * *

Adam stared at Claire. He couldn't think. Couldn't move. When his eyes had locked onto her moments ago, something strange had flickered inside his head. Images of her smile and laugh as they'd danced around the park—

Natalia's gasp snapped him back to the present. She grabbed Claire's hand. 'Quick. Let's get outside.'

Adam didn't argue as Natalia ushered them onto the verandah.

'Okay, what's this about?' Claire asked.

Adam exhaled. 'Look, I know you've been away and

probably haven't heard what's going on, but I need you to tell me what happened that night.'

'Oh.' She blinked. 'All right. I mean, I know you were drunk, but—'

'I think someone spiked me. And because I don't remember, Jordan's saying I'm the father of her kid.'

Claire blinked again. 'Wait. You're not?'

'I don't know, you tell me!'

Natalia placed her hand on his heaving chest, her gaze on Claire. 'No one seems to remember being with Adam in the park that night, and from what Jordan's saying, we're worried that she may have either spiked him or taken advantage of Adam's intoxicated state to—'

'Holy shit!' Claire's eyes widened. 'That bitch! And here I thought it was true!'

His breath caught. 'It's not?'

Claire recoiled. 'God no!'

The tension he'd been carrying for months evaporated as Adam pulled Natalia to his side.

'I mean …' Claire reached for his arm. 'I don't think it's true. And I'm sorry, I know you were drunk, but I'd never considered that it was more than that. I was tipsy myself.'

'You didn't suspect drink spiking?' Natalia asked.

Claire shook her head. 'I remember that night clearly. I was out with a few workers from Dad's farm and you were already quite pissed when you joined us at Smithy's. When they closed, we went back to the Royal. You and I were hitting it off, but then Jordan tried to interfere.'

'So, she was there?' Not that he'd doubted it.

'She was working. Most of my friends left when the Royal closed, but Sven and I went with you to the park because …' Claire's eyes widened. 'Oh my God.'

Adam's heart leapt. 'What?'

'It makes perfect sense ...'

Natalia stamped her foot. 'Claire!'

'Sorry.' She shook her head. 'Yes, we were in the park and you and I were having a pretty good time. Part of me had hoped for more but—' she frowned '—I guess that's when you started acting stranger. I just thought you were drunker because you'd got hold of a bottle of rum. That's when Jordan forced her way in, and I swear she only kissed you to piss me off. But you kept pushing her away and eventually, she stormed off.' Claire placed her hand on his shoulder, her eyes serious. 'Jordan did not come back, Adam.'

'Are you sure?'

'Positive.' Claire sipped her wine. 'So maybe the rum could have been spiked because I didn't drink any of that.'

'I'd suspect the rum,' Natalia agreed.

'And Jordan gave it to you as we left the Royal,' Claire added. 'She didn't have any and Sven stuck with vodka. I let him go crash at my place, but I stayed because I was having too much fun watching the unimaginable.'

Adam frowned as she broke into a grin. 'What do you mean?'

'Well, you won't like this, but you were partying it up pretty hard with Paul Kelly.'

Adam jerked back. 'I was *what*?'

'Oh my God ...' Natalia breathed.

'Oh, come on! Even though the rest of the night is disturbing, *that* part is kind of funny.'

'You left Adam in the park, drunk, with his sworn enemy?'

'I didn't leave him and you guys were far too drunk to remember you hated each other. At one point, you were singing "Duncan". You know? "Duncan" by Slim Dusty?'

Adam exhaled, his gut roiling as the altered words flashed through his head. *I love to have a beer with Paul* … 'Fuck me.'

'So, you see why I couldn't leave, right? You even hugged! It was the funniest thing. But eventually, you guys passed out and I stayed 'cause I couldn't be bothered going home. I tried waking you in the morning, but you were both out of it, so once I got a grunt out of you, I figured you were both okay and went to work.'

Natalia slowly shook her head. 'So, it really was a lie.'

Adam's teeth clenched as it all came rushing back. The unknown mate he remembered singing and drinking with hadn't been a mate at all. 'Blow me down …'

Claire smiled softly. 'I'm glad I could help. But I'm sorry I didn't realise the rum had been spiked. If I had—'

'Never mind that now.' Adam pulled Claire into a hug and squeezed her tight. 'You don't know what you've done. Thank you.'

She had been the faceless woman. He'd kissed Claire that night. Jordan hadn't taken advantage of him. He wasn't going to be a father.

Thank fuck!

'No worries. I felt bad for you when I thought you'd knocked up Jordan, but honestly …' She pulled away and grinned at him and Natalia. 'I'm so happy for you both. Is there anything else you need to know or—'

Natalia took her hand. 'No. Thank you, Claire.'

'Good. In that case, I'm gonna find another guy to dance with and leave you to it.'

Claire sashayed back inside. Adam turned to Natalia and pulled her close. 'Can you believe it?'

Her eyes glistened. 'I'm so happy that it's a lie.'

'I meant partying with Kelly.'

Natalia choked back a laugh. 'I know. But that's not what you need to think about, Adam. The important thing is, Jordan didn't assault you.'

'She spiked me though.'

'Yeah ...' Natalia exhaled. 'We'll figure out how to prove that, but at least you don't have to worry about her having your baby.'

Adam didn't have the words to describe what a relief that was. Tightening his grip around the beautiful woman in his arms, his chest swelled until it hurt. 'You, Natalia, are amazing.'

'I haven't done anything.'

'Yes, you have. You've stood by me. You believed me even when other people didn't. You kept me sane.'

'I couldn't stand by and let someone use you.' Her hands slipped down his shoulders to rest on his chest, her eyes sparkling. 'To let her think it was okay to take advantage of you, or for you to process that knowledge alone.'

'I know.' He swallowed, but the words longed to be free. 'Which is why you're the most incredible woman I've ever met. You're kind, compassionate, sexy as hell. And I love you.'

She stiffened in his arms, but the brightness remained in her eyes. 'You do?'

'I do. It sounds cliché to say at a wedding, but I've been thinking it for a few days now. You are the best thing that's ever happened to me.'

Rising onto her toes, she pressed her body to his as her mouth curved in the most beautiful smile he'd ever seen. 'And you're the best thing that's happened to me. Moving to Elizadale scared me, Adam, because I honestly wasn't sure how I'd cope in a small town. But now, I never want to leave because I love you too.'

The words were music to his ears. Relief and hope rose through him as he kissed her with a passion unlike any he'd ever known. This woman. His angel. How had he got so lucky?

Later that night, they lay side by side, his arm around her as they stared up at the dark ceiling. The words escaped before he could stop them. 'You want to move in with me?'

Squealing, Natalia rolled and flopped onto his chest, her blonde hair tumbling over their faces. 'Are you serious?'

'Sure, why not?' Yeah, it was impulsive, but what was stopping them? 'I love you, Nat, and I want to share my home with you. It'll make things a lot easier and I think Rusty will like it too.'

'Oh, I must be nuts,' she muttered, her eyes glittering as her mouth met his in a hot kiss. 'Yes. I'll move in. Tomorrow?'

'First thing. There's already space in the wardrobe.'

'There is?'

'No big deal. It's been empty forever.'

She laughed as he flipped their positions. 'Well, I'll happily fill it with all my pretty clothes.'

'Clothes you love to wear.'

'Clothes I'm confident to wear thanks to you.'

'You've always had that confidence, Natalia, but I'm glad you found it again and that you're happy. I'll live to make you happy.'

She tightened her arms around his neck. 'I'll be happy as long as I'm with you.'

Chapter Thirty-Six

Natalia squeezed her mum tight as they stood outside Jackson Villas. 'I hope we see you again soon.'

'You can count on it. I'm so pleased you're moving in with Adam. But what's happening with this place?'

'I'm not sure.'

'Do you think I could take it?'

Natalia blinked. 'What?'

Nadia laughed. 'I can't stay in Sydney while you and Ana are here raising my grandbabies without me.'

'Well, I can't speak for Ana, but there's no need to rush as I'm not having babies anytime soon!'

'Either way, you and Ana are all I have. So, if you don't mind …'

'Not at all!'

When Ana and Liam arrived, Nadia shared her news and Ana squealed.

'Oh, Mama! You'll love living here!'

Grinning, Natalia waved them off as they left for the airport, then decided she better get packing. But she didn't even make it off the driveway when Adam returned from wherever it was he'd needed to go so secretively. He jumped out of the ute, raced towards her, and lifted her off her feet.

'Righto, I got all I need.'

'You can't just take me! I need my stuff!'

He sighed heavily. 'If you insist. Good thing I got a ute. Let's get you out of here.'

It didn't take them long as Adam upended drawers into boxes with little finesse. Alone in the bathroom, Natalia packed up the cupboards, then picked up her rubber duck. Holding him in both hands, her throat clogged as she stroked his yellow head. 'This is it, Surge. This time, we're going to our forever home.'

Joy erupted through her as she placed Surge on top of the basket and carried it downstairs. Then she tackled the rest of the packing with the same vigour as Adam until the unit was void of her belongings. She shoved the last of her things onto the backseat of her Rav-4, climbed behind the wheel, and followed Adam out of the driveway. After the detour to pick up Steph and Louis, they headed home to Shadow Creek.

Parking outside the picturesque house overlooking the water, Natalia couldn't shake the smile from her face. Living here wasn't so scary. With acres of bush surrounding her, their own creek, and no neighbours for miles, she'd spend her life in pure bliss with her man. Her strong, respectful, and gorgeous man.

Her smile widened as Adam led Steph and Louis into the backyard, then strolled over and wrapped his arms around her waist. 'Welcome home, Natalia.'

'I can't believe it.'

'Neither can I, but I've never been happier. And I've got a present for you.' He led her into the shed and picked up a potted plant, his eyes gleaming as he offered it to her. 'Your frangipani tree.'

Natalia's hand flew to her mouth. 'Really?'

'Yeah. Went and grabbed it this morning after pleading with the nursery owners to open for me. We needed to do something to celebrate you moving in.'

Tears prickled her eyes as she wrapped her arms around his neck, squishing the plant between them. 'You are the most thoughtful man I've ever met, Adam Maguire.' She kissed him. 'And I love you.'

He beamed. 'I love you too. So, decide where you want it. I'll grab the shovel.'

* * *

Elanora sat in Natalia's office, her eyes bright as she said, 'I have an appointment at the fertility clinic next week.'

Natalia grinned. 'That's wonderful. Has Shane finally come around?'

'He said he'd come and it *seems* like he's accepted that it's the next step for us. But then ... I don't know.' Elanora sighed. 'Over the past few days, he's been distant again. He's supposed to be here now, but I don't know what's keeping him.'

Natalia had wondered as they'd both been scheduled into the appointment book. 'Maybe he got held up at work?'

'Maybe. I've messaged him, but he hasn't answered. I made this appointment mainly for Shane because the clinic wants him to get blood tests done, which he got quite defensive about. I assured him that it's standard procedure, but he insists there's nothing wrong with him.'

Natalia nodded slowly. 'And there may not be, but I'm glad he's coming around.'

'Well, he was until last week when—' Elanora frowned at the same moment Natalia heard raised voices in the waiting room.

'No, I can't see her. Can you call Joanne in?'

Natalia sighed. Great. Another person who refused to see her. When would this stop?

'Paul, take me to Mareeba. We'll go and—'

A cry of pain echoed through the building and Natalia and Elanora leapt to their feet.

'That sounds like Jordan,' Elanora said, her eyes widening as Natalia crept towards the door and opened it a crack.

'I'll speak with Nat.' Footsteps approached and Natalia stepped back as Grace slipped inside the consult room and closed the door behind her.

Natalia twisted her fingers together. 'Is she …?'

'Abdominal pain. Not sure if it's serious. I've called Emma, but she'll need a doctor.'

Nodding slowly, Natalia let out a deep breath. What was she going to do? Of all the days for Joanne and David to take advantage of the school holidays to go strawberry picking in Atherton, Jordan Kelly needed urgent care.

Natalia ran her fingers through her hair. She wasn't supposed to talk to Jordan while the complaint was being assessed, but what choice did she have?

'Do you want—'

'It's fine.' Natalia turned to Grace. 'I can see her.'

Conflict of interest be damned. This was a small town, she was a doctor, and despite what Jordan Kelly had put her through, the woman needed medical attention.

Natalia turned to Elanora. 'If you don't mind waiting—'

'Not at all. I'll just check on her.'

Natalia didn't stop her as Grace opened the door and Elanora hurried over to her sister. Then with an encouraging smile from the nurse, Natalia strode into the waiting room. Harrison paced while Paul and Elanora sat on either side of Jordan, who hunched over in a chair.

She glanced up as Natalia approached, her eyes wide. 'Don't touch me. I don't want to see you.'

Paul's jaw clenched. 'Jordan, come on.'

'No! She'll probably help me miscarry!'

'No, she won't,' Harrison said.

Taking a deep breath, Natalia crouched in front of Jordan and met the woman's terrified eyes. 'I hear you, Jordan. Emma is on her way and she will check out your baby. But you are in pain and something may be wrong. You have come here for care, which you can refuse, but I am a doctor and I can help you if you let me. That is my only job right now. So, will you come with me or do you want to go to Mareeba?'

Natalia didn't break their gaze. She didn't want to do this and if she were anywhere else, she wouldn't have to. But this was what she'd signed up for. She was it. And she'd take care of Jordan even if it killed her.

'Jordan, go with the doctor,' Elanora said kindly.

Jordan's eyes closed and shoulders slumped. 'Fine.'

Natalia shot to her feet and stepped out of the way as Nikki helped Jordan into a wheelchair. She entered the ward where Grace was setting everything up.

'Good job, Nat.'

Natalia's heart pounded as she washed her hands. 'No one is to leave me alone with her. How far away is Emma?'

'A few minutes, I'd say.'

The midwife was there by the time Nikki and Grace had

Jordan in the bed. Natalia wrapped the blood pressure cuff around Jordan's arm, asked her questions, and made notes in the chart. She left Emma to do most of the examination, grateful more than she could say for her help.

'Is my baby okay?' Jordan asked as they observed the small ultrasound. It wasn't great for pictures, but the heartbeat echoed steady and strong.

'The baby seems happy and healthy,' Emma said with a smile.

Jordan exhaled and fell back against the pillow. 'Good.'

The genuine relief in Jordan's tone almost made Natalia smile. 'Based on your examination, I think you may be experiencing some stretching of the uterus or early Braxton Hicks contractions. There's nothing to indicate that either of you are in any danger.'

'You must think I'm pretty stupid,' she muttered.

'Not at all. You don't know what these things are until you experience them.'

'I guess.' Sheepishly, she met Natalia's gaze. 'Thank you though. For not turning me away.'

Natalia interlocked her fingers below the bed where Jordan wouldn't see. 'I could never do that. I take care of people, no matter what.'

'Yeah.' Then as quickly as it had appeared, the gratitude vanished from Jordan's eyes. 'So, can I go now?'

'In a minute.' Natalia's spine steeled as she gazed down the small ward to where Emma was making a show of being busy. Adam might have wanted to talk to Jordan, and while knowing that he was out of Jordan's clutches for good was enough for Natalia, as a medical professional, she couldn't pass up the chance to help. Jordan may not deserve her compassion after the misery she'd caused, but that didn't matter. This was her job.

Natalia cleared her throat and forced a soft smile to her face. 'Jordan, I'm worried about you. I believe that the story you're telling people about your baby's conception may get you into trouble.'

Jordan frowned. 'How? I didn't do anything wrong.'

'No?'

'I know you don't want to hear it, Natalia, but I screwed Adam that night.'

'After you spiked him?'

'Look, if he took anything, that's on him. But we—'

Natalia's hands clenched. 'Jordan, you know he didn't consciously take anything. And I'm concerned that if you had sex with Adam while he was that intoxicated, then you risk facing sexual assault charges.'

Jordan snorted. 'What? You think I—'

'Raped him. Yes.'

'That's ridiculous! He was drunk. We had sex. It wasn't the first time.'

I took all of Natalia's strength to remain calm. 'You've already stated you were quite sober.'

'I'd had a couple of drinks. And it was just sex. You … you can't …'

Natalia raised her eyebrows. 'Can't what? Rape a man?'

Jordan opened her mouth, but no words came out as she ran her hands down her rounded belly.

The tension in Natalia's shoulders eased. 'Jordan, rape isn't always a violent act. The definition is "being made to penetrate". Now, I'm sure you've heard of consent and a person needs to be in a sound mind to give that.'

'Yeah, but it's Adam. He always wants it. And you know men, they—'

Natalia's fingernails dug into her palms. 'Jordan, you and I both know that men can have erections they don't control. Ones they don't plan to use. But that doesn't mean you jump on and take a ride!'

The colour drained from Jordan's face. Natalia gave her a moment, then took a steadying breath. 'So, my concern is this: did you rape Adam or—'

'Fine!' Jordan threw her hands in the air. 'We didn't have sex!'

Natalia barely resisted her smile. 'I know that. So why lie?'

'Because I had no other choice! I wanted to tell the real father, but then everyone would hate me. Adam was the perfect solution until you came and fucked it up.'

'So, you wanted revenge by lying about me to the Health Ombudsman? Because you and I both know I didn't tell Adam anything. He came to you that day with no knowledge of your pregnancy and we can prove it.'

Jordan's lips curled into a snarl. 'I guess it won't do much. You won't leave town even if you do get deregistered.'

Natalia raised her eyebrows. 'Is that what you want? Because, no, I won't. I'll stay in Elizadale whether I'm a doctor or not.'

Jordan hopped off the other side of the bed. 'Fine, I'll retract the complaint too. Then will you and Adam leave me the fuck alone?'

Natalia unclenched her hands. 'I would be very grateful.'

'Good. Anything else?'

'Did you spike him?'

'Oh, for fuck's sake.' Jordan ran her hands through her hair and pulled. 'Why can't anyone accept he was *just drunk*?'

'Jordan.' It took all of Natalia's effort to remain calm. 'We know you gave him the bottle of rum. Adam remembers most of the night until meeting up with you and a person is far more likely to suffer amnesia by mixing substances than on alcohol alone.'

'And what? That's your "medical" opinion?'

'Yes.' Her voice rose a notch. 'It is.'

'Then Adam's lucky he has someone so smart like you.' Jordan shoved her feet into her shoes. 'But you can't prove anything, so I'm leaving.'

Since she had no medical reason to hold Jordan there, Natalia didn't stop her as Jordan strode across the room and yanked open the door. Natalia followed, watching as the Kellys rose from their chairs. Strangely enough, Elanora reached for Jordan first.

'Are you okay?' she asked. 'The baby?'

'I'm fine. So's the baby.'

'Good. I'm glad to hear that.' Elanora glanced at Paul and Harrison. 'Will you two take Jordan home? Shane and I have an appointment, but he's not here yet.'

'Sure,' Paul said. 'Everything okay with you two?'

'We'll be fine,' Elanora said before glancing back at Jordan. 'Can I come and see you later? To chat and see if there's anything you need?'

'Ah …' Jordan glanced uncertainly between her siblings. 'If you must.'

Natalia smiled softly, proud to see Elanora was trying. It wouldn't be easy for her. With any luck, she too would soon be on her way to becoming a mother and Natalia was keen to continue that conversation. But since it was almost five o'clock and Shane was nowhere to be seen, Natalia began to doubt that he shared his wife's commitment to their family.

* * *

Hope filled Adam's heart as he drove to the surgery to pick up Natalia. He might not have all the answers, but he had the ones that mattered. He would talk to Jordan this week, tell her he knew the truth, and give her one more chance to confess to the spiking. Since he couldn't prove it, he doubted she'd suffer any consequences, but that was a problem he'd discuss with Cade later. For now, all he wanted was to pick Natalia up and take her home.

Adam strode into the surgery with a spring in his step. But instead of finding the waiting room empty and staff getting ready to leave like usual, he was met by the hard glowers of both Kelly brothers.

'Now you show up,' Paul sneered. 'Great timing, as usual.'

'Do you know what you've done to my sister?' Harrison yelled, gesturing towards Jordan.

Adam glanced past the Kellys to where Natalia stood in the doorway of the treatment room. What had he walked into? But as she smiled softly and nodded, strangely enough, he understood what that meant. Somehow, she'd begun to set things right. So, Adam placed his hands on his hips and glanced at Paul, Harrison, and Jordan. He almost blinked at the sight of Elanora standing behind them. 'I've done nothing.'

'Damn right! You've done nothing to help her! Or care! Some man you are when you can't own your fuckups and leave a woman to fear for your kid's life alone!'

'Harry—' Jordan said, but Harrison paid her no attention.

'You say you don't remember that night, but you only have yourself to blame,' Paul said, advancing on Adam. 'Next time, you might think about how your actions can hurt other people.'

Adam stood his ground. 'Thanks to a friend, I *do* know what happened that night. Just like you do, Paul. So, let's put an end to this once and for all. I am not the father of Jordan's baby.'

Paul rolled his eyes. 'Bullshit, you were—'

'He's right.'

Paul spun towards Jordan. 'What?'

'He's not the father?' Harrison asked. 'But you said—'

Jordan threw up her hands. 'I know. I wanted Adam to be the father, but he knows we didn't have sex that night and now it's all fucked up. So, I'm going before—'

Paul held up his hand. 'You lied to us?'

'Jordan!' Harrison cried.

'It was better than telling you the truth! Now, I really must—'

'I think you owe us an explanation,' Adam interrupted. 'Or me, at least. Why did you try to trick me? You put me through hell, Jordan! And for what?'

Jordan crossed her arms over her chest. 'You'd have accepted the story if that city bitch hadn't showed up.'

Adam's eyes narrowed. 'You don't think I would have questioned it? That I wouldn't have thought you'd taken advantage of my intoxicated state?'

She held up her hand. 'I've already had the third degree from your stupid girlfriend. I don't need it from you too. You only have yourself to blame after you decided you could ditch me like that.'

Adam's jaw clenched. 'Is that why you spiked me?'

'Like I'd need to spike you.'

'You said it yourself, Jordan. I kept turning you away, so

you needed to do something to get me back. But from what I heard, I still said no even when I was doped up. So, you tried to use me to cover your arse with this pregnancy! Why?'

Adam's heart pounded, but he held her gaze. He wanted answers and this time, he was going to get them.

'And why did you lie to us?' Harrison asked as Paul sank into a chair.

'Because! It was the only way I wouldn't hurt you! Not that it fucking matters now. Adam went and lost interest in me and then—'

'So, you spiked me with fuck-knows-what?'

'I didn't spike—'

'Diazepam,' Paul said, and everyone stopped shouting. Jordan stilled. Harrison stared at his brother while Adam exchanged glances with Natalia. Her eyes widened.

After what felt like an age, Paul rose to his feet, his steeled eyes on Jordan. 'You laced that rum with diazepam,' he said, anger lacing his tone.

All Adam could do was blink.

Jordan opened her mouth. Closed it. Cleared her throat. 'You can't prove that.'

'Yes, I can,' Paul said, approaching his sister. 'I woke that morning sick as all shit and left Maguire there thinking he deserved to sleep off whatever crap he liked to party with. I went to the doctor and was bloody furious to find I had diazepam in my system, but I figured it was my fault for sharing drinks. But Adam wasn't to blame, Jordan. You spiked him! Spiked both of us! Maybe Claire and Sven too!'

Jordan's mouth twisted. 'I didn't mean to spike you!'

'For fuck's sake, Jordan!' Paul roared. 'Don't you see your actions have consequences? Now tell us! Who is the father?'

'None of your business!'

'Jordan,' Elanora said calmly, moving towards her sister. 'We respect your privacy, of course, but I think you owe Adam and Paul an apology for spiking that rum.'

'Where'd you get it? The diazepam?' Natalia asked, frowning.

'Oh, please.' Jordan rolled her eyes. 'Not all doctors are as perfect as you. Pay them a few favours and they'll prescribe anything.'

'Jordan!' Harrison cried. Elanora gasped and Adam's eyebrows shot up. Natalia didn't look surprised.

Paul cleared his throat and turned to Adam. 'I don't know what you want to do, but can you give me some time before you take the spiking further? I'll need to think about this.'

Adam nodded. He could hardly believe what he'd just witnessed, but he knew one thing. 'You're the one with the proof, so just let me know what you decide to do.'

Paul paused. 'Thanks.'

Jordan snorted and crossed her arms. 'You won't press charges.'

Paul slowly lifted his finger her way, his eyes heating. 'Don't you test me.'

'We're all witnesses, Jordan,' Harrison said. 'You committed a crime—'

'Several, I'd say,' Natalia interjected.

'—but I still want to know why you lied to us.'

Paul nodded. 'Tell us now or later, but I want to know who the father is.'

The doors opened behind Adam and Shane Campbell strode in. 'El! Good, you're still here. We need to ...' His gaze drifted from Kelly to Kelly. 'What's going on?'

Elanora moved towards him. 'Where have you been? Our appointment was an hour ago!'

'Aren't doctor's always late?'

'No, but it's okay because Natalia had to take care of Jordan. She was in pain.'

'Shit.' Shane was at Jordan's side in a few quick strides. 'Are you okay? The baby?'

Jordan's eyes lowered. 'We're fine. I just want to go home.'

Shane glared at Paul. 'Then take her. Or I will. El?'

She nodded. 'Yeah. Maybe we can all go because Jordan needs to explain why she lied to us.'

'About what?'

'Adam's not the father,' Elanora told Shane before turning to Jordan. 'But it'll be okay, Jordan. If you tell us, we'll help you. Right?'

Elanora glanced at her brothers, so she didn't see the look on her husband's face as he asked Jordan, 'You were going to tell them?'

Adam's eyebrows shot up. Paul stepped forward.

Jordan scoffed. 'No …'

Shane spun to Elanora. 'Maybe we should go—'

'You're not going anywhere,' Paul growled.

Everyone stilled. Elanora glanced at her husband. Then she turned to Jordan.

And screamed.

Chapter Thirty-Seven

Natalia moved quickly as Elanora stumbled backwards with her hands over her mouth.

'No. No, no …'

Shane reached for her. 'El—'

'Don't touch me!'

'Don't fucking touch her!' Paul roared.

Harrison grabbed Jordan by the shoulder. 'Is this true?'

Natalia helped Elanora into a chair as she covered her face and cried heart-wrenching sobs. Sitting beside her, Natalia held Elanora tight while she watched the fallout.

Paul grabbed Shane by the collar. 'Did you cheat on Elanora?'

'It wasn't like—'

Paul knocked him to the floor with one punch. Jordan shrieked. 'Shane!'

Natalia bit down on her lower lip, heart racing as Elanora's cries echoed through the building. Oh God, what was she going to do?

'How could you, Jordan?' Harrison yelled.

Jordan reached for Shane and helped him up. 'Oh please. She brought it upon herself.'

Paul's jaw hardened. 'Are you serious? You're blaming El?'

Shane wiped his bloodied mouth. 'If she didn't want a fucking kid so much—'

'Don't make me knock you back on that floor!'

Elanora shook, her cries intensifying, and Natalia drew her close, holding her more like a friend than a doctor as she struggled to hold back tears herself.

'Fuck off, Paul. El—'

Natalia narrowed her eyes, shotting daggers at Shane as he stepped towards them. 'I think you should leave.'

Paul grabbed him again. 'Listen to the doctor and get the fuck out of here. Else she'll be stitching up your bloody face.'

'Fine.' Shane shook himself from Paul's grip. 'El, I'm … I'll be at home.'

He moved towards the door. Elanora shot out of Natalia's grasp and onto her feet.

'You better not be there when I get back!'

'El—'

'You heard her.' Paul's long strides pounded over the tiles and Shane scrambled out of the building. 'Don't make me come around with my shotgun! And you!' He spun to face Jordan. 'What were you thinking?'

Jordan shrugged, her arms crossed over her belly. 'He was lonely and wanted to have some fun. She was making sex boring. It just happened.'

Elanora sank back into her chair and Natalia took the tearful woman back into her embrace, glaring at Jordan. How could she be so callous? Was Jordan even sorry?

Elanora dropped her face to Natalia's shoulder. 'Get her out of here.'

Harrison took Jordan by the elbow. 'I think you've made a big enough scene.'

'Oh, don't worry. I'm going.' She shook free of Harrison's grip and strode towards the door, but not before stopping in front of Adam. 'Happy now? You're off the hook.'

'Wouldn't say I'm happy,' he said, slipping his hands into his pockets.

Jordan snorted. 'Whatever. None of this would have happened if you'd believed my story.'

Adam merely raised his eyebrows. 'Bye, Jordan.'

She left. No one stopped her.

* * *

It took all of Natalia's strength not to cry as she sat in the consult room and held Elanora's hand while she wept. The woman was inconsolable, so Natalia simply sat there, handing Elanora tissues while offering useless words of reassurance. There was nothing she could say that would be remotely comforting when Elanora's whole world had been shattered.

Natalia shook her head. Why were some men such bastards? She'd met many people since moving to Elizadale and had consulted with many patients, but she'd connected with Elanora. She was a friend. Natalia had believed in her, had longed to help, and now …

Her husband was having a baby with her sister.

Natalia wanted to punch Shane Campbell in the face.

She probably would have if Paul hadn't beaten her to it.

'I'm so sorry, Elanora,' Natalia said for the umpteenth time, brushing the damp hair from Elanora's face. 'Are you sure you don't want me to call anyone?'

She knew Paul had stayed in the waiting room. He'd agreed

to call their mother when Harrison had gone to 'help' Shane move out of the house.

Elanora was almost hyperventilating. 'I ... I can't ... what the hell, Natalia?' She glanced up over her fist full of tissues. 'I don't understand. I know she's always hated me, but why? I never did *anything* to her!'

'People like Jordan are complicated.' It was the best explanation Natalia could come up with because even though she'd done her rounds in psychiatry and wanted to be a good counsellor, she didn't think she would ever understand people like Jordan.

'She's always wanted everything that's mine. My clothes. My horse. Now, she has my husband and my ...' Elanora's face crumpled back into the tissues. 'A baby! They're having a baby!'

Natalia's heart clenched and she drew Elanora into a tight hug. Forget being professional. This was a small town. Her town. Her friend. She wasn't going anywhere and would be there for these people in any way she could. There was more to working in rural practice than simply being a doctor.

'I don't know what to say, but I'm here for you, El. I'll talk with you any time.'

Elanora managed to nod and continued to cry. It wasn't for another hour that she was strong enough to leave Natalia's office. Night had fallen and the staff had long gone home, but Adam was still there, as were Paul and Liz Kelly.

'Thank you, Natalia.' Elanora squeezed her hand and smiled softly. 'For everything.'

'Any time. Call me, okay?'

'I will,' she said. Elanora left with Liz and Paul, and Natalia locked the door behind them.

It wasn't until she turned to Adam that her shoulders slumped. He opened his arms and her tears broke free.

* * *

Adam held Natalia tight as she wept against his chest. He couldn't believe what had gone down tonight, but at least they had their answers. Change had been possible. He had a woman he loved, was now a *de facto*, and for the first time in his life, Adam felt like he could do anything.

Although Natalia crying would always wound him. 'It's all right, Nat.'

She drew back and wiped away her tears. 'I didn't think it'd be so hard. I don't become emotionally attached to patients, Adam. It's not professional. But it's impossible here. I know too much. Everyone's secrets, hopes, and dreams. And I became attached to Elanora. I wanted her to have a baby as much as she did.' She shook her head. 'I shouldn't even be telling you this.'

'It's okay. Everyone knows that Elanora wants a baby. But you did a great job with her tonight.'

'That was probably the most difficult consult of my life, and I didn't even do anything. I didn't know what to say. I so badly wanted to help her and now Jordan ...' Her eyes flashed. 'How could she do this?'

'I'm not surprised,' Adam said honestly.

'It's disgusting!'

'Yep. But if Shane had wanted Jordan, she'd have taken him. No matter how wrong.'

'Clearly,' Natalia muttered. 'Right now though, I just want to go home.'

Natalia grabbed her things, then they left the surgery, travelling most of the way home in silence.

'One good thing happened though. Jordan said she'd retract the complaint against me.'

'Good.'

'Although are you sure you don't want to go to the police about the spiking?'

Exhaling, Adam nodded. 'I'll chat with Cade, but I'll leave pressing charges in Paul's hands for now. She's his sister and he has more evidence than I do.'

'Jordan deserves to be charged.'

'And I think Paul will do it. But either way, I've got everything I need.' He reached for her hand and Natalia smiled softly.

'You do. Although I'm going to have my work cut out for me helping Elanora through this. Sometimes it isn't easy being a doctor.'

'I wouldn't expect it to be.'

They pulled up outside their house and climbed out of the car.

'But I do like my job here, Adam. Despite how people have treated me, it's been good.'

'People will stop talking now, Nat. They'll see what Jordan did was wrong, that I'm not a total bastard, and that you're a good doctor. And I'm sure you'll do a great job of helping Elanora through this.'

'I'll try,' she said as they stepped inside. Rusty greeted them and Natalia scooped him into her arms before sinking onto the lounge. 'At least I'll keep my job and remain valuable to the community. That's all I want.'

Adam sighed and sat beside her. 'And I finally know what happened on my birthday.'

'Yeah. Diazepam makes sense, although I hate that there are still doctors out there illegally prescribing. And mixing it with alcohol could easily have caused your amnesia, especially as we can't be sure of its quantity.'

'But what is it?' Adam asked.

'Valium. Should be used for short-term anxiety treatment, but it's a medication that's often abused. I don't know where Jordan got it from, but she was obviously doctor shopping. Despite the attempts at real-time prescription monitoring, drug-abusers are still getting away with it. You're lucky you weren't sicker.'

'Yeah. Paul told me he was pretty wiped out and that he didn't remember much either. Sounded like I got off lightly, actually.'

'The important thing is that you were both okay. But even though I feel terrible for Elanora, Paul, and their family, I'm so glad it's over. And that this baby wasn't yours.'

'Yeah. Having a baby with Jordan wasn't what I wanted.'

Her hand paused on Rusty's back and she glanced up. 'What do you want?'

Heart swelling, Adam pulled her closer until she had no choice but to throw her leg over his and straddle him. Rusty jumped away with a huff. 'I want you, Natalia. I want to spend the rest of my life with you. I want to marry you.'

Her tear-stained face broke into a grin. 'Really?'

'Really.'

Excitement skidded through his veins as she gave a little bounce in his lap. 'Then are you going to ask me? Or tease me and make me wait?'

Grinning, Adam brushed the hair from her face. 'Oh, you know I love teasing you. But I hate waiting. So … will you marry me, Natalia?'

Everything inside him relaxed as she softened and pressed her body close to his. 'Oh, Adam. Of course, I will.'

She crushed her mouth to his and Adam's hands hardened on her back as his body sank into the lounge in the shared relief that he'd never thought they'd feel. They were free and he wanted to revel in it.

Rusty jumped back up and Natalia drew away, grinning at the little dog. 'Hey, boy! I'm going to be your mama!'

'Oh, God.' Adam rolled his eyes as Natalia drew Rusty into her chest, squishing him between them. 'Really?'

'Yep.' She kissed Rusty's head. 'I'll be his mama even if you're not his daddy.'

Adam's shoulders slumped. 'Fine. I'll be his bloody daddy. 'Cause I do love the little rascal.' He rubbed Rusty's ears, then returned his gaze to hers. 'But I love you more. And I'm going to marry you.'

'Soon?'

'Very soon. Because Natalia … you're the only woman I want to have babies with.'

Her eyes softened. 'And I want to be the only woman to have your babies.'

He grinned. 'Soon?'

She blew out her breath. 'Give us a moment, Adam! We just moved in together and are already engaged! Plus, I have my fellowship and … well, I know you've had some time to think about it, but I don't think I'm ready for kids.'

He laughed. 'Righto. But can we at least practise?'

Natalia pressed her gorgeous body closer to his, her eyes gleaming. 'We can practise all you like.'

'Good.' Adam tightened his hold around her and stood. Natalia laughed and plopped Rusty onto the lounge as she wrapped her arms around his neck. Joy burst from his chest as for once in his life, he hadn't fucked it up. He'd left his past behind, had made a name for himself as a woodworker, and had the most beautiful woman in the world in his arms. The woman with whom he'd live out his days in their house by Shadow Creek.

Author's Note

It is an occupational hazard as a health professional to weave science and examples of healthy living into my books. As authors, we often write about the things that interest and inspire us. When I redeveloped the Shadow Creek series in 2021, it was an obvious choice for me to rewrite Natalia as a vegan based on her father's cardiac history. While most cases of high cholesterol are passed through families not by genetics but by learning unhealthy eating habits, familial hypercholesterolemia is a real chromosomal condition. Slim, active people as young as their higher teens have been diagnosed with elevated cholesterol levels through little fault of their own. Diet is the only conservative way to control blood cholesterol levels and in Natalia's case, she chose the plant-based diet to manage her health and reduce her risk of sudden cardiac death like her father.

Nathan Pritikin, an American nutritionist, was one of the first scientists to promote high carbohydrate, low fat diets filled with unrefined grains, fruits, and vegetables to reverse heart disease. His research was based on studies indicating that people in primitive cultures who observed a primarily vegetarian diet showed little prevalence of heart disease.

Pritikin developed an institute that helped people with death sentences live decades longer on this earth simply by changing their diets and encouraging regular exercise. In the 1980s, The China Study was a groundbreaking research project that examined the link between the consumption of animal products and chronic disease. By studying people who lived in rural China, scientists concluded that whole-food vegan diets reduce and reverse the development of numerous diseases. Scientific studies continue to prove this fact today.

When I'm not writing, I work as an exercise physiologist in cardiac rehabilitation. This involves helping people recover from heart attacks, stent insertions, valve replacements, and coronary bypass surgery by administering a graded aerobic exercise program. I monitor their aerobic and cardiac response to exercise and promote healthy living in the hope of reducing their risk of further cardiac complications. Yet, exercise is not the key to reducing the prevalence of heart disease and if only people adhered to the basics of nutrition, I would be out of a job. So I do not share this knowledge with an agenda. I enjoy my work, but I'd rather that people didn't suffer from heart disease. If this were the case, I could sit back and write romance novels all day long.

However, I am grateful to have discovered the power of plant-based nutrition as it has enhanced my skills as a clinician, improved my own health, and the health of some dear friends. I am in no way affiliated with these associations, but I would recommend nutritionfacts.org and Dr Michael Greger's book *How Not to Die* for more nutritional information.

Ana does not carry the same chromosomal abnormality as her sister and therefore isn't as strict with her animal protein. However, she continues to observe a vegetarian diet for improved health outcomes and won't say no to baked goods made with cow's milk and enjoys it when Liam brings home ice cream.

Acknowledgements

I burned many dinners while writing this book and forgot to turn the oven on a few times too, such is the curse of a solitary writer. Nevertheless, later dinners meant more writing time, and this story was both a pleasure and a headache to write. However, I couldn't have produced this book without the help of some fabulous people.

Thank you always to Mum and Ian for your support and encouragement as my writing career unfolds. I wouldn't have managed to save this story without you, especially when everything went pear-shaped. Thank you for your reassurance, confidence boosting, and for all of your help with book events and fruit farm research trips. Mum, you have done so much for me, especially during the months leading up to the release of this book. You always have an ear I can chew to help me formulate ideas, and that helps me more than I can say. Thank you simply for being my mum. Thank you also to my brother Chris for being the one I can turn to when I need a Norwegian rock band and for trying to 'funny up' my stories by asking why Adam's missing his pocket on the cover. I'm sorry I didn't include the story about a possum stealing an apple from Adam's pocket and ripping it off in the book, so here it is.

I also couldn't have done this without the encouragement of my friends and writing network—Dee West, Linda Wright, Bec Cole, Matt Lewis, Barbara Strickland, and Jill Staunton. You are always there for me and you picked me up when I was down, so thank you for being my cheer squad.

Jill and Barb, thank you for your invaluable feedback and for being my friends. To have you both in my corner means the world to me and I've learned a lot from both of you. Barb, your encouragement continues to push me, so thank you for your support. Jill, this book would not have been the same without you. Our many discussions around your beautiful mango table have changed me as a writer, so it's no wonder that such an object managed to inspire Adam's story as a woodworker. I cherish our friendship, your advice, and I thank you for being the person I can turn to.

I drew upon various aspects of my life for this story, so I'm grateful for my job where I have learned the highs and lows of being a general practitioner. This insight into managing drug seekers, doctor shopping, overprescribing, and complaints to the medical board helped me improve this story and shape the characters of Natalia and Jordan.

I'd also like to thank the supportive organisations of Romance Writers of Australia and Romance Writers of New Zealand for the fabulous networking and learning opportunities that you bring to writers. And thank you to the Australian Romance Readers Association for helping writers reach readers through the wonderful community you've created. I am also very grateful for those who attend my Popular Fiction writers group and I thank you for letting me share my knowledge to help us all become better writers.

On the technical side of things, a big thank you goes to my awesome cover designer Danielle, who did another stunning job with this book. And thank you to my editor Nicola, who found the flaw I would never have seen after spending so many years with this story. Thank you for your structural report and notes that created a much more intriguing read. It never ceases to amaze me how fresh eyes can make an overly polished dull manuscript finally shine.

A shout out also goes to Timmy, my fox terrier who is no longer with us but helped inspire the character of Rusty. Thank you for protecting us from the brown snake, whip snake, and killing any rat that dared invade our home. I will always remember your happy smile, warm cuddles, and cheeky attitude. I will continue to keep my final promise to you that day you went to sleep—you will live forever in my books. More are to come.

Thank you also to Jacob, my border collie, who is well trained in 'writing time' and provides me with a fluffy foot rest as I write these books. You are truly a wonderful writing companion.

Last but not least, thank you to all the readers who bought *Home Among the Palm Trees* and couldn't wait for the next adventure in Elizadale. Your support keeps me going and helps me bring you the Maguire family's stories. As you see, they are a big family, and everyone will have a chance to find their happy ending.

The *Shadow Creek* series

The Pub with No Food
Grace and Luke
A spinoff prequel

Home Among the Palm Trees
Ana and Liam

The Man from Shadow Creek
Natalia and Adam

Waltzing Maguire
Meg and Jack